# The sight sent a jolt of fear through her.

"He's back." Lacey pointed at the snowmobile on the mountain. "And he has a rifle."

As they took cover in a snowdrift, Lacey pushed aside the panic that filled her.

Jude faced her, but neither of them dared make a sound. They listened to the snowmobile grow closer. Just a few more minutes and it'd be past them.

She looked up and her breath caught. "He has her! He has the girl!"

"The roads must be open. He's taking her out of here." Jude reached for his gun. "We have to stop him." He fired a shot.

He jerked his head to one side. Before she even had time to look up the mountain to whatever had alarmed him, a thundering roar surrounded her.

Avalanche.

They bolted downhill but couldn't outrun the wave of snow. In seconds, her body was picked up and tossed around. Snow cascaded around her, enveloping her, and stole her last breath.

# DEADLY MOUNTAIN TRAP

## USA TODAY BESTSELLING AUTHOR

# SHARON DUNN

# &

# SARAH VARLAND

Previously published as *Mountain Captive* and
*Alaskan Mountain Murder*

## LOVE INSPIRED
### INSPIRATIONAL ROMANCE

## LOVE INSPIRED®
INSPIRATIONAL ROMANCE

Recycling programs for this product may not exist in your area.

ISBN-13: 978-1-335-46622-8

Deadly Mountain Trap

Copyright © 2021 by Harlequin Books S.A.

Mountain Captive
First published in 2020. This edition published in 2021.
Copyright © 2020 by Sharon Dunn

Alaskan Mountain Murder
First published in 2020. This edition published in 2021.
Copyright © 2020 by Sarah Varland

This edition published by arrangement with Harlequin Books S.A.

For questions and comments about the quality of this book, please contact us at CustomerService@Harlequin.com.

Love Inspired
22 Adelaide St. West, 40th Floor
Toronto, Ontario M5H 4E3, Canada
www.Harlequin.com

**Printed in U.S.A.**

# CONTENTS

Ever since she found the Nancy Drew books with the pink covers in her country school library, **Sharon Dunn** has loved mystery and suspense. Most of her books take place in Montana, where she lives with three nearly grown children and a hyper border collie. She lost her beloved husband of twenty-seven years to cancer in 2014. When she isn't writing, she loves to hike surrounded by God's beauty.

### Books by Sharon Dunn

### Love Inspired Suspense

*Cold Case Justice*
*Mistaken Target*
*Fatal Vendetta*
*Big Sky Showdown*
*Hidden Away*
*In Too Deep*
*Wilderness Secrets*
*Mountain Captive*
*Undercover Threat*
*Alaskan Christmas Target*

### *True Blue K-9 Unit: Brooklyn*

*Scene of the Crime*

Visit the Author Profile page
at Harlequin.com for more titles.

# MOUNTAIN CAPTIVE

## Sharon Dunn

Weeping may endure for a night,
but joy cometh in the morning.
—*Psalm* 30:5


I cried by reason of mine affliction unto the Lord,
and he heard me; out of the belly of hell cried I,
and thou heardest my voice. For thou hadst cast me
into the deep, in the midst of the seas; and the
floods compassed me about: all thy billows
and thy waves passed over me.
—*Jonah* 2:2–3

For Shannon, who brings so much humor and adventure into my life. So glad you are my son.

# ONE

Private Investigator Jude Trainor gripped the steering wheel of his SUV as it hugged the upward side of the narrow mountain road. One small overcorrection and he ran the risk of sailing off the road and down the steep incline. Windshield wipers beat out an intense rhythm, wiping away the increasing snowfall. The radio forecast an unexpected blizzard, the worst Montana had seen in fifty years.

He could just make out the red taillights of the car he'd chased for miles. The car matched the description of the one believed to have been used to kidnap an eight-year-old girl over a week ago from her home in North Dakota. There was no way to match it to the driver because it had been reported as stolen a day before the kidnapping.

Was the girl being held in a remote cabin in these mountains? Jude doubted the suspect would lead him to the girl. What he hoped for was to take the driver into custody and get him to confess. But the driver had not stopped when they were on the highway. Now with only the two of them on this road, he must know he was being tailed. Jude prayed for an opportunity to stop or disable the car.

The car had surfaced around various parts of Montana, but this was the closest Jude had gotten to the suspect.

The road curved and the red taillights disappeared.

Snow cut Jude's visibility. He let up on the gas until he was moving at a crawl. Wipers cleared his windshield only to have it fill up again with snow. All he saw was white everywhere. The car couldn't have gotten that far ahead of him. The wind blew with such force, he could barely make out the tracks where the other car had been.

Headlights filled his field of vision. Adrenaline flooded his body. The other car had gotten turned around and was headed straight toward him on the one-lane road. He tensed, ready for a fight for his life.

Jude shifted into Reverse. He drove more by feel and instinct than by what he could see in his mirrors. His car hugged the upward side of the road.

Through the snowfall, all he saw was the glowing orange of the headlights as they loomed ever closer to him. He prayed for some sort of shoulder to pull off on. Bushes scratched the driver's side window because he was so close to the bank.

Though the other car was moving at a crawl as well, it closed the distance between them.

He checked his mirrors and then craned his neck. The snowfall cleared for a moment, so he had a view of the road. He couldn't see a safe place to pull over. He pressed the gas even harder, guessing at where the safest route was.

He felt a thud against his front bumper.

He set his jaw and gripped the wheel. No, this could not be happening. He was not going over that incline.

Jude shifted into First. He revved the engine and pushed toward the other car, which was only a few feet away. If this guy wanted to play demolition derby, bring it on.

The other driver backed away a few feet. Jude brushed his hand over the gun in his shoulder holster. For the kidnapped girl, he needed the suspect brought in ready to talk. Even if he injured him to capture him, it meant a delay in finding the child.

An idea struck him. He turned off his headlights and continued to back down the mountain.

The other car backed away, as well. Now he saw the flaw in his plan. The guy would back up until he got to the place where he was able to turn around and then take off. With his lights still off, Jude edged forward. The headlights of the other car faded in and out as an intense wind gusted.

They came to a straight part of the road. The other car barreled toward him at a dangerous speed. He hit Reverse again. His windshield filled with blinding yellow light right before metal crashed against metal. The whole car seemed to be vibrating and creaking. His back end fishtailed. And then he was sliding sideways. His hand gripped the wheel. He pumped the brake. The car slipped off the edge of the road. He felt weightless as the seat belt dug into his chest and the car rolled twice before coming to a stop right side up.

The crash had taken the wind out of him. Still numb, he unclicked his seat belt. His door was too bent to open. Though he was in pain, he didn't think he'd broken anything.

He pulled his phone out. No signal.

Jude dragged himself toward the passenger side door.

He clicked the handle and pushed it open. A gust of snow chilled his face as he crawled out.

He heard the zing of the rifle shot before he heard it hit the metal of his wrecked vehicle. His heart pounded. He could just make out the silhouette of the possible kidnapper standing in the headlights of his car, aiming a rifle down the mountain at him.

Adrenaline surged through Jude's body as he crawled around to the front of his car for cover. His bright colored ski jacket would be easy to spot even in the storm.

The freezing cold enveloped him. He'd kept his winter coat on, but he had no hat or gloves. He wrestled with the thought that he might die out here. That his life would come to nothing. And that the little girl would not be brought home safe. That bothered him more than the reality of his own death.

Another shot rang through the air. Glass shattered.

The possibility of bringing that little girl home safe to her parents had felt like a shot at redemption to him. He wasn't a private investigator by choice. At the age of twenty-one, ten years ago, he'd washed up as a rookie officer when a domestic call he'd been sent on had ended in the murder-suicide of husband and wife. Their ten-year-old daughter had witnessed the crime. The last he'd heard she was under a psychiatrist's care. Her life would never be the same. The guilt weighed on him every day.

If only Jude had said the right words as he'd talked to the husband through the open window. If only he'd chosen a different tactic. If only…

Jude peered around the side of his car. The man with the rifle was nothing more than a dark spot, but he was still there waiting to take another shot at Jude.

The cold seeped into his muscles as he wondered if he had the strength to make a run for it into the unknown down the mountain. The winding road was the one he'd just come up in his pursuit. Maybe there was somebody down there, a hunter perhaps. For the first time in ten years, he said a quick and desperate prayer.

*Lord, send help or show me a way out of this.*

Wildlife biologist Lacey Conrad put the binoculars up to her eyes and scanned the winter landscape until her view landed on a ridge where she expected to see elk appear within the next hour. She gripped the binoculars a little tighter. She wasn't going to see anything with the storm moving in. Not a good day for research and observation. She let the binoculars fall around her neck. Even on days like this, she loved her job. She preferred being outside and the research allowed her to move around Montana. Since the death of her parents and little brother in a car crash when she was in college, she had lived like a nomad, never putting down roots anywhere. That was the way she liked it.

The wind died down for a moment and movement much closer to her caught her attention. On the mountain road above her, a car had rolled off the road. She'd heard the muffled sound of a crash only moments before. Now as the wind died down, the noise made sense.

She saw a man crouched in front of the car. Her heart squeezed tight. A man holding a rifle was headed down the steep incline. She'd thought the shots she heard before were from a hunter somewhere on the mountain.

The man by the car bolted to his feet. She could see the bright colors of his ski jacket even when the wind picked up. Panic filled her body. It was the man in the ski jacket who was being hunted. The man must have seen the orange of her hunting vest. He made a beeline toward her.

Another shot was fired. The man in the ski jacket fell in the snow. Her heart lurched. Had he been hit?

She ran toward him. Her boots sank into the snow. She looked up the mountain seeing only white. The neutral colors the man with the rifle wore made it harder to see him.

The man in the ski jacket got to his feet. She ran toward him, nearly crashing into him.

He gripped her arm. The fear she saw in his face turned to relief.

A thousand questions raged through her head. Was this some sort of drug deal or other crime gone bad? Was she helping a criminal? Was the man shooting at a hunter who had lost his marbles?

Another shot rang through the air. She scanned the landscape in the general direction the shot had come from, but she could see nothing through the blowing snowfall.

The man in the ski jacket would have to explain later.

The only thing that was clear to her was that his life was in danger.

She tugged on his sleeve. "This way." Her truck was parked down the mountain in a grove of trees.

They half ran and half slid down the mountain toward the next section of winding road. She hurried through the evergreens to her truck. She yanked open the driver's side door. The man in the ski jacket got into the passenger side of the truck.

She glanced over at the stranger sitting across from

her. Her heart was still racing from running from the shooter.

He met her gaze. His eyes looked honest, anyway. "Thank you," he said. "You saved my life." He was still trying to catch his breath.

She wasn't sure what to think about this stranger. She pulled through the trees and out onto the road. The heavy snowfall on the unplowed road meant she had to go slow. "I'll take you as far as Lodgepole where I'm staying. There's no law enforcement there. Tiny town, only two hundred people." Her voice dropped half an octave. "Obviously, you have something to report. There's a sheriff in Garnet about fifty miles from Lodgepole."

He nodded but offered no further explanation. "Again, thank you." He let out a breath. "I'm Jude, by the way." His voice had a soft melodic quality.

"Lacey. I'm a biologist doing research on elk." She hoped he would return the favor and explain what he was doing up in these mountains.

He nodded but didn't say anything.

She maneuvered the truck through the heavy snow that had already piled up on the road. An object hit the truck with a violent thud. Her heart pounded as every muscle in her body tensed. The man with the rifle had thrown something at the truck.

"He must be out of bullets," said Jude. "I think he threw a rock at us."

Lacey glanced out of the driver's side window. The man was close enough for her to see his face. He ran toward them, rifle raised to be used as a blunt instrument. She saw him clearly. He was maybe ten feet away, a hulking mass of a man. The white-and-gray hair, the beard, the eyes that were filled with a murderous rage. A face she would not easily forget. The man looked right at her. A chill skittered over her skin.

She pressed the gas even harder, accelerating to a dangerous speed. She swerved.

Another blow struck the back end of the truck. In the rearview mirror, she saw the man raising his rifle to hit the truck again with the rifle stock.

Lacey gripped the steering wheel and chose the path of least resistance where the snow wasn't as deep. All the same, her truck drifted toward the edge of the road. She straightened her steering wheel, finally gaining control.

"Good job," said Jude. "That takes some skill." He still had a white-knuckle grip on the dashboard as he glanced nervously out the back window.

She had no idea what to think about this man sitting in her truck. He had a lot of explaining to do. She had never been a good judge of character. As her grandmother used to say, her people picker was broken. She did better with wilderness and animals.

"You handled the whole thing really well," said Jude.

"Thanks. So was that guy some sort of crazed landowner or something?" She really wanted to give Jude the benefit of the doubt, but she needed to know whom she had just rescued.

He took a moment to answer. He ran his fingers through his wavy brown hair. "No, it's a little more complicated than that. I'm a private investigator. That's all you need to know." He turned away and stared out the window.

Okay, so he wasn't going to tell her much. At least he was on the right side of the law.

When she checked the rearview mirror, she could no longer see the man with the rifle. But his face was burned into her memory. Though she could not say why. She had the feeling she had looked into the face of a murderer.

# TWO

Lacey could see the tiny cluster of lights that was Lodgepole as she drove toward the base of the mountain. By the time she pulled onto Main Street, the wind and snow had intensified.

"Probably too dangerous to drive into Garnet to report what happened to you. Might have to wait until after the storm." She searched for a parking space.

"I suppose I can phone it in." His voice lacked commitment as he stared out the window. He seemed distracted. His mind must be on something else.

"If you can get a signal. Maybe we should do that together. I saw the guy pretty clearly."

Jude perked up. "Really?"

Downtown Lodgepole was all of five blocks long. Many of the businesses did double duty. She rolled past a post office that was also an information center for tourists. The hardware store advertised that you could get your car fixed there. There was one café next to the hotel where she was staying.

The Davenport Hotel had probably been the talk of the town when it was built at the turn of the century. Meant to be an elegant stopping place for weary railroad travelers, it was now run-down with only a few rooms still being used. Much of the hotel was boarded up and closed off. The railroad didn't come through Lodgepole anymore. No one came through here except the occasional hunter or hiker. She glanced over at Jude. And the occasional tight-lipped private investigator.

The residents of Lodgepole were not used to strangers and had a suspicion of them.

If she included the people who lived in remote cabins outside of Lodgepole, the population count might tick up by fifty. She'd been here for only a few days.

She pointed at the café. "We can find out about road conditions by going in there. The locals will give a better report than any weather channel or app on your phone. Are you hungry?"

"I really need to track that man down. I'll need to get another car. And I need you to describe him for me." A sense of urgency entered his voice. "I can't wait around here in this town."

"Sure, I can describe him. But honestly I don't think anybody is going anywhere." He seemed almost nervous now. Lunch might give him an opportunity for him to explain himself.

She headed toward the café which was also a sort of community center and place to get gossip and news. In addition to the cars parked on the street, there was probably an equal number of snowmobiles. Because the snow stayed almost year-round at this elevation and roads sometimes didn't get plowed quickly, snowmobiles were the preferred mode of transportation for most of the residents.

The second they pushed open the door and the tiny bell above it rang, the place fell silent. All eyes were on

Jude and her. The chatter resumed almost immediately, but she felt the shift when she stepped into the café.

They weren't used to outsiders. She was still an outsider, and Jude wasn't from here either. Her research would keep her here for at least a month. People might warm up to her a little.

She searched the room for an empty table but didn't see one. All the seats at the counter were taken, as well. As she passed by the table, the talk was about the storm. She heard enough of the conversation to know the roads were already impassable.

She patted Jude's shoulder. "Looks like you're stuck here for a while."

The news didn't seem to sit well with Jude. His expression hardened.

A table opened up at the back of the café.

The teenage waitress came over and plopped down two menus. "We're out of the patty melt, but the tomato soup isn't too bad." The girl whirled away.

"Boy, she really sells that soup." Jude seemed to be mildy amused by the waitresses's casual behavior.

Lacey laughed and leaned forward, glad that he seemed to relax a little. "They probably just open up a can. It's not like the fresh produce truck makes its way up here." She liked the warmth she saw in his eyes and appreciated his effort at lightening his mood. "Maybe I could help you if you could tell me why that guy was after you."

Jude's forehead creased. He looked slightly off to the left. Then he leaned closer to her and spoke in a low voice. "A girl has been kidnapped. Part of the initial communication from the kidnapper was that the FBI not be contacted. But her father couldn't do nothing, so he hired me. Her father is a fairly well-known millionaire real estate developer in North Dakota. It's all got to be under the radar, or something bad might happen to the kid."

Lacey's breath caught in her throat as she absorbed the gravity of what he had just told her. Now she understood why he wasn't crazy about contacting the sheriff or being trapped in Lodgepole.

"It helps my case, but I'm concerned about you being able to identify him." He twirled the pepper shaker.

She spoke slowly. "You think he might follow us into town and try to hurt me?" Her old truck was distinct enough and Lodgepole was the only town for miles. It wouldn't be hard to figure out where they'd gone. Her heart squeezed tight.

"I don't know." Jude shook his head. "I just wish I wasn't stuck here. I was so close to catching him."

Lacey stared at the jelly packets and tried to process what Jude was implying. The man, who was probably a kidnapper, might come after her. "One good thing. If the roads are impassable for us, then he's stuck too. Either on that mountain or in town. Anyway, there are people around. I'm sure he wouldn't try anything." Her voice sounded weak, like she was trying to convince herself that she was safe.

Jude was grateful when the waitress walked back over to them before Lacey could ask him more questions. He'd already told her too much. He would be forever grateful to her for saving his life. She had been an answer to a very frantic prayer.

The waitress twirled a strand of her hair. "So, what will you two have?"

He hadn't had much time to study the menu. "A burger sounds great."

"I'll have the club sandwich." Lacey closed the menu and handed it over to the waitress.

He noticed the ketchup stain on his menu as he lifted it so the teenager could take it. This place had a certain uniqueness to it.

He turned his attention to Lacey. She kept her auburn hair tied up in a braid. Soft wisps of red hair framed her face. She offered him a brief smile when she caught him staring.

"You're not from around here?" he asked.

"I move around a lot for my research work." She rearranged the jam packets that were in the metal container.

"How about you tell me about your research."

Her eyes lit up and her whole face seemed to brighten. "I'm tracking the migrations and feeding patterns of an elk herd that mostly hang out on Shadow Ridge. I'm looking at how human activity might affect that." She continued to share details about her job. He liked the way she became so animated when she talked.

They continued to visit until most of the patrons had left the café. A silence fell between them.

Jude cleared his throat. "Are you okay with telling me what the man who shot at me looked like?" Though he didn't like making her revisit the attack, he needed to know if he was to find him.

Lacey stared at the table. "Yes, I can do that. Broad shoulders, built like a wrestler but older, gray-and-white hair, a beard. The expression on his face was…such rage." She shuddered.

He leaned toward her and patted her shoulder. "I still can't thank you enough for getting me out of there."

She nodded before glancing around the nearly empty café. "Looks like we closed the place down. I suppose we should get going. There is only one hotel in town."

When they stepped outside, it was pitch-dark. The wind had picked up, creating little tornadoes of snow swirling down the street. Jude buttoned his coat up against the cold. "I really want to have a look around this town. If that guy did follow us down the mountain, he probably hid his car, but I could knock on a few doors with some kind of story. Maybe check some backyards. If there is only one hotel, I doubt he'd stay there."

"I don't think you would get very far in the dark and cold."

A gust of wind hit him. His eyes stung from the intensity of the cold. He could only see a few feet in front of him. His jaw clenched in frustration. "Okay maybe you're right. So, what is this hotel?"

"It's called the Davenport Hotel," she said.

"Guess I should stay there too." More than anything, he wanted to get back to tracking his suspect. Things were more complicated now that the suspect knew he'd been made and could be identified. He feared for the little girl's safety. If she was being held in one of the houses on that mountain road, would the man just leave her there to come into town after him and probably Lacey?

Several snowmobiles putted by, their headlights cutting through the blackness. Leaning into the wind, Lacey and Jude crossed the street and entered the hotel.

An old man slept in an overstuffed chair in the lobby. "That's Ray. He's the manager. Rather than wake him, I think we can just grab a key and leave him a note that you've got a room," she said. "You can pay him later or just leave the money in an envelope by the note. It's fifty dollars a night."

"Okay, if that is how it's done." The informality of the place only added to its charm. Jude pulled some money out of his wallet while Lacey found an envelope and paper to write on.

A wide sweeping staircase with an ornately carved bannister filled up most of the lobby. Though everything looked dusty, there was still a yesteryear elegance to the place. A huge mural of forest and wildlife, with a train puffing through it, took up one wall. Faded by time, it was nevertheless impressive. The trim on the ceiling looked like it had been carved by hand. The red carpet and matching velvet curtains indicated this had been quite the classy joint at one time.

Lacey walked behind the counter and grabbed a key. "You can have room ten right next to me. I'm in twelve. Some of the rooms aren't used anymore, but I know that one is."

They walked up the stairs together. Though frustration over being stranded made his jaw ache, meeting Lacey had been a nice reprieve. Lacey went back and forth between warmth and seeming guarded. Still, having dinner with her had been fun. *Fun* was not a word that was in his vocabulary much anymore...not for ten years.

She turned to face him. "Ray told me earlier today that two hunters checked in to the hotel this morning. Other than that, it's just us."

He touched a bannister, which was dusty. The whole place was probably not up to code. "They're probably glad to have your business."

"They gave me a deal since I'm going to be here a

while doing research." She turned her key in the door. "Well, good night." She entered her room and closed the door behind her.

Jude sat down in his room. Though everything looked dated, it was very clean. He opened the bed-side drawer and pulled his handgun out of the shoulder holster. He stared out the window as the snow fell with increasing volume and velocity. He didn't need to form any attachment to Lacey however temporary. He was here to find a kidnapped eight-year-old girl who was the daughter to millionaire George Ignatius.

Before becoming a private eye, Jude had been a po-lice officer. He'd used his contacts in the department to get a trace of the vehicle that had abducted eight-year-old Maria. The home across the street from where she'd been kidnapped had a camera to record who came to the front door. Jude had isolated the time of the abduc-tion on the recordings. The vehicle that took the little girl appeared in the background.

That trace on the vehicle had led him here. And now he couldn't do anything. From where he sat on the bed, he rested his elbows on his knees and his hands on the sides of his head. The rising frustration tied his stom-ach in knots.

This whole investigation might have gone sideways. His phone still wasn't getting a signal. If there was a landline, it probably wasn't working either. He couldn't call George. He'd never forgive himself if something happened to that little girl.

Again, he opened the drawer where he'd put his handgun. He hadn't noticed the Bible there before. Stan-dard-issue even for this hotel. Not that he would ever open that book again. Not only did not being able to prevent the murder-suicide sideline his career, it stole his faith. He didn't know what he believed in anymore. That frantic prayer on the mountain when Lacey had shown up was the first time he'd prayed in ten years. And God had answered.

Jude lay down on top of the covers, staring at the copper ceiling, waiting for sleep to come.

He rubbed his chest where it felt tight. Though the kidnapper had not yet made a ransom demand, the clock was ticking for little Maria. A day ago the kidnapper had contacted George to let him know Maria was alive.

This storm moving in would delay his chance to search the residences that were on that mountain road. Even as the wind rattled the window, he could feel his chest tighten. He had to bring the girl home safe. In a way, he felt like his own life depended on that.

With the storm picking up intensity outside, Jude closed his eyes and willed himself to go to sleep. His last thought was of the auburn-haired Lacey. She was a hard woman to read, but she intrigued him. What was her story?

The heaviness of sleep invaded his muscles and he felt himself drifting off. He awoke to the sound of a woman screaming. Lacey was in trouble!

# THREE

Lacey screamed when she awoke in total darkness, sensing that someone else was in her room. A footstep thudded in the darkness moving toward her.

Heart pounding, she fumbled for the bedside light. It didn't click on. The storm must have taken out the electricity. Her flashlight was in her backpack across the room. The curtains were pulled tight. She couldn't see anything. The darkness and being awakened from a deep sleep left her disoriented.

She could hear someone moving around the room.

"Who's there?" She cleared her throat, trying not to give away her fear in her voice. "What are you doing in my room?"

She swung around and let her feet fall on the carpet. What obstacles lay between her and that flashlight? She couldn't remember. She took two steps before she hit a piece of furniture.

A body brushed up against her. Terror paralyzed her in her tracks. She could sense someone moving very close to her. Her heartbeat drummed in her ears.

Hands wrapped around her neck.

She twisted to one side before the attacker could grab hold of her.

Her heart beat so wildly, it felt like it would jump out of her chest. The man or woman reached out and tugged at her shirt, probably trying to grab her again or feel their way in the darkness. She whirled away, crashing into more furniture.

Someone pounded on the door. "Lacey, is everything okay in there?"

It was Jude.

She opened her mouth to speak but no words came out. Terror had stolen her voice.

She could hear the intruder fumbling around. Jude was shaking the doorknob.

"Lacey, come on, open up."

She stumbled across the dark room, feeling along the wall until she found the doorknob. She unfastened the dead bolt and swung open the door.

Jude shone a flashlight into the room. "What's going on?"

The light bounced around the room. Lacey got only a glimpse of her intruder before he exited out of the other door on the other side of the room. All she could say for sure was that he was a tall thin man. Not the broad-shouldered man she'd seen on the mountain.

Lacey grabbed Jude's flashlight and ran in the direction the man had gone. The door where the intruder had escaped was ajar. The place was so low security it had been unlocked. She entered an adjoining room that was not occupied but must have been part of a suite that connected to her room at one time. She shone the flashlight all around. The man was gone.

Jude came up behind her. "What's going on and can I have my flashlight back?"

"Sorry." She handed it back to him. "There was somebody in my room."

"I'll see if I can catch him." Jude's footsteps pounded up the hallway and then faded.

She was left in the dark. A rush of terror over the assault, which may have been an attempt on her life, caused her knees to turn to mush.

Jude returned. "I couldn't see anyone. I don't know the layout of this place. There are a bunch of boarded up areas. I searched as best I could. I think he must have escaped."

"I'm sure there is more than one door he could have slipped out of." Her voice still vibrated with fear.

Jude's words filled with compassion. "I would have gotten to you faster from my room. It took a minute to find my flashlight in the dark. Why don't you come back and sit down?" He led her gently back into the room and pointed her toward a chair. He stood at the window and pulled back the curtain. "Looks like the power is out all over town."

She stared out the window. Her room faced the back of the hotel, so they were looking at residences. All the windows in the houses were dark. She saw only the occasional tiny glow of light coming from a flashlight or a lantern or maybe even a candle.

She wrapped her arms around herself, still trying to process what had just happened.

Jude patted her hand before sitting in the chair opposite her. "Did you get a look at him? Was it the man who came after me?"

She shook her head. "I didn't see his face. But he was the wrong build for the man we saw on the mountain."

"Hate to say it, but sometimes people take advantage of blackouts and decide to rob people," Jude said.

"I suppose I would be a prime target since I'm not from around here." She touched her neck, remembering that the man had tried to grab her or maybe he'd just been fumbling in the dark. But she was not able to shake off the fear that had sunk into her bones that the attack was connected to what had happened on that mountain road. "Or the man who came after you has an accomplice." She couldn't stop shaking.

Jude touched her shoulder. "Hey, it's all right now. You're safe."

She appreciated his kindness, but her heart was still racing.

Footsteps pounded on the stairs and Ray, the old man from the lobby, appeared in their open doorway holding a camping lantern. He held it close to his cheek, so half his face was in shadow and the other half was lit up. "You two are awake. Heard a ruckus up here." He looked at Jude. "You the fella that left a note?"

Jude nodded. "Yes."

"What's all the noise about?" Ray leaned forward to peer in the room.

"Someone was in Lacey's room," said Jude. "Did you see anyone?"

"No," said Ray. "Only two other people are staying at the hotel."

Ray stood still, holding the lantern, studying both their faces while his was still half-covered in shadow. Did he think they were making this up?

"All I know is someone attacked Lacey," said Jude.

Ray took a step back. "Electricity is out all over town. Got a fire started in the ballroom and some snacks," said Ray. Without waiting for their response, he disappeared down the hallway. The old man either didn't believe him or didn't want to deal with another problem right now.

The wind rattled the windows. Lacey got to her feet. "We might as well go downstairs. I'm not going to fall back asleep."

The signs indicated that the ballroom was in the west end of the hotel. The room was huge with wooden floors. Two chandeliers hung from the ceiling. Lacey could picture the parties, dances and banquets that must have taken place here.

Now it was completely empty except for a table, couch and comfy-looking chairs that surrounded the crackling fire. The air smelled like wood polish. Another lantern had been set up on the table. Store-bought cookies, cold cuts, cheese and crackers had been set out. There was also a camp stove with a teakettle on it. All the fixings for cocoa and tea sat beside the stove.

A moment later, two men entered the ballroom and found a seat. Lacey's heart fluttered. Both the men were the same build as the man who had attacked her. Come to think of it, so was Ray.

The older man pointed to the younger. "I'm Eddie and this is my son Jonathan. Looks like we are in for a long night."

Lacey and Jude introduced themselves.

Lacey grabbed a paper plate and some food. When she sat down in a high-back chair, the heat from the fire calmed her. The men made small talk while Lacey stared at the fire.

Ray entered the ballroom. "Things have gotten even worse in the last twenty minutes. It's whiteout conditions outside. A man could walk only a few feet, get disoriented and freeze to death," said Ray. "Until this storm subsides, you cannot go outside. You'd be taking your life in your own hands."

Lacey's throat constricted. "So if someone was in the hotel, they couldn't leave, right?"

"Not unless they wanted to risk death," said Ray. "Nope, the smart thing to do is to stay put until this thing dies down."

The cookie Lacey was nibbling didn't taste so sweet anymore. She stared at all the men. The only one who was off the hook for attacking her was Jude. He'd come to the door and spoken while the other man was running away.

It was possible too that the three men were innocent and the attacker was hiding somewhere in the hotel. Both alternatives sent a wave of terror through her.

As he snacked on his cheese and crackers, Jude noticed a shift in mood for Lacey. She stared at the fire and gave one-word answers when anyone tried to include her in the conversation. She rubbed her feet together as though nervous.

He felt a little restless himself. How was eight-year-old Maria doing? Was she safe? Was she alone and hungry? His only comfort was that if he was trapped, maybe the kidnapper was too. Once the storm broke, he might still be able to search the houses that connected with that road. Maybe Maria had even been in the car when Jude had been shot at. The kidnapper could have brought her down here and was hiding her somewhere. There were too many unknowns. All he knew was that the longer he was delayed, the colder this case got and the less of a chance that Maria would be returned alive.

Maybe Lacey was right. Maybe the kidnapper had an accomplice. Lacey could identify him, but Jude was the one who had been on his tail. Jude figured it was only a matter of time before he became a target too.

When there was a lull in the conversation, Lacey bolted up from her chair. "You know, I think I'll go upstairs. Are you coming, Jude? I need to talk to you about something."

"Sure." What was she up to?

Jude nodded his goodbye to the other men and then walked with Lacey across the expansive wood floor.

Once they were out of earshot in the hallway, Lacey turned toward him. Desperation filled her voice. "Help me search the hotel."

"What are you talking about?"

"Ray said there was no way anyone would go out in this. Whoever attacked me must still be hiding in this hotel. He must have snuck in before the storm got so bad," she said. "I want to know what he was doing in my room. And I want to know that it won't happen again because he's been caught."

He heard the fear in her voice. "Sure. It's not like I have a busy social schedule." He hoped the attack on Lacey wasn't connected to the kidnapping. It was a thin hope at best. He didn't like the idea of Lacey being in danger after she had risked her life to save his.

"Okay, come with me so I can get my flashlight out of my room," she said.

She headed toward the stairs, moving outside of the cone of illumination his flashlight made.

"I don't want the others to know we're looking. Just

in case it was one of them who was in my room." She stepped on the first stair and turned, waiting for him to come toward her with the light.

They hurried upstairs. While Lacey got her flashlight, Jude retrieved his gun from the nightstand drawer. He shoved it in his waistband at the back and untucked his flannel shirt so it would be covered.

Had Lacey been chosen at random to be robbed? Had she been chosen because as a woman she was more vulnerable? Or was this connected to what had happened on the mountain?

They met in the hallway, both of them holding flashlights. "Let's search this floor first," she said. "He ran off this way. At the time, I just assumed he took a back entrance and escaped out into the night."

He spoke in a low voice as they made their way down the hallway. "Is there something controversial about your research?"

She swung the flashlight back and forth after stepping into an area that may have been some sort of meeting place for hotel guests. There was a fireplace in the center of the room and a very dusty-looking oriental rug. A couple of cardboard boxes were stacked in a corner.

"I don't think there is anything controversial about my research. If anything, it helps hunters and campers. Why are you asking?"

"Just trying to figure out a motive for the attack." He really wanted the attack to be unconnected to the kidnapping.

"Motive for the attack? You sound like a cop." She shone her flashlight in his direction.

"I used to be." The comment was friendly enough,

but he could feel himself retreat emotionally. "Let's just leave it at that."

"Sure, Jude." She swept past him and up the hall, then looked over her shoulder. Even in near darkness her auburn hair had a glossy sheen to it. "I told you everything about my job, but you don't want to talk about yours."

He hurried after her. "I said I used to be a cop."

"So why did you stop being a cop?" She stood in front of an ancient-looking elevator with an out-of-order sign. Her gaze rested on him, waiting for a response.

He reached out and touched the out-of-order sign that looked like it might have been hung during the Carter administration. "Let's take the stairs." Jude felt like someone had stirred his insides with a hot poker. Thinking about the past did that to him.

He'd kept all the pain from his past at bay, but here was this redheaded woman showing curiosity about who he was as a man. A part of him wanted to open up to her just to have another person bear the burden with him.

Lacey bounded down two flights of stairs. "He probably wouldn't hide on the main floor since it is the most used." At the bottom of the stairs was a large wooden door.

Jude pushed on it. It screeched open, revealing a dark corridor with a series of doors and walls made of stone.

Lacey held the flashlight up to her chin and spoke theatrically. "The belly of the whale."

He laughed. Her sense of humor was infectious. "You go first, my lady. I'll back you up." Maybe too, the humor covered up the fear she must be wrestling with.

They brushed away cobwebs and stepped into the hallway. Their footsteps echoed on the concrete. Each room they searched revealed various items: stored furniture, a broken chandelier and some kitchen appliances. All of it looked like it hadn't been used in a long time. Lacey stepped into the room where a stove was stored. She shone a light on the dusty surface. Her body went rigid.

Jude stepped toward her. "What is it?"

"This looks fresh to me." She aimed her light on the dusty stove top where there was a handprint.

Jude shone his light all around the concrete room. All the other rooms had had an abundance of cobwebs but not this one. "Yeah maybe someone was in here recently."

He saw the fear in her eyes. He patted her shoulder, hoping to comfort her. They continued their search. "It could have been Ray for whatever reason."

The only room that looked like it was used on a regular basis was the laundry room, which was clean and contained folded linens, three washing machines and two dryers. Some towels hung over a drying rack. They had worked their way down the entire corridor to the other end of the hotel where there was another staircase leading back to the main floor.

"Let's head back upstairs," he said.

She rubbed her forehead, still standing at the base of the stairs. "The one thing I know for sure is that someone was in my room and that at one point they had their hands around my neck." Her voice faltered.

He leaned a little closer to her. "I know an attack like that can be really scary. I think the best thing to do would be to try to get some sleep. If it would help at all, I can sleep in the chair in your room."

"Thank you. I think I need that." She turned to face

him. "We were strangers less than ten hours ago. I guess we're in this together for now."

He did feel a bond growing between them. It was unusual for him to have an instant connection with anyone. His relationships with women seemed to fall apart before they ever got started. There wasn't much he could do about liking Lacey other than enjoy the time they did have together. His work here would be finished soon enough, hopefully with a happy ending. He'd head back to North Dakota. His gut twisted into a tight knot when he thought about the kidnapped child.

They made their way upstairs, taking a little time to search the main floor. Laughter spilled out from the ballroom. When they peeked inside Ray and Eddie had set up a chessboard. Eddie's son must have returned to his room.

They stepped away from the ballroom and headed back to their rooms. They stood on the mezzanine looking down on the ornate but worn carpet in the lobby.

The most likely scenario was that whoever had been in Lacey's room had been there to rob her. All the same, he could not shut off his cop mind. "Is there some reason why someone in this town might be mad at you or your family?"

"I don't have any connection to this town. I'm from the other side of the state." She leaned forward, gripping the railing with her hands and staring off into space.

"I thought you said that you moved around a lot?"

"I do. I live in forest service cabins and campers mostly. I grew up in a little town called Jasper." Her voice faltered. "Haven't been back there in years."

There was a depth of emotion to her comment that he could not begin to plumb. He suspected that there was a tragic amount of pain to her statement. "What about your mom and your dad?"

"They're dead along with my little brother. The only family I have is my grandmother. Honestly, I don't think my family has anything to do with why I was attacked."

Jude felt as though all the air had left the room. He picked up on her defensive tone. "I wasn't prying. I'm just trying to figure this thing out."

Lacey turned toward him. "Sorry, it's a time waster to ask questions about my family, okay?"

Just like him she'd grown defensive when talking about the past.

Jude cleared his throat. He stepped away from the bannister. "Why don't we try to get some sleep. If he is still here in the hotel, I'll keep watch for him."

She studied him for a long moment. "Okay...thank you." She walked the few feet to her room and shut the door behind her. Jude returned to his room to grab his phone, which had a book on it he'd been reading. He knocked on her door. Lacey opened it.

He collapsed into the chair. She got into bed and rolled over.

Jude read for about twenty minutes, dozed and woke up. He'd left the flashlight on to provide some light. A small tattered Bible sat on her nightstand. Maybe her tragic loss had deepened her faith instead of stolen it. It seemed though that both of them had been running each in a different way. Her job meant she didn't put down roots or connect to a community. After the shooting, he'd quit the force and closed himself off, preferring to put his energy into his work. Lacey was the first person he'd felt any connection to in ten years.

He couldn't begin to sort through the emotional rupture that had risen up between them. Right now, he needed to focus on keeping Lacey safe. The storm continued to rage outside as Jude struggled to calm his restless mind.

# FOUR

Lacey awoke. She turned sideways. Jude was no longer in his chair. Even though he might have just slipped out to get something in his room, she felt less safe when he wasn't close. His agreeing to sit watch was the only reason she'd slept at all. Early morning light shone in from the window. The storm had let up, improving visibility, but it was still snowing.

She heard a noise outside her door.

Her heart beat a little faster. "Jude, is that you?" She ran to the door and flung it open expecting to see him. There was no one on the mezzanine. Now she realized that maybe the noise had come from downstairs. She stepped toward the banister. Down below, she watched as a tall thin figure hurried through the lobby and slipped outside. He'd been wearing a hat, so she couldn't see what color his hair was.

That had to be her attacker.

She stood on the mezzanine as she reached out for the wall for support.

Lacey's heart thumped in her chest. The man had taken advantage of the letup in the storm to escape. Fear permeated her whole being.

A heavy silence enveloped her as she fought the terror that raged through her. Seeing the man brought back the trauma of the attack.

Jude came up the hallway and she fell into his arms.

"Hey, Lacey, what happened?"

"I saw him. He left the hotel. He was here all night." Her voice must have given away how upset she was.

"Hey." Jude gave her a tight reassuring hug and then stepped back to look at her. Jude led her over to the plush velvet chairs that were outside the hotel room on the mezzanine. "Sit down and catch your breath. How long ago? Maybe I can catch him."

"It's been a few minutes. I'm sure he's gone by now." She placed her hand on her heart and took in a deep breath. "Where did you go, anyway? I woke up and you weren't there."

"I just went down the hall to use the facilities." The hotel was so old that there was only one bathroom per floor. He rested his hand on her shoulder. "I'm sorry."

His hand lingered on her shoulder, and the warmth of his touch soaked through the fabric of her shirt. She'd always thought of herself as a free spirit, someone who didn't need anyone. But given what had happened to her, she kind of liked having Jude around. Just his presence seemed to smooth over the agitation and fear.

"If he is connected to the kidnapper, why hasn't he come after me?"

She turned to face him. "There you go again being a detective."

"I'm trying to figure this thing out." Jude shifted in his chair.

She crossed her arms over her chest. "Maybe I'm just the easier target." She slumped back in the chair. "I do know one thing. I don't like feeling like I'm trapped in this hotel." But going outside meant the tall thin man might come after her.

Ray walked into the lobby holding a box. He shouted up at them. "Storm won't be the worst of it. It's the aftermath. Be a few days before the plows dig us out and the roads are passable." Ray must have heard what she'd said.

Jude let out a heavy breath.

Ray rested the box on the counter and pulled out a package. "Got some beef jerky here if you folks are hungry."

Jude rose, leaned over the railing and held up his hands. Ray tossed him a package. "Fine dining at its best."

Ray pointed to the box. "There's more food in here if you want to top off the meal with some granola bars. Bottled water is in the kitchen." Ray pointed to a door on the other side of the checkout counter. "Eddie and son have already helped themselves."

"So they are both still here?" said Lacey.

Ray drew his head back, so his chin touched his neck and a look of confusion crossed his features. "Sure, why wouldn't they be?"

Lacey shrugged.

Ray walked over to the window and placed his hands on his hips. "Four or five more hours. This should clear up enough to walk around town at least." He turned back to face them, rubbing his chin. "Still won't be any electricity."

Ray, the bringer of bad news, ambled away.

Jude rose to his feet and held out a hand for Lacey. "Might as well make the best of it."

She took his hand, feeling the strength of his grip

and the calluses on his palms. She met his gaze for just a moment, his soft eyes resting on her.

After finding food and water in the kitchen, Jude and Lacey returned to the ballroom to wait the storm out by playing a game of chess. They played two games.

"That's it. You beat me," Jude said.

"So we're even. You beat me last time. Want to go for a third game to see if we can determine who the true champion is?"

Jude yawned. "You know I think I might just close my eyes for a minute. I didn't sleep much last night."

"Okay." Of course, he was tired. He'd stayed up half the night watching over her.

She got up and wandered the ballroom toward a far wall where other books and games were stored on shelves. She pulled a book from the shelf that looked like it might hold her attention and then sat down in the easy chair opposite Jude, who was already snoring. He looked kind of cute sleeping with his mouth open. His wavy hair flopped over his forehead.

She'd never spent this much time with another person. Other than her little brother when he was alive. Pain shot through her as though a sword had been driven through her chest. So much had been ripped from her life. She knew that there was a part of her that just didn't dare open her heart again to ever caring about another person.

She liked being with Jude. He was funny and easy to be with. But theirs was a temporary and fragile arrangement. All she needed was God, her job and her beat-up truck.

She thanked God for the brief reprieve she'd gotten from his company.

She read for a while, threw another log on the fire and then dozed herself. Her nap was interrupted by Ray towering over her.

"Put your snow gear on if you like. People are starting to dig out and emerge. Most people are congregating over at the school on the other side of town, up a few blocks. They have a generator and food. Any announcement that town folk need to hear will be made there."

Jude had stirred awake, as well. It took them only minutes to race upstairs and get into their boots and coats. They both emerged from their rooms laughing.

"I didn't realize how bad my cabin fever was until now," he said.

Lacey and Jude bounded down the stairs and out into the open. Her elation changed to fear. The tall thin man was out here somewhere.

The snow had drifted in front of some of the doors of the shops and in the street, as well. Some snow still twirled out of the overcast sky. But she could see structures and people.

He tugged on her coat. "I have no idea where the school is. First let's take a look around and see if we can spot the man you saw at the hotel. If that other guy did come down off the mountain, I doubt he'd be out in the open, but he's my lead for finding Maria. I have to search for him and his car."

Lacey tensed as a wave of fear rolled over her. "I didn't get a good look at the tall thin man."

"I'll stay with you, promise." He squeezed her arm just above the elbow and then winked at her, which made her smile. "I have to do my job even with this storm."

It looked like she and Jude were going to continue to be together for safety if nothing else.

In her brief survey of the town as she'd driven toward the hotel when she'd first arrived, she didn't remember seeing any buildings that looked like a school. She tilted her head toward the sky and let the flakes melt on her cheeks.

"Ray said the school is not on Main Street. I'm sure we can ask someone to get more specific directions if we can't find it, but let's have a look around."

"Just describe the man you saw and say you're looking for him. No one needs to know about Maria," Jude said.

He stopped to ask several people who were outside their homes clearing away snow if they had seen the car or the man from the mountain. He offered a description. None of them had.

Lacey stared down the street. "What if we split up. I can go this way up the street."

"Okay, but stay on this street so you're in my sight," Jude said.

Lacey worked her way up the street knocking on several doors. One was occupied by an old woman and another by a woman with kids hanging on her skirt. None of them had seen the man she described or the car. When she peered around the side of the houses she didn't see a car that resembled the one that had run Jude off the road. The Davenport was the only hotel in town. If the man was in town, he must be hiding out in a house or maybe there was an abandoned building somewhere.

She walked past an empty lot where a house may have been at one time. When she glanced up the sidewalk, Jude was knocking on another door. The final house she came to was a weathered-looking blue Victorian. She ran up the creaking steps and knocked, waited and knocked again. She stepped down the stairs and peered into the big front windows. It didn't look like anyone was home. Movement on the upper floor window caught her attention. A man with jet-black hair and a beefy build stared down at her. He locked her in his gaze and then slipped back into the shadows.

Her skin tingled. Why hadn't he answered the door?

Jude was coming up the walk toward her. She ran to meet him, brushing off the rudeness of the man at the upper window. Some people were just antisocial. She met Jude in the middle of the block.

"There's some more houses over there we can check out," Jude said, pointing at a group of houses that lay just beyond an open field.

She followed him with a backward glance toward the blue Victorian house. They wandered toward a side street and then into an open field that was probably for baseball or soccer. The field was set apart from the rest of the town, but there were houses on the other side of it some distance away.

All around them she could hear the sounds of the town coming to life. She heard children laughing in the distance and snowmobiles motoring around.

They were midway across the wide field when the sound of a snowmobile caught her attention. She looked up to see a snowmobile headed straight toward them.

It took a second for it to register in Jude's brain that the driver of the snowmobile intended to plow them down. He grabbed Lacey and pushed her toward a snowdrift, landing beside her as the vehicle whizzed past them. The driver had on a helmet with a dark visor.

Heart racing, he pulled Lacey to her feet.

Again, the roar of an engine surrounded them. The driver had turned around and was making a second pass at them, barreling toward them at a high rate of speed. Both of them crawled over the drift and ran toward a grove of trees.

The clang and rumble of the snowmobile engine engulfed them as they sprinted toward the safety of the trees. The grove wasn't that big, maybe fifty feet across. The snowmobiler circled around it as though taunting them that they could not escape.

Out of breath, Lacey touched her gloved hand to her chest. "What in the world?"

He gathered her into his arms and held her close. Partly to quell her fear but also because having her close made him feel less afraid.

The snowmobile did another circle around them. The noise of the engine was menacing and oppressive.

"Either people in this town really don't like outsiders, or someone is after us." Her voice trembled.

He held her close even as the noise of the snowmobile echoed through the trees. The guy wasn't just going to give up and leave.

He glanced through the bare trees at the snowmobile. "When he gets to the back side of these trees—" Jude pointed out across the field where the houses on the edge of town were visible "—I say we make a run for it."

"I don't know if I can."

When he looked into her eyes, he saw the fear there, how shaken she was by all this. Jude touched her cheek with his gloved hand. "You can do this. Those houses are not that far away. I doubt he'll come after us in broad daylight with people around."

"It's got to be the same guy who was at the hotel. Don't you think?"

"Probably. Let's just get to where it's safe." He watched the snowmobile circle around behind the trees. "Now, Lacey, now." He grabbed her hand and pulled her through the trees.

Their boots pressed into the deep and drifted snow slowing them in their flight. Behind him, Jude could hear the snowmobile growing louder.

He hoped he had not made a mistake and put Lacey in even greater danger. He could see the backyards of the houses up ahead. But no people.

Gripping Lacey's hand, he sprinted even faster. She kept pace with him. The mumbling roar of the snowmobile pressed on his ears drawing ever closer.

Then suddenly it stopped altogether.

Jude glanced over his shoulder. The snowmobiler had parked, still perched on the machine with the engine running. Then Jude drew his attention to the scene in front of him. They were still about fifty yards from the backyards of the houses. A man had come around with a snowblower and was trying to clear a path while his children played behind him.

The snowmobiler revved his engine and was turning away, disappearing on the other side of the trees, so the guy didn't want any witnesses.

Out of breath, Lacey and Jude slowed their pace, reaching the houses on the edge of town. The snowblower was too loud and the man too focused to get his attention. Jude and Lacey approached the three children. Two were lying in the snow making snow angels while the third caught snowflakes on her tongue.

Jude's heart was still racing as he walked toward the

girl catching snowflakes. "Did you guys see that guy on the snowmobile?"

The girl, who was maybe seven, wiped moisture off her forehead. "Yeah."

"I don't suppose you know who owns that snowmobile." Jude leaned so he was closer to the girl.

The girl studied him with dark pensive eyes. "Everybody has one. They kind of all look alike."

It had been a long shot. There was nothing distinct about the snowmobile, no paint job or custom design that would make it stand out. The driver as well had been in a brown snowsuit and black helmet.

"Can you point us toward the school?" Lacey stood beside Jude, their shoulders touching.

One of the snow-angel makers, a boy, sat up, "That's where everyone is going. We're headed up there as soon as Dad makes a path." The boy pointed to the man with the snowblower.

The girl pointed up the street. "You go back to the street where the restaurant is and then turn and walk up."

"Thanks." Jude trudged up the sidewalk which was still filled with snow. Lacey walked beside him. "Why are we going to the school?"

"I'm thinking it would be safer with people around," Jude said. "Maybe I can borrow a snowmobile to get out of town and search that mountain."

"You're probably right." She looped her arm through his. Maybe it was just because she'd had such a fright that she wanted to be close to him. All the same, he liked that she trusted him that much.

The houses were still mostly dark. He saw only a faint light here and there in windows from a candle or lantern. An overcast sky veiled the full intensity of the sun. It felt a little like they were under a dome.

They found their way back to Main Street where there were more signs of activity, more people digging out. Still no cars moved up and down the street. Some men shoveled around where their snowmobiles were buried beneath several feet of snow. The café where they had met was dark as they walked past it.

They trudged about two blocks before what was clearly the school came into view. A front school yard filled with very dated play equipment made of metal and a brick building with another smaller stick-built house next to it. He suspected that at one time the house had been where the schoolteacher lived though it might not be used for that now.

Light glowed from every window and there was a steady stream of people coming from different parts of town headed toward the wide concrete steps.

Lacey jerked.

"Are you okay with this?"

"I'm not sure what choice we have." She tilted her head to look into his eyes.

She looked kind of cute with the snow falling all around her, her beanie hat, red hair framing her porcelain face.

"That guy on the snowmobile, whomever he is, doesn't want witnesses. We should be pretty safe staying here," he reasoned. He wanted to search more, but he knew he couldn't leave Lacey alone.

"Well, one thing is for sure. I'll go crazy if I have to hang out in that hotel," she said.

He laughed. Both of them could agree on that. They headed toward the steps. Jude nodded at the other people going inside. Plenty of them were tall and thin. He wondered if any of them had come after Lacey and him intent on harm less than twenty minutes ago.

Or was the culprit hiding out somewhere in some dark home, waiting for another chance to strike?

# FIVE

A tension twisted through Lacey's chest, making it hard to breathe. Yes, there was a good chance whoever had entered her hotel room and then tried to mow Jude and her down with a snowmobile was among the people going into the school. And there was a chance he was the kidnapper's accomplice.

They stepped into a sort of lobby area where there were cubbies and places for kids to hang up their coats. There were two doors on either side of them and a wide hallway in the middle with two large doors at the end. A woman in a sweater that had light-up reindeer on it stepped toward them. Her graying blond hair was piled on her head in a series of twists and braids.

"You two look lost," the woman said, stepping toward them. "This must be your first Lodgepole snowstorm."

"Yes," Jude said. "I guess we kind of stick out from everyone else."

The woman had a warm smile. "Not to worry. Most people in the classrooms are just socializing. We have coffee and tea set up. The rest of us are in the gym trying to put some hot food together to feed everyone."

Lacey tugged on Jude's sleeve. "We'll come give

you a hand with the meal." That way they could stay together. Lacey had worked in enough small towns to know that the way to win people over was to pitch in with whatever work was at hand. Plus, if Jude wanted to borrow a snowmobile, he'd have to win the trust of the townspeople first.

The woman's face lit up. "Oh delightful. We can use all the help we can get. I'm Terri by the way," the woman said.

"I'm Jude and this is Lacey."

"Follow me." Terri spoke over her shoulder as she walked down the wide hallway. "Don't tell me you two came here on your honeymoon to cash in on the winter activities."

"Actually, we didn't know each other until a day ago," Jude said.

Jude shot Lacey a look, raising his eyebrows. She shrugged. So, they had given Terri the impression that they were a couple.

Terri pushed open one of the wide doors. They stepped into what was a sort of all-purpose room for the little school. There was a gym floor marked off for half-court basketball and a stage at one end. A piano sat in a corner.

Terri pointed to a door off to the side. "The kitchen is in there. There's plenty of chopping and mixing to do." She looked at Jude. "And in a little bit we'll need to set up some tables and chairs."

They entered the kitchen where several older women and two teenagers, a boy and a girl, were at work. The boy, who was loading a dishwasher, was too chubby to have been her attacker.

"We're here to help," Lacey said to the elderly woman who appeared to be in charge.

The woman smiled and pointed over to where the girl was chopping vegetables. "We're hoping to get some kind of meal for a crowd thrown together." She eyed Jude. "You look like you would be good at cutting up chicken."

Lacey set to work with the teenage girl chopping vegetables while Jude aided in dicing chicken. From the talk of the other women, the plan was to make some pots of chicken soup and some salads. The women were warm and welcoming. The older women had stories to tell about previous snowstorms. They asked Lacey questions about her work. Quite a switch from the earlier reception when she'd first come into town. Maybe it just took a while for people in Lodgepole to warm up to strangers. Nothing like a snowstorm to draw out the best in people.

She noticed that Jude still wasn't volunteering much information. He must be tight-lipped with everyone.

As the ladies joked and laughed, she caught herself stealing looks at Jude who seemed to be enjoying the company, as well. He met her gaze for just a moment. Other people, strangers, had looked at them and thought they were involved. Her heart fluttered a little when he caught her in his gaze. Maybe there was an attraction there.

One of the older women tapped Jude on the shoulder. "You look big and strong. If you go down in the basement, there's a pantry. I'm going to need one of those bags of flour to make my biscuits. I can't carry such a heavy thing up the stairs."

Jude glanced in Lacey's direction. Whatever the reasons for the attacks, these people were not dangerous. She could stay in the safety of the kitchen until Jude got back. "Sure, no problem."

Another woman caught Jude on his way out and handed him a piece of paper. "Before you go. I wrote down some other things we'll need from the basement."

Jude took the note and headed out the door.

Once Jude was gone, one of the older women sidled up to Lacey and knocked her shoulder against Lacey's. "Hubba-hubba."

"What?"

The older woman tilted her head to where Jude had just gone. "If I was a little younger. How wonderful for you. He's handsome and he likes to help out in the kitchen."

Heat rose up in Lacey's cheeks. "No, we're not…" Oh, what was the use? These women were convinced she and Jude were together. Maybe they were seeing something she wasn't willing to admit. She and Jude had been thrown together because they were outsiders and now she appreciated the protection he offered until they weren't stranded in this town and they could let law enforcement know about the attacks. But Jude was just as guarded as she was. Once the roads opened up, she suspected they would part ways.

Jude returned a few minutes later with the flour and the promise that he would bring the other stuff up. He disappeared again. While the pots of soup boiled, Lacey helped chopped vegetables for a salad. At least ten minutes passed with no sign of Jude. She grew worried that something bad had happened to him.

She excused herself and searched for the door the women indicated led to the food storage area. She headed down the stairs. There were rows and rows of shelves stocked with all sorts of canned goods as well as some in plastic tubs with labels on them like flour and sugar. Another shelf had first aid kits, water and thermal blankets. The town was clearly prepared for disasters like a snowstorm.

"Jude?"

It looked like there was a hallway on the other side of the storage room.

"Jude? Are you down here?" Above her, she could hear people stomping around and laughing. There was a scraping sound like tables and chairs being set up. She heard footsteps on the stairs she had just come down. She couldn't see around the shelves. The footsteps came toward her. Fear encroached.

A young pregnant woman came around the first wall of metal shelves. "Oh, I didn't know someone else was down here," the pregnant woman said. "I was just looking for some napkins. We should be eating here pretty soon."

"I think I saw some a couple shelves over." Lacey helped the woman find the napkins. She listened to her footsteps tap up the stairs.

Convinced that Jude must have gone somewhere else, she was about ready to head back up the stairs herself when she heard a screeching noise deeper in the basement.

She stepped out into a hallway where she'd heard the sound. "Jude?"

Someone grabbed her from behind, cupping a hand over her mouth and dragging her down the hallway. She struggled to break free or at least scream for help. The man held her in his tight grip, dragging her farther down the hall.

She kicked and tried to twist free.

He let go of her. She felt herself being pushed. A door slammed. Cold enveloped her. She was inside a walk-in freezer. A single lightbulb hung from the ceiling. She banged on the door and shouted for a full five minutes. Her fists hurt from pounding.

Already the chill had sunk into her skin. She could feel her body shutting down. Her mind fogged.

Above her, she could hear people moving around. Settling in to eat a meal together. The cooking was done. It was unlikely anyone would come back down the stairs for at least twenty minutes. By then she would freeze to death.

Jude stared around at the throngs of people as they shuffled into the gym. Some stood in line to get their food. Others were already sitting down enjoying their soup. He didn't see Lacey anywhere.

He'd gotten tangled in a conversation he couldn't get out of for just a few minutes.

He popped his head in the kitchen. Only two of the women remained. "Have you seen Lacey?"

Both of them shook their heads.

"She might have gone looking for you," one of the women said.

Jude hurried down the stairs to where the food and supplies were stored. He called Lacey's name. He raced around the tall shelves.

A pounding noise led him down a hallway to a walk-in freezer. He swung the door open and Lacey fell into his arms. She was crying and shivering.

"Stay here, you're going to be okay." He ran back to the supply shelves and grabbed one of the thermal blankets. He enveloped her with it. She tucked in close to him as he led her up the hallway.

She backed up against the wall and slid down to the floor. He pulled the blanket over her shoulders and sat next to her.

"Someone pushed you in there?"

She nodded, still unable to speak.

He wrapped his arms around her and held her close. After a while, she stopped shivering.

"This has to be connected to what happened on the mountain. The people in this town might not like outsiders but they're not killers." She turned her face toward him and wept.

She swiped at her eyes.

He continued to hold her as her tears dampened his neck. He rested his hand on her shoulder. "I don't know what is going on here, Lacey. But you are safe now. I'm here." And it was clear he needed to stay close to her no matter what, for her protection.

She pulled away so she could make eye contact, her gaze searching. "I thought I was going to die in there."

"But you didn't." He looked into her eyes.

"That thing about your whole life flashing before your eyes is true." She drew the blanket around herself. "I mean, it's not like I saw everything that happened to me. But I could feel my body and my brain slowing down. And I just wondered if the life I'd lived mattered. To other people, to God especially."

He pulled away. "God and I are kind of not on speaking terms."

"But you were at one time?"

Jude took in a deep breath. He had to tell her the truth. "It's a long story. Two people died on my watch back when I was on the force. I prayed I would be able to prevent it." He shook his head as the bitter taste over what had happened, over what he could not stop, rose up inside of him. "There was a child who witnessed the murder-suicide. She will never be the same."

"After my parents and my brother died, I just figured I could get through with just me and God." She tilted her head toward the ceiling where they could hear the sound of people enjoying food and fellowship. She shrugged. "Now I don't know. Maybe that was wrong thinking. I really thought I was going to freeze to death in there."

The experience had made them both want to share more about themselves.

He hugged her and held her close. "I'm glad you didn't." He hesitated but then plunged forward even as fear wanted to steal his words from him. "This last day or so with you, Lacey. It's been nice…in an unexpected way."

She elbowed him playfully. "Thanks. You've been a good surprise too."

Jude stared at the ceiling, tightening his arms around Lacey. Her soft hair brushed his cheek. While he relished this moment they had together, it was clear that wherever they went in this town they were not safe.

# SIX

Lacey turned to face Jude, staring into his brown eyes. His expression had grown serious as he pulled away from her. He stared at the floor and then rose to his feet.

The warmth of his embrace faded. She liked being close to him. Nearly dying in the freezer made her realize how much she'd missed out on in life. Some part of her had closed off and shut down after her parents and brother died. Her life had become about surviving. She didn't want to live that way anymore. She pushed herself off the floor and reached out to touch Jude's arm. Lacey felt as though she was on some kind of crazy roller coaster ride. She had no idea how to live differently. The irony was that now that she wanted a more abundant life, her physical well-being was under threat. Someone wanted her dead. "What do we do now?"

He turned to face her. "Are you hungry? First of all, we should maybe go upstairs and find some food."

"I'm starving," she said.

He tilted his head toward the ceiling. "While we're up there, look closely at everybody around us. One of them could be the tall thin man. Try to remember anything you can."

Her stomach had tightened into a hard knot.

"Let's just be practical here, okay? We both need food in our bellies." He must have recognized the fear in her expression. His voice held a note of tenderness. "I'll stay near you."

"I didn't see him…at all this time." She wrapped her arms around her body, feeling herself going numb. She didn't want to think about any of this.

"Try to remember anything you can about today and last night's attack, a smell, an article of clothing." He touched her arm lightly at the elbow. "Food first. Let's go upstairs."

She managed a nod. Upstairs, most people had finished eating but many continued to sit and visit. The cacophony of voices made Lacey wince. Jude led her to a seat. He patted her shoulder. "You just sit. I'll get the food."

Lacey sat staring at the table, then she lifted her head and looked around. There were plenty of tall thin men. She saw the two hunters from the hotel. They nodded in recognition at her.

Jude set down a steaming bowl of soup in front of her along with a spoon, napkin and roll.

"They're out of the salad," he said.

He sat down beside her with his own bowl of soup.

She still didn't feel like her brain was working at a hundred percent. She studied Jude's face. Worry lines formed around his mouth and forehead. Much too intense for a man so young. Always, from the first time she'd met him, there was a warmth in his eyes that made her feel drawn to him. He wasn't wrong about her needing to stay close to him.

She tore the roll in half and dipped it in the soup. It

tasted salty and comforting. She took several spoons full, relishing the warmth of it.

A man dressed in snow gear stepped up on the stage and tapped on a microphone that had been set up. The chatter in the room tapered off.

The man spoke in a clear voice. "I trust all of you have filled your bellies."

The people nodded and laughed.

"For the few of you who are not from Lodgepole I am the mayor. I've been in radio contact with the weather service and we are looking at two more days before the roads are passable by car at the very least."

Everyone groaned.

"If you are low on food or other cold weather supplies, please see my wife, Nancy, and she will issue you some. Another meal here at the school is planned for tomorrow. Right now, the most pressing thing is for us to check on the welfare of people in the cabins and homes outside the city. There may be people who need medical attention or food or they may not have heat. The roads should be passable by snowmobile. I need five sets of volunteers, two people in each team, to check on the residents and report back."

Jude perked up. He squeezed Lacey's shoulder. "We should do that."

His remark caught her off guard.

"I can't leave you here alone. It's not safe." He leaned closer and whispered in her ear. "I think the little girl might be in one of those houses that connects with that road."

"Okay." What else were they going to do, sit in their hotel room wrapped in blankets, watching in case someone tried to break in? Hang out with the townspeople so the attacker could have another crack at her? She was used to being outside in adverse conditions; she thrived on it. The safest place was with Jude.

They both raised their hands. The mayor nodded at them while several other people raised their hands, as well.

"Good, meet me back at my office in fifteen minutes. We'll get you suited up and ready to go."

She followed Jude out of the school into the whirling snow, realizing that a little girl's life might depend on what they found at the houses.

Jude only had to ask one person on the street to find out that the mayor's office was inside the bank because the mayor was also the bank manager. They hurried across town to the bank which had a single light on inside. The mayor came to the door and let them in.

"So glad you volunteered. You didn't have to, being from out of town and all." The mayor held out his hand. "I'm Lev Stevenson by the way."

There was another team of two men coming up the street, as well. One of them was tall and thin. Jude needed to make sure they searched the cabins on the mountain road where his car had been run off the road. "I'm a little bit familiar with this area. I've driven on Mountain Sun Road close to Shadow Ridge."

"You can have that area, then," said Lev. "Come with me." He led them to a back room that had snowsuits and helmets. "Find your size. The city owns several snowmobiles. They're in the back lot. I'll print out a list of the residences that connect with that road and the landmarks to look for. I'll show you where they are on a map, as well."

Lev pointed out that there were four homes on that road. Two that were occupied by locals and two that were seasonal cabins. The other two men came in and suited up. Jude watched Lacey shrink back.

"I don't know if either of those cabins were occupied at the time of the storm," said Lev.

One of those cabins had to be where the man was keeping Maria. Lev seemed like an honest man and he was not tall and thin, but he couldn't say anything to Lev while the two other men were within earshot. "We should be able to hit all four residences?"

"Weather and conditions permitting," said Lev.

Twenty minutes later, he and Lacey were suited up. Lev loaded a backpack of emergency supplies to the back of the snowmobile. He handed Lacey a radio as she got on behind Jude.

Several other teams had shown up, as well. Some were inside suiting up. Others already on their snow-mobiles.

Lev pointed to the radio. "You can communicate for limited distances with that."

"Thanks," said Lacey as she put the radio in an in-side pocket of the snowsuit. Both of them got into their helmets. Lev gave them a thumbs-up.

Lacey wrapped her arms around Jude and he took off on the snow-covered road. Snow had drifted across part of the road causing the snowmobile to bump along and catch air. Lacey held on even tighter.

Jude hoped that he had made the right decision. He couldn't wait until the roads were cleared to try to find Maria. Every second counted. Since he could not com-municate with George Ignatius, he had no idea if the ransom demand had been made yet. Maybe he could find the little girl, break her out and get her to safety.

He hoped too that he had made the right decision for Lacey's safety. Staying back in town seemed to guarantee another attack. He suspected that it was just a matter of convenience to go after Lacey first at the school. She was more vulnerable than him. The kidnapper and whomever his accomplice was sure didn't want him to solve this case.

Jude leaned forward, tucked in behind the snowmobile windshield as the cold stung the exposed part of his neck. The mountain road wound up and up. They passed the grove of trees where Lacey had parked her truck.

He twisted the throttle as the road became even more precarious. Lacey pressed in close and held on tight.

He slowed when they came to the place where his car had gone off the road. It was covered in drifts and barely visible. There were deep dents and grooves where he'd slid and then rolled over. He probably wouldn't be able to get it towed out until spring, the least of his worries.

He'd studied the map before taking off. This main mountain road connected with several spur roads where there were houses. He had an obligation to check on the residents, but what he really wanted to do was see if anyone was in the cabins. Someone could be up here for hunting season, but they could also be holding a little girl in one of them.

Up ahead, Jude spotted a handmade signpost, a piece of wood shaped like an arrow. The wood looked like it may have at one time had something painted on it, but it was now too faded to make out. That had to be the first spur road. Lev had said that an old man lived there by himself.

Jude took the turn on the road. The road wound through forest that grew denser cutting out much of the midday light. Up ahead he saw a house. There was no smoke coming out of the chimney and the windows were dark. Not a good sign.

He stopped the snowmobile twenty feet from the front door. Lacey got off first, and he followed. They pulled off their helmets. The wind chilled his skin.

"Let's hope he is open to having some visitors," said Jude.

"Let's hope he's okay," said Lacey.

They approached the dark house. Their boots crunched in the snow. Jude pulled his glove off, raised his hand and knocked on the door.

# SEVEN

Lacey felt a tightening in her stomach as Jude pounded on the door. He pulled his hand away.

"What if he's…frozen or hurt?" She turned to look around the place. There was one car now half-covered in snow, and no sign of a snowmobile. The wind rustled through the upper branches of the pines. It sure was isolated out here.

Jude raised his fist and knocked again. The knocking seemed to echo. He stepped back, letting his hands fall at his sides.

His expression was pensive.

"We should probably check around the property before we try to get inside, don't you think?"

He put his finger to his lips indicating she needed to be quiet. "Do you hear that?"

She leaned toward the door, tilting her head. There was some sort of noise, far away but growing louder. Then she recognized it as the sound of several barking dogs. The barking increased in volume until they were right on the other side of the door.

"What did Lev say this guy's name was?"

"Mr. Wilson. Angus was his first name."

Jude stepped closer to the door and shouted to be heard above the dogs. "Mr. Wilson, are you in there? We're from Lodgepole. We've come to check that you are safe."

The dogs barked and then quieted. She could hear them moving around and whining.

Lacey pictured Mr. Wilson lying dead somewhere in the house.

"Mr. Wilson?"

A man came around from the side of the house dressed in coveralls, a knit cap and holding a rifle, which was aimed at them.

On impulse, Lacey threw her hands up. Her heart pounded wildly at the sight of the rifle.

Jude stepped in front of her. "Mr. Wilson?"

"Who wants to know?" the man said.

"We were sent from Lodgepole to check on your safety. We have a few supplies with us," Jude said.

The rifle went slack in the man's arms after he sized up Lacey and Jude. "I'm doing just fine. Sorry about the rifle. Some people use the storm for an opportunity to rob folks."

Jude thought Angus's place was a little bit inconveniently located for a robbery, but he understood the man's fear, being alone and older.

"Is there anything you need?" Lacey stepped toward him. "The house is dark and there was no smoke coming out of the chimney."

"I'm fine. I've been holed up in a little shed in the back that is easier to heat. I've got a little generator." Angus Wilson tilted his head toward the sky and then stared down his long road. "I imagine it will be a few more days before the plows get up this way."

"The mayor said it would take a couple days to open up the roads around town," Lacey said. "Are you sure there is nothing we can help you with?"

"Naw, I've lived here for forty years. Storms come and storms go. I'm prepared." Angus stepped toward the porch. The dogs were still making noise on the other side of the door.

Jude put a hand out to help Angus up the steps. "Mr. Wilson. I know there is one other occupied house that connects with that main road and some cabins that are often empty. I'm wondering if you've noticed any strange vehicles coming and going in the last few days when you were out on that main road."

Angus Wilson studied Jude for a long moment. "I ain't seen nothing strange. 'Course I mind my own business, which is what everyone should do."

Lacey felt like there was a warning in Angus's words. "You don't know if anyone is in the cabins up the mountain and who they might be?"

"You ask a lot of questions," Angus said.

"Just want to make sure everyone is safe," Jude replied.

The old man shook his head. "Those folks who come up to the cabins are rarely very friendly to the locals."

The dogs continued to scratch and whine at the door. Angus opened it, so they could get out. He closed it quickly. "I left them in the main house. They were making me crazy in that little shed." There were three dogs: a border collie, a Lab-looking dog who moved like she was older and a white short-haired dog that must be some sort of pit bull cross.

Jude thanked the man, and he and Lacey returned to the snowmobile. Lacey grabbed her helmet, waving goodbye to Angus Wilson before getting on the snow-mobile behind Jude. She wrapped her arms around his waist. He patted her gloved hand.

The gesture was one of familiarity. It touched her heart. She felt so comfortable with him. Despite her resistance, they were growing closer. After she lost her family, she had dated some. Any time things seemed to be getting serious, she'd requested a research job that would take her to somewhere else. Forming attachments meant feeling pain. It would probably just be the same with Jude.

The snowmobile lurched to life and Jude got it turned around and headed back to the main road. He drove for a while before pulling onto a shoulder. She got off, wondering why he had stopped.

Jude dismounted as well and removed his helmet. He spread the map Lev had given them out on the seat of the snowmobile. He pointed to a spot on the map marked with an *X*. "That family we're supposed to check up on is way back here from the road. The cabins are directly off the main road but farther up. I feel like the clock is ticking. I have to know if that little girl is in one of those cabins. If she is up there, I might need your help extracting her." He stared at her for a long moment.

Lacey's heart skipped a beat as she considered the potential danger. Jude had protected her, she needed to be a support to him. "A little girl's life depends on us. I'm all in."

His features softened, and it was as if a light had been sparked beneath his skin. He clamped a hand on her shoulder and squeezed. "Okay, good. Let's do this."

Before he put his helmet on he turned back toward her. "Thank you."

Once they were on the snowmobile, Jude sped up the winding road through the deep snow. Lacey held on and prayed that the little girl would be brought home safe. If she was in one of those cabins, Lacey prayed she and Jude would be able to free her without losing their own lives.

Jude switched the headlights to the higher beam.

They had maybe three hours before it grew dark. They couldn't stay out here much past sunset. It would just be too hard to see potential hazards in the road.

Jude rounded a bend. He slowed. She peered over his shoulder. The intense headlights of another snow-mobile filled her vision.

Jude slowed down even more. He waved.

The other driver did not wave back. It sped up, coming straight toward them. Lacey tensed as she held on to Jude and peered over his shoulder. Did this man mean to crash into them?

To avoid being hit, Jude performed a sharp turn. He was no longer on the road but headed cross-country.

As they turned, she got a look at the other snowmo-bile, not the same one that had come after them in town. This one had bright colors—orange, yellow and red.

Jude twisted the throttle. Lacey glanced over her shoulder. The other snowmobile was following them and closing the distance between them. They were being chased down.

Jude peered ahead. It was hard to read the terrain. The whiteness of the snow nearly blinded him even with the polarized visor of his helmet. If the sun had been at its apex, he might not be able to see anything. Though the helmet muffled the sound, he heard the roar of the other snowmobile intensify as it drew closer.

Because it was hard to see what was beneath the snow, there was a danger of hitting a rock or some other object that could catapult them off the snowmobile. He dared not slow down though. The other driver was bent on chasing them. This could only mean one thing—the girl must be in one of those cabins. Word must have gotten to the kidnapper that searchers would be out to check on people.

Jude checked his mirrors. The other driver was within feet of them. They bumped through some drifts, catching air and landing hard. Jude accidentally bit his tongue. He tasted blood. His heart pounded.

In his peripheral vision, he saw the lights of the other snowmobile. He had to do something radical to shake this guy.

He turned sharply, making his way down the mountain in a serpentine pattern until they were on the road again only lower on the mountain. The other snowmobile slipped in behind him though he'd managed to put some distance between them.

He veered off the road and into a grove of trees praying there would be a way through. Once he was hidden by the trees, he switched off his headlight and slowed down to a crawl. The snowmobile putted along until there was no visible way through other than going back the way they'd come. Even then, getting turned around would be a challenge. He switched off the engine.

Lacey flipped up her helmet and he did the same. They could hear the other snowmobile circling around.

He hadn't followed them into the dense forest probably fearing an ambush or getting stuck.

The other snowmobile sounded like it was idling.

"Do you think he's going to wait for us to come out?"

"I doubt he'll come on foot in here to find us. We'd have the upper hand unless he is armed." There was a high probability of that since they were probably dealing with the same man who had shot at Jude with a rifle. Jude turned in a half circle studying the thickness of the trees. "This was a big section of the forest. He can't watch every inch of this forest."

The other snowmobile was back in motion accelerating, circling around the grove of trees. The engine noise grew louder, then dimmed and grew louder again.

"Maybe we can find another way out," Lacey said.

While the other snowmobile continued to run patrol, they searched the forest for a clear path. Jude found a sort of trail where the trees were not as thick. From where he stood, he could see the edge of the forest.

Lacey stood beside him. "Do you think the snowmobile can fit through there?"

"It's our only choice," Jude said. "We can't hope to escape on foot. Come on, let's clear some of this brush and get back to the snowmobile."

Once they were on the snowmobile, Jude looked down at the gas gauge. Escaping the other snowmobile had used up a lot of fuel. Even if they could shake their pursuer, there wouldn't be enough fuel to get up to those cabins and back to town. Frustration caused a tightening through his chest.

Lacey spoke over his shoulder. "You all right?"

"Let's head back to town before we run out of gas."

Being stranded on the mountain with a kidnapper nipping at their heels would not do anyone any good.

He started the snowmobile but kept the headlight turned off. He maneuvered through the narrow path. He cranked the throttle to get over a mound of snow. Up ahead, he could see the fading daylight and an opening through the trees.

Jude took in a deep breath. He couldn't hear the other snowmobile at all. But that didn't mean it wasn't close. They came to the edge of the trees. He sped up, zooming out into the open. He looked side to side not seeing the other driver.

He had to get back up to the road. He circled around the trees. Lacey held on tight as the snowmobile climbed up the hill. The terrain was rough. The engine revved and groaned as they navigated around the drifts and snow-covered bumps that might be rocks or fallen logs.

The landscape evened out. He took in a breath when he saw the road up ahead. Lacey pounded on his shoulder. In his mirror he saw the other snowmobile some distance behind them but closing in. The kidnapper must have been waiting for them on the road.

Jude sped up as the other driver drew closer. Jude went even faster, rounding a curve at a dangerous speed. The sparse lights of Lodgepole came into view. Almost there. He looked behind. No sign of the other snowmobile.

They rumbled along the road and he relaxed a little.

His snowmobile clanged and sputtered. When he looked down, the gas gauge read Empty.

# EIGHT

Even before the snowmobile came to a complete stop, Lacey knew they were out of gas. Jude swung off the snowmobile and tore off his helmet. He glanced nervously up the road.

She didn't see any sign of the other vehicle. Could they hope that he had given up the chase because they were so close to town? That seemed unlikely.

He tugged on Lacey's jacket while she was pulling her helmet off her head. "You have the radio?"

She nodded and placed a gloved palm on her chest where the hard plastic had dug into her skin.

"Let's hide in the trees. Hopefully we're close enough to town to be able to call for help."

Heart racing, Lacey zipped open the backpack and grabbed a packet of food which she slipped into her coat pocket. She took the food on instinct. She didn't know if they would be out here for only a short time or if they would be dodging the man on the snowmobile for hours and walking back to town.

"Come on, hurry." He grabbed her hand and they raced toward the trees.

Their footsteps made almost a mushy sound in the

soft snow. Her boot sunk down deep. Progress was slow. Jude held on to her hand.

The trees loomed up ahead. She thought she heard the sound of a motor but couldn't be sure. They entered the forest and kept running. Lacey took in jagged cold breaths as her legs grew tired. Jude kept going. They were moving farther and farther away from the road.

Jude came to an abrupt stop. They were far enough in that they couldn't see the road anymore. She pulled the radio out of her chest pocket and clicked it on. The green light glowed. She prayed they would be able to reach someone. She pressed the talk button and cleared her throat. "This is Snow Team One. Is anyone there?" She let up on the button, feeling the tension coil inside her belly.

"Try again," said Jude.

She pressed the button. "This is Snow Team One. We need help." She let up on the button, hearing only static.

Though the sound was faint, she could hear a snowmobile putting along and then stopping. The kidnapper was out there probably looking at their snowmobile. Their boot tracks into the forest would be easy enough to follow. Her breath caught in her throat. The man had a rifle. He'd used it before on them when Jude had wrecked his car. She hadn't gotten a good enough look to know if he had a rifle with him now. He hadn't come after them before when they'd hidden in the trees. Maybe he wasn't armed.

A voice came across the line. "Snow Team One. This is Lev. What's your problem?"

Lacey breathed a sigh of relief at the sound of Lev's voice. "We've run out of gas. I don't know exactly where we are, but we can see the lights of Lodgepole, what there is of them."

"I can send someone up with gas to get you home."

"That sounds good. There's something else." She looked at Jude, not sure how much she was supposed to tell.

Jude took the radio. "Listen, someone has been after us, chasing us. It's not safe for us to wait by the snow-mobile and you need to approach with caution. He's dangerous."

Static came across the line. Lev was probably trying to process what he'd just been told. "Don't worry about us. Some of us will be armed. So…how will we find you?"

Lacey was glad Lev didn't ask too many questions. He was just focused on getting people home safe.

Jude pressed the button. "We'll listen for the sound of your snowmobile approaching. We'll come out of the trees then."

"Okay, we're losing daylight here. How many houses did you get to?"

"Only one, Mr. Wilson is okay."

"We'll send you or another team out again tomor-row," Lev said. "Hold tight. We'll be up there as fast as we can."

Jude pushed the disconnect button and handed the radio back to Lacey. "At least we know we can trust Lev. He's too large to be the guy who attacked you in your room. Now I'm thinking maybe we should let him in on the possibility that Maria is being held somewhere around here."

Lacey gestured toward the road. "Do you think it's safe just to wait here?"

"I don't know. He must know we're hiding in the trees."

"I was thinking if he has a gun, he might come in after us," she said.

"Let's keep moving. We're going to have to get closer to the road to hear that snowmobile coming from Lodgepole."

"If the driver leaves right away, it will take at least twenty minutes for him to get up here."

Some distance through the trees, Lacey heard the sound of a branch breaking. Her heart stopped, and her breath caught.

Jude must have heard it too. He gestured for them to move deeper into the trees. The noise could be an animal or the wind. But they couldn't take any chances.

They stepped cautiously, trying not to make noise. If the kidnapper had been close by, he would have heard them talking on the radio. As they moved, Lacey studied the trees. She squinted to discern shadow from substance in the dim light of evening.

Jude seemed to be moving in a sort of arc that would lead them back to the road. They stopped where the canopy of the evergreens cut out nearly all the remaining daylight.

She pressed her back against a tree trunk. She glanced at Jude who seemed to be tuned in to his surroundings. They dared not speak and give away their position.

She listened as well and studied the trees for any sign of movement. All of her senses were heightened. Her heart pounded. She heard the creaking of tree branches as the scent of pine filled her nose. She tasted fear, metallic and cold. She tensed up, ready to run if she had to.

A growling stomach caused her to touch her belly,

afraid that even that noise would tell their pursuer where they were.

She pulled the food packet out of her pocket. She had to remove her glove to open it. The chill stung her fingers. She opened the packet slowly and handed a piece of the protein bar to Jude who nodded a thank-you.

They hadn't heard the sound of a snowmobile starting up, which meant their pursuer was out there watching and waiting or he was searching the forest for them. Either way, he was still a threat.

Once they had eaten their food, Jude gestured for her to follow him. He worked his way back toward the edge of the forest. As the trees thinned, the setting sun shed light on them. Jude came within a few feet of where the evergreens no longer grew. He slipped behind a tree with a thick trunk and peered out.

She chose a tree that provided her with a view of the road. Their snowmobile was parked there in the middle of the road. About ten feet away and off on a shoulder was their pursuer's snowmobile. The man who had chased them down was nowhere in sight. Was he searching for them? Or had he taken up a position with his rifle, ready to shoot as soon as they came out into the open?

A gust of wind sent a miniature tornado of snow toward them. She closed her eyes and shrank back behind the tree. Both of them pressed their backs against their respective trees. Waiting. Listening. She was not able to get a deep breath.

Jude turned his head so he was looking at her. She couldn't see his expression clearly. He shrugged his shoulders and shook his head.

Would the sound of the snowmobile from town ap-

proaching be enough to scare their pursuer away, or
would the kidnapper see their rescuer as collateral damage and take him out too?

Having to be still and wait with danger so close by
was harder than running. She was aware of her heartbeat drumming in her ears and the tightness through
her chest.

Then she heard it. The faint and faraway sound of a
snowmobile drawing closer. She let out a heavy breath.
Jude rose to his feet. She did the same but remained
with her back pressed against the tree.

Then they heard the sound of another snowmobile
starting up and fading. The kidnapper was leaving. She
pushed off the tree. Jude reached out a gloved hand to
grab hers.

She supposed it was a natural protective gesture.
He didn't mean anything by it. Still, it was a reminder
of the affection that had blossomed between them and
that she felt herself draw away from. The approaching
snowmobile grew louder. They headed down the snowy
bank and stepped out onto the road just as headlights
became visible around a curve.

She glanced up the road and didn't see the pursuer's
snowmobile. But if she tuned in to the noises around
her, she thought she detected the distant sound of an
engine as the kidnapper's vehicle drew farther away.

She turned her attention to the approaching snowmobile. A spark of fear surged through her. The driver
was tall and thin. She reached out for Jude's hand.

His posture stiffened, as well. He squeezed her hand.
"We don't know anything yet. We have to get back to
town."

The driver came to a stop but left his snowmobile idling.

Lacey pressed her lips together as the driver tore off his helmet. She relaxed. It wasn't a he at all. The driver was a tall thin lady with gray hair pulled back in a ponytail. "I got some gas for you folks," she said, turning toward the container she had strapped on the back of her snowmobile.

Jude stepped out toward the woman and took the gas can. "Thank you."

The woman tilted her head toward the darkening sky. "We better hurry. Don't have much daylight left. I'll wait to make sure your snowmobile starts up. I'm Nancy by the way. Lev's wife."

Lacey stepped toward the older woman. "Nice to meet you." She held out a gloved hand. There was something trustworthy in Nancy's expression.

Nancy pointed at the rifle she had mounted on the snowmobile. "Lev said there might be trouble. Over his objections, I volunteered. I'm the best shot in town, almost made the Olympic team as a biathlete when I was younger."

Jude poured the gas into the tank and started up the snowmobile. He gave Nancy the thumbs-up.

She nodded and gave him the thumbs-up. "Stop by the bank when you get into town. Leave the snowmobile there. Pop your head in. Lev wants to make sure you made it back safe."

"Got it," said Jude.

Nancy got back on her snowmobile, zoomed a ways up the road until she found a wide spot to turn around and then headed back down the mountain. She disappeared around the curve just as Lacey and Jude got into their helmets.

Jude stared down at his gauges. "Looks like just enough gas to get us back into town."

"That's the plan, right?"

Jude glanced up the road where the kidnapper had sped away. "That little girl must be in one of those cabins. We have to get to her…somehow."

Lacey couldn't argue with him.

"I'm going to take you back into town and then I'm going to see if I can talk to Lev. I'll let him know the whole story. See if he is open to going out with me to search the cabins."

"It'll be dark soon." Even as she spoke, she knew she couldn't argue with him. This was a child they were talking about.

"I know navigating at night has more hazards, but I don't think we can wait."

Jude got on the snowmobile and Lacey slipped in behind him. He twisted the throttle and sped down the road. She rested her head against Jude's shoulder, feeling the fatigue settle into her muscles. She knew that she didn't have the energy to brave the cold and the dark again. That meant she would be left alone while Jude went out. She didn't much care for that idea either.

Jude was not wrong. Time was of the essence in finding Maria. Still, the thought of being alone in Lodgepole struck a chord of terror inside her.

Jude was glad to see the lights of the town grow closer though they were much sparser than the last time they'd come into Lodgepole. Up ahead, he saw Nancy's taillights as she came to the edge of town and turned off on a side street.

Much of the snow had been removed from Main Street.

He wrestled with the choices that lay ahead for him. To leave Lacey behind meant she might be in danger. But he couldn't wait until morning to search the cabins where Maria might be held.

Even through the padding of his snowsuit, he could feel the weight of Lacey resting against his shoulder. She might already be asleep.

He pulled up by the bank where there were still lights on inside. He could just make out Lev's silhouette as he stood watching. As they stopped and pulled helmets off, Lev came to the door and held it open for them. "Glad to see you made it. You're the last team to come back."

Jude stepped toward the warmth of the building. "Sir, I need to talk to you."

Lev's shoulders drooped. He was probably tired too. "Come on in."

Lacey followed behind.

He turned to face her. "I'm not sure what to do. I don't think going back to the hotel will be safe for you."

"I'd rather stay with you until I know what the plan is."

Jude felt like his insides were being ripped apart. He didn't blame her for being afraid to be alone. "Maybe we can ask Lev if you can stay at his place. You'd be safe there."

She nodded. "You must be tired too."

He was exhausted but that didn't matter.

Lev ushered them into the back room where they could get out of their snowsuits. A lantern had been set up to provide some light. He'd seen some lights on in town but not many. Maybe people had backup generators.

Lev sat on the bench.

Jude took in a deep breath and explained everything. That Maria was probably in one of the unoccupied cabins. That he had been unable to communicate with Maria's father, George Ignatius. That he had no idea what the kidnapper might do. He told Lev about the attempts on his and Lacey's lives while they had been in Lodgepole as well as while they were on the mountain. "So you see, Lev, I've got to go back up there. And I need to go with someone I can trust. This can't wait."

Lev rubbed his chin. He stared at Jude for a long moment. "You're not going back up there in the dark."

"But, sir…"

Lev raised his hand. "You're exhausted. You'll end up having an accident. I will search the cabins with some men I trust. You and Lacey can stay at my house with Nancy."

Even as Lev spoke, Jude knew he didn't have the energy to make it back up that mountain. Lev was right. He'd end up wrecking the snowmobile or worse. Lev gave them the directions to his house. "If you run into the man who is holding her, there might be violence."

"I have a gun," said Lev. "I can radio Nancy and let her know you are coming over." He patted Jude on the shoulder. "Get some sleep."

Jude nodded. Still, his guts felt tied up in knots. Staying with Nancy was safer than being at the hotel and at least he could stay close to Lacey. "Wake me as soon as you get back into town."

Lev nodded. "I'll get up there as fast as I can. I just need to find someone to man the radio for me."

He and Lacey headed out to Main Street. All the windows in the businesses were dark. They turned onto the side street and no one was walking around. The quiet hush offered a sort of comfort. They found Lev's house. Nancy stood at the window, looking out as they made their way up the snowy walk.

She opened the door for them and welcomed them. "Come on in."

They stepped inside. There was a fire going in the woodstove that made the living room toasty warm. The furniture was rustic in style with lots of natural wood and leather. The lights on the wall must have been battery operated.

Nancy gripped her bathrobe at the neck. "I'm afraid I have limited things to offer. We are trying to ration our use of the generator. I can warm you up some water on the cookstove if you want a hot beverage."

Lacey glanced over at him. "I think we both would just like to get some sleep."

Nancy pointed toward the woodstove. "The warmest place is in the living room. I've made up the couch and I was just going to grab a pad and a sleeping bag. Be right back."

"You can have the couch," Jude said.

She smiled faintly. "Thanks."

Her expression brought back some of the warmth and good feelings he'd had when they'd first met. He shook his head. He'd come to Montana to do a job. Maybe that was where he needed to keep his focus.

Lacey took her boots off and placed them beside the couch. She lay down on the couch, adjusted the pillow and pulled the blankets around her, staring at the fire through the glass door of the woodstove.

Nancy returned and handed Jude the bedding. "You don't want to sleep too close to the stove, you will wake up in a pool of sweat. I'll try to have some breakfast for you in the morning."

Jude thanked Nancy. She nodded and disappeared down a hallway.

Lacey had closed her eyes. He laid out the pad and sleeping bag. A noise outside alerted him. He rose to his feet. The window that faced the backyard looked out on a road. Three snowmobiles sped by. That had to be Lev and whoever he had recruited to search the cabins in the dark.

His stomach twisted into tight knots. He wasn't sure if he'd even be able to sleep until he knew what the men found. He glanced over at Lacey whose relaxed posture indicated she had fallen asleep.

Still restless, Jude moved around the room making sure the doors were locked. At least he could keep Lacey safe tonight. He settled down on the pad, unzipped the down sleeping bag and crawled inside. He set his gun off to one side but within reach. He stared at the ceiling for a long moment trying to pray. The prayer on the mountain when he was being shot at had been out of total desperation.

Though he was not in danger or in fear of losing his life, a sense of desperation invaded his mind. Desperation for Maria to be returned safely to her parents, and for him to feel like he'd redeemed himself from ten years ago.

He pulled the sleeping bag up close to his neck. The down surrounded his body and warmed him. He struggled to make the words of the prayer form. Did he only need God if he thought he was going to die? His faith had been so solid at one point in his life.

Lacey rolled over, so she was facing the back of the couch.

He listened to the gentle sound of her breathing.

If he was totally honest with himself, he wished too that there could be something between him and Lacey. He loved her easy laugh and the way her face got all animated when she talked about her work. But what did he have to offer her? He was a washed-up cop with only a fraction of the faith she displayed.

He stared at the ceiling, not able to form the words of a prayer but knowing that God understood anyway. His eyelids grew heavy, and he drifted off to sleep.

Hours later, his eyes fluttered open. Though he could not tell if he had dreamed it or if it was really happening, he thought he'd heard noises. He sat up. Alarmed, he rose to his feet. From what he could see, Lacey was not on the couch. The blanket that had covered her lay on the floor. Panic spread through his body as his senses tried to absorb what was happening.

It was still night outside. His eyes had not adjusted to the dark room. He heard muffled noises. As he glanced across the floor, he could see only shadows. He ran toward the noise in the next room just in time to see a dark figure unlock the back door in the kitchen from the inside and swing it open. The man disappeared into the darkness and he had Lacey with him.

Jude stepped into the first pair of shoes he saw. They were too big for him. The move had cost him precious seconds, but he wouldn't get far barefoot. He yelled once for Nancy to come help him. He didn't have time to find her room in the house.

A cold wind hit him as he stepped outside to search. In the dark, he could just make out boot tracks and two parallel lines. Signs of a barefoot Lacey being dragged away.

How could anyone know they were even here instead of at the hotel unless they'd been followed from the bank?

Someone had gotten to Lacey, probably taking her to a quiet place where killing her couldn't be heard.

# NINE

Cold seeped into Lacey's bare feet as she struggled to get away from her abductor. Everything had happened so fast. A few minutes before in the house, the man had put a gun to her head probably intending to kill both her and Jude while they slept. She had managed to knock the gun out of his hand. Jude had seen she was being taken. He couldn't be far behind.

Her kidnapper still held a hand over her mouth and the other suctioned around her waist as he dragged her through the snow. The chill seeped through her thin layer of clothes. She tried to get traction with her feet but to no avail. She twisted her head and torso to break free. She fell on the cold ground in a heap.

She couldn't see the house. Her kidnapper had dragged her behind a bunch of trees.

Her abductor grabbed her by the collar and lifted her up. Already she was shivering. She reached out toward his face. He was wearing a ski mask. He was tall and thin. Again, he wrapped his arms around her waist.

"Jude…somebody," she tried to yell, but her voice was paper thin.

He clasped a gloved hand over her mouth. "Be quiet!"

His voice held a note of rage that scared her even more. She had no doubt that his intent was to kill her.

As he continued to drag her through the snow, she spied the backyards of the houses on the same street they had searched. The run-down blue Victorian house was set off from the others. The tall thin man must be looking for a hiding place to kill her before Jude found them. When she looked where they had been, she saw no sign of Jude. The back sides of the houses looked very far away.

She had to get away. His grip around her waist was like iron. He swung her around and planted her feet. He gripped her wrist. "We need to run." He yanked her arm, pulling her through a cluster of trees. They ran for at least five minutes before he stopped. She stood before a set of stairs leading to a door that belonged to what looked like a single wide trailer. The trailer was off by itself, and it was not visible through the trees.

"Get in," he barked.

Her heartbeat drummed in her ears. Once she was inside, she was a dead woman. She turned and took off running. Her bare feet sunk down in the snow, chilling her to the bone. She took five steps before he was on top of her, tackling her to the ground. Her stomach pressed into the snow.

He rolled off of her. "Get up."

In what felt like one swift motion, he pulled her to her feet and pushed her into the trailer. Though she could not see much in the dark space, it was clear the trailer hadn't been occupied for some time. The place smelled like dust and mold. Cupboard doors hung on single hinges and what she could make out of the furniture, lopsided chairs and a couch with no cushions, indicated no one lived here.

She gripped the corner of the counter. He pushed on her back from behind. She took a step and felt a sting to her foot.

She lifted her leg. "I think I cut myself."

He pushed her again. "Like it's going to matter."

She limped forward. The house was nothing more than shadows. But there had to be a back door. She bolted down the hall as pain from the cut shot up her leg. The fact that her feet were already cold numbed some of the potential pain.

Because of all the junk and broken furniture, the house was like a maze. She crashed into furniture. She ran into a room and flipped open a window, preparing to crawl out.

He found her and pulled her back in. He pushed her to the ground and his arms were around her neck. He squeezed tight as she struggled for breath.

Her hands reached out for something…anything. Fingers wrapped around an object, something metal. She lifted it and hit him in the back. The blow was enough to make him let go of her and cry out in pain. She rolled away and scrambled to her feet, hitting him again but this time in the shoulder. She ran down the hallway.

*Please, God, let there be a back door here.*

She saw it then at the other end of the trailer, a door swinging on its hinges. She stepped through it expecting stairs. Instead she found herself falling through space and landing on the ground. Her knees hit first and then her hands.

Behind her, she could hear the noise of her abductor crashing through the trailer.

She rose to her feet and started to run, back toward Nancy's house, back toward safety. But she was disoriented. She'd run in the wrong direction and now she was surrounded by trees. She turned in a circle, trying to get her bearings.

A voice came to her ears, calling her name. Somewhere out in the darkness. It was Jude.

"I'm here. Jude." Her voice sounded faint and far away like it hadn't even come out of her throat. She hurried toward the sound of his voice.

She glanced over her shoulder as she ran. Where had the tall thin man gone?

Jude was suddenly there. Out of breath, she pressed herself against his chest. He wrapped his arms around her. "It's all right. I've got you."

"Do you see him back by that trailer?"

Jude still held her but lifted his head and turned slightly. "He's gone. He must have run off when he saw me coming toward you."

She felt both relief and rage. Relief that she was safe for now but rage that he was still out there in the shadows, waiting for another chance to come after her.

"Let's get you back to the house." Jude squeezed her shoulder.

She took a step forward her leg collapsed under her. Her feet were numb from the cold, and one of them was bleeding.

Jude looked down at her feet. "You're in no condition to walk." He swept her up in his arms and carried her toward the house.

She nestled her face close to his neck, breathing in the scent of wood smoke and musk. Her hand rested on his chest. She could feel herself getting light-headed. It wasn't entirely because of her injuries. Being held by Jude's strong arms made her feel like she was a balloon floating on the air.

She heard Nancy's voice. "Oh my, let's get her inside and warmed up." Though Laccy didn't think she'd managed to make much noise, Nancy must have been awakened. Maybe Jude had yelled for her help.

A door creaked open. Jude's boots made a different sound as they pounded across the wood floor. Nancy said something about heating up water and getting a first aid kit. Jude gently placed her on the couch. He grabbed the blanket and lifted it, so it covered her shoulders.

He kneeled and looked at her feet, then rubbed her uninjured foot between his hands.

"I can't see very well. Are your toes tingling?"

"No, just numb." She could feel the warmth of his fingers as he squeezed her foot. "I don't think I have frostbite. I'm just very cold." She drew the blankets even tighter around herself.

"You're probably right." He lifted her other foot. "It's this one I'm worried about. It looks like you have a cut on the side of it."

Nancy arrived with the hot water and first aid kit. "Let me get a lamp so you can see better." Lacey listened to her footsteps pad away and then return. "I'll hold the light." She brought it down closer to where Jude held her injured foot.

He washed her foot with warm water. The gentle touch soothed her. As the memory of the attack encroached, she was able to stay calm.

His finger pressed into the bottom of her foot. "You must have scraped it on something." He pulled something out of the first aid kit. "I need to disinfect it. It's going to sting a little."

"I can take it." She pressed her lips together.

"I know you can. You're one strong lady." He winked at her.

His playfulness sent a wave of electricity through her despite the pain she was in.

He pressed his thumb into the bottom of her foot and squeezed out the disinfectant. A sharp pain played across her nerves and then dissipated.

"Got it," he said.

"I think there's a bandage in there too," said Nancy.

Lacey closed her eyes as he pressed the bandage on.

"Is she going to be all right, Doctor?" Nancy's tone was joking.

"Yes, Nurse Nancy."

Lacey rested her hand on her chest, finally able to take a deep breath.

"I'm a little worried that man might come back." Nancy gripped her bathrobe at the neck.

"I'll make sure the house is secure and I'll stand watch until Lev gets back. Get some sleep, Nancy," Jude said.

After a moment's hesitation and nervous glance toward the kitchen, Nancy disappeared down the hallway.

Lacey could feel the heaviness of fatigue and the fallout from her attack weighing her muscles down.

"Why don't you try to sleep too." Jude stood up. "I'm going to make sure that window can't be opened again."

Lacey lay her head on the pillow and pulled her legs up toward her chest. She could hear Jude rooting around and then there was the sound of a hammer. By the time he returned, she was half-asleep.

She opened one eye. Jude had settled down on the pad and pulled the sleeping bag around himself while he stared at the fire in the woodstove.

"It's okay, you know," she said. "There's probably no way you could have prevented that guy coming in here."

"I should have stayed awake. I shouldn't have let my guard down. The reason why he's after you is because of me. Because you helped me."

"You were as tired out as I was." Even as she spoke, she could feel the tension between them again. It seemed that guilt ruled much of Jude's life. He must have felt a huge sense of responsibility ten years ago. That it was his job to save the husband and wife and now this kidnapped girl. "Jude, you're not invincible. You need sleep too. I know you would have prevented that guy from coming in here if you could have."

"I shouldn't have been sleeping so deeply."

"You're a human being. You need to eat and sleep like the rest of us. I'm just glad you came for me when you did. So quit beating yourself up…over everything."

He took a long moment to answer. "Okay." His tone suggested he didn't really mean what he said.

She pulled the blanket up toward her neck and stared at the ceiling. It seemed as though Jude had carried the weight of the world on his shoulders for a long time. Would he ever forgive himself for what had happened ten years ago? "I know that you did everything that you could with that husband and wife. You always do the right thing. You're a good man, but that doesn't mean bad things won't happen."

Jude didn't answer for several moments. "You might be right. I never thought about it that way."

Lacey drifted off to sleep not knowing if her words

had made a difference. She awoke hours later to the sound of heavy pounding on the front door.

Jude had only been half-asleep when he heard someone knocking at the door. He doubted the assailant would try to come back a second time and he certainly wouldn't knock.

Jude jumped to his feet just as Lacey opened her eyes. He peered through the window of the door. Lev stood outside in his full snowsuit gear but holding his helmet. Jude unlatched the door, feeling a tightness in his chest. It was just Lev on the front steps. No other searchers. No Maria.

Jude clicked back the dead bolt and twisted the doorknob. Early morning sun shone in his eyes.

"Forgot my key," Lev said as he stepped inside. "We usually don't have to lock our doors."

"What did you find?" Fear zinged through him like a Ping-Pong ball. He prayed Maria hadn't been killed or left to die.

Lev placed his helmet on the table by the door. He turned to face Jude. "Nothing."

"Nobody was up there?"

"There was evidence in the vacation rental that someone had been there recently. The other place was locked up tight. I don't think anyone has been there in months."

Jude tried to process what Lev was telling him. Lacey sat up on the couch, stretching and yawning. Maybe the kidnapper had panicked and moved Maria from the vacation rental. But where would he go? His travel would be as limited as theirs was. The roads were still not plowed.

Lev pulled off his gloves. "Did you two get some rest?"

"We had a little excitement here. Someone got into the house and grabbed Lacey."

Lev looked at Jude and then at Lacey who had risen to her feet. "I'm sorry about that. You know, there are men in this town I trust with my life. We can start questioning guys who are tall and thin…maybe get to the bottom of this before the sheriff shows up."

"I don't want the whole town knowing what is going on. The tall thin man would probably just go into hiding," Jude said. "There is one more home to visit on that mountain road. I can go up there and check it out and then I need to take the time to look around myself. That car that was used to kidnap Maria was on that road for a reason."

"You can't go up there alone," Lev said.

"Lacey's foot is hurt, so she might need to stay here with someone watching her."

Lacey stepped toward them, favoring her cut foot only slightly. "It doesn't hurt that bad. I'd rather be helpful and go back out with Jude. I'm in danger no matter what. Might as well make myself useful. I feel safest when I'm with Jude." She stared at him with those wide round eyes.

Jude appreciated the vote of confidence, but he'd already messed up once. "Are you sure?"

She nodded.

Her words from the night before came back to him. Did he allow himself to be a human being who made mistakes? His intention was always to do the right thing. That had been his intention ten years ago. He had asked God a thousand times why things had gone so wrong.

"I don't know if I like this plan." Lev shook his head. "It concerns me that that man came into my home and grabbed Lacey. I think maybe we should have her under some protection."

Lacey touched her hand to her chest. "Lev, I don't know if the man who came after me is someone from Lodgepole or an outsider who is in hiding. You're a good guy and I am sure most of the people in Lodgepole are good people, but right now Jude is the only one I trust."

Jude studied Lacey for a moment. Morning light from the window gave her auburn hair a golden tone. She wanted to be with him, if only for safety. She believed in him even if he didn't believe in himself.

Lev took a moment to answer. "It's your call, Lacey." He turned to face Jude. "I assume you carry a gun for your line of work."

Jude padded his chest.

"Okay, you can go up there again. Make sure when you take one of the town snowmobiles that you are fully fueled up."

"We'll grab some breakfast and head out so we have the full day. No need to wake Nancy. We can find something to eat," Jude said.

"I'd appreciate it. I'm pretty worn-out myself. I need to get a couple hours shut-eye before I deal with everything that has to be done." Lev nodded and disappeared down the hallway.

Lacey and Jude ate from the food supply that Nancy had set out on the counter. She heated some water for oatmeal and instant coffee. She handed him one of the steaming mugs after she'd stirred the coffee in.

"Not exactly a mocha with whipped cream, but it will warm your belly and give you some energy," she said.

"I'm sure my stomach will say thank you." He lifted the steamy mug in a toast.

While they sipped the coffee, Lacey got the map out that Lev had given them with the house that needed to be checked in on. She laid it out on the table and pointed. "That last house is the farthest away from the main road. It will take a while to get to."

"Yes, that's the one where that family lives off the grid. Lev said we'd have to park the snowmobile and hike in."

The both stared at the map. "Besides those two cabins, there are no other residences that connect with that mountain road." Jude shook his head. "It doesn't make any sense. Where would he have taken her? He was on that road for some reason."

She pointed at the map. There are primitive roads that go off toward the other side of the mountain. "Maybe he was holding her on the other side of the mountain and going the long way to avoid detection."

"I don't know," Jude said. "I just know I have to keep trying."

They both stepped into the living room where they'd tossed their snowsuits and other winter gear. While they suited up they continued to talk.

"Maybe she was never in the cabin." Lacey sat down to pull on her boots after she'd zipped her suit up.

"Then why was he so bent on me not making it up that mountain road in the first place?"

She shook her head. "I don't know. Maybe he has a camper up there."

They stepped outside into the crisp clear morning.

For the first time in days they could see blue sky even though the temperature felt like it might be hovering around zero.

"Just a second." Jude pulled his cell phone out. "I think I have a signal. I have to call George Ignatius. At least try to make contact. I'm sure he's sitting in his home in North Dakota worried to death about his missing daughter."

Lacey nodded, sat sideways on the snowmobile and tilted her head toward the sun.

The phone rang several times. He heard a man's voice on the other end of the line. "George? It's Jude Trainor."

George's voice faded in and out. Jude thought he asked if Maria had been found yet.

"No, but I think she is being kept somewhere on Shadow Ridge. Has a ransom demand been made yet?"

A blast of static hit his ear. He thought he heard George say "Yes." And then all he could hear was warbled speech. "George, I can't hear you." He listened a moment longer before giving up.

They got onto the snowmobile, which revved to life. They refueled at the grain silo, where Lev had told them they would find some gas pumps, and headed back up the mountain.

The sun shining somehow renewed his hope and energy. They had at least eight hours before it got dark. It wouldn't take that long to check on the last home. He didn't doubt that Lev had not seen anyone at either of the cabins, but maybe there was some clue that would tell him that Maria had been there.

The snowmobile wound up the mountain past the first turnoff where they had checked on the old man and his dogs. They came to a fork in the road. He slowed the snowmobile and turned. He'd traveled maybe a quarter mile before the road became a trail.

The deadfall of forest and the heavy snow made it clear that if they tried to go any farther, they'd just end up getting stuck. He stopped the snowmobile.

Lacey got off first, grabbing the backpack that contained emergency supplies. Jude pulled his helmet off and looked around. "How crazy does someone have to be to live in such a remote place?"

"Lev didn't warn us in any way about them. Some people just don't want to be all caught up in modern life. I like it when my research takes me up to a cabin or campsite where I can't see the light of civilization anywhere, only the stars. It has its appeal."

There was a heaviness to her words. They had both been hiding, running for years just in different ways. "I suppose we all need to get away now and then." He reached toward her. "I'll carry the backpack."

He slipped into it and led the way through the trees. After a while, there was no clear path. They stepped around fallen logs and pushed the branches of bent-over trees out of the way.

He smelled wood smoke but couldn't see anything through the thick undergrowth. They stepped into the clearing where the smoke from a chimney twirled through the blue sky.

Lacey stepped forward and stood beside him. "That's a good sign. They are able to keep their house heated."

He liked that she stood so close to him. "I'm glad you decided to come out here with me."

"Honestly, Jude, I meant it. Being with you is the safest place for me."

"Thanks." He reached out and squeezed her gloved hand. Jude turned his attention back to the smoke though the house was still not visible. "Let's go make sure this family is okay."

If everything went according to plan, they would have plenty of time to search the area for any clues as to what had happened to Maria. He could not accept that she had never been on the mountain at all.

The kidnapper or kidnappers had communicated with George to set a ransom. If the kidnappers had demanded cash, assuming that Maria was being kept somewhere on the mountain, the exchange couldn't happen until the roads were open. That meant Maria was still alive. It also meant time was running out to find her.

# TEN

Lacey heard the sound of children laughing even before she saw the house that belonged to the Johnsons. The forest thinned, and a structure that looked like it had been made from recycled materials came into view. Part of the dwelling was an old bus with rooms and walls extending out from it. Though the place looked like square footage had been added as needed, it was probably quite large inside.

Two boys, one maybe eight years of age and a teenager, threw snowballs at each other while a brown dog leaped in the air at the snowballs and yipped. The boys stopped and stared at Lacey and Jude when they stepped free of the trees.

Jude waved. "We're from Lodgepole. We're here to check on your safety."

The younger boy spoke up. "I'll get my dad." He ran, disappearing around the side of the house.

The older boy picked up an ax and chopped wood while Lacey and Jude drew closer.

Lacey stepped toward the teenager who brought the ax down on a log. "Is everyone here okay?"

"We've been fine. Dad reckons we'll be able to dig out of here in a couple of days."

Several more children came to the window and looked out. Two girls and a blond baby who sucked his fingers as they watched with interest.

A man who looked like the teenager, only with a mustache, came around the corner of the house. He held out his hand to shake both Jude's and Lacey's hand. "I'm David Johnson. You came up from Lodgepole to check on us?"

"Yeah, it's something Lev feels needs to be done."

"Good ol' Lev. I think we're pretty well set."

Lacey noticed a truck still covered in snow. "You're able to drive out when the roads are clear?"

David turned toward his truck. "Yeah, there is a road on the other side of the property that leads into Garnet. That's where we get most of our supplies. Gonna be a few more days before the forest service plow makes it up this far. But we have a generator, lots of wood, stocked shelves and a greenhouse. I can get around on the snowmobile. We're ready for anything. I used to live in Seattle, worked as a financial guy. The stress was killing me, and I never got to see my kids." He cupped a hand on the teenager's shoulder. "Trying to teach them self-sufficiency."

"Dad, what about some aspirin for Winnie?" The teen pointed at Jude's backpack.

"Oh yes, if you have aspirin in that pack, we'd take that."

Jude slipped out of the pack and started rooting through it. He opened the first aid kit and pulled out two packets. "Probably only going to be three or four in each one. It's not a children's aspirin."

"We can cut it in half." Johnson took the packets. "Thanks. My wife likes to use herbal medicine, but sometimes you can't beat good old-fashioned aspirin. You folks are welcome to come in if you like. Wife said something about making a pecan pie."

Lacey glanced at Jude. They couldn't waste any time. "That sounds tempting, but we need to get going."

David offered them a tip of his hat. "Take care and say hi to Lev for me."

"You got it," Jude said. He turned to go but then turned back around. "Have you noticed any strange vehicles around here before the storm hit?"

David shook his head and then looked at his older son who also shook his head.

Jude still wasn't going to give up. "I don't suppose you've seen anyone headed up toward those two cabins that are above you or signs of someone camping out?"

Again, David shook his head. "One of the cabins is owned by some organization. The members can use it. The other is a vacation rental. Sometimes in the summer I run into people. If they are out here to hunt, they might come by and introduce themselves. But no one has made themselves known lately."

"Thank you," Jude said.

The younger boy and a girl about the same age emerged from the house. Lacey and Jude walked back toward the growth of trees with the sound of laughter and wood being chopped fading as they hurried along.

"They seem like a happy family," Lacey said. She hadn't meant for her voice to be tinged with sadness. "I suppose they exist in this world. Happy families. I used to think that I would get married and have kids, but now I don't know."

Jude stopped the galloping pace he'd been setting and turned to face her. "Yeah, I understand about life being derailed. I used to think I was going in that direction too, but then when I couldn't stop that murder-suicide." He shook his head. "I don't know…it's like I lost my way." He reached out and squeezed her arm, offering her a faint smile.

From the moment she'd met Jude, she'd been drawn to the bright dancing quality she saw in his eyes. The slightly upturned mouth that suggested a mischievous side. She felt so conflicted. She was attracted to him and had been right from the start, but he stirred something up inside her that made her want to run. They had only known each other a short time. Maybe she was drawn to him because they both had suffered great loss. But part of her wanted the past to remain buried.

An uncomfortable feeling, a tightening through her stomach, made her start walking again.

Jude kept pace with her. "Maybe if we talked about this. I don't know. Both of us had bad things happen. It sounds like we both gave up on a normal life because of it, marriage, kids, a home."

She walked even faster. "I don't know what there is to say. Talking about it just makes me hurt all over again." It felt like a rope was being wrapped tight around her chest.

Jude dropped back a few steps behind her. "Okay, I'll let it go."

She hurried through the trees toward the snowmobile. They came to where it was parked. Now things just felt tense and awkward between them.

"I'm sorry," she said.

Jude's attention was on the snowmobile.

"What's wrong?" she asked.

"Someone has been here." He pointed to a wet spot in the snow. "They punctured the gas tank." He leaned forward to have a closer look. "Could be a couple of bullets shot through it to make it leak out." He stood back up.

Both of them tilted their heads. Lacey listened as tension filled her body.

A rifle shot rang out. The sound bruised her eardrum. Jude pulled her to the ground, seeking cover behind the defunct snowmobile. Her belly pressed into the cold hard snow. Jude turned his head so he was facing her.

"Let's try to get back to the Johnsons'."

Lacey wasn't sure if that was a good idea. That might put the family in danger.

They jumped to their feet together and took off running toward the trees. Another shot zinged through the air. And then another.

Jude grabbed her arm and pulled her toward a ditch surrounded by trees. He searched the forest. "Judging from the noise, whoever is shooting at us is really close." He pointed. "Shots came from over there. He's between us and the Johnsons' house. We can't get back to there."

"He'll stalk us through the forest." Her throat had gone tight with fear.

"We'll have to head the other way," Jude said. "Maybe we can work our way down to Mr. Wilson's house."

That was miles from here.

Neither of them moved.

"The Johnsons might hear the shots," she said.

"Maybe. It is hunting season. What if they don't think anything of it?" Jude continued to stare out, probably looking for the next place to take cover. She searched the trees where the shots had come from but saw no movement. Jude pointed back toward the snow-mobile.

She nodded. They pushed up from the ground and ran back toward the snowmobile, diving behind it. The silence surrounded them. She lifted her head just above the seat of the snowmobile. At least when they were being shot at, she knew where the would-be killer was.

Jude tugged on her sleeve and they sprinted toward another cluster of trees. They ran for some time, making their way out close to the road though they stayed close to the forest to provide cover. Several times shots pinged off trees. They ran silently down the mountain.

The forest ended, giving them no choice but to dart out into the open. Lacey peered over her shoulder. The shooter was behind them. His muscular build and gray hair told her he was the first man they'd seen on the mountain. He lifted his rifle and aimed.

Her heart froze in her chest. She turned to face forward just as she felt herself falling through space. She'd come to a steep drop-off and fallen. She hit the ground and rolled head over heels. A mini avalanche followed in her wake sending a wave of snow behind her. She stopped rolling and landed in a sitting position with snow covering her legs.

Fortunately, her snow gear had kept her warm. Only her face was chilled. The field of white that surrounded her was blinding. She glanced above her, expecting to see the shooter taking aim. He hadn't made it to the edge yet.

She rose to her feet, not seeing Jude anywhere. Had he fallen too or had he stopped fast enough to avoid the steep drop-off? She dare not call out to him. A hundred yards down the mountain was an outcropping of trees. She headed toward it. The softness of the snow had broken her fall. She wasn't bruised, only fatigued.

Where was Jude?

She had only run twenty paces when she noticed a dark object partially covered in snow. Heart racing, she ran toward it, fearing that Jude had been buried in the little avalanche. As she drew closer, she saw that it was the backpack Jude had been carrying.

Terror warred with panic. Was Jude suffocated by the snow?

She leaned down. The backpack was not attached to a body. He must have fallen too and this had become detached as he rolled. She looked all around, not seeing Jude anywhere. She slipped the backpack on.

Movement out of the corner of her eye drew her glance upward. The shooter had come to the edge of the cliff and was taking aim. He lifted the rifle.

She couldn't make it to the trees before he got a shot off. She dove to the ground and crawled through the field of white. A shot came very close to her. So close it must have lodged in the backpack.

A light breeze brushed the skin of her exposed face as she made her way toward the trees. Crawling solider style. Heart racing. Body tensed. Again, the silence surrounded her. She peered over her shoulder. The shooter fell partway down the cliff when some snow broke off. He'd dropped his rifle above him.

This was her chance to make a run for it while he climbed back up, got his rifle and lined up another shot.

She bolted toward the rocks and trees. Her boots pressed into the snow. She pumped her legs as her heart pounded. She fought for breath, running even harder, faster.

Like a baseball player sliding into home plate, she dove toward the cover of the evergreens. A bullet hit the tree in front of her. She hurried deeper into the trees. She peered out at the field of white.

Where was Jude?

Jude opened his eyes staring at the clear blue sky. He lay flat on his back. His head rested on a rock that protruded out of the snow. He must have been knocked unconscious. He remembered only the snow breaking beneath him, the ground giving way.

He'd been out so long, that despite the warm winter gear, he could feel a chill seeping into his skin. In his tumble, he'd lost a glove and the backpack. He unzipped his snowsuit and placed his frozen hand close to his chest to warm it. His gun was still there.

Jude pushed himself off the ground. When he heard what he thought were rifle shots, he lurched forward. The shots hadn't come anywhere near him. His heart squeezed tight. Lacey was in danger.

A line of trees blocked his view of where the shots must have come from. He ran toward them. Once on the other side of the trees, he was faced with an uphill climb. He must have rolled some distance in his fall.

He dug his feet in the side of the hill to get some traction, feeling a sense of urgency as another gunshot shattered the silence. He worked his way up the snowy hillside. As he came to the crest of the incline, he saw the shooter, the broad-shouldered man, standing on the edge of the steep drop-off that Jude must have rolled down. He followed the line where the rifle was aimed just in time to see Lacey disappear into the trees.

He saw now the furrows he must have created when he rolled down the hill. Other than that, a field of pristine snow lay before him. In his fall he had rolled completely out of view of the shooter. In order to get to Lacey, he'd have to become a target himself.

Jude shrank back down the hill, running out of view for as long as he could. His cover ended. He took a breath and stepped out into the open. Dropping to the ground might make him harder to hit, but it would take forever to crawl across the white expanse to the trees where Lacey had disappeared. He opted instead to run fast and hard, moving in a zigzag pattern and dropping to the ground for short intervals so it would be hard to line up a shot on him.

His boots sank down in the snow as he hurried toward the safety of the trees. In his peripheral vision he saw the shooter step back, lift his rifle and take aim. Jude darted sideways just as another shot rang through the forest. Heart pounding, he kept his gaze on the edge of the trees. Another shot by his upper arm nearly knocked him over and took his breath away. He waited for the excruciating pain of a gunshot wound to disable him altogether, but the pain never came. It must have gone through the thickness of his snowsuit at the padded shoulder where it felt like he'd been punched hard.

Just as he reached the edge of the trees, he glanced up. The shooter had backed away. But Jude had a feeling he'd merely gone back to his snowmobile so he could meet Lacey and him on the other side of the forest. Just because the shooter had opted not to tumble down the steep cliff where he and Lacey had fallen didn't mean the kidnapper had given up.

Jude entered the trees, his eyes searching. "Lacey." He sprinted. The canopy of branches meant that there was less snow beneath the trees. Still, he scanned the ground hoping to see her boot print. He kept running, shouting her name several more times.

Desperation filled his awareness. Where had she gone? She hadn't seen him. She probably thought she was on her own out here. The sound of the snowmobile grew louder. He kept on running, searching. Fear gripped his heart. What if the shooter caught up with Lacey before he did? What if she'd been shot before she got to the shelter of the trees? She might be lying somewhere bleeding, unable to respond to his cries. He pumped his legs, willing himself to go faster. He wasn't going to let anything bad happen to Lacey. Choosing a path that looked most like a trail, he wove through the trees, running for at least ten minutes.

She nearly crashed into him.

"I thought I'd lost you." Her hand rested on his chest. She tilted her head to look into his eyes. She was out of breath from running.

He gasped for air too as relief flooded through him. "I was afraid too." He touched her cheek with his ungloved hand, relishing the warmth of her skin and the radiance of the affection he saw in her eyes. The prospect of losing her had made him realize how much he cared about her. More than anything, he wanted to kiss her and to hold her close.

She studied him a moment longer and then cast her gaze downward, breaking the heat of the moment between them.

Snow started to twirl around them. Their clear blue sky had become overcast. In the distance, a snowmobile engine revved.

"He's still after us, isn't he?" Lacey took a step back away from him, turning a half circle in the forest, probably trying to come up with a plan of escape.

He was grateful to see that she had recovered the backpack of supplies. "You have the radio still?"

She padded her chest. "Yes, but we're not close enough to get a signal. I don't think. I lost my bearings when we rolled down that drop-off. Do you think we could get back to the Johnsons'?"

He wasn't exactly certain of their location either. "I think that we might end up even more lost. If the Johnsons heard the shots, maybe they'll come out and see the sabotaged snowmobile." He knew they shouldn't count on help coming for them. He stepped forward and squeezed her arm just above the elbow. The snowmobile grew louder. Though it made sense to try and find the road that lead back to town, it would make them too easy to track down. "We just have to go where that snowmobile can't go." He took several steps deeper into the trees, turning to look back at her. Her auburn hair had worked loose of whatever had fastened it into place, framing her face and making her brown eyes seem even more filled with light.

He had a flash of memory. She'd pulled away when that electric moment had passed between them a few minutes ago. She didn't want to talk about the tragedies that defined both their lives. The walls around her heart were just too high. He'd have to hold on to that warm wonderful memory of being with her in the café, knowing that that was all there would ever be for the two of them.

Why was he even thinking about that? They were lost. He turned back around, tracing a pathway through the trees with his eyes. He wasn't quite sure where they were at in relation to the road. Maybe if they worked their way downward they would get to a place where they could radio for help.

Once they didn't come home in the evening, a search party might be sent out for them. Even if Lev or somebody else found the sabotaged snowmobile, it would take some tracking skills to figure where he and Lacey had ended up and by then it might be too late.

# ELEVEN

Lacey stared at the back of Jude's head as she trudged a few paces behind him. They'd been walking for over two hours with no sign of any landmark to tell her where they were. What if they were moving away from the road? All she saw were trees, trees and more trees. The terrain had leveled off. The only good thing was they had not heard the snowmobile for at least twenty minutes.

The tension between them was palpable. She'd looked into his eyes, and the affection there had frightened her.

She stopped, planting her feet. "I don't think we are making any progress here. We might actually be moving deeper into the forest and getting more lost."

He turned to face her. His forehead wrinkled. "What do you suggest?"

She picked up on the ire in his words. She suspected his irritation wasn't about where he was leading her. It was about her pulling away in the heat of the moment. She wanted to tell him that she had felt the electricity between them too, but it had made her afraid. Instead, she responded with an impatient suggestion. "I think we need to work our way back to the road so we can figure out where we are. I know it's not safe to just follow the road but knowing where it is would be the best way to navigate."

He tilted his head toward the sun in the sky, which was barely visible through the thickness of the trees. "You know he is still out there looking for us. He's not going to give up. Someone from town should come searching for us once we don't come in at sunset."

"But they won't know where to find us, Jude."

"I'm doing the best I can." Jude placed his hands on his hips.

Hearing the frustration in his voice made her soften. "I know you are. I'm sorry. I just don't think we could survive if we had to spend the night out here."

"Tell you what. Let's walk for another ten minutes or so and then head out toward the edge of the tree line to see if we can figure out where we are."

"Okay." She tilted her head to see where the sun was. To the best of her recollection the road was east from where they were at. She pointed. "Probably the best choice would be to go that way."

Jude changed direction, instead of moving due north he cut across the forest in a more eastward direction.

He continued trudging through the trees, taking the path of least resistance since there was no clear trail. It had snowed off and on throughout the day, just a light snow that never turned into a full-on storm. If another snowstorm moved in, they for sure would not be able to survive the night outside. They had a few hours before it got dark.

They walked for several hours, stopped to eat and drink from the supplies in the backpack and then kept going. As the sun set low in the sky, she was giving up hope of ever coming out of the forest. It seemed to go on forever.

"Let's try the radio and see if we can get anything?"

He stopped and nodded.

She pulled the radio from inside her snowsuit and pressed the button that activated it. "Hello, is anybody out there? This is Snow Team One." She let up on the button and heard only static. She pressed the button again. "Hello?" She spoke more slowly as a sense of hopelessness invaded her mind. "This is Snow Team One. We're in some trouble."

The silence on the other end of the line caused a tension to twist through her chest and stomach. She squeezed the radio a little tighter.

"Nobody is there, Lacey." Jude's words were soft and filled with despair.

She glanced in his direction. He turned away and crossed his arms over his chest. "We got a little more daylight left. Let's use it while we can."

Lacey put the radio back in her snowsuit and followed as Jude set an even faster pace through the trees. She stopped in a clearing that looked like a tornado had gone through—broken tree branches and muddy snow.

"What happened here?" Jude looked around.

She looked closer at the tracks on the ground. "Herd of elk went through here. See the tracks? When there is a bunch of them, they're like bulldozers."

"Where were they going?"

"Maybe looking for food. Maybe some hunters scared them."

It felt like the research that had brought her to Lodgepole in the first place was some faraway dream.

They continued to walk, still not finding an end to the forest or seeing any sort of landmark that might orient them. As darkness fell, the snow and the wind increased. She zipped her snowsuit up tighter. Jude placed his ungloved hand inside his snowsuit to keep it warm.

The sun slipped out of view, and the night grew cold. Wind blew snow in her face. She stumbled.

Jude turned around to look at her. "You okay?" He was carrying the backpack, which he took off. "I'll see if there is some kind of light or something in here. Maybe some flares. They'd be spotted now that it's dark."

He set the pack on the ground, leaning close to see. She kneeled as well as he turned over the objects that were in there. Food, water, medicine.

"There's a lighter in here." He held it up so she could see. "We could build a signal fire."

"What if it's spotted by the wrong person?"

"We could at least build a small fire to keep warm." Jude took one of the bandages out of the first aid kit and wrapped it around a stick, then poured the rubbing alcohol on it before lighting it to make a torch. "This will burn out after a while, but we can at least see a little better."

He handed her the torch to hold while he zipped the backpack up and slipped into the straps. Again, they took off at a steady pace. The landscape never seemed to change: evergreens, fallen logs, the occasional clearing with no sign of the road.

From time to time she heard a strange sound in the forest, some sort of wild animal maybe. She couldn't quite place the noise, not a bear or a mountain lion. At first it was faint and infrequent.

Jude must have heard it too. "A fox maybe? Whatever it is, it sounds like it's in pain."

"Foxes sound like crying babies when they're in pain. That's not a fox." Fear infused her words.

They kept moving. Jude's makeshift torch illuminated the ground in front of them. The path was wide enough for them to walk side by side. The strange noise died out altogether.

They walked for another twenty minutes. The sound from the animal returned, this time closer and more distinctive. Jude turned one way and then the other. The noise was clearly howling and yipping, a canine sound.

"Are there wolves around here?" Jude asked. The flame from the torch flickered on the side of his face.

A chill ran up her spine like a thousand tiny spiders. "Yes. They're the primary predator of the elk."

"They move in packs though?"

"Usually unless they have been kicked out." Her throat was dry from fear. "Wolves aren't that noisy when they're hunting."

The barking was very close but still they couldn't see anything. She caught a flash of movement in the trees. "There." She grabbed the torch to aim it. Jude still held on to it.

She saw a flash of dark fur.

It was a canine and it did look like a wolf and now it was being quiet. Was it stalking them?

"What if it's a dog?" Jude stepped forward. "Hey buddy, come mere, puppy." He aimed the torch at sectors of the trees.

It could be a dog that had been abandoned because of the storm, left to fend for itself. "Mr. Wilson had dogs."

Jude whistled and called for the animal again. They

heard yipping and then a black border collie with white markings emerged from the trees. The dog wagged its tail and jumped up and down.

Breathing a sigh of relief, Lacey knelt down and pet the dog who licked her face. The dog had tags. "This is Mr. Wilson's dog. It says his name is Bart."

"Maybe we're far enough down the mountain that his place is just around a corner."

"But why is this dog out running through the forest with another storm on the way?"

"I don't know. We must be close to Wilson's house. Maybe he'll lead us to it." Jude handed Lacey the torch and rummaged through the backpack for another long bandage. He tied it around Bart's collar. He petted the dog's ears. "Come on, boy, lead the way."

They took off. Bart put his nose to the ground running at first and then slowing down. Though he seemed content to stay with them and didn't mind the makeshift leash, his movement seemed random and erratic.

The wind blew, and the snow fell more intensely. Her face grew cold as they worked their way through the trees and across a clearing. The temperature was dropping.

The dog sniffed the ground from time to time but really didn't seem to be leading them anywhere. They were now headed downhill, but she wasn't holding out hope that they would find Mr. Wilson's house.

They kept walking. The torch died out, slowing their pace. Her nose and cheeks felt numb from the cold. Bart grew excited, barking and twirling in circles, jerking on the leash.

He might just be chasing the scent of raccoons or

some other nocturnal creature. All the same, she kept pace with the excited dog.

The back of Mr. Wilson's house appeared first as shadows. There were no lights on at all. Though Bart continued to yip and pull on the leash, they slowed their pace.

Mr. Wilson had a rifle, and he was paranoid about being robbed.

As they approached the house, another dog came out of the shadows and greeted them. The old Lab was glad to see them and Bart. They circled around the house and knocked on the front door. No answer.

"Didn't he say he was staying in a back room because it was easier to heat?" she said.

The Lab disappeared around the side of the house. Jude untied Bart and let him go. "They must know how to get in. Let's follow."

She could barely make out Bart's dark fur against the blackness of night. The wind howled, and the snow had started to come down sideways. The dogs led them to a door that was ajar. The tiny room was more of a shed, maybe ten by ten feet and it was separate from the main house.

Jude knocked on the door. "Mr. Wilson?"

The dogs yipped and barked and wagged their tails. Jude tried the door. The knob turned.

"Mr. Wilson, it's the people from Lodgepole. We checked on you yesterday."

The silence was eerie. Lacey tensed as Jude opened the door farther. The room was dark though she could make out the outline of a woodstove.

Despite the storm still raging, they searched all

around the outside of the house and a little ways into the forest. She was shivering.

"We can't stay out here much longer," Lacey said. "Let's get warmed up and then we can look some more for Mr. Wilson."

They returned to the little room with the dogs trailing behind them.

They stepped inside. Jude touched the woodstove and opened the door on it. "Fire is out but the stove is still warm, so it went out recently." He grabbed some of the chopped wood stacked in the corner and lit the stove.

The dogs came inside and lay on the beds that had been set up for them in the corner. Lacey fumbled around until she found a lantern and lit it. When she shone the light around, she saw Mr. Wilson's rifle propped against the wall. Would he go anywhere without his rifle? She wondered too where the third dog was, the white one that looked like it was part pit bull. All of this was concerning.

With the stove blazing, Lacey reached her hands out toward the warmth, shifting from foot to foot. Jude picked a blanket up that had been resting on a small nightstand. He stood beside her. His shoulder pressed against hers. "There's only one blanket. You can have it."

The fear she'd felt earlier was no longer there. There was something comforting about having him close. "We can share it."

He wrapped the blanket around his shoulder and then around hers. His hand brushed over her back. Jude had left the door on the woodstove open. Both of them stared at the crackling fire.

The dogs settled down on their beds. Bart whined before lying down.

"We're going to have to go looking for Mr. Wilson once we're warmed up."

"I know," she said. Now that they had a quiet moment, the memory of him looking into her eyes came back to her. There was a part of her that wanted him to kiss her. Her jaw tensed. Why did she feel so conflicted about this?

"Mr. Wilson wasn't a young man. Maybe he wandered away from the property and had a heart attack," Jude said. "He must have gone pretty far. We looked everywhere. Maybe he went to a friend's house."

"Maybe, but the door was left open. That's why the dogs got out. That is the action of someone leaving in a hurry," she said. They'd worked together to get here. Over and over, Jude had shown her that he would protect her and not leave her. She wasn't sure what to say. "I'm sorry I didn't want to talk about losing my family."

Jude turned, grabbed another log from the stack and tossed it into the fire. "I understand. It's painful to open old wounds. I sure don't want to do it." He settled back down beside her.

Tears welled up in her eyes. "I guess I've been kind of closed down since the accident. I cut people out of my life who cared about me. I worked and moved around so I didn't have to think about it." The tears flowed. "I feel like I wasted the life God gave me. I don't want to do that anymore."

Jude took her in his arms and held her.

She sobbed, resting her face against the flannel of his shirt. His arms held her while she cried. She felt a release…anger, guilt and sadness that she'd been holding in for years. Finally, there were no more tears. She rested her face against his chest while his heart beat in her ear.

His fingers touched under her chin. She lifted her face to look into his eyes. He bent toward her and brushed his lips over hers. She drew closer, feeling the hunger of his kiss and wrapping her arms around his neck.

The blanket fell from her shoulders. She felt the warm smolder of attraction…and maybe something deeper. His arms held her as he kissed her again. When he finally pulled free, she felt light-headed but so alive.

It was as if she had spent the years since the accident in walking paralysis. Functioning but numb with pain.

He rested his forehead against hers and then kissed her cheek before shifting back. His hand found hers and he squeezed it tight.

She closed her eyes, enjoying the moment.

Jude's hand pulled away. She opened her eyes. Something in the corner of the room caught his attention. The look on his face was one of shock.

As she watched him rise to his feet, her mood shifted to fear. Jude picked up the object in the dark corner of the room. It was a small stuffed animal, a lamb. Holding the toy, he turned to face Lacey. "This was the toy Maria was holding when she was kidnapped."

# TWELVE

Jude stared down at the toy he grasped in his hand. It felt as though his world had been flipped on its side and then turned upside down. Maria's mother said she always had the toy with her. The picture he'd been given of the child showed her holding it.

Lacey rose to her feet. "I'm sure there are a lot of stuffed toys like that around. Maybe Mr. Wilson has grandchildren or maybe the dogs play with it."

He shook his head. "It can't be a coincidence. Mr. Wilson must have been holding Maria here."

"Do you think he's in on the kidnapping?"

"It looks that way."

The dogs stirred from their beds, barking and flinging themselves at the door. Something had them excited.

Lacey moved toward the door. "I hear another dog barking."

While the dogs continued to bounce around, she and Jude got back into their boots. Jude grabbed a flashlight that rested on a chair. Lacey eased the door open only a slit so they could slip through but the dogs couldn't get out. Outside the wind was still blowing and the snow came down sideways.

The barking of the third dog grew louder as he emerged through the trees. The dog ran toward them, jumped in circles around them and then headed back toward the trees.

"He's trying to tell us something." Lacey hurried after the white dog.

Jude ran beside her, shining the flashlight. The conditions were not a whiteout. All the same, it was not a good idea to get too far away from the house.

As they ran following the dog, the intensity of the kiss they'd shared lingered in his memory. How quickly the mood had been destroyed by his discovery.

His feet pounded through the snow. Frustration rose up inside of him. When they'd checked on Mr. Wilson, he may have been only a short distance away from Maria and not have known it. Or maybe she'd been brought down here from the cabin. Though they still needed to search the property, he had the feeling Maria was not here any longer. Had Mr. Wilson taken her somewhere else?

The dog led them into the trees that surrounded Mr. Wilson's property. He stopped at what looked like a fallen log, sat back on his haunches and howled. Lacey and Jude sprinted toward the dog, arriving at the same time. Jude shone the light all around. The object that he thought was a log was not. The light washed over a body lying facedown. The white hair indicated that it was Mr. Wilson.

Lacey let out a sharp gasp and took a step back. She reached for Jude's arm. Jude stepped closer. The body was frozen but there were clear bloodstains on the back. "He was shot."

"So he wasn't involved?" Lacey's voice faltered.

Jude straightened his spine as his stomach twisted into a hard knot. "Mr. Wilson lived a very austere lifestyle. I'm sure a little cash would have persuaded him to watch a child."

"His conscience must have bothered him. So he was shot," Lacey said. "Maybe he threatened to tell the authorities."

"Or maybe that guy on the snowmobile just eliminates anyone who could turn him in. We need to search the rest of the property. I doubt Maria is still around. But there might be some clue as to where she's been taken. That car that I was chasing must be parked somewhere."

The dog whined and yipped and then paced. Something was upsetting him.

A bright light shone on the body and then on their faces. A man in silhouette stood not more than twenty yards from them.

Lacey's voice filled with panic. "He's come back for the body."

And now they'd been spotted. The dark figure advanced toward them. He was the same build as the man on the snowmobile, the broad-shouldered man.

"Run," Jude said.

Both of them sprinted toward the house. As he ran, he lost sight of Lacey. Several shots were fired. The proximity and power of the shots hurt his eardrum. He sprinted toward the house, shining the light in the trees. Without a flashlight, Lacey would be forced to move slower. He didn't see her anywhere. His heart squeezed tight with fear.

Another shot zinged by his head. Jude switched off the flashlight. It made him too easy of a target. The dog that had led them to the body continued to bark.

Without any light to guide him, Jude slowed his pace. He slipped from tree to tree. The kidnapper was close enough that Jude could hear his footsteps. Light flashed into and out of the trees.

Jude pressed his back against the thick trunk of a tree. The kidnapper's steps crunched in the snow and landed on branches that crackled as they broke underneath his boots. Jude feared his raging heart and heavy breathing would give him away. He stood still as a rock. The kidnapper's flashlight continued to jump around.

He heard another set of footsteps moving rapidly. Lacey. Now the kidnapper turned his light toward where that sound had come from. Jude caught a flash of Lacey running and the kidnapper falling in behind her right at her heels. Jude could see the kidnapper's back as he raised the gun to take aim at Lacey. He had to stop him before he shot Lacey. There was no time to draw his gun. Jude ran toward the kidnapper, leaping on his back and taking him to the ground. The two men wrestled. The kidnapper hit Jude in the head. The blow stunned him as he lay on his back.

The other man had risen to his feet moving toward where he'd dropped his rifle. He'd lost the flashlight in the struggle, leaving them both in the darkness. Jude rolled away into the brush, pushed himself to his feet and fired a shot. It was too dark to see if he'd hit his target. Another shot whizzed by his arm.

He needed to find Lacey.

He sprinted toward the dark shadows of Mr. Wilson's house. He peered over his shoulder. The kidnapper must be looking around for his flashlight. It bought Jude a few precious seconds. His legs pumped as he neared the house. Where was Lacey? She might go back to the room where the dogs were to get that rifle. But she wouldn't stay there. There was only one way in and out. That would make her a sitting duck. And he didn't think she would run haphazardly into the forest either. There were piles of rubble and building materials and an old car on the back side of the property in addition to the car that was parked out front.

"Over here," came a whisper.

He heard Lacey's voice but had no idea where it had come from. Light flashed as the kidnapper appeared around the corner of the small shed. Jude dove toward a pile of rocks. The man stomped past him, shining the light everywhere.

It occurred to Jude that the man must have come on his snowmobile. Where had he parked it? If he could find Lacey and figure out where the snowmobile was, they could get back to Lodgepole. The kidnapper would be stranded. Wherever he had hidden that car, it wasn't going anywhere.

The kidnapper trudged back toward where Jude was hiding, swinging around his flashlight. Jude crouched lower as the man passed him.

The footsteps stopped. Jude could no longer see the light. He lifted his head, trying to figure out what had happened. The dog that was still outside had stopped barking. Silence fell around Jude like a shroud. He studied each sector of the yard looking for any indication of where the kidnapper may have gone.

Jude bolted up, still not seeing any movement. He turned.

A light flashed in his peripheral vision by the little shed. He crouched back down.

"I think you better come out wherever you are. I got your girlfriend here with a gun to her head."

The blood froze in Jude's veins.

From the loft where she was hiding in the main house, Lacey peered out. She couldn't believe what she was hearing. The kidnapper was trying to lure Jude out into the open with a lie. She watched in horror as Jude rose to his feet and stepped toward the little back room where the voice had come from. She had to warn him, but shouting would only alert the kidnapper to her position. She reached behind her and grabbed the first object that her hand touched, a metal mug. She tossed the mug close to Jude. It fell in front of him. He stuttered in his step then looked up. She waved, hoping he would see her in the dark. The attic space where she was hiding had a window-like opening but the glass had been replaced with plastic that she had torn away when she'd first cried out to Jude.

Jude studied the house, his head tilted up.

A shot reverberated through the winter cold. Jude ducked back down but then he took off running toward the front of the house. He'd seen her. She needed to meet him downstairs. She heard the door open just as she stepped on the top step that lead down to the main floor.

She hurried down the creaking steps, which were old and not stable. She could hear footsteps now in the other room. Though her heart pounded with excitement at seeing Jude, she dared not cry out. The kidnapper had no doubt seen which way Jude had run and was on his heels.

She was on the third to last stair when the board broke and her foot fell through. She tried to pull it up, but her boot was wedged in place. She was going to have to slip out of the boot and then reach through and get it.

Jude entered the room and ran over to her.

"I'm stuck. We don't have much time."

"Boy, am I glad to see you." His hand rested on her cheek and he gave her a quick kiss.

Even in the frenzy of needing to get away, the gesture melted her heart. She pulled her leg through without the boot.

From the other room, an intense banging sound filled the whole house.

"I locked the front door, but it's just a matter of minutes before he breaks it down or goes to the other door." Jude pointed at the back door, which was in the same room as the attic stairs.

There was no further banging at the front door in the living room. Was he waiting for them to burst through that door so he could shoot them, or was he running around to the back of the house to use the other door?

Lacey gripped Jude's arm. "We've got to go out through the attic window. It's the only safe option."

Jude nodded.

Lacey slid back into her boot, flipped around and climbed up the stairs. "These aren't real strong."

Jude was right behind her. "I see that."

They reached the floor of the attic just as they heard the back door swing open and bang against the wall. While they scrambled across the attic floor, she could hear the kidnapper stomp through the house. They had only minutes before he would check the front door and potential hiding places. Once he saw the stairs to the attic, he would probably figure out where they'd gone.

Lacey glanced around for something to use as a rope

to lower down with. She had counted on being able to find something in the space that was stuffed with unwanted items.

The kidnapper's boots pounded on the wooden planks as he entered the kitchen and stopped. He was no doubt looking at the attic stairs.

Jude bent a foam mattress cover and shoved it through the window. "Come on, we're jumping."

There was no time to think. No time to argue. Jude disappeared in an instant and she was right behind him. She stuck her legs out the window and pushed off. She landed hard on her knees. The snow and the mattress cushioned the impact.

Jude grabbed her hand. "We have to find his snowmobile or there is no way we'll be able to escape."

They ran toward the little shed. The third dog was waiting outside it, sitting and looking up expectantly. The dogs were warm in there and they had food. Jude stopped and opened the door so the third dog would be safe until help could come for them. His two compatriots greeted him with excited yipping and bouncing.

The move had cost them precious seconds. But it made Lacey admire Jude even more. They rounded the corner of the little shed just as another bullet whizzed past her. They ran into the forest. Without a flashlight, they couldn't see and were forced to slow down once they were in the trees.

Jude pointed. "He came from over there. We need to follow his tracks."

Lacey knew without looking that Mr. Wilson's body was off to the side. They moved as fast as they could in the darkness. She peered over her shoulder. The bobbing light behind her told her that the kidnapper had just entered the forest.

Jude chose a route. She stepped in behind him. When she glanced back, the bobbing light was no longer there. "Jude, I think he figured out we're trying to find the snowmobile and he's going to try to get to it first by swinging around that way."

Jude stopped and tilted his head, probably thinking or listening. He scanned the whole area around them. Though it was hard to make out much in the darkness, Lacey didn't see a snowmobile, only tracks that led out of the forest.

"Let's try to get there first." He glanced over his shoulder, then took off running. The steady rhythm of their footsteps crunching through the snow was all she heard.

There was no good choice here. They couldn't go back to the house and wait out the night. The kidnapper would come for them. Staying out in the elements without transportation wasn't a good idea either.

The forest ended, and they were faced with an uphill trek. They followed the tracks. The ground leveled off. They were on a sort of side road. She could see the tracks leading toward the forest and the parallel grooves that a snowmobile would make, as well.

She sprinted to keep up with him despite the deep snow. She could feel her leg muscles fatiguing.

The yellow-white glow of a headlight blared at them. Coming at full speed. The kidnapper had made it to the snowmobile before them. They ran to the side of the road and headed back downhill. She slipped and fell, rolling part of the way. The snowmobile came down the hill after them.

Jude found her and reached both hands out to pull her to safety. They ran. The snowmobile could only follow them as far as the edge of the forest. The trees grew too close together to get a snowmobile through.

Before they even got to the tree line, the snowmobile veered back up to the road. They entered the forest and slowed down.

She stopped to catch her breath. Her heart pounded wildly from fear and exertion. She could see Jude's breath as he sucked air in and out. He stood with his hands on his hips.

"Do you think he's going around to the other side to catch us when we come out?"

Jude shook his head. "Let's just keep moving. We should be able to hear him if he is close and still on that snowmobile."

"Thanks for saving me back there," she said.

He took her in a single-arm hug, squeezing her shoulder. "No problem."

They moved slower, walking single file. Lacey listened for the sound of a snowmobile motor. She thought she might have heard it behind them. She dismissed the noise as just being her imagination.

They stepped out of the forest. "I say we go to that room where the dogs are. It's warm and the rifle is there. If he hasn't gotten to it already. I have a few bullets left in my gun. One of us will have to stand guard at all times. If he comes through that door…"

Jude didn't complete his thought, but she knew what he meant. If the kidnapper wasn't already back on the property waiting for them, they could wait until daylight in the little room, but they'd have to shoot the kidnapper if he tried to get in. It wasn't a bad idea. The dogs could alert them to anyone approaching.

All the same, the thought of having to shoot another human being, even someone on the wrong side of the law, sent chills down her spine.

They approached Mr. Wilson's homestead with caution, moving from one place of cover to another looking for the kidnapper or his snowmobile.

# THIRTEEN

Jude peered above the pile a snow. Lacey pressed close behind him. He could feel her breath on the back of his neck. Though much of it was covered in shadows, the little back room was within their view.

He couldn't see any movement anywhere, but their pursuer could still be lying in wait. He could have gotten back to the homestead way faster on the snowmobile than they could on foot. "Should we make a run for it?" They had one final sprint to get to the room where the dogs were.

"I'm with you." She patted his shoulder.

Jude burst to his feet, half expecting to be shot at. Lacey was right beside him. When he got to the door of the little room, the dogs barked on the other side. He touched the doorknob and pulled his pistol out. His heart squeezed tight. There was a chance the kidnapper was waiting inside for them.

Lacey stood off to one side. He did as well, turning the knob and pushing the door open. The dogs burst out, yapping and jumping on them.

Lacey laughed. "Someone is glad to see us."

Jude looked around the dark room searching the corners. The lantern must have gone out. "I think we are in the clear."

He stepped inside.

"I'll stay out here for a minute with the dogs so they can go potty."

Even that made his chest tight with fear. "Not too long in the open, Lacey."

He fumbled around until he found the lantern. The fire was still going, which provided some light when he opened the door. He relit the lantern and came to stand at the door with Lacey who was pressed close to the wall.

The dogs ran around sniffing all the new smells. Jude whistled and two of them came running. The third dog, the white dog who had been in the forest with Mr. Wilson's body, lagged behind.

They stepped inside, closing the door once the last dog had come in and settled on the beds with the other dogs. Jude turned the lantern on low. If the kidnapper did come back, he'd see the smoke from the woodstove and know that they were there. Maybe they should just let it die out. The room looked to be well insulated. They'd probably stay warm until daylight.

He put his own gun back in the shoulder holster. Jude stepped across the floor and grabbed the rifle, which was still propped in a corner. He checked to see that it was loaded. "I'll take the first watch." When he glanced over at Lacey, he read fear in her expression. "Why don't you try to get some sleep?"

She nodded and settled down by the fire, pulling a blanket over her body as she lay on her side. Jude chose a position opposite the door where if the kidnapper came through, he'd have a clean shot. The little room had two windows on opposite walls from the door. He'd have to watch those too.

He jumped up to see if he could lock the door from the inside. He could not. The toy that had belonged to Maria still sat in the corner of the room. His chest squeezed tight and he prayed that she was still alive. The prayer came easier this time. The roads weren't plowed yet, so the kidnapper could only move Maria somewhere else on the mountain or hide her in Lodgepole and she'd have to be transported via snowmobile. Maybe she had been in one of the empty cabins and moved here once the kidnapper feared they would be searched.

Lacey drew the blanket tighter around herself and tossed from one side to the other before growing still. Her breathing slowed. Bart, the border collie they had met in the forest, came and sat beside Jude. The dog licked Jude's cheek and then lay down close to his legs. It gave him some peace of mind to know that the dogs would alert if anyone drew close.

He watched the door for what felt like several hours. When he could no longer keep his eyes open, he woke Lacey so she could stand guard.

He handed her the rifle. "You know how to shoot one of these?"

"It's required for my job. Just in case I have to deal with aggressive wildlife." She took the rifle. He touched her cheek with the back of his hand. Her eyes were soft and welcoming, glowing with affection.

"I'll be okay," she said. "Get some sleep."

He lay down where she'd been and pulled the blanket over his body. It took him only a few minutes to fall asleep. He slept until light coming through one of the windows woke him.

He rolled over. The rifle was propped in the corner and Lacey was gone. Panic filled his awareness as he sat up and tossed the blanket to one side. He took in a breath. The dogs were gone too. Maybe she had just stepped outside to watch the dogs. He opened the door and glanced around. His chest felt tight again until he heard dogs barking.

Lacey came around the corner of the main house with the dogs trailing behind her. She held something in her hand. She smiled when she saw him. She ran toward him and held up two granola bars and an apple. "I found us something to eat at the main house."

His stomach rumbled at the sight of food. "Thanks." He looked around.

Both of them lifted their heads at the same time. Though it was faint they could hear the sound of a snowmobile engine. It could be someone from town searching for them or it could be the kidnapper coming back to look for them in the daylight.

"We better get out of here." At least now, he knew where they were in relation to the road.

They ran back to the little room, leaving the dogs inside but the door ajar so they could get out if they needed to. Once they got back to town…if they got back to town, they'd have to make sure someone came up to rescue the dogs. Jude grabbed his one glove and tossed Lacey hers. He stuffed the granola bar in his pocket.

They sprinted toward the trees. They were only a short distance into the forest when Jude saw why the kidnapper had given them a brief reprieve. Mr. Wilson's frozen body was no longer there. They had gotten maybe five hours' sleep total. That was how long it took to hide evidence like a body. He suspected that the kidnapper would continue his search until he killed both Jude and Lacey, thereby wiping out any chance that he would be caught.

The snowmobile motor noises stopped. Though he could not see through the trees, he had to assume that the kidnapper had come back to search the property for them since it was the most likely place for them to hide.

"They have got to be looking for us by now," Jude said. "Let's see if we can get to the road and be spotted before the kidnapper finds us."

The cold air chilled his face as they ran parallel to the side road that led to Mr. Wilson's property. Lacey kept pace with him. He pushed a tree branch out of the way and jumped over a log. Both of them were gasping for breath when they heard the snowmobile start up again. The trees had thinned enough that he could see the road up ahead.

They stepped out into the open. Behind him he could hear the approaching snowmobile. They had a view of the road as it wound down the mountain. He glanced up the road where there were several sets of snowmobile tracks.

"What should we do?" He detected the fear in Lacey's voice as she gripped his arm.

His mind reeled. The unexpected. They needed to do the unexpected. "We're heading back toward the house through the trees, but we will loop around it and then up the mountain. The kidnapper is expecting us to head down the mountain toward the road. We're just going to have to trick him."

Their tracks in the snow would tell the tale to the kidnapper, but he would have to follow them on foot once he figured out they hadn't gone back to the house.

They were only a short distance back in the trees when they heard the sound of another snowmobile. Without a word, both of them turned and ran back toward the road. In the distance coming down the mountain was a different snowmobile.

Thank you, God.

They stood out in the road knowing that the kidnapper would stay hidden to avoid being caught. The snowmobiler stopped and flipped his visor up so they could see his face. "I'm from town. Lev sent me. We've all been looking for you."

"Boy, are we glad to see you." Without knowing why, Jude felt some hesitation.

"Hop on, it'll be a tight fit, but I'll take you back down the mountain." The driver flipped his helmet back down.

What were their options? None really. They could stay up here with the known kidnapper.

"We should go," Lacey said. Her voice held a pleading quality.

Lacey got on the snowmobile. He let go of his suspicions and squeezed in behind her. The snowmobile lurched forward.

He was glad to be headed back to safety and warmth, glad to be holding Lacey. Without a helmet his face got cold. He nuzzled in close to Lacey's neck. She patted his thigh.

His positive thoughts hiccupped. It seemed a little strange that the snowmobiler hadn't radioed the other searchers that he and Lacey had been found.

Tension threaded through Lacey's chest when the snowmobiler veered off the road that lead back to town.

She pulled away from the driver's back where she'd been nuzzled in close to cut the wind on her face. Something was wrong.

She angled her head to try and see where they were going.

The driver took them up over a berm. The snowmobile caught air and landed hard, skidding to one side. All three of them fell off. Lacey rolled as a whirlwind of snow encased her. At least the landing was somewhat soft. Her face was chilled from the wind and she'd lost her hat in the fall. The flurry of snow died down and she saw Jude on all fours trying to get up. It appeared the driver had caused the accident on purpose.

The snowmobile engine was still running. The driver jumped to his feet and ran toward the snowmobile. He intended to leave them behind. She still wasn't fully able to figure out what was even going on. They were in a sort of bowl surrounded by forest above them.

Jude had gotten to his feet and was chasing after the driver of the snowmobile. Jude tackled him. They rolled around in the snow and then Jude pinned the man down. "What is going on here?"

Lacey pushed herself to her feet and ran toward where the two men were.

Still holding the man down by resting his knees on the other man's stomach, Jude nodded toward Lacey. "Take his helmet off."

Lacey kneeled down, took her gloves off and reached to press the buttons that opened the helmet. She pulled it off. The man underneath the helmet had short blond hair. His eyes darted back and forth, filled with fear.

"What are you up to?"

"Please, I needed the money."

"What are you talking about?" Jude leaned closer to him.

Lacey stared at the man. His snowsuit had made him look bulkier than he actually was. Was it possible this was the tall thin man who had attacked her while they were in town? It wasn't the same snowmobile that had come at them. This snowmobile looked like one that was owned by the city. Of course, he wouldn't have come for them on a snowmobile he had tried to mow them down with.

"Someone paid you to try to kill us?"

The man looked like he might cry. "My wife has cancer. We had no way to pay for the treatment." The man coughed. "I can't breathe."

Jude took his knees off the man.

Still gasping, the man sat up.

"Somebody hired you? Who?"

The man stared at the ground and then lifted his head to talk. His eyes grew wide and then he fell over backward. A single bullet had pierced the middle of his forehead.

All the air left Lacey's lungs. As she stared at the dead man, her stomach churned. She feared she might throw up.

A numbness settled into her mind and body and everything felt like it was moving in slow motion. The snow by the man's head turned crimson. Jude grabbed her by the elbow and sprinted toward the snowmobile.

More shots were fired from above them at the rim of the bowl. Now she saw why they had been taken here. It made them easy targets. She suspected it was the broad-shouldered man shooting at them. He must have radioed the tall thin man to pick them up and bring them here to be shot. Now she understood what the phrase *shooting fish in a barrel* meant. The tall thin man was probably just supposed to leave them there. But when the shooter saw that he was talking to them, he'd been eliminated. Before they could even get on the snowmobile, shots hit it. The engine stopped running. Liquid, probably gasoline, leaked out onto the snow.

Jude slipped over the side of the snowmobile and crouched. She rolled off the seat and pressed in beside him. Her heart pounded. She still wasn't able to fully process what had happened.

How long were they safe here using the snowmobile as cover before the shooter repositioned to have a clean shot at them? She surveyed the trees, catching some movement, a flash of white. The shooter must be in snow camouflage. "He's there. I think he went deeper into the trees."

"He must be moving to get another shot at us." Jude stared up at the untouched snow that led to the tree line. "We can't stay here. We have a few minutes while he repositions."

That plan would only work if he didn't come back out from the forest and see them running up the bowl to get to the trees. They'd have to run for some distance out in the open before they got to the trees that were on the opposite end of where they'd seen the shooter, even then they'd have to hope they didn't encounter him in the forest.

They took off, slowed by the depth of the snow. Lacey glanced nervously at the edge of the forest, seeing nothing. Though fatigued, she lifted her legs and kept going. They made it to the forest without being shot at again. Once at the safety of the trees, she stopped to catch her breath and listen. Bands of light streamed through the evergreens.

Jude tugged on her sleeve.

She was fully aware that they might encounter the kidnapper at any time. Their tracks in the pristine snow would reveal exactly where they had gone if the shooter slipped out to check their position. Maybe he had predicted which way they would run and was waiting for them. It wasn't like there were options.

A crackling sound somewhere deeper in the trees reached her ears. Her heart pounded. It could be human.

Jude put his finger up to his lips. He stepped carefully, and she followed. They moved slowly past one tree and then another. It was cold enough that she could see her breath.

She glanced around. Breath came out from behind one of the trees less than twenty feet away.

"Run." Her voice came out in a hoarse whisper. The rifle shot nearly drowned out her command. Her eardrum rattled from the percussive impact of the bullet breaking through the air.

Jude took off through the trees. She sprinted as well, running on a slightly different path. If they stayed close together, it would be that much easier to shoot them both.

She ran for several minutes, breathing heavily from the exertion. She'd lost sight of Jude but could guess at where he was. The pathways through the trees were limited.

Another shot knocked a tree branch above her off. It hit her shoulder before falling to the ground. The trees seemed to go on forever. She wondered if she should move toward where the forest opened up to get an idea of where they were in relationship to the main road. That was their best hope for finding help.

Lacey glanced over her shoulder. Where had the shooter gone?

They ran as fast as the deep snow would allow. The snowmobile ride that had ended in the driver's death had gotten her completely turned around. The sun was in the middle of the sky, it was hard to get her bearings.

She hurried after Jude, glancing over her shoulder and wondering what had become of the man with the rifle. It had to be the same man who'd been after them all along, the broad-shouldered man who had run Jude off the road.

It was just a matter of time before he caught up with Jude and her.

# FOURTEEN

Lacey fought for breath as she hurried downhill after Jude through the trees. Jude seemed to know where he was going. Both of them continued to look over their shoulders.

After jogging for what felt like more than an hour, Jude slowed down. They hadn't seen or heard the shooter or the snowmobile.

They trudged, not talking. She was tired and hungry. She'd witnessed a man die right in front of her. "I need to rest." She slouched down using a tree trunk as a backrest.

Jude sat down beside her.

She wanted to cry but no tears came.

He wrapped his arms around her. "I know it's all been a bit much."

She lay her head on his shoulder. "That man who died in the bowl. It sounds like he did all this for the money for his wife."

They couldn't stay here. They had to keep moving. It got dark by five o'clock. That gave them some time. It felt good to rest and to be here with Jude even though their situation was not good.

Jude glanced at the sky again. "How far off the main road do you think that guy took us when we ended up in that bowl?"

"Not long. Maybe ten minutes before we got there." It was hard to even calculate. Walking was so much slower than going by snowmobile.

He squeezed her shoulder. "Lev and the others must be looking for us. They will widen their search when they don't find us on the main road."

Lev and the town of Lodgepole had limited resources and they were in a crisis situation. And the man who had shot at them in the bowl was still out there. "I'm sure they'll do all they can." She couldn't hide how hopeless she felt.

She turned to face him. He held her. She liked that he didn't tell her everything was going to be okay, because that wasn't necessarily so. He touched her ear and cheek with his palm. She closed her eyes relishing the warmth of his hand.

She let out a heavy breath and tilted her head toward him. He kissed her forehead and then her lips. He pulled back and gazed at her and then hugged her close. She let out a breath and relaxed.

He spoke into her ear. His voice barely above a whisper. "We have to keep moving."

"I know," she said. She pulled back and removed her glove so she could touch his jaw. "We should try to get to a high place, so we can try to see any landmarks that might help us figure out where we are."

He nodded. They rose together and headed uphill. The wind intensified as the temperature dropped and the sun slipped lower in the sky. They huddled close

together as they walked until they came to a high spot
that provided a view of the mountain below.

The sky had turned gray and it was hard to see much
more than the outline of mountain formation and forest. Far off in the distance, the twinkling golden lights
of Lodgepole were just barely visible.

She felt a mixture of relief and despair. "So far
away," she said.

"But at least we have an idea of where we're at."

The cold made her face feel numb and her stomach growled. She turned in a half circle, hoping to see
some lights that indicated a house or cabin close by.
They could head toward the lights, but at some point,
they'd descend into a valley and the mountain in front
of them would block their view of Lodgepole. In a few
more hours they would be in total darkness. She saw no
sign of the mountain road that led into town.

She turned toward him. "I'm not sure what to do."

"Let's hike a little farther up and see if we can spot
anything else." He offered her a comforting smile.

She knew that Jude had made the best decision in a
terrible situation. They could not stay out here all night.
They'd freeze to death. She knew also from having
worked outside in the winter that every step they took
expended precious energy.

They trudged a little farther up the mountain through
a grove of aspens. Though there were no leaves left on
the trees, their white trunks glowed in the darkness.
They came to another vantage point and peered out.
The lights of the town were still visible.

Far below them, she saw a moving light. "That has to
be where the road is." At this distance there was no way

of knowing if the snowmobile belonged to a searcher or to the man who had tried to kill them.

Jude squeezed her arm. "That's where we go, then."

They headed down the steep incline. She angled her foot and dug her heels into the snow to create a secure foothold. The snow seemed to be cascading around them. She was aware that this high up, with as much snow as there had been, the avalanche danger was significant.

The snowmobile headlights disappeared from view probably rounding a corner on the mountain road. In the nighttime silence, the hum of the snowmobile motor echoed up the mountain.

They headed downward in a straight line. Several times they encountered snowmobile tracks that weren't on the road. People had been all over the mountain, maybe searching for Jude and Lacey. Once they were down in the valley, they could no longer see the lights of the town. They trekked back up the mountain. Fatigue had settled into Lacey's leg muscles. She couldn't stop thinking about sleep and food. Several times her eyes bobbed shut and then she jerked awake as she walked. The important thing was to keep moving. The sound of the snowmobile faded.

Finally, they stepped out onto the road. The lights of Lodgepole were again visible but still very far away. Jude reached over with his gloved hand and squeezed hers. He'd stuck the hand that didn't have a glove into his pocket.

"We should pray," she said. Why did things have to get to this point before she even thought to reach out for the help that was always there, always available?

They walked side by side. "God, we are afraid and

cold," Jude said. He took several more steps without saying anything.

"We know that You are the God who can do anything," she said and then she fell quiet. Her breath came out in cloud-like puffs. She listened to their muffled footsteps on the soft snow. The fabric of their snowsuits made a swishing sound as they moved along the road.

Jude picked up the prayer, asking God to give them the strength to keep going. And then he recited the first lines of Psalm 23. "The Lord is my shepherd. I shall not want."

She said the next line.

And so they walked reciting the psalm that offered so much comfort and promise of God's care. Each of them saying a line and then walking in silence for several seconds before the other voiced the next part of the psalm.

Once they were finished, they trudged without talking until Jude cleared his throat. "I owe you a debt of gratitude for restoring my faith."

"I didn't know that's what I did."

The wind blew snow around. The stars twinkling above them offered only a little light to see by. In spite of the bleakness and the cold, she felt her hope renewed.

Jude stopped for a moment and lifted his head. "I think I hear something."

She couldn't hear anything but the wind rushing through the treetops of the evergreens that grew close to the road. The odd mixture of joy and then dread flooded through her. Was the snowmobile they heard coming to rescue them or kill them?

Jude's mind shifted into high gear. He tuned his ears to his surroundings trying to detect if the snowmobile he heard was above them or below them. He was keenly aware that his feet and face felt numb. His legs weighed a thousand pounds. He was beyond exhausted.

The sound faded rather than grew closer but the echo effect of the mountain made him uncertain if he was hearing correctly. The only thing he knew for sure was that there was a snowmobile somewhere close.

Then the sound faded. He listened, thinking maybe he would hear it again. His hope deflated like a balloon losing air. An intense gust of air hit them. He turned slightly and put his gloved hand up to his face to protect it.

The wind died down. He peered out. First at the lights of Lodgepole and then down the mountain. A lump in the snow several turns down the mountain road caught his attention. He walked to the edge of the road squinting to make sure he was seeing clearly. His spirits lifted. "I know where we are."

She stepped toward him and he pointed down to where the lump was. She followed the direction of his hand. "Your wrecked car." Enough of the snow had blown away to make the top part of the car visible.

"We must be close enough to radio the base station."

Lacey touched her chest, her voice filled with pain. "I took the radio out of my suit when I slept in Mr. Wilson's little shed. I forgot to grab it in all the excitement. I can't believe I did that."

"Don't beat yourself up," Jude said. "We'll figure this out together. The car will provide some shelter for us."

They cut off from the road and moved in a straight line toward the half-exposed car. Once they got to it, it was clear the front doors were too buried in snow to open. They dug away at a back door with their hands.

He stuck his ungloved hand in his pocket to warm it and kept digging one-handed.

Out of breath from the frenzy of digging, Lacey stood back. Jude reached for the door handle, stepping aside so Lacey could get in first. He crawled in after her.

The entire front windshield was covered in snow. They both sat trying to catch their breaths.

"Do you have, like, a winter survival kit in here?" Lacey slumped against the seat.

He thought for a moment. The morning he'd taken off to tail the car the kidnapper had stolen felt like an eon ago. He shook his head. And then he turned to the cargo area in the back where he had a blanket for his dog. He handed it to her.

"What about in the front seat? Any food or anything that might be useful? I'm smaller. I can crawl through and look."

Again, he searched his memory. "There's a flashlight in the glove compartment."

She crawled over the front seat, opened the glove compartment and handed him the flashlight which he shone so she could see better. She opened the console that was in between seats and laughed. "Ketchup packets. A couple of sugar packets."

Jude rubbed his hands together. "We will dine in style."

She let out a little laugh before shoving the packets into her pocket. "Food is energy at this point." She searched around a little more before joining him again in the backseat. "Maybe save it for when we hike out."

They both got underneath the blanket for warmth. He wrapped an arm around her. She rested her head on his chest. "God is funny, isn't He?"

"What do you mean?"

"We prayed thinking the answer to our prayers would be for one of the snowmobilers to find us."

"But God saw another option." He nestled close to her. They'd be able to stay warm enough until daylight. "I'll take first watch." The man with the rifle was probably still searching for them. He listened to the steady soft sound of Lacey's breathing as she slept. He turned his head slightly to stare out at the darkness.

His eyelids felt heavy. He nodded off and shook himself awake. Outside it was still dark. Lacey stirred awake. She pulled away from him.

"I feel more rested. I'll sit watch, so you can get some sleep," she said.

He was grateful for her offer. He leaned his head back and closed his eyes. His brain fogged from exhaustion and he felt himself relaxing as he fell into a deeper sleep.

He awoke one time in the night. Lacey had moved away from him and was resting her cheek against the door. He saw no lights outside. When he rolled down the window in the backseat all he heard was the wind. He had only a view out the back window where he saw no snowmobile lights.

He fell back asleep, waking when the sun shot through the window and warmed him. Lacey was already awake.

She touched her stomach. "Boy am I hungry." She drew out the sugar and ketchup packets and divided them evenly. They ate quickly. Jude pushed open the door they had dug out of the snow.

They ran straight down the mountain, connecting with the road as it wound toward Lodgepole. They'd only gone a short distance when they heard a snow-mobile above them.

Jude glanced up.

"I saw him," Lacey said. "He has a rifle with him. He must have been waiting for us. I wonder why he stayed away all night."

Her words sent a bolt of fear through him. He looked around for a hiding place as the sound of the snowmobile grew louder.

# FIFTEEN

As they hurried toward a snowdrift that would provide some cover, Lacey pushed aside the panic that filled her. They slipped behind the drift, pressing close together.

If the man with the rifle stopped to look over the edge of the road, they would be spotted, their brightly colored snowsuits easy enough to see in a field of white. If he kept going down the road, there was a chance he would whiz past them.

Heart racing, she bent forward hoping no part of her showed above the drift. Jude faced her, crouching low, as well. He stared into her eyes. Neither of them dared make a sound. Though her legs were starting to cramp in the tight position, she remained still. They listened to the snowmobile *putt putt* along. The guy must be looking all around to be going that slowly.

The motor was the loudest as it passed by them on the road.

She stared into Jude's eyes. Just a few more minutes and they would be in the clear as long as he kept heading down the mountain. She raised her head getting a glance at the back end of the snowmobile before it disappeared. Her breath caught. There was a second smaller passenger on the snowmobile. Maria.

"He has her! He has the little girl. That's why he didn't come after us last night."

Jude's eyes grew wide and round. "The roads must be open. He's taking her out of here." Standing, he reached in his snowsuit for his gun, but thought better of it. He couldn't risk hitting Maria. "We have to stop him."

He jerked his head to one side. Before she even had time to look up the mountain to whatever had alarmed him, a thundering roar surrounded her.

Avalanche!

All that snow and then days of it warming up a little had caused them to be in the wrong place at the wrong time.

They bolted and headed downhill trying to outrun the wave of snow. She felt her body being picked up and tossed around. She saw flashes of color. Jude's snowsuit. She landed on her bottom. The snow cascaded around her, enveloping her. She had a terrifying moment of not being able to breathe. The wall of snow moved past her and then she felt herself thrust upward. Though she was covered in snow from head to toe, she was upright. She wheezed in a shaky breath.

A pile of boulders in front of her had created a sort of pocket where the snow had gone around her. Her stomach and her cheek were pressed close to one of the rocks. Lacey stood up brushing the snow off her face and sleeves. She traced the pathway of the snow which now blocked part of the road. She'd been right on the edge of the avalanche. Frantic, she looked around for Jude. All she saw was a field of white.

With some effort she climbed up on the rocks and

looked all around. She prayed that Jude was not buried. It would be only minutes before he suffocated. Whiteness everywhere. The kidnapper hadn't gone that far down the road before the avalanche hit. She saw his taillight far away down the road. He was getting away and he had Maria with him.

Her priority was finding Jude.

She saw some thirty feet from her a spot of pink in the white field. It was a hand. The depth of the snow slowed her down as she raced toward where Jude was. As she drew closer, she deduced that the force of the avalanche had ripped his boot off. His pink foot stuck out, as well. She sank deep into the snow. Pulling her leg up, she took as big a stride as she could. Each step was laborious. By the time she reached Jude, she was out of breath. She dug furiously where she thought his head might be. She saw curly hair and then a forehead.

"Jude?"

He didn't open his eyes or move. His lashes were white with snow. His face red and lifeless from the cold. Her emotions plummeted to the depths of despair as she pulled off a glove and reached a hand out to touch his cheek.

He wheezed in a breath, and his eyes shot open. He stared at her as though not comprehending who she was.

"Jude." Her voice filled with elation. "Let's get you dug out of here."

She freed both his hands first and then his upper body so he could help dig out his lower half. His body had twisted at an odd angle and she feared something was broken and he just wasn't feeling the pain of the injury because he was numb from the cold. She scraped the snow away from the leg that no longer had a boot.

She stood back and reached for his hands to pull him up. "Is anything broken?"

Jude still had a dazed look on his face. He shook his head slowly.

He was shivering. She unzipped her snowsuit and slipped out of the top part of it. She was dressed in layers. She pulled her sweater off leaving only a T-shirt. She pointed for him to sit back down and wrapped the sweater around his bare foot. The makeshift boot was awkward, but the wool would wick some of the moisture away at least.

He was probably weak from being buried alive. "Can you walk?"

He nodded. She reached a hand out to help him get to his feet again.

They walked a short distance. When they were free of the deep snow the avalanche had brought down, he stopped and leaned against a tree.

He reached out and touched her face. "Thanks for digging me out."

His hand was cold on her cheek. "I'm just glad I found you in time," she said.

His expression changed. His jaw hardened, and he drew his eyebrows together. The light still had not come back into his eyes. "I almost died back there…just like you in the freezer."

She leaned toward him. "It's not like your whole life passes before you, but you do have a moment of wondering if you made the right choices."

"Yeah, exactly." Jude seemed to be very far away in his thoughts.

She touched his face. "We have to keep moving. I'm afraid you're going to end up with frostbite."

"Yes, we have to get to town. Alert the authorities about the kidnapper having Maria. I doubt he's headed to Lodgepole. We can't catch him now." He touched his side. "It hurts when I breathe. I wonder if I broke a rib or something."

Though progress was slow, they found a path where the snow was smashed down, probably by deer, outside the perimeter where the snow had cascaded down the mountain.

They walked for at least a half hour before Jude needed to rest against a tree.

She heard a tremendous roar. She left Jude and stepped out into the clear where she had a view of the road down below. It took several minutes before she saw four snowmobiles headed up the mountain. They must have seen the avalanche from town and come up to assess the damage. She hurried back to get Jude.

Jude still sat slumped by the tree. His eyes had life in them again. She sat down on the ground, as well. Her heart pounded. They needed to get out to the road to be spotted by the snowmobilers.

Knowing that the avalanche risk was still high and could be triggered by the noise of so many snowmobiles would the men even come up this far? She caught a flash of movement through the trees. Several deer stepped out into the open, tails flicking nervously as they looked around and then took off running. The avalanche had stirred them up.

It sounded like the snowmobiles were still headed up the mountain.

She tuned in to the sounds around her. Her heartbeat drummed in her ears. She tensed, drawing her lips into a tight line. She prayed another avalanche would not be triggered by the snowmobiles.

Because of the echo effect, it was hard to tell exactly how close the snowmobiles were. Jude leaned forward. From where he was sitting, he must have a view of the road. He motioned for her to get up.

They ran through the trees and out to the road. Two snowmobiles were a hundred yards away but headed toward them. The others must have remained behind. Lacey thought she might collapse from relief. She peered over her shoulder just as the deer disappeared back into the forest.

The men stopped. One of them was Lev. He pulled his helmet off. "Boy, are we glad to see you. Thought for sure you were goners. Is the road blocked off farther up?"

Jude nodded.

Lev glanced down at Jude's foot wrapped in her sweater. "You two probably need to be looked at. Get on and we'll take you back to town."

Jude pointed down the road. "The man who took Maria is escaping with her. He'll have an hour head start on us."

"The roads are just now opening up. I can make some calls to have law enforcement be on the lookout for a man with a little girl."

"Okay, but nothing that draws attention. The kidnapper threatened if law enforcement was involved something bad might happen to Maria," said Jude.

"Can do." Lev's voice filled with compassion. "Let's get you to a place that is safe and warm. We've got another man missing."

Lacey opened her mouth to explain that the missing

man was dead, but she was experiencing a sort of shock now that they were safe.

"Is the man tall and thin with short blond hair?" His voice as well sounded weak.

"Yes, his name is Dale. He volunteered to go out and look for you two," said Lev.

"He's dead. The man who has Maria shot him," Jude said.

Lev stared at him for a moment. He lowered his voice. "I didn't know Dale. He kind of kept to himself. He was new around here."

Jude's voice was solemn. "He said his wife had cancer."

Lev nodded. "I heard that too." Lev let out a heavy breath. "Sounds like you have quite a story to tell the sheriff over in Garnet. My priority has to be your safety."

Jude stood for a long moment. His jaw set tight. But then, he nodded. Maybe accepting Lev's plan.

Jude took Lacey's hand and led her toward the second snowmobiler. She got on and he patted her back. The gesture of care touched her. He walked with some effort over to Lev's snowmobile and got on. He looked like he was about to fall over from exhaustion.

The trip down the mountain went by in a blur. At some point the two other snowmobilers joined them.

Lacey felt herself nodding off as the edge of Lodgepole came into view. She had a vague awareness that the snowmobile had stopped. A moment later, someone picked her up and carried her. She opened her eyes briefly to see Jude's soft smile. He was clearly as worn-out as she was, not only from lack of sleep but from all the trauma.

She felt herself being placed somewhere soft and a blanket was put over her. Jude's voice sounded very far away as she heard him saying he needed to talk to the sheriff.

She recognized Nancy's voice telling him he needed to be looked at by a medical professional. Her sleep felt more like she was passing out.

She awoke when the growling of her stomach overwhelmed her need to rest. She sat up. She was alone in Nancy and Lev's living room asleep on the couch. The curtains were drawn and the lights were out. Hushed voices came from another room.

She rose to her feet and entered the kitchen where Jude and Nancy were sitting at the kitchen table. Jude rested his hand on a cell phone that he must have borrowed. An empty bowl sat beside him.

Nancy smiled. "I'm sure you're hungry. Have a seat."

Lacey nodded and sat down beside Jude. He had dark circles under his eyes and his skin looked sallow. "Did you get a doctor to look at you, Jude?"

"Later. We've got things to take care of. I've been on the phone to the sheriff over in Garnet."

Nancy sat a bowl of soup down in front of Lacey. She pushed some crackers that were on the table toward her.

"Jude's foot looks like it has some frostbite," Nancy said. "His ribs are bruised too. I tried to tell him that getting over to the sheriff could wait a few hours. The sheriff has put out an all-points bulletin for the kidnapper and the little girl."

"I need to talk to the sheriff in person. I want to help with the search for Maria," Jude said. "I haven't been able to get hold of George yet. He's not picking up."

Lacey spooned up the soup. The warm liquid soothed her empty stomach.

"Lacey, would you be willing to go with me since you can identify the kidnapper? I gave the sheriff a basic description over the phone based on what you told me. But can you look at mug shots so we can put a name with the face?"

Lacey nodded. If she still felt tired after a short rest, Jude must be beyond exhausted.

"It's an hour drive to get to Garnet," Nancy said. "Why don't you at least let Lacey drive so you can sleep?"

"That would work." Jude turned toward Lacey. "Nancy is loaning us her SUV. We need to hurry."

"I'll finish my soup so we can go."

"I'll go warm the car up for you." Nancy rose to her feet. "And, Jude, grab a pair of Lev's boots from the closet by the door. He has big feet, so your feet might be swimming in them but at least you'll have boots. I'll get some extra pairs of socks." Nancy left the room.

Lacey heard the outside door open and close.

She finished her soup. The meal had strengthened her. Ten minutes later, she was behind the wheel of Nancy's SUV. Jude crawled in the back along with a blanket Nancy had given him.

Lacey backed out of the driveway. "I know you have a lot on your mind, Jude, but Nancy is right about rest."

"I know," Jude said. "But I don't want this guy to get away with that kid. Who knows what he has planned?"

She rolled up the street toward the edge of town. Would the man with the rifle hide Maria somewhere and come after them? She checked her rearview mirror as she came to the city limits and pulled out on the two-lane road that led to Garnet.

Damage from the snowstorm was still evident. Snow was piled high on either side of the road and there were cars covered in snow that must have slid off. She prayed that the people in the accidents had made it to safety.

"I talked to Lev while you slept. The man who was shot in the bowl was from Lodgepole and his wife was in a hospital in Denver. Lev said Dale was antisocial and not mentally stable. He lived in a run-down old Victorian on a big lot. Lots of junky cars in the front yard. Kept to himself."

"I remember walking by that house when we were searching." And she remembered seeing the dark-haired man standing by the window who had slipped out of view. Maybe he was Dale's paranoid brother. "Did he live alone?"

"I don't know. I didn't ask. Why?"

"There was someone else in that house, a dark-haired man."

"A friend maybe?" Jude's voice grew weaker as exhaustion had set in.

She drove for another five minutes passing only fields with drifted snow.

She looked down at the gas gauge. She should have thought to fill the tank before leaving town. Conditions were still not perfect. She drove slowly. Several cars passed her. An equally cautious driver in a black van eased by her. A sign indicated that a gas station was up ahead.

She pulled in. When she peered over her shoulder, Jude was fast asleep. She filled the gas tank up. She had only cash, so she went inside to pay. The clerk was a lanky teenage boy who leaned over the counter flipping through a magazine. She handed him the cash and waited while he made change.

A news program on a television, mounted to the wall, droned in the background as the kid counted out her change and excused himself. He exited out the side door. He had smelled of smoke so maybe he was out having a cigarette.

Her eyes were drawn to the television set as a breaking local news story flashed on the screen. Her breath caught and she looked around for the remote control to turn up the volume. She found it behind the counter. She pressed the volume button.

She couldn't believe what she was seeing. The news story was about how Maria Ignatius had been returned safe and sound to her parents in a Montana town. A news story that should have made her happy. Should have made her want to run out to Jude and shake him awake so he could hear the good news.

As she stood alone in the gas station though, she knew something was terribly wrong. On the screen flashed a scene of little Maria with her father, George. Lacey felt like an elephant had just sat on her chest. George was the man she'd seen at the window of the Victorian house where Dale lived. George had been in Lodgepole at the time of his daughter's kidnapping, and he knew Dale.

He had led Jude to believe the calls were coming from out of state. Was it possible that George was somehow connected to his own daughter's kidnapping? Why?

Lacey hurried outside to tell Jude. She swung open the back door of the SUV. Jude wasn't there.

A hand went over her mouth.

A gruff voice spoke into her ear. "Where's your boy-friend?"

She shook her head.

"Fine, we'll just use you as bait."

The scenery whirred around her as she was dragged across the icy gravel lot. A door clicked open and she was shoved into the back of a van. She caught a glimpse of her kidnapper just before he slammed the door. The black van must have followed them from Lodgepole or just outside of it. She recognized the man as the one who had hunted her and Jude from the beginning on the mountain, the gray-haired muscular man. He must have turned Maria over to somebody who did the exchange giving him time to come after Lacey and Jude. The van smelled like grease. Her hand touched dirty carpet.

She wasn't tied up. She could still get away. She lurched for the side door that had just been opened. Her hand reached for the door handle. She slid it open.

Jude was just coming around the side of the build-ing. A look of horror spread across his face.

A man shoved her back in and slammed the door. She caught sight of Jude running toward the van.

The front door opened and shut. The motor of the van roared to life.

She heard a fist pounding on metal and Jude shout-ing her name as the van gained speed. Would the infor-mation that George Ignatius was somehow connected to his own daughter's kidnapping die with her? Lacey collapsed on the dirty carpet.

# SIXTEEN

As he raced toward Nancy's car, Jude had the sensation of being punched in the stomach and hit in the head at the same time. He jumped into the cab and turned the key in the ignition. He'd awakened to find the car stopped and assumed Lacey was inside paying for the gas. He'd noticed the bathroom on the side of the building and gotten out of the car to use it.

He used the restroom and then wandered around the back to stretch his legs where he found a teenage boy sitting on milk crates staring at his phone. He'd exchanged a hello with the kid and then gone to get back in the car. In those brief minutes, Broad Shoulders had had time to grab Lacey. The van may have already been parked there. He wasn't sure. He was still groggy from his deep sleep and not as observant as he should have been.

He pressed the gas and sped up after the van. Jude was able to stay close to the van as it sped down the highway. He pulled the phone Nancy had loaned him from his pocket. If he drew his concentration away from the road, it meant slowing down to call the sheriff. He pressed the button on the phone and put it on speaker, informing the deputy who answered as to what was going on.

The distance between himself and the van increased. He ended the call and pressed the gas. He drew close to the van and then increased his speed to come alongside it and maybe run it off the road. An oncoming car made him slip back behind the van again. He stayed close to the van's bumper looking for his chance when the van turned suddenly onto a side road without signaling. Jude took the turn to follow at a tight angle, sliding sideways. This road was paved and plowed but still icy. The piles of snow on either side of it made it into almost a one-lane road. There was no way to run the van off the road. He could only tail it and wait for the road to widen. Several times, he tried to ram the van from behind to make him go into a snowbank, but he only managed to tap the bumper before the van gained speed.

They passed a house with several barns and outbuildings and then the landscape flattened out. Though the fields were covered in snow, they were probably used for planting in the spring.

Jude continued to follow the van. The driver maintained the same distance between them. Clearly this was some sort of trap to get both of them to a vulnerable and isolated place. All the same, he could not abandon Lacey. He had to find a way to free her.

He slowed and tried the phone again. The sheriff would be looking for him on the main road. Before he could press the call icon, the phone slipped out of his hand and fell on the floor of the passenger side.

Jude gripped the wheel and maintained his pace. They drove for what seemed like at least twenty minutes. In all that time, the only living things they encountered were a field of sheep. The road turned from paved to gravel.

He began to wonder what the guy in the van had in mind when he pulled over on a shoulder, the first one they'd encountered.

Jude hung back on the road waiting to see what the man was going to do. His gun was still in his shoulder holster which was in the backseat. He'd taken it off when he'd lain down to sleep. Jude turned to try and reach it. His fingers were inches from it.

He glanced back. Broad Shoulders had gotten out of the van and was opening the side door. What had the man done with Maria? He'd had over a two-hour lead on them. Maybe she was in the van with Lacey? Broad Shoulders reached in and grabbed Lacey, yanking her toward the road as he drew out a gun and pointed it at Lacey's head.

Jude had the awful feeling that neither one of them was going to get out of here alive. Both of them could identify this man. Though the evidence against him for being connected to the kidnapping was circumstantial, he had probably killed Mr. Wilson and Dale. He had repeatedly tried to kill Jude and Lacey.

No, his intention was clear. He was going to shoot both of them.

The man nodded his head, indicating that Jude needed to get out of the cab of the SUV. Jude glanced back at his gun.

With Lacey in tow, holding her by her ponytail and pressing the gun to her temple, the man marched toward the car. Lacey's expression was filled with anguish. And then he saw her close her eyes and her features softened.

She was praying.

He needed to do the same.

He pushed open the door even as the words tumbled through his head.

*God, help me find a way to get Lacey free and us to a safe place.*

He stepped out and put his arms up in the air.

Broad Shoulders pointed the gun at him. "Open your coat. I need to see that you're not armed."

Jude held his coat open.

"Turn around," the man commanded. "Lift your coat up."

Jude did as he was told and then turned to face the man. Satisfied, the man put the gun back on Lacey's temple.

His teeth showed when he grinned. "So which one of you wants to die first?"

*God, please.*

Broad Shoulders grimaced. The rage Jude saw in those eyes was scary.

Jude's gaze moved upward for just a second as relief spread through him. The man was standing almost underneath a tree whose branches were heavy with snow. One of the lower branches had a chunk of snow that looked like it might slip off at any second.

"Please, there must be something we can work out between us." Jude kept his hands in the air but took a step toward the man, knowing that it would make the man take a step back. One more step and the man would be right underneath the branch. He needed to buy some time.

"There is nothing to work out. I'm not going to jail," the man said.

"Do you think they're not going to find any evidence

that links you to those two dead men on the mountain? Let alone the kidnapping of Maria Ignatius."

The man raised his eyebrows in a quick spasm. Again, it wasn't solid evidence but what Jude read in that expression was guilt.

"I have a way to get out of the country so fast, I'll be somewhere they can't find me before they even bring the body bags in…if they ever find them."

Fear shot through Jude. "What have you done with Maria?"

Something flashed across Lacey's features and then was gone. She shook her head. A movement so slight that only he would notice it as he faced her. She knew something about Maria.

Without moving his head, Jude gazed upward. The snow was hanging, ready to slip. He just needed the man to take one more step back.

"Please, let's try and work something out." Jude took a step toward the man.

The man held his ground and pressed the gun tighter against Lacey's head. Lacey closed her eyes, but this time she wasn't praying.

The laden branch above creaked as the snow started to slide. Jude lunged toward the man. The man stepped back, dragging Lacey with him. The snow fell on them, but because he was taller than Lacey, the bulk of it landed on the man's head. The man let go of Lacey. The moment of distraction was enough time for Jude to leap toward him and land a blow to his jaw and a second punch to his stomach.

The man held on to his gun. He aimed it at Jude and pulled the trigger. Lacey leaped on his back, which made the shot go wild. The man hit Lacey on the side of the head with the pistol. She toppled to the ground, not moving.

Shock spread through Jude at the sight of Lacey's still body. He lunged at the man before he had a chance to aim the gun at him. Both men fell on the snowy ground and rolled around.

The man was on top of Jude though he'd dropped his gun. He hit Jude several times in the face. Pain radiated through Jude's jaw. His vision blurred.

He slammed his fist into the man's stomach. And then sitting up, he put his hands on the man's shoulders and pushed him back. Jude tried to get to his feet. The man was already standing. Broad Shoulders glanced around searching for the gun. While Jude was still kneeling on the ground, the man kicked him in the stomach.

Lacey had begun to stir from the shock of the blow she'd sustained.

Once the man found his gun, they would both be dead.

He crawled toward Lacey.

The man stomped around kicking at the snow, still unable to find his gun.

Jude reached Lacey just as she opened her eyes. She sat up, taking in the scene. He scrambled to get to his feet and reached down to help her up.

The man's body slammed him, knocking him to the ground. Jude's face was buried in the snow. He heard punches being thrown. He flipped over. Despite a valiant effort, Lacey was no match for the man who had grabbed both her wrists as they faced each other.

Jude picked up a hefty branch and landed it across the man's back. The man remained upright but the blow was enough to stun him into inaction for a moment. Jude grabbed Lacey's hand and they raced back toward the SUV.

He could hear the man running behind them, right at their heels. Jude swung open the driver's side door. Lacey got in and scooted across the seat. As he moved to get into the car, the man grabbed him from behind. Jude swung around and punched him several times. The man wobbled and took a step back.

Jude got behind the wheel. Lacey had already started the SUV.

Broad Shoulders ran toward his own vehicle, stopping a moment to pick something up. He'd found his gun.

Lacey was safe with him. Now they just needed to get back to the road that led to Garnet. Their attacker ran toward his van. The shoulder they were parked on was too narrow to make a U-turn without sliding off the side or getting stuck in the deep snow. Jude sped ahead past the parked van, knowing that there had to be a place to turn around somewhere on the road.

Their attacker jumped into his car and raced after them.

Lacey gripped the dashboard and craned her neck. "How are we going to get turned around with him so close to us?"

Jude gripped the wheel and stared out at the flat terrain and the straight narrow road with a berm of snow on either side of it. He didn't know the answer to that question. His foot floored the accelerator and he sped down the road into the unknown.

Frantic, Lacey gulped in a breath of air and looked over her shoulder. The other car was drawing dangerously close to them. It was close enough that she could see the man behind the wheel, his teeth bared in rage.

The other car lurched forward and tapped their bumper. The impact jarred her body. She bit her tongue accidently. Her lower jaw stung with pain.

The man hit them a second time. Their car fish tailed, hitting one of the snowbanks. Jude held the wheel steady. "I can't shake him."

He sped up.

She feared they'd hit a patch of black ice. At this speed there was a danger of sliding into the snowbank. They came to a crossroads. Jude took a sharp left. The move put a little distance between them and the van.

They drove for several miles. The van remained behind them.

The tension in her chest made it hard to get a deep breath. "He's not going to give up until we're dead."

"I know," Jude said. "This road has to open up or lead somewhere."

"Jude, I saw something back at the gas station on television. Maria is home safe with her parents."

"That's good news. How did they get her back? Did George pay the ransom?"

"I don't know the details. All I saw was the tail end of the news story."

He glanced over at her. "Why do you look so grim?"

"Jude, I didn't know what George Ignatius looked like until I saw the news story. George was in Lodgepole. I saw him in the window of the house where Dale lived."

Jude shook his head. "Why would he lie to me? He called me from out of state."

"What if he had something to do with his own daughter's kidnapping?"

"That doesn't make any sense, Lacey. Why would he hire me if he was involved?"

Before she could answer. The attacker's car rammed their bumper once again. Jude swerved on the road, heading straight toward a snow pile. Her side of the car skimmed the edge of the snow berm. He straightened the wheel and righted the car.

The van remained close for another mile or so.

Jude slowed down. Up ahead, a farmer was moving his sheep across the road. The farmer along with a younger-looking man on a horse stood watch while a border collie ran circles around the sheep nipping at their heels. The men were some distance away from the road. Jude came to a full stop. The attacker stopped his car, as well. He wouldn't harm them with witnesses around.

"What if we asked that farmer for help?"

"We'd have to run all that way across the field out in the open." Jude rubbed his forehead and then tilted it toward the van. "We know he's already killed two other people. I don't see a farmhouse around here anywhere. It just seems like we'd be risking the guy's life and that kid's and I don't think we could get to them before the shooting started."

If they could get to town where there were lots of people, they'd be safe.

Jude checked the rearview mirror. "Looks like he's making a call. Must be cell service out here." He pointed at the phone on the floor of the passenger seat. "The sheriff's number was the last one I called. Tell him where we are and that we need help."

She took the phone. "I'm not sure where we are."

"I don't know exactly either. It was the first right turn off the main road after that gas station."

She laughed. "That's real precise."

In spite of their situation, he laughed too. "I know we've been driving for a long time. It might be hard to locate us. Maybe they can use GPS to find the cell." He glanced back at the van. "The sheriff needs to know. Just in case."

He didn't need to finish his sentence. She knew he meant just in case they didn't make it to Garnet. She spoke while the phone rang. "Wish I could remember the name of the gas station."

"There can't be that many between Lodgepole and Garnet."

Lacey spoke to the deputy who answered the phone, giving him all the information she had. She wasn't sure how to explain about seeing George Ignatius or if she even should. They had no evidence that George was connected to the kidnapping, only that he had lied about where he was at. The connection dropped out before she could explain. The last sheep made it across the road. Jude shifted into First and rolled forward. The van remained behind them the whole time though it seemed to be hanging back and just following them.

Lacey stared at the phone. "Do you suppose I can figure out where we are with the maps feature on this phone?"

Jude shrugged. "Worth a try."

The road widened a bit. A truck was in front of them for several miles and then turned off.

Lacey stared at the map on the phone. "It looks like

there's a town not too far from here. It's called Stage-line."

She looked up. Jude's face had drained of color. She stared at the road ahead where a car was parked facing forward, blocking the road. The road was so narrow, there was maybe a foot of clearance on either side.

"I guess we know who the guy in the van was talking to."

A chill ran down her spine as she stared straight ahead. Now she knew why the man hadn't tried to ram them once they were out of view of the farmer. "Looks like he called in reinforcements."

# SEVENTEEN

Jude's heart pounded. The car up ahead completely blocked the road. There were two men in the front seat. The berm of snow on either side of the road was pretty steep. And there was still snow in the flat field beyond. The van behind them blocked the possibility of hitting Reverse and backing away.

"We don't have a lot of choice," Lacey said.

She must have been thinking the same thing he was thinking.

"Can you crawl in the backseat and get my gun?" Jude asked. "We might need it."

"Sure," she said.

Jude drew closer to the car speeding up. Maybe the guy would think he was playing chicken and back up. When he was within twenty feet of the other car, he turned the wheel sharply and gunned the engine, heading toward the open field.

The SUV hung at the top of the snow berm. One of the back wheels was spinning.

Lacey sat back up in the passenger seat, holding the holster in her lap. She glanced out her window. "One of the men is getting out of that car that is blocking the road."

Jude pressed the gas and turned the wheel. Three of the tires still had traction. He could get them out of here. "You might want to pull that gun out of the holster." Jude spoke through gritted teeth.

He let up on the gas, hit Reverse, rolled back a foot and then sped forward. This time the SUV broke free. They lumbered over the berm and out into the field.

Lacey pulled the gun from the holster and ducked down. He caught only a glimpse of a man moving toward them before a bullet pinged off the metal of the car. He slipped down in the seat, as well.

The snow in the field was deep enough that it slowed them down, but he was still moving forward. In his rearview mirror, he could see the man with the gun climbing the berm and running after them.

The snow had grown heavy and slushy which slowed them even more.

The SUV chugged like they were driving with square tires. It took him a minute to realize it wasn't just the consistency of the snow that was slowing them down. One of their tires had deflated. The man with the gun must have shot at it. They weren't going to get much farther in the car.

"We're going to have to make a run for it." Jude turned the SUV so it was facing sideways. Lacey's side of the car was the farthest from the approaching gunman. They could use the car as cover until the shooter got beyond it. "Give me the gun."

She handed it to him and pushed open the car door, dropping to the ground. He crawled out behind her and caught up with her as she ran. The shooter was still about thirty feet from the car. Ahead of them lay an open field filled with melting snow.

The shooter had only a handgun which didn't have the same range as a rifle. As long as they kept twenty feet between them, he wouldn't be able to get a clean target. If he shot and ran at the same time, the possibility of getting an accurate shot was low. He'd have to stop and aim which meant they could put even more distance between them.

Along the road, the van was backing up, maybe to try and head them off if they tried to circle back to the road. Because there still wasn't a spot wide enough to turn around, the van had to continue to go backward.

The second car did not move.

They hurried as fast as they could. The bottom of his pant leg was weighed down from the moisture of the slushy snow. Jude glanced over his shoulder. The shooter had stopped and shoved his gun in his jacket. The van started to rumble forward, and the car shifted into Reverse.

A farm truck hauling a load of hay was behind the van. It was too far away for them to hope to wave it down. But the presence of the stranger was enough to make the men hide what they were up to.

The delay bought them precious minutes. They ran through the field. Jude veered off toward the east where a windbreak of trees stood in a straight line. The deciduous trees were barren and gray. Judging from the wide circumference of the trunks, the old oaks had to be at least fifty years old. They slipped in behind the trees. Both of them were gasping for air. Jude stared out at the field and then along the road. He couldn't see the van or the farmer's truck anymore, but the car was rolling down the road. It must have pulled off on a shoulder while driving backward and let the van and the farmer's truck go by.

The man with the gun was still headed across the field toward them.

Jude tugged on Lacey's sleeve. "Let's keep going." Though not a direct route, they were headed back in the direction they had come from toward the main road and the gas station though it had to be at least ten miles. They ran until the side road was no longer in view. The terrain turned from flat to rolling hills. Every time they came to the crest of a hill, Jude looked down to see the shooter still dogging them but never catching up. He was a lean man who appeared to be in very good shape. Was he just waiting for them to drop from exhaustion? Jude's leg muscles screamed from the amount of exertion.

They stopped only briefly to catch their breaths and then kept running. Their footsteps smacked through the damp heavy snow. He was grateful for his waterproof boots or his feet would have been as soaked as his pant legs.

He wondered if they would just be running forever, never being caught, but never able to get away either. Up ahead, he saw a field populated with huge round hay bales. This might be the chance they were looking for. They could hide behind one of the bales and try to ambush the shooter. Or, maybe the shooter would run right by them.

After glancing over his shoulder and not seeing their pursuer, he sprinted toward the middle of the field. Lacey ran beside him. Their boots made squishy sounds on the half-melted snow. He crouched behind a bale and Lacey slipped in beside him, pressed close to his back. He pulled the gun from his waistband. He could feel Lacey's breath on his neck and the heat of her touch as she rested her hand on his upper shoulder.

Time seemed to slow down as he watched and listened. The rhythm of Lacey's breathing matched his own. His leg muscles started to cramp. He switched to a more comfortable position on his knees which meant his pants would get even more wet.

Lacey whispered in his ear. "I'll keep a lookout on the other side of the bale. I'll signal you if I see him coming."

Jude nodded. The less they talked, the better. The guy might have figured out their plan and was already creeping through the field.

Jude angled his head around the bale so he could see more. His gaze moved from one open area to another and then he studied each of the hay bales. A crow fluttered down on top of one of the other bales picking at whatever morsels of food he could find.

The distant cawing of other crows filled the air. Jude glanced at the slow-moving clouds in the blue sky. The calm he saw there stood in sharp contrast to his pounding heart and tensed muscles.

He turned to glance back at Lacey. His heart froze. She wasn't there. He had a moment of fear that she'd been snatched. But no one could be that quiet. She would have put up a fight. She'd moved for some reason.

He studied the area around him. Lacey stuck her head out from the side of a bale not too far from him and gave him the okay sign. She had probably reasoned that they could see more if they were split up behind different bales.

The wind ruffled his hair and he adjusted his grip on the gun. The crow on top of the bale flapped away. Jude went on high alert as his gaze darted everywhere. The crow may just have had his fill of grain or he may have been frightened by something.

Jude heard movement, footsteps, off to his side. He rose up and lifted his gun. Lacey had run from one bale to the next. His breath hitched. Now he knew what she was doing. She must have spotted the shooter and was making herself bait to draw him out. No wonder she hadn't said anything. Making her a target was a plan he never would have agreed to.

Jude sprinted toward another bale. He heard swishing movements but couldn't see anything.

At the sound of the first gunshot, his heart squeezed tight and he prayed for Lacey's safety.

Jude sprinted toward the next bale, still not seeing anything.

Lacey was pretty sure that first shot had lodged in the hay bale she was hiding behind. So the shooter had seen her. Her heartbeat drummed in her ears as she rose up and prepared to run to the next bale. She could not see the shooter or Jude, but she heard squishy footsteps all around her.

Crouching low, she sprinted out into the open. The next bale was only fifteen feet away, but it felt like a thousand miles while she was vulnerable and exposed. She was sure that Jude would realize what her plan was. As she ran, she looked from side to side. She caught a flash of movement. Someone slipping behind a bale not too far from her. He'd disappeared before she could tell if it was Jude or the shooter.

She ran to hide behind the next bale but stuttered in her step. The shooter with his back to her crouched one bale away. She scrambled to the side of her bale so he wouldn't see her. That meant that it was Jude who had gone behind the other bale. Their positioning formed a sort of triangle. Jude at the apex of the triangle and the shooter and her at the lower angles.

Lacey took in a breath and rested her palm against her raging heart. She could try to jump the shooter from the back. But if he heard her coming, he could turn and shoot her. At that close a range the shot was bound to be fatal.

She crept around to the other side of the bale that was closer to where she'd seen Jude. She sprinted out toward the next bale, pressing against the side of it that was the farthest away from the one where she'd seen the shooter.

Fear raged through her at the same time she felt a surge of strength. She ran to the next bale. She was one bale away from where she'd seen Jude when a volley of gunfire shattered the silence around her.

She pressed into the bale as terror froze her in place. The straw was itchy against the back of her neck. A deafening silence fell around her. The beating of her own heart seemed to be the only thing she could hear. And then she detected the distant cawing of the crows and felt the breeze on her face. She shook herself free of the paralysis, scrambled toward the edge of the bale and peered out to see if she could figure out what had happened.

She looked everywhere, not seeing or hearing anything. She feared that Jude lay on the cold wet ground bleeding to death, and the shooter was just waiting for her to find him so he could take her out too.

She thought she heard footsteps off to the side of her. She ran the other way toward the nearest bale. Her own footsteps seemed to be getting louder. She slowed and stepped more lightly.

She pressed against the side of the cylindrical hay bale and tilted her head to the sky and listened. She'd worked her way almost to the end of the field. Ahead she could see another windbreak of trees and a barbed wire fence. She wasn't leaving without Jude. She had to know what had happened. If the shooter had taken him out, he was probably still stalking the field looking for her.

She crawled to the top of the hay bale, lifting her head only slightly to try to get a view of the field. One more shot was fired, followed by the deafening quiet, no cries of pain, no indication that anyone had been hit. She recoiled but managed a deep breath, still studying the field. She could guess the direction the shot had come from, several bales back from where she'd just been.

To run to where the shot had been fired from meant she might be running directly toward the shooter. She waited and watched. In the midst of this standoff, someone had to move sooner or later. Even slight movement caused the straw to make noise. She pressed her belly against it and willed herself to be still.

Her gaze darted from one bale to the next and then to the open areas. After what felt like forever, she saw Jude's head for only a moment before he was hidden again.

Heart racing, she crawled down and ran to the edge of field on the side where she'd spotted Jude. She risked running into the shooter, but she worried that Jude would be distracted wondering about her safety. If they were together, they could take on the shooter.

Jude was three hay bales up from the edge of the field. She darted to the end of the first cylinder of straw, stopping only to take in a deep breath before she ran to the next one. Her fingers pulled straw out to release some of the tension building up inside of her. Her stomach had coiled into a tight knot.

She prayed that Jude hadn't already repositioned again. This deadly game could go on forever if he had. She ran toward the last place she'd seen Jude.

When she got there…the space was empty.

She heard footsteps behind her. Before she could turn around, an object hit her head and a view of the ground filled her vision.

# EIGHTEEN

"Jude, I have your girlfriend. Come and get her."

The mocking tone of the shooter tore Jude to pieces. Gritting his teeth, he squeezed his eyes shut.

"I'll give you to a count of ten and then I'm going to put a bullet in her."

Was it possible the shooter was lying to lure him out? Jude stood up and shouted, "I need to hear her voice."

"That's not possible. I call the terms of this arrangement."

Was Lacey already dead? Or maybe unconscious.

Judging from the volume of the shooter's voice. Jude was within one or two bales of where the man was. He took in a deep breath to try to loosen the tightness he felt in his chest. He peered around the bale where he was hiding, still not seeing anything. He didn't have a clear plan, all he knew was that he needed to get to Lacey.

If she was conscious, close and not being held at gunpoint, she would have heard the shouting and responded in some way to warn him. He studied the field and the fence and trees beyond. Could she be hiding out there?

Too many questions, too many unknowns. He hurried to the next bale in the general direction the man's voice had come from. He ran to another bale and looked out. Adrenaline surged through him as he raised his gun. The shooter was turned sideways. Lacey lay on the ground beside him.

Before he could pull the trigger, the shooter raised his gun. Jude dove behind the bale for cover and fired a shot. When he looked out, the man was no longer out in the open. Lacey lay motionless on the cold wet snow. No doubt, the shooter was somewhere he could watch her, so running to rescue her would only get them both killed.

A strange mumbling reached his ears. Jude lifted his chin, listening. It sounded like the shooter was on a phone. The voice grew louder then softer. Like he was pacing.

He touched his own pocket where his phone should have been. It must still be on the console of the SUV from when he'd had Lacey call in to the sheriff.

From the sound of the voice, the man was getting farther away. That didn't make sense. Wouldn't the shooter at least be where he could see Lacey?

Lacey's body jerked. She must be coming around. The intense need to run to her, to make sure she was safe, overwhelmed him. The shooter had to be using her as bait. Jude glanced all around, not seeing any movement or any sign of the other man. The voice had faded altogether.

Lacey stirred even more. Her legs moved and she lifted her head slightly. She must be cold lying there on the ground for so long. She opened her eyes. Her expression changed when she saw him. Her features softened, and warmth seemed to come into her eyes.

He rose up to run to her when he heard footsteps

behind him. He turned but saw no one. The man was on the other side of the hay bale. Jude glanced over at Lacey, who was still struggling to get to her feet. Her hand went to the side of her head.

The next few minutes seemed to unfold in slow motion. The broad-shouldered man came out of nowhere and grabbed Lacey before she could get to her feet. He pulled her by her hair and held a gun to her stomach. A look of terror crossed her features as she reached out a hand toward Jude and was dragged away. He jerked to move toward her.

Jude had been so focused on Lacey and what the shooter was up to, he hadn't seen the van driven by Broad Shoulders lumbering across the field to park behind the windbreak.

Broad Shoulders lifted his chin in a challenging way as his gaze darted toward the gun that was held on Lacey. Jude watched in horror as the man's finger moved to the trigger. Lacey's eyes grew wide with fear.

Breath caught in Jude's throat.

Broad Shoulders looked out beyond Jude. His grimace went slack as he withdrew the gun from view but still was controlling her by pushing the gun into her back. Jude glanced over his shoulder.

The farmer they'd seen earlier had driven into the adjoining field where cattle rested. His truck rolled forward while he threw rectangular straw bales off the back of it.

Jude felt something hard push against his back. A gun. The shooter who had chased them across the field spoke in a low voice. "Get moving and don't try anything."

"You won't shoot me," Jude said and tilted his head

toward where the farmer was. "I know you don't want witnesses."

"Shut up," the man who had chased them said. "It would be nothing for me to drag you behind that hay bale and put a bullet through you."

That might be true. But the farmer would still remember seeing two strange men in the field and if a body was found later, he would connect the dots. Broad Shoulders had disappeared behind the windbreak. The van was nearly camouflaged by the bare trees. He didn't see the other car or its driver anywhere. Maybe he had left.

"Okay, I'll go." All Jude knew was that Lacey had just been loaded into that van. He wasn't about to abandon her. Even if he could get away and get the farmer's attention, Lacey would still be held captive. She would be killed and her body dumped somewhere else.

The farmer, focused on feeding the cows, had not looked in their direction other than a quick glance. Men and a woman in a field had to look out of place.

They walked across the snowy muddy field to where the van was. The shooter swung open the side door of the van and shoved Jude inside. Lacey was there. Her back pressed against the wall of the van. Her hands tied in front of her.

"Stay away from her. No talking."

The man who had captured Jude got into the passenger seat of the van and slammed the door.

"Thought I was going to have to leave without you," Broad Shoulders said.

"Like you would," the second man, who had buggy eyes, said. His red hair stuck out beneath his winter hat.

There were no windows in the back of the van and

Jude couldn't see much out the front window without lifting up. He raised his eyebrows as a way of communicating with Lacey. She gave a slight nod in response.

"What are we supposed to do with them now?"

"I'm sure boss wants us to find a place to get rid of them."

Jude wondered who the *boss* was referring to. Had it been the man who was the driver in the other car? Jude had not seen him at all. Was it like Lacey had speculated, George Ignatius had conspired in the kidnapping of his own daughter?

"Off the road somewhere should be fine. Just find a concealed area," Bug Eyes said.

The words sent a chill through Jude. Did they have only minutes to live?

"Don't you think you should tie him up too?"

"Why? This will be over soon enough. Let's just get this done. Then, I want to go into town and grab a burger."

The callousness of the men sent a new shock wave of fear through him. His hands weren't tied. He had to act. He glanced around in search of a weapon. Lacey seemed to understand, as well. She looked from side to side and shook her head.

The van went from rolling smoothly to bumping along. He didn't have much time. He jumped up and reached for the driver, knowing the other man had a gun. All the same, if they were distracted by a potential wreck, he and Lacey might have a fighting chance.

Lacey jumped up as well, moving toward the man in the passenger seat. Jude wrapped his hands around the neck of the driver while Lacey pummeled the passenger with her bound hands.

The driver took his hands off the wheel in an attempt to free himself from Jude's stranglehold. The van swerved.

Broad Shoulders wrestled free of Jude's hold. The passenger had subdued Lacey by gripping her bound hands and pushing her down. Through the windshield, Jude saw the farmer in the truck driving toward them.

With Lacey under control, both men pounced on Jude.

The passenger, the man with buggy eyes, glanced nervously through the windshield. "Get him out of sight," Broad Shoulders said.

Jude felt a hard object hit the side of his head. Black dots filled the edges of his vision as his view of the orange carpet in the back of the van loomed toward him.

He heard Lacey scream.

"Shut her up before that farmer gets here."

With his cheek pressed against the carpet, he saw feet moving toward where Lacey lay. His eyelids were as heavy as lead. He fought to remain alert. The darkness closed in on him.

Lacey tried to crawl away as Bug Eyes lunged toward her. He placed his hand over her mouth and slid out of view behind the seat. Up front, the driver rolled down the window. "Hey there."

There was a pause and then an unfamiliar voice spoke up. "Is everything okay here?" That must be the farmer she'd seen driving toward them. His voice was filled with suspicion.

"Oh, sure. I'm just a little lost. I'm not from around here…trying to get to town."

"Weren't you with some other people?"

"They're laying down in the back. We've been driving for hours. That's why we were out in that field. I'm sure you saw us there. We just needed to stretch our legs is all. We didn't mean to trespass."

Lacey twisted from side to side, trying to escape. She reached her free hand up to claw at the man's fingers. If she could just get his hand off her mouth, she'd be able to cry out. The man pressed even harder against her mouth.

Again, there was hesitation before the farmer said anything. "You sure everything is all right?"

"Oh sure, if you could just point me toward the nearest town."

"Stageline is just up the road a piece."

"Thanks."

Lacey heard the window close. The driver shifted into Reverse. Bug Eyes released his hold on her and jerked her around. He removed a winter scarf from around his neck and used it as a gag.

He put his face very close to hers. "Just in case you get any ideas."

Before taking his place in the front seat, he tied up Jude, as well.

After a few minutes, the driver spoke up as he glanced in his rearview mirror. "Would you look at that. That stupid farmer is following us."

"What kind of do-gooder citizen is he?" Bug Eyes said.

"Well, I guess we got to go into Stageline or he's going to report us. I was hungry anyway," Broad Shoulders said. "What are we supposed to do with those two?"

"We could shoot them now and dispose of the bodies later."

Lacey's heart beat faster at the suggestion. Sweat trickled down her back. She pressed her head against the back of the driver's seat.

"I can't risk being caught in a car with two bodies. Mr. Do-gooder Farmer already thinks we're up to something. He can identify this vehicle. He's probably written down the license number. He knows what I look like. I'm not going back to prison. That was not the deal I made."

"We need to have a plan here," Bug Eyes said. "First thing, we shake Farmer Joe. Do you think he'll give up once he sees we're turning into town?"

"I don't like being in the van with these two. This is way more than I bargained for. I was supposed to be out of the country by now. This whole thing is a mess. Get on the phone to the boss," Broad Shoulders said.

Lacey listened while Bug Eyes told the man on the other end of the line what was going on. "Look, we're being followed. This is way more than we signed up for. Way more than we agreed to. Okay fine, soon as we throw this guy off, they're your problem. You need to get over here to this town… Stageline." He turned the phone off.

The van picked up speed as it turned onto what must have been a paved road.

"Do you suppose that farmer has already phoned in to the law?" The driver sounded nervous.

"Could be," the passenger said.

A tiny bit of hope blossomed for Lacey. The sheriff in Garnet knew what was going on. She didn't know if Stageline was big enough to have any law enforcement. If a call came in, maybe the sheriff in Garnet would put two and two together and know where to look for them.

"All he has to go on at this point is his own suspicions. He's probably following us to see if he can find a reason to report us."

"I say we can't take any chances," Bug Eyes said.

The men drove on in silence. Several times Bug Eyes turned in the passenger seat to check on her and Jude, who had not stirred from being unconscious yet. He raised his gun in her direction to let her know she dared not try anything.

The van slowed down. They must have been within the town limits.

"Put that gun away," the driver said. "I don't want anyone seeing you with it through the window."

"So what do we do now?"

"We told that farmer we were going to find a bite to eat, so let's do that." The turn signal beat out a droning rhythm. When she lifted her head, she could see some houses and a gas station.

The passenger twisted in his seat. The gun was in his lap. His face was red with rage. "Get back down."

The two men were clearly on edge.

"I suppose it's too much to hope for a drive-through in a town this size," Broad Shoulders said.

"Over there." The passenger pointed through the window. "You can get us some food to go. I'll wait here and watch these two."

"Is that farmer still following us?"

"He's parked. Watching us from across the street."

"Suppose he's not going to give up until he sees at least one of us go inside," the driver said. "Watch her close. I don't want any chance that she can draw someone's attention."

Bug Eyes crawled back and put his face very close to hers. "Don't try anything."

"I'll order something quick. I want to ditch these guys," Broad Shoulders said. "This is the end of the line for me. I need to get out of the country before this whole thing blows up. Once I got that kid off the mountain that was supposed to be the end of my job."

Broad Shoulders left the car. She wiggled snakelike across the carpet. She could just lift her head above the console between the seats.

"Hey, get down," the man in the passenger seat said.

There was only one other vehicle in the parking lot and it was parked at the other end. She slipped out of view. It seemed there was no way to get anyone's attention and no way to escape the vehicle.

With her bound hands, she reached out and touched Jude's head, brushing the lock of golden-brown hair out of his eyes. Though she could see his pulse throbbing on the side of his neck, it concerned her that he had been out for so long.

She scooted a little closer to him, knowing they both did not have long to live.

# NINETEEN

Jude awoke to the sound of Bug Eyes and Broad Shoulders talking. The tension in the van was palpable. Lacey sat with her hands tied. She smiled at him when he opened his eyes.

"I think that highway patrol car is following us," Broad Shoulders said. "There is no way we can pull off and get rid of these guys."

"There hasn't been any place for him to turn off. It's miles of straight road. Maybe he's just headed in the same direction as us."

Broad Shoulders sped up. "Wrong. His lights are flashing."

Bug Eyes glanced in the side-view mirror. "We can't be caught with these guys. This was supposed to be an easy job."

"I don't like this. I'm not going back to prison." Broad Shoulders accelerated even more and then took a tight turn. "This is way more than I signed up for. We're not that far from where the boss is. I say we shake this guy and make those two in the back his problem."

"Okay, if that is what you want to do," Bug Eyes said.

He noticed that Jude was awake. He aimed the gun at him. "I'm watching you."

Jude caught a glimpse of a sign that said they were in Stageline. Broad Shoulders took several sharp turns, weaving through city and residential streets. He drove for another ten minutes.

Broad Shoulders checked his rearview mirror. His shoulders relaxed. "Good, looks like we lost our friendly law enforcement."

The van climbed a long winding hill and came to a stop. Jude lifted his chin. He could just see a garage door and a large cabin. A car that looked a lot like the one that had dropped Bug Eyes off was parked outside.

Bug Eyes opened his door and disappeared, then returned a moment later. Broad Shoulders rolled down the window.

"He's not happy about seeing us. But he says bring them in. Hide the van in the garage just in case that cop gets eager again and starts to search this neighborhood."

Lacey and Jude were pulled out of the van. "Put them in different rooms so they don't get any ideas," Broad Shoulders said. Lacey's eyes filled with fear as they were both brought into the kitchen and then she was taken to another room. He was shoved in the room next to the kitchen. The man they referred to as the boss had yet to make an appearance.

The curtains were drawn in the room where he'd been tossed, and the lights were out. His hands were tied in front of him. Though his head hurt from the blow he'd received, he pushed himself into a sitting position. He wondered where they'd taken Lacey.

He waited for his eyes to adjust to the darkness. He was in the rec room of some sort of cabin. The heads of animals were mounted on the walls. He had been placed on a couch. There was a shelf with games and books and a big fireplace that took up most of the wall. There were no personal items anywhere and the decor, from the leather couch to the cow skin rug and the stuffed animal heads, suggested a Western theme. He speculated that he might be in a vacation rental.

He could hear an argument taking place in the next room. Broad Shoulders yelling about how he had already done the job he was paid to do. Jude heard stomping and a door slamming. A vehicle started up and peeled away.

He rose to his feet. His legs were stiff and numb. He pulled aside a curtain and stared out into darkness. Off in the distance, he saw the twinkling lights of several other houses. A car whizzed by, headed down the hill. That must be Broad Shoulders leaving. Even farther away was a cluster of lights that suggested a small town. Again, he wondered what had happened to Lacey. He tried to open the window thinking he might crawl out. He pulled the latch forward but with his hands bound was unable to lift the window.

Voices in the next room drew his attention. He stumbled across the wood floor. When he tried the doorknob, it was locked. He pressed his ear close to the door. This time whoever was talking must be right outside the door. He could hear them more clearly.

"We can't do away with them here. It doesn't matter that I didn't rent this place under my name. My DNA is all over this place. There can be no link between me and their deaths because all of that will point the finger at me being involved with Maria's kidnapping."

Jude slid down to the floor. He knew that voice.

George Ignatius. His words confirmed what Lacey had speculated about.

"Okay, so we move them and dispose of them," said a second voice that belonged to Bug Eyes.

"They've seen too much. If law enforcement is out looking for them, we have to hurry," George said. "Reed took my car. You're going to have to take the van. Get rid of the bodies and get rid of the van. I'll make arrangements for you to be picked up."

Reed must be Broad Shoulders.

There was a moment's hesitation before Bug Eyes responded. "So all the risk is still on me. No way."

"I'll make it worth your while."

"There is not enough money in the world at this point."

"Fine, I'll help you," said George.

"And double my fee," said Bug Eyes.

"I don't have much choice at this point," said George.

One of them stomped across the floorboards coming closer. Jude darted back to the couch. The door swung open. George Ignatius stepped into the room and stalked over to where Jude sat.

Muscular and over six feet tall, George was an imposing figure with his jet-black hair and angular features. "You must have heard the conversation."

"I get it." Jude cleared his throat. "I'm going to die."

George lifted his chin in a show of dominance. "Do you think I'd be standing here in front of you if that wasn't the case?"

But it seemed as though George's goons were losing their enthusiasm.

"Why did you hire me?"

"I had to make it look like I was trying to get Maria

back even if the kidnappers threatened to kill her if I got the FBI involved." George crossed his arms. "I have to say I'm impressed with you. I didn't think a washed-up cop would get as far as you did."

The remark was meant to hurt, but it didn't. He knew he was no longer the guy who had given up on life. Being with Lacey had renewed his faith and his confidence. And all that they had been through and overcome showed him he wasn't washed-up. "Why kidnap your own daughter?"

"She was never harmed, and she was never afraid." George's words sounded defensive as he took a step toward him. "My wife holds the purse strings. Let's just say there were some big expenses she couldn't know about."

Jude could feel the rage toward George growing inside him even as he fought off the rising fear. What kind of evil man would put his own daughter through such a trial just to get money from his wife?

George narrowed his eyes at Jude as he leaned toward him. Even in the dim light, Jude could see the wildness in his eyes. Greed was a funny thing that consumed the hearts of men. "I hadn't counted on that snowstorm stranding me and delaying the ransom drop-off and Maria's return."

"Where are your wife and daughter now?"

"They're waiting for me back home. I needed to make sure all the loose ends on this thing were wrapped up. They think I'm on a business trip," George said. "Soon as I get rid of you and that woman, we'll be one big happy family again."

Jude swallowed, trying to produce some moisture in his mouth. The rising panic would not own him, not today or any day. Adrenaline pumped through his body. He jumped up and, using his head as a blunt object, slammed into George's chest.

It was wrong, immoral to do what George had done. A desire for justice gave Jude strength.

The move knocked George off his feet. He fell backward on his behind. Rage over what George had done surged through him. Jude jumped on the older man and pummeled him in the face and stomach with his bound hands.

He knew too that the rage was toward himself for having fallen for George's deception. Bug Eyes ran into the room and pulled Jude off George.

George rose to his feet, squared his shoulders and brushed his sleeves off. "Get him and the girl loaded up. We'll get to where there are no witnesses and the bodies won't be found or connected to this place and then we need to make sure that van is sunk in a lake or set on fire."

Jude twisted back and forth fighting to break free of the hold that Bug Eyes had on him.

George glared at Bug Eyes. "This wasn't supposed to go down this way. You shouldn't have come here."

"We did the best we could," Bug Eyes said through gritted teeth. "We didn't know they'd put up such a fight."

Jude sensed the tension between the two men.

"We'll take the back roads where the van isn't likely to be spotted," George said. "Let's go. We need to discuss the best way to get rid of them and get some things together. I don't want to be linked to this." He stomped out of the room.

Bug Eyes shoved Jude back in the room. Jude heard

the lock on the door click shut as he slumped down on the couch. He was grateful that Lacey was still alive. Where they were keeping her, he didn't know. Probably somewhere in the house in another locked room.

His head was still throbbing. He had to find some way to get Lacey and him out of here. There were houses just down the road. He rose to his feet, heading over to the bookcase that contained games and books. He walked the room looking for some way to cut through the rope that confined his hands.

The rock on the stone fireplace would maybe provide a sharp enough edge to free him. He positioned himself so he could rub the rope back and forth on the corner rock. How much time did he have? Ten minutes? Half an hour?

He had no way of knowing.

He rubbed the rope with a furious intensity. He could hear George and Bug Eyes arguing in the next room. The second man was demanding more money.

Dale and Mr. Wilson were killed by the man they called Reed. He hoped that man would not get away. Jude doubted the man who was still with George would turn him in no matter how mad he was about the situation. Only he and Lacey could tell the story that would put George and his associates behind bars.

He prayed that that secret would not die with him and Lacey. They had to get out of here and tell the sheriff all they knew and all they had seen. Justice would not be served until George Ignatius was behind bars.

Lacey stared at the ceiling in the bedroom where she'd been locked. She could hear two men downstairs arguing. Her hands were tied in front of her. At least they had taken the gag out of her mouth. She'd been placed in a chair. The curtains were drawn, but she could see through a slit that it was nighttime.

She'd watched them haul Jude away, but she had no idea where he was in the cabin.

She steeled herself and rose to her feet. She walked toward the dresser and pulled open a drawer, which contained a Bible and a brochure about the area. Apparently, they were in one of the guest cabins outside of Stageline. The guest cabins connected with a golf course and indoor swimming facility. She walked into the bathroom. Opening drawers with her hands tied was a bit of a challenge. She found nothing that would help her cut her hands free. The personal items in the shower indicated the bathroom had been used recently. In desperation, she kicked over the garbage can hoping to find a used razor. Nothing but paper. She looked around. The metal frame that surrounded the glass shower door was bent up in one spot. She placed her hands on it and sawed back and forth cutting through the rope.

The sound of footsteps coming up the stairs sent a surge of terror through her. She heard the door unlocking just as she locked the bathroom door. She opened the bathroom window.

"Hey. What do you think you're doing?" Bug Eyes pounded on the bathroom door and jiggled the doorknob.

She flipped open the window and pushed the screen out.

A tremendous thud shook the whole room. The man seemed to be slamming his body against the door. She stared down at the dark ground below. Two stories was a ways to jump, but what choice did she have?

She climbed out of the window and hung on for a moment before letting go, praying for a soft landing. Some barren bushes broke her fall but scratched her up. The man must have given up breaking the door down and was headed down the stairs and outside. She rolled toward the darkness of the bushes that surrounded the house.

She heard two men shouting at each other. One of them came and stood beneath the porch light. It was the man she'd seen in Lodgepole and then later on the television, George Ignatius.

Another man, the bug-eyed one who had been in the van, came up to George again. They shouted at each other before resuming their search for her.

She glanced around. The lights of other houses glowed, the nearest one was maybe a quarter mile away as the crow flies.

They could get to help, but first she had to find Jude. She ran toward the house, peering inside. She saw a kitchen and living room. Then she came to a room where the curtains were drawn but the window was open. She stuck her head in. It was some sort of rec room with a fireplace, couch and shelf filled with books and games. No one was inside.

Footsteps pounded off to the side. She glanced around spotting a tarp, which she rolled under just as the footsteps reached the side of the house she was on.

"She has to be here somewhere," George said. "Find her."

"How do you know she's not already headed down the hill to get help?"

"She wouldn't leave without him."

More footsteps. "I think we got a problem. Looks like he's gotten out too."

"Find them. Find them both." George's voice filled with rage. "I'll see if I can spot them headed down the road or anywhere around it." George lifted a gun and then shoved it in his waistband.

Lacey lifted the tarp to a view of a pair of white cowboy boots that belonged to Bug Eyes. The man paced.

The man stopped with the boots facing her. Then took a step toward the tarp. Her breath caught in her throat. Of course, the tarp looked like a good hiding place. There was no way to escape.

The boots stopped about three feet from the tarp, turned slightly and then Bug Eyes ran off. Something had caught his attention.

Heart racing, she lifted the tarp. The cold night chilled her. She still had on her winter coat but no hat or gloves. Lacey hurried toward the edge of the property where there was a fence. She circled around one side of the house searching for Jude. She stayed back in the shadows knowing that she might encounter Bug Eyes.

She came around to the second side of the house. Jude might be hiding in the shadows, as well. How were they ever going to find each other? Maybe the smart thing to do would be to head down the road but not where George would see her. She could get help. But would she get back in time to save Jude? It was too risky. She had to find Jude.

Still not seeing anything, she ran around to the next side of the house. From this vantage point on the edge of the property, she could see George walking down the road shining his flashlight. He aimed the flashlight in the bushes. Her breath hitched. Had he seen movement? Was Jude down there?

She'd circled around to three sides of the property and still had not run into Bug Eyes. Maybe he'd gone back inside for some reason.

Lacey ran around to the fourth side of the house. No Jude and no Bug Eyes. She was facing the back door. She saw movement inside. A man crouching as he walked past the kitchen window in the dimly lit house. She could not tell if it was Jude or the other man. Both men must be inside.

She stepped into a mudroom area. She heard footsteps in the adjoining room which had to be the kitchen.

Lacey pressed against the wall, trying to find the courage to step into the dark kitchen and face the danger there.

# TWENTY

Jude slipped out of the kitchen into the living room. All the lights were off, but the curtains were not drawn like they had been in the rec room. He hurried to hide behind a couch just as he heard footsteps behind him entering the living room.

"I know you're in here," Bug Eyes said.

Jude pressed against the side of the couch knowing that any noise would give him away. Bug Eyes must have seen Jude through the window when he was upstairs looking for Lacey. Jude had gotten out of the house through the window, but he'd slipped back in to search for Lacey through an unlocked door on the main floor. When he'd looked upstairs for Lacey, he found a room with a broken bathroom door, an open window and the cut rope that had bound Lacey's hands. Speculating that she must have gotten out too, he hurried downstairs to find her but had encountered Bug Eyes before he could get outside.

The man switched on the lights.

Jude braced himself. It was only a matter of seconds before he was found. He listened to the slow footsteps. From where he crouched, he watched the man as he checked behind the curtains. The man still had his gun in his waistband. His white cowboy boots pounded on the wood floor like a funeral dirge.

Jude crawled to the front of the couch, staying low. He had a straight shot to the door that led into the kitchen. Could he get there before the man pulled his gun and aimed? He doubted that Bug Eyes cared about George not wanting the bodies connected to this rental. It was the only option he had. He took in a breath and prepared to run when the lights in the kitchen flashed on and off.

Bug Eyes cursed and ran into the kitchen just as the lights were turned out again. Jude heard a muffled thud and then the man yelled. Leaping to his feet, Jude ran into the kitchen. Lacey hit the man with a golf club. The man grabbed the golf club and yanked it out of Lacey's hand. Jude dove toward the man before he could attack Lacey, balling his hand into a fist and smashing it against the man's jaw. In response, Bug Eyes swung the golf club and hit Jude in the shoulder. Pain vibrated down Jude's arm making his fingers tingle.

Lacey jumped into the fray slapping Bug Eyes on the face and chest. The blows were not strong enough to disable the man, but they served as a distraction. Jude maneuvered around him and reached for his gun. Before he could get it, the man had swung around unleashing the full force of his rage on Jude. Hitting him on the head and in the stomach before pulling his gun and aiming it at Jude.

The man spoke to Lacey but kept his eyes on Jude. "Take one step closer to me, and he gets a bullet through his chest."

Lacey put her hands up.

"George doesn't want us to die in this house," Jude said. "Those are his orders."

Bug Eyes took a moment to respond. "I'm tired of his orders." He tilted his head and pointed the gun at Lacey. "Go and stand by him."

The only chink in the armor of George's plan was that his goons were losing heart. One man had driven off and the other's enthusiasm for helping George was fading.

Keeping her arms in the air, she walked across the floor and positioned herself by Jude.

The man was breathless from the altercation and his face was red. He pulled the phone out of his front shirt pocket, still keeping the gun on them.

"Phone George and tell him to get back here." He extended the phone in Lacey's direction. "It's the last number I called, listed just as GI."

Lacey took the phone and pressed the required buttons. She cleared her throat. "He has us both. You can come back and stop looking."

Jude could hear George's laughter even though he wasn't on speaker. Once George got back and loaded them in the van, it would be all over for them. Their bodies might not be found for months or maybe never.

Lacey hung up the phone.

"Good girl." Bug Eyes never took his eyes off Jude, probably judging him to be the bigger threat. "Now put the phone back in my pocket and don't try anything."

Lacey did what the man asked. And then stepped back toward Jude. The man indicated the kitchen chairs. "Why don't you both sit down, turn the chairs so they face me?"

With the gun pointed at them, they had no choice but to do what he requested.

They had only minutes before George got back and it would all be over.

"George has put you through a lot," Jude said. He knew he couldn't win the man over, but maybe he could weaken his resolve.

"He's paying me extra."

"Yes, but is it worth it?" Lacey said. She must have picked up on his game plan. He doubted the man would turn on George, but maybe they could make him let his guard down enough for them to overpower him. "Your partner left, didn't he?"

"Yeah, he got mad and took off," Bug Eyes said.

"What is your name, anyway?" Jude said.

"Does it matter?" The man lowered the gun a little.

Jude could tell from the man's body language that he was softening toward them. All the same, they didn't have much time.

"You look tired," Lacey said. "George is asking a lot of you."

The remark made the man's posture soften even more.

While the man focused on Lacey, Jude glanced around the room to where the golf club lay. He couldn't get to it before Bug Eyes pulled the trigger.

Jude waited for the moment when the man's gaze rested fully on Lacey. Jude grabbed a chair and swung at the man. Lacey dove for the golf club. The man let go of the gun as he fell to his knees and it slid across the floor out of sight. They heard a door open.

George would be coming through the mudroom and into the kitchen any second. They'd have to take the other door. The man remained on his knees, conscious but dazed. As they hurried toward the other door, which was actually the front door, Jude heard George step into the kitchen.

The door they went through looked out on the golf course and several outbuildings which were only silhouettes in the nighttime darkness.

They ran across the snowy rolling field toward the first building. When he peered inside, he saw that it was a storage area for golf carts. The door was locked.

They had to find a way to get turned around so they could run to one of the houses and get help. Maybe there were other houses connected to other holes on the golf course, but he could not see any lights that indicated that.

When he looked out the side of the building closest to the rental house, he saw one man moving toward them on foot. That meant the other man, probably George, must be watching for them to try to connect with the road that led to the other houses.

"The brochure I saw said that these are vacation rentals that had a golf course and swimming facilities." Lacey pointed. "That other building must be where the swimming pool is."

"We don't have much choice." Jude grabbed Lacey's hand and squeezed it before taking off running.

The half-melted snow had crusted up and frozen in the low night temperatures. They slid but did not fall down. When Jude glanced over his shoulder, he could see a man drawing closer to them. Bug Eyes ran at a steady pace toward them, shining a flashlight.

Jude hurried around to the far side of the building hoping to see light that might indicate a house on this side of the building. He saw only a line of trees and more rolling hills where the golf course was spread out.

Lacey shook the doorknob. "Maybe we can hide if we can find a way in." The door didn't budge. "This is a big building. There are two of us and only one of him. Maybe we can take him out before George gets here."

Jude cupped a hand on Lacey's shoulder. "He's getting closer."

She stopped shaking the door and followed him to the side of the building. He crouched along the wall of the brick building. There was a concrete pad connected to part of the facility. They could hear footsteps as Bug Eyes drew near.

"Let's split up. You go that way around. Maybe we can catch him." If they could get one guy out of commission, it would be that much easier to get to help.

Lacey disappeared into the darkness. Jude turned back around and headed in the direction that he'd heard the footsteps. He pressed his back against the brick building and eased around the corner. Bug Eyes was standing there looking out with his back to Jude. Jude took cautious footsteps, trying to hide beneath the shadows that the eaves on the building provided. The man stepped away from the building but continued to look in the opposite direction from where Jude was. He thought he heard another set of footsteps, faint and barely discernible. Lacey.

Bug Eyes must have heard them too. He drew his pistol. Jude leaped toward the man and landed on his back, taking him down to the ground. Jude braced the man in place with his body despite his twisting and kicked to get away as he lay on his stomach.

"Lacey, I got him. Find something to tie him up with."

Bug Eyes groaned beneath Jude's weight.

"Lacey?"

Jude looked up hearing more footsteps. Laccy stood over him. "I can't find anything."

"Get his coat off. We'll use the sleeves to time him up."

The man continued to struggle. Lacey ripped fabric and handed pieces to Jude. They tied his feet and gagged him, as well.

Both of them jumped to their feet. Jude grabbed the man's gun. It was a different gun than the one he had dropped in the kitchen.

Headlights glared at them from the road. George was getting desperate if he was taking the van out. Of course, if he mowed them down with it and then got rid of it and their bodies, the evidence left behind would not be substantial.

They took off running across the golf course which was still covered in snow. George lumbered toward them in the van.

Though the snow slowed George down, they would be no match for him on foot. They circled back around to the brick building where the pool was.

They ran around to the far side of the building and pressed against it. The van made a rumbling noise as it made its way across the snow toward them. Then he heard it. Wheels spinning. George had gotten bogged down in the melting snow and mud.

Jude gripped the gun. "Now's our chance. I'll go get him."

"I hope he's not armed," she said. "I'm going around the other side."

Jude crouched and moved along the building until he reached a corner where he could peer out. George had gotten out of the car and was stomping toward the swimming pool building.

It didn't look like he was holding a gun.

Jude listened to the sound of the approaching footsteps, waiting for the right moment.

The footsteps slowed down. Then stopped.

Jude's heart pounded.

Was George trying to figure out where Jude had gone? Or did he know and was waiting to jump him?

Taking in a breath Jude angled around the building and lifted the gun. "Hands up, George. It's over." George was maybe five feet away.

"You got me," George said. But he didn't raise his hands.

Jude tensed.

"But not really. I gave that gun to my associate when he lost his in the kitchen. I happen to know it has no bullets. We were in a hurry. I figured a gun pointed at you would be enough to stop you."

Was he bluffing? Jude pulled the trigger. Nothing happened.

Fear pierced Jude's heart as George lunged toward him, but then crumpled to the ground.

Lacey stood behind him holding a golf club that she had used to hit George on the head.

"Where did you find that?"

"In the outside garbage can by the pool. Someone must have been frustrated with it and tossed it."

"Give me the golf club. I'll watch him. You run over to that stuck van and find something to tie him up with."

Lacey returned a moment later. "All I could find were the cords they use to plug things in."

George stirred and groaned but didn't try to sit up.

Lacey tied George up and helped him into a sitting position.

"I'm going to need George's phone to call the police."

Lacey searched his coat pockets and made the call. "The police are five minutes away. They picked up that other guy based on the description the farmer gave. He ran a red light. They've been looking for us ever since we didn't make it to the sheriff's office."

Jude leaned close to George. "I want to know. If you wanted to keep your hands clean of the kidnapping, why even be in Montana at all? You might as well tell me. It's over for you."

"The ransom had to be in cash. After Reed took his cut, I needed that money to cover a debt before my wife found out. The snowstorm trapped me there. My wife couldn't get the ransom to my associate until the storm cleared. I met Dale. I saw how desperate he was for money. I got him to help me."

Exhausted, they both slumped down on the ground.

They sat with their shoulders touching. "I'm not a washed-up cop, you know," Jude said to George. "I'm a good detective and I'm thinking about going back on the force."

"Really?" Lacey said.

"When I almost died in that avalanche, I realized I needed to start living again. I cut people out of my life. I gave up on the job I loved. It's like I've been treading water for the last ten years."

"I know the feeling. That's not living and it's not what God wants for anyone. After my family died, I think I didn't want to risk loving someone ever again," she said.

Jude's hand was resting on his knee. She reached over and placed her hand on top of his. The gesture made him believe that she was feeling the same way he was.

He twisted his hand around so he could squeeze hers. "Maybe I can find a cop job in Montana."

Her voice filled with affection. "I'd like that, Jude. Maybe I can get a job that doesn't involve moving all the time, put down roots somewhere."

They could not say much else with George glaring at them, but he had a feeling they were going to be spending more time together…if she felt the same way about him that he felt about her.

The flashing lights of several law enforcement vehicles brought a sense of relief for him.

Lacey let out a breath.

Hours later, they sat in the sheriff's office in Garnet. George and his accomplices were locked in jail cells.

Once they'd given their statements, the sheriff pushed his chair away from the desk. "When you two didn't show up, we went out looking for you. Took a while to put things together. Call from a farmer about two guys in a van acting suspicious. Still, I don't know that we would have found you if you hadn't phoned once the van gave highway patrol the slip."

They thanked the sheriff and stepped outside, bathed by the early morning light.

"I'm glad that's over," Lacey said. She stared into Jude's eyes. "So what happens now…to us?"

He touched her cheek and pulled her into a hug. "What say we both get jobs in the same town and maybe work on building a life together? I love you, Lacey."

She pulled back from the hug. Her eyes filled with warmth. "I love you too."

"Well, then." He leaned in and kissed her. He pulled back and touched her cheek, gazing at her. "I could stand a lifetime of kisses like that from you."

"Me too." Lacey wrapped her arms around Jude and he swung her around and then set her down.

"Here's to being alive again. With you," Jude said. "I don't know where all this is going but if we do end up married, let's honeymoon at the Davenport Hotel."

They both laughed.

\* \* \* \* \*

**Sarah Varland** lives in Alaska with her husband, John, their two boys and their dogs. Her passion for books comes from her mom; her love for suspense comes from her dad, who has spent a career in law enforcement. When she's not writing, she's often found dog mushing, hiking, reading, kayaking, drinking coffee or enjoying other Alaskan adventures with her family.

### Books by Sarah Varland

### Love Inspired Suspense

*Treasure Point Secrets*
*Tundra Threat*
*Cold Case Witness*
*Silent Night Shadows*
*Perilous Homecoming*
*Mountain Refuge*
*Alaskan Hideout*
*Alaskan Ambush*
*Alaskan Christmas Cold Case*
*Alaskan Mountain Murder*

Visit the Author Profile page
at Harlequin.com for more titles.

# ALASKAN MOUNTAIN MURDER

Sarah Varland

If we confess our sins, he is faithful and just to forgive us our sins, and to cleanse us from all unrighteousness

—*1 John* 1:9

To my family. Thank you for everything.

# ONE

The sight of the front door hanging open, crooked on its hinges, was the first time Cassie Hawkins let herself consider that something might be really wrong. As she sat in the relative safety of her rental car staring at her aunt's home, she wondered if she should go in this late at night. She'd gotten the phone call as her aunt's next of kin—more like a daughter than a niece after all the years Cassie had lived with her—that she was missing. But it was Alaska, people went missing often in innocent ways that still had them coming home eventually. Hikers got lost. Plans changed and independent Alaskans forgot to tell their friends.

Cassie couldn't say that she'd heard of many disappearances beginning with open house doors that ended well. She swallowed hard and started to step out of the car. She had one foot on the Alaskan ground she'd sworn years ago never to return to when she hesitated, climbed back into the vehicle. Was it safe to go inside?

Her gaze went to the seat behind her, where six-year-old Will was dozing soundly, his cheek pressed against the headrest of his high-back booster. He'd fallen asleep just after they'd left the airport in Anchorage, before they'd headed south on the Seward Highway. She'd driven the familiar curving road in silence, appreciating the sweeping views of Turnagain Arm and the mountains that guarded it, even as her chest tightened at the idea of being this close to Raven Pass. To home.

To Jake Stone.

She exhaled a long breath, all the weariness of the last few days tangled up in it. She couldn't leave Will in the car, not when no one seemed to have a good answer for how her aunt had disappeared. If there was foul play involved—and the state of the door on the house made her uncomfortable—she couldn't risk her son. He was all she had.

That and an overwhelming sense of guilt that her former fiancé had no idea he existed.

Her stomach turned and she swallowed hard. She should go to Jake's house first, before she did anything else, before she let Will out of the car and small-town tongues started talking. She hadn't meant to keep Will from him, not really. But as she'd let more time pass without having that necessary conversation—one that was too important for a phone call but that she'd never worked up the courage to have in person—it had gotten more difficult to face the inevitable.

He needed to know.

Cassie climbed back into the car, shut the door and pulled out of the driveway, checked her rearview as she navigated back onto Raven Pass's main road.

There. Behind her on the side of the road. Hadn't she seen that gray car before? It had been behind her on the highway earlier. And hadn't they stopped for gas when she'd stopped in Girdwood, just fifteen miles or so back?

And now they were in Raven Pass too, right here near her aunt's house?

She took a deep breath, felt her heartbeat slow and steady as she braced herself for a crisis. Cassie had many faults, she was well aware of them, but when something went wrong, it was like her mind buckled down, readied itself for battle.

It was what had made her want to be a doctor all those years ago, the suggestion she could use that skill to help people.

If only she'd gotten the chance. But life was too short to waste on regrets. And besides, she wouldn't trade Will for all the degrees and dreams in the world. Jake would tell her that God had a way of redeeming situations and turning challenges into blessings. He'd always said things like that when they were dating, spoken of God like He cared about her.

Cassie? She'd never been sure.

Out on the road, she put the rental car back in Drive and headed forward, toward Jake's house, her eyes flitting between the road in front of her and the rearview mirror.

The gray car followed.

Cassie swallowed hard, increased her speed as the other car did the same. She led the car back out of town, onto the Seward Highway. Her eyes went once again to Will's sleeping face. She'd do anything to protect her son. But what if it wasn't enough? She couldn't lose him.

*Please, God.* She fumbled with the words. Jake had tried to introduce her to the God he loved, but Cassie had never quite understood. How could Jake talk to God as though He were right there, a friend, and not a

far-off Being who created the world and existed somewhere far away.

Still, it was worth a try. Hopefully that would count
for something and if He was there as Jake insisted He
was, He'd help her somehow.

The car edged closer and Cassie reached for her cell,
which was sitting on the dashboard. She'd not bothered
to sync it to the rental's Bluetooth system when she'd
picked up the vehicle. Keeping her eyes on the road,
she wrapped her fingers around the slick, cool phone.

It slid from her hand to the floorboard. She glanced
down, looked back up again in time to swerve back right
and miss the truck she'd almost hit head-on in the attempt to get her phone.

She'd have to call the police later. Right now she
was on her own.

There were no turnoffs that were a good place for
losing the tail, not unless she could drive around Girdwood and lose him in one of the neighborhoods filled
with houses and vacation cabins.

Otherwise her option was to drive on the dangerous
Seward Highway all the way back to Anchorage with
him on her tail. Some of the curves of the road hugged
rock cliffs on one side, where the mountain itself had
been blasted to build the highway, and the ocean on the
other. It wasn't a risk she was willing to take.

She'd have to try to lose him. Cassie turned right
onto the Alyeska Highway, a generous name for the
two-lane road that led to the resort town of Girdwood,
the town nearest to Raven Pass, and pushed the engine
as far over the limit as she dared. Drawing someone's
attention with her speed could help her, but on the other
hand, this was a town where many people walked and

rode their bikes and she didn't want to risk hitting anyone. Even this late at night people could be out, though it seemed hardly anyone was.

No matter how many turns down obscure neighborhood roads she made, Cassie couldn't shake the tail. And she couldn't make out any of the driver's facial features either.

This had to stop. Every minute that swept by her heart beat faster and she felt her body temperature rising. She only had so much longer to be able to hold it together.

She'd go back to Raven Pass, to the police department there. She should have thought of that in the first place. She'd just been so determined to try to lose her tail. All she could do was try to make better decisions now, and that started with finding a police department. Since Girdwood had no department of its own, Raven Pass was her best bet. She needed to go back.

Pressing the gas pedal hard and gripping the steering wheel like she had NASCAR aspirations, she drove hard, back toward town.

She'd just made it past the Welcome to Raven Pass sign when the gray car accelerated, and Cassie hit the gas but braced herself for impact in case she'd reacted too slowly.

She had.

The crash was an instant of crunching metal and pain in Cassie's head, and the car threatened to spin out as she fought the wheel for control. After seconds that seemed like minutes, she won, and the sedan slowed to a stop on the side of the road. She was grateful it hadn't been a hard enough jolt for the airbag to deploy. There were no other vehicles in sight, probably because she'd had the brilliant idea to come to town right after her flight got in, which meant it was just past midnight, not exactly the prime traffic time of day. She should have spent the night at a hotel in Anchorage and waited until day to head to Raven Pass, but then how could she have known she'd be followed? Run off the road?

Cassie twisted in her seat to look in the back, thankful to see that Will looked uninjured. He was awake, his eyes wide, his cheek still marked with wrinkles from being pressed against the booster seat, an image that turned her heart upside down with sheer love.

She had to keep him safe.

"Did we get in a wreck?" he asked, his eyes wide, voice wavering.

If only she had the time to reassure him fully, but the door of the gray car behind them was opening. And she had no choice but to run.

"Listen, baby," she said as she unbuckled his seat, "when I open your door, I need you to run as fast as you can, okay? We're going into the trees there." She motioned with her finger toward the dark spruce woods. Memories fought to surface—hiking the woods with Jake, finding places where they could talk—and not talk—without interruption. Would the memories always feel so suffocating? She'd felt numb in Florida. Up here though, she felt everything as deeply as ever. Every ounce of love she'd ever had for him, the regret at her rash decision to leave town.

But time couldn't be turned back.

And right now her focus was keeping her son—and herself—safe.

"Ready?" she asked him, taking a deep breath.

"Ready, Mom." His little voice was confident. Trusting.

*Please, God, don't let me let him down.* She tried another prayer, remembering the way Jake had talked to God.

"Go!" She threw her door open, then quickly yanked his wide, and they both took off into the woods.

"Hey!" her attacker yelled—the voice was male, but she didn't notice any more than that in her hurry to escape—but they didn't turn around. Instead they ran, straight for the path Cassie remembered, which would take them to town—where it came out she couldn't remember, but someone would help her. It was a tight-knit community, where you could count on your neighbors.

And hopefully find safety.

They ran until Will started to lag and then Cassie picked him up, his head resting on her shoulder as she pushed herself as fast as she could with a sixty-pound boy draped across her.

Ignoring the burn in her legs, the sharp pain in her lungs as she gasped for breath after breath, exhaustion and adrenaline fighting for dominance, Cassie closed the gap between where she was and town, glancing back now and then to see if she was being pursued. Once she'd seen someone, large and tall, dressed in dark clothes with a ski mask, and since then she'd pushed her pace harder. As the woods grew thicker, her pace slowed by necessity, and she stepped off the trail, staying close enough to it that she knew where she was—at least she thought so—but hoping her pursuer wouldn't be able to find her, even if he did catch up. The path she made through the trees was tight but it worked, twisting around large stalks of the thorn-laden devil's club plant.

The darkness of the woods grew thicker as she approached Fourteen-Mile River. The main trail had a bridge, but since she'd been avoiding that path, she'd have to run through the river and soak her legs. Better than being caught by whoever had been after her.

She splashed through the water, the icy cold like a thousand needles in her skin as she ran. Not far now, maybe a quarter of a mile till the path would end. She just needed to figure out where she was going to come out in relation to town, and plot her path to the police station. Or just find the first house and ask for help and a phone to call the police. She'd decide which when she got there.

Cassie glanced back one more time, saw the tall man dressed in dirty jeans and a jacket, a ski mask on his head. He was closer now than he had been, and she could see a large gun in his right hand.

Any doubts about whether she was justified in running, about whether or not her aunt had disappeared naturally, fled from her mind.

Something was going on in Raven Pass, something that had put her aunt, and now Cassie and her son, in danger.

She was fueled by adrenaline now, keenly aware that it would fade soon and then she'd be at his mercy.

Cassie was determined not to let it happen. So she kept running, pushing through the last bit of crowded forest onto a gravel path, lifting her eyes to look straight at the house in front of her.

Light green with dark green trim. An octagonal window above the front door on the second story.

She'd run straight to Jake Stone's old house. Just like old times, like she could still count on him to sweep her into his solid arms and tell her everything was going to be okay.

Those days were long gone, and Jake had surely moved out of his parents' old home, but she needed help, and needed it now. She felt convinced whoever was after her wouldn't hesitate to snatch her even from here, on the edges of town where someone could see. Why else would he have worn a mask to conceal his identity?

She needed to get inside that house. Call the police. Sort this out.

So she didn't hesitate any longer. She sprinted across the street, and threw open the door, just like she would have without hesitation seven years ago—when the Stones had treated her like part of the family, when it had been assumed she and Jake would follow through on their engagement and maybe one day live in this adorable house in Raven Pass.

Back before everything blew up. And Cassie had been left holding the fuse.

She could only pray his parents had forgiven her, but even if they hadn't, they were decent people. They would keep her safe, she was sure of it.

She shut the door hard behind her and locked it, then set a wide-eyed Will down beside her.

"Are we okay, Mom?" he asked in a shaky voice.

"We will be, sweetie. Stay right here, okay?" Cassie moved toward the kitchen, hoping they still had a landline.

And ran straight into a solid person. Tall. Much, much too solid to be Jake's dad.

And found herself looking right into the sky blue eyes of the man whose heart she'd broken seven years ago. Jake Stone.

"Cassie?"

Jake barely managed to sputter out her name, the one he hadn't spoken aloud more than a handful of times in years. He'd imagined what it would be like to see her once more, maybe even let himself have the slightest daydream about her being against his chest like this again.

But deep down he'd known the latter would never happen, and the former probably wouldn't either. He'd heard her aunt was missing and he'd let himself wonder if Cassie would come but hadn't really thought she would.

Now she was in his house. And there was a little boy standing beside her.

A little boy who looked… Jake swallowed hard. Seven? Six?

She hadn't said a word to him about the boy yet, but Jake saw his eyes in the boy's face, saw his own childhood expression mirrored.

"What are you doing here?" He put his hands on her upper arms, gently, and stepped back, looked her over. Her brown-sugar hair was tangled around her face, which was red, like she'd been exercising.

"My aunt is gone. I'm in town because of that, but when I went to her house the door was open and I don't know why. Someone followed me here." Cassie turned quickly, looked behind her though nothing was back there.

"And you ran here…?"

"I didn't come here on purpose." Her cheeks reddened further. "Listen." She cleared her throat, her tone switching to the all-business one she used when she was uncomfortable. "I'm sorry to have bothered you, but I went to my aunt's house and the door was open, and there was a car and they followed me and ran me off the road…" She glanced back again. "They chased me through the woods, even through Fourteen-Mile River when I crossed it. I needed to get help and this was the first house I saw. I'm sorry, but please. Don't send us away yet, not until the police come."

Jake felt his defenses rise, his shoulders tense. She'd hurt him, sure, probably more than anyone realized. He glanced at the small boy beside her who still hadn't said a word. Swallowed hard. Either way, this was another layer to the hurt. Had she cheated on him? Or...

It wasn't outside the realm of possibility that they could have made a son together. Jake had had good intentions, had his standards and his plans to wait until they were married but it had grown harder and he hadn't resisted temptation as well as he should have.

Cassie didn't share his level of faith, and had said she loved him and that was what had mattered. But still, whether she believed in God or not, it had been his job to keep their relationship on track. He'd failed her.

Had that been the beginning of the end?

"Jake?" Her nervousness was displayed across her features.

What kind of cruel person did she think he was to wonder if he would send her away while she was in so much danger? Especially when she had her son with her. If anything, with the way he was feeling right now, it would be a struggle to let her leave.

Not that she needed to know that. No, she'd lost the right to know his innermost feelings and thoughts when she'd left him and Raven Pass in the dust years ago. Besides, the first thing he needed to do was call the police. He slipped the cell phone out of his pocket, dialed 911 and reported the incident as Cassie had told it to him. He thought he noticed her relax a little from her place beside him, but she still looked behind her several times a minute, her grip on the boy's shoulders seeming to get tighter. The boy squirmed. "You're squashing my bones, Mom," he finally said in a dry tone.

"Sorry, sweetheart." She looked down at him, squeezed him against her in a hug. Cassie as a mom. The sight was a gut punch. She seemed good at it, comfortable with motherhood. He'd always known she would be, despite her doubts because of her own upbringing.

"Do you have any kind of description of the guy who was after you? That might help the police." Why that was the question that came out when he had a hundred others overwhelming his mind, he didn't know, but she looked relieved. Because she wanted to think through the trauma she'd just been through and start to process it? Or because she was glad he hadn't tried to steer the conversation to anything personal?

She shook her head. "It was a man, probably six feet or taller. But he had a ski mask on, so I don't know anything about his appearance beyond that."

This wasn't a spur-of-the-moment crime then. He'd been prepared. Had he been intending to snatch Cassie? Kill her? Or had it just been his plan to watch her and then something had triggered him to go after her?

After them? Did her would-be attacker know she had a son?

"Wait, did you say your aunt's door was busted open?" He frowned. He'd been over there the day of her disappearance with the Raven Pass Search and Rescue Team, of which he was a part, and her house had been in pristine condition, just as she'd left it, with the exception of the few odd things they usually found when people disappeared or died suddenly—a cereal bowl in the sink, a glass on the counter, signs of a life paused midstream.

"Yes I knew she disappeared, but I was led to believe it could have been accidental, not…whatever this is." Cassie shook her head and Jake watched as the frown between her brows deepened, small wrinkles on her forehead pinching as her expression darkened.

"Her door wasn't open the other day," he said, wondering as the words left his mouth if this was the best way to let her know that he was involved in the search for her aunt. Too late now, he guessed. Cassie wouldn't have appreciated being danced lightly around anyway. She'd always insisted she could handle the truth straight. And maybe she could. Jake had tried that once, had told her the dreams he'd had of the two of them, the family he imagined, and though they'd been engaged, she just left. Had she not wanted kids? Had the future overwhelmed her so much? Or had it been him?

He didn't know, but the irony was inescapable and cutting. She'd gone. Had a kid without him.

It was a knife in his chest, one he felt every time he took a breath.

"Why were you there?"

May as well answer her. "I'm on a search-and-rescue team and we've been looking for your aunt."

"I thought the police were looking?" Her eyebrows were raised.

"They are. It's not unusual for them to utilize our resources out here. It's rough country, you know that. Teamwork helps people get home safely."

"Search and rescue? What happened to med school?"

The knock at the door announced the police officer's arrival, and Jake was spared at least that question. This conversation was exhausting to have with the woman he'd loved enough to want to spend the rest of his life with, now that she was acting like a virtual stranger. But one who was intensely familiar with his past.

*Was* his past.

Jake moved to the door but noticed Cassie had tensed, her shoulders edging toward her ears as she pulled the boy closer to her again. "Cassie, it's the police, okay?" he said once he'd confirmed the assumption through the peephole in the door. "You don't have to worry right now."

She swallowed hard and he watched her light green eyes flick glances around the room. She'd delivered her account of what had happened with remarkable calmness and clarity, but she was rattled, no doubt about it. Seven years ago he would have sat down with her, made her some coffee that was mostly cream, the way she liked it, and then listened while she processed out loud, the way she always did.

But everything between them had changed now and he felt like someone who didn't understand what his next step should be. There was too much between them—had been at one time anyway—for him to be comfortable just sending her off with the police and not seeing her again, not following up at all. Then again, she'd left, hadn't she? Left *him*. Who was to say she wanted him to care anymore, on any level?

He needed to remember to keep ahold of his feelings, remind himself that she hadn't come to his house on purpose. It was coincidence, maybe some part of her subconscious at the absolute most. But she didn't want *his* help. Not specifically. That was critical for him to remember.

However, at the same time…they needed to have a conversation. There were two explanations for the boy with her—either he was his father, or she'd betrayed him worse than he'd imagined, being with someone like that so soon after their breakup, or even before. One way or another he needed to know, and he couldn't even wrap his mind around either option being true. But at the moment his main focus was on reporting this to the police and getting together a game plan to make sure Cassie didn't have to have that kind of fear in her eyes again.

The knock came again, more forceful this time, and he hurried to open the door, having confirmed that it was the police.

"Jake. Morning." Levi Wicks was one of the officers Jake knew best, having worked with him on a search-and-rescue case several months back. Of all the officers who could have responded, Levi was the one most likely to welcome Raven Pass Search and Rescue's help.

"Morning, Officer Wicks."

Levi rolled his eyes at him, but Jake wasn't teasing him by using the title, just wanted his friend to know he respected his position and didn't take their friendship for granted.

"Good morning, Jake." The other officer, Christy Ames, smiled at Jake, then looked past him. "Cassie?" Her eyes widened. Jake sometimes forgot that some of his friends now had been *their* friends when he and Cassie were a couple. Raven Pass had grown and changed enough in the years that she'd been gone that he sometimes lost track of how many people had been in high school with them, watched them fall in love and then been around to witness the aftermath of Cassie's departure.

"Hi, Christy." Cassie attempted a small smile.

"You two know each other?" Levi shook his head. "I'm never going to get used to how small towns work."

"We went to high school together," Christy explained, then looked to Jake. "This is the woman you called and told us about who was almost abducted? And you didn't specify *who* it was?"

"I figured you'd find out when you got here." Jake shrugged.

Christy gave a slight shake of her head, then moved toward Cassie. "Rather than have this conversation standing in the entryway, why don't we move to the living room. Sound good to you, Jake?" Christy led the way, having visited his house in high school with Cassie. His parents had left town several years back, choosing to move deep into the Alaska wilderness near Anaktuvuk Pass. Most people his parents' age left Alaska for the warmth of the south. They didn't opt for *more* Alaska when they moved, but that was just his parents. If he could be half the adventurers they'd always been, he'd be happy with his life.

Without consciously meaning to, he looked at Cassie. At the little boy beside her.

Once upon a time, he'd assumed being happy had meant being with Cassie. Funny how dreams changed. Some came true and some disappeared quicker than frost on a late spring morning.

All he could do was move on. Just like he'd been trying to do for years.

Only to end up where he was today, with Cassie back in his house, tangling up his thoughts and feelings, and making him feel like no time had passed at all.

# TWO

Both officers, Levi Wicks and Christy—who Cassie was having a hard time believing was the same person she'd known in high school—were kind in their questioning, but Cassie still felt as if her head were spinning. If only she'd gotten a better look at the man. She'd done everything she could, they assured her, and while Cassie knew in her head that their words were true, she still couldn't quite shake her guilt for putting Will in that situation. She'd had no inkling they'd be facing this kind of threat in Alaska, or she'd have… What? She had friends in Florida, ones she'd trust with Will, but not for such a long period of time. So she'd had no choice but to bring him with her. He was in the room with them now, hearing things no six-year-old should about danger, but he was playing a *How to Train Your Dragon* game on her phone, which Officer Wicks had brought since they'd stopped by the scene of Cassie's accident on their way, so she could only hope his little mind was full of Night Fury dragons and not this conversation she was having with the police.

"We've been working this as a typical missing persons case, but no one had reported the damage to the house that you've just told us about," Officer Wicks told her. He glanced down at his phone. "Excuse me just a minute."

He stood and walked to another room to take the call, then came back.

"That was one of the other officers confirming what you said about the door and telling me about the rest of the house."

"Was it more than just the front door?" Cassie asked, having not gotten far enough in her thoughts to wonder about that.

"Yes, the house has damage in several rooms. The office and the bedroom look like a tornado blew through, but jewelry and electronics are still there, so it's not a random break-in."

"Which means we need to change the way we are running the search also," Jake said. "We've been looking for her, but the assumption was that there was a good chance it was a hike that went wrong."

Did that change how the search-and-rescue team worked? Cassie wouldn't have guessed so, but then again she didn't know much about that kind of work.

Office Wicks spoke again. "The sooner you can meet with your team and brief them, the better. They need to know to be on guard also, in case any evidence they might uncover could make them targets."

Jake nodded. He was still worried; she knew by the way the corners of his eyes crinkled, the blue in them shadowed ever so slightly. He looked at Christy, who seemed to understand better than Cassie what was bothering him. A fact which bothered Cassie far more than it should have when this was a man she'd given up every claim to years ago. And had driven a bigger wedge between them by keeping Will a secret, something they hadn't talked about yet but would need to. Jake had been kind to Will, calm in his presence. Had he guessed his age? Could he see a resemblance and know it was his son? Cassie didn't know—she'd never considered how any of this would play out, at least not in any realistic sort of way. Or did Jake think she'd been unfaithful?

That idea hurt. She would have never been untrue to him. She'd loved him, completely.

"Cassie, you need to stay with someone." Christy didn't bother softening the words with any kind of preamble.

"I had been planning to stay at my aunt's house." She scooted forward to the edge of the couch she'd been sitting on. "If you're done with me now, I'll just head that way." Because if the police were finished taking her statement, then they'd be leaving soon, and no way was she sitting here alone with Jake. The conversation they needed to have could be done…another time. Right? She'd already been in his house too long and she couldn't deal with the growing tangle of confusing feelings inside her, the guilt tormenting her.

*God, forgive me. I should have told him about Will sooner.*

A third prayer to a God she had never been sure existed. Cassie wanted to sort those feelings out later, figure out why it was starting to feel natural. She wished she could talk to Jake about it.

Looking over at him, his broad shoulders that had always been there to help her carry any burden she'd faced, his clear glacier-blue eyes that had never once lied to her, it was hard to remember why she'd left.

And then she remembered it had never been Jake. He'd never been the reason.

It had been all her.

They'd had their future planned. She'd doodled her first name and his last name all over her wedding notebook, had filled it with ideas for their day. And then somewhere along the line she'd realized she wasn't just planning a wedding, wasn't just falling in love. She was about to spend the rest of her life as someone's wife. *Jake's* wife. She'd been raised by just her dad—well, he'd had some help from his sister, her aunt who was now missing—after her mom had left him when she was two. He'd done an amazing job and had tried to give her everything she could ever need, but she had still never quite felt like part of a *family*. Not the kind like Jake had. Maybe that was why she'd gravitated toward him in the first place, his idyllic life, though as she'd gotten to know him and had started a relationship with him, she'd fallen head over heels for the man himself.

And then she'd realized that as much as she wanted a family, she had her mom's DNA, her blood in her veins and…what if she turned out like her? Left Jake and some sweet blue-eyed baby? Besides that, here in town people would have expected her to be his support as his wife. She'd had dreams of her own, wanted to be a doctor just like Jake had. She couldn't reconcile her dreams with being a traditional wife, and she'd wondered if that's what had sent her mother away, wanting more, feeling trapped, even by love. She'd panicked. So she'd left, given them both space to pursue their dreams.

But she'd left without explanation, and she could only assume she'd broken his heart. She'd certainly broken her own.

They were all staring at her, she realized after a minute or so of being lost in her own personal memory lane.

"Would you be open to the possibility of staying somewhere else?" Officer Wicks asked, and she guessed she should be thankful he was asking and not ordering her. Not that police were allowed to order people around for no reason, but she understood the fact that she was risking her safety by going back to her aunt's house.

But what other options did she have?

"If you both feel it's necessary, I can consider something. I certainly don't want to endanger Will." She addressed her comment to the officers, hoping that despite what she'd heard about Jake getting his *team* involved, whatever that meant, that he'd stay out of this particular conversation.

"Then it's settled, you'll stay here," Jake spoke up.

She felt the blood rush to her head and a wave of dizzy panic hit her. Cassie swallowed hard, blinked the feeling away. "I'm not staying…"

"All nice and professional. My parents turned the upstairs into sort of apartments. You'll have privacy but I'll be close by. The two of you will be safe there."

Cassie opened her mouth to argue. Closed it again.

Seeming satisfied, Christy and Officer Wicks both stood and moved toward the door before Cassie could decide what to say, how to protest. She wanted to stop them, demand that they stay, but what, was she afraid to be alone with him? Surely not. Even if her…feelings hadn't dissipated over the last decade, she was an adult. She knew when relationships weren't healthy, and she wasn't good enough for Jake. That should keep her away from him no matter how much looking at him, being in the same room with him, made her wish she could forget all the reasons she'd ended it in the first place.

And she would stay away from him.

Even if it was going to be infinitely harder to do while living in his house.

"Remember, if you think of anything else that could help, description-wise, give us a call anytime, okay?" Christy handed her a business card, which Cassie took as she felt herself nod. Then she stuck the card in her back pocket.

"Thanks for coming out," Jake said, then the two officers left. Jake shut the door behind them.

And it was just the three of them. Mother. Son.

And Father who didn't know he was one.


"We need to talk." Jake could feel the charge in the air between them, a thousand levels of awkward and the invisible scarring that came from being so close to someone in the past only to have your shared life ripped in two and not see her again for seven years.

And she came back in danger. Needing your help.

And with a son.

"We do." She agreed before he could follow his train of thought any further. His heart skipped a beat. Nodded. He waited for her to start, looked over at the kid who was still playing on the cell phone.

"Will?" Cassie waited until he looked up to continue. "We're going to stay here. I… I knew Jake when I lived here before."

He nodded. "Okay."

"We're going to stay here, okay?" she repeated, as if stalling for time.

"Because the guy was chasing us earlier?"

"Yeah. It's safer if we aren't alone, all right, bud?" She moved closer to him, pulled him into a hug and kissed the top of his head, then drew a breath.

"Maybe we could stream a movie for him?" she asked Jake. Jake nodded, understanding that whatever way this was going, Will didn't need to hear the conversation. He turned Netflix on, scrolled through the kid options until he got to one about dragons, at which point the kid reacted enthusiastically and he offered him his Bluetooth headphones. There, they were now functionally alone. At least enough to finish this conversation.

"So…" Cassie trailed off as she took a seat on one of the chairs, her shoulders tense as she perched on the edge of the cushion. She wasn't in any better shape than Jake was. He took a deep breath, tried to convince his shoulders to un-hunch.

"Please don't do that, Cassie. Just…" Just what? He couldn't very well tell her to spit it out, not when it was something this important.

"Sorry. I'm sorry. You need to know." She took a breath. Jake braced himself the best he could.

"He's yours, Jake."

He'd have said five minutes ago he was prepared to hear either, but there was no way a man could process this well. At least not that Jake could figure out. He stood, walked across the room. Back to the chair. Across.

Run. He could go running. His feet on the trail through the woods, using his body and his mind to the limit would help, but he couldn't leave Cassie right now. Or Will.

*His son.*

Air. He needed air. He walked to the kitchen, as far

from Cassie and Will in the living room as he dared to go without feeling like he was putting their safety in jeopardy.

After a few minutes he started back toward her. "Cassie…" He trailed off. What was there to ask? He let his eyes go back to Will, took in his features with the knowledge that he was his. *His son.* Again, the words echoed in the hollow spaces inside him, the ones Cassie's leaving had caused. He had more family? Someone counting on him?

He opened his mouth to ask her another question when someone knocked on the door. He watched her shoulders tense.

"I'll answer." He stepped toward it, willing it to be someone who'd go away quickly. He didn't want this conversation interrupted.

# THREE

A knock sounded at the door before he could ask whatever question had been on his mind. Cassie sat up straighter, feeling every muscle in her back and shoulders bunch up and ache. Logic told her the man after her wasn't the kind to knock, but the idea of facing him again, or facing anyone unexpectedly, made her tense.

Jake opened the door. Stepped outside. Cassie waited. A girlfriend he wanted to prep for Cassie's sudden reappearance? She hadn't even let herself consider that Jake could be in a relationship, but of course it made sense. Jake was a good man, the kind who deserved a family. One that lived with him, let him be the husband and father he'd always dreamed of being.

He stepped back inside, blew out a breath.

"Someone you need to talk to?" Cassie tried to keep the hurt out of her voice, reminded herself she deserved anything she had to face. She'd made her choices and believed fully that meant she had to live with them.

"They want to talk to both of us actually." He ran a hand through his hair. Cassie had rarely seen him so rattled, but of course the news of his son, her appearance, the threat against her...it made sense it would take a toll.

"Who?"

"My team. The one I mentioned earlier."

"The search-and-rescue team?"

Jake nodded. "They brought dinner." He laughed. "A really late dinner."

Cassie inhaled, held her breath for a second and let it out slowly. "Okay."

"We'll talk more later?"

His eyes, the ones she'd once loved looking into, losing herself in, were unreadable. Maybe it was good for him to have time to process her news, but Cassie needed to know if he forgave her. There was no way to have that conversation when there were people here, and Cassie understood that the case took priority. Assuming they'd come to work, she needed to let them do so.

"Okay," she said again. She nodded. Jake held her gaze for one more second, looking like he was staring straight down to her heart and reading her thoughts the way he used to. But neither of them said anything. Whatever connection they'd had once was severed now.

Wasn't it?

Jake opened the door.

"Two pepperoni pizzas, and one ham and pineapple!" A woman walked in, tall and blond, and held the pizza boxes up with a flourish. Then her eye caught Cassie's.

"You must be Cassie. Awful night you've had." Immediately her expression changed from triumphant and teasing to compassionate. "I'm Piper McAdams."

More people pushed in behind her. Two more women, one with dark hair and skin that was a shade or two more tanned than Cassie's Alaska-toned coloring. And one man who was a little shorter than Jake's six feet three inches, but not by much. He had broad shoulders, like a swimmer.

Piper kept talking as they entered. "This is Adriana Steele—" the woman with dark hair smiled at Cassie "—and Ellie Hardison." The second woman waved at Cassie. She looked like her eyes had a story and Cassie was curious about it. Of course, she was curious about all of these people. None of them was familiar to her, so they must have moved to the area within the last decade. "And Caleb Gaines." Piper pointed to the last man.

Jake took the pizza boxes from Piper and set them on the table. "This is the team, Cassie. Raven Pass Search and Rescue."

Cassie was impressed. Already, less than a minute in their presence, she could tell they all had very different personalities, but they must have figured out some way to work together in their searches. That took a unique kind of teamwork and community and she was excited to see it in action. It was the kind of group that would be interesting to work with. She may not have become a doctor as planned, but she'd gone to school at night, finally gotten her BSN and enjoyed working as a nurse. She knew from those experiences how important good teams were, how working in sync with each other led to good outcomes. Of course, pediatric nursing wasn't quite the same as helping with possible medical emergencies in the backcountry and she knew that, but it would be interesting to try.

If she'd stayed, would she have changed career paths and become a nurse despite her initial plans? Life didn't turn out like you planned; she'd learned that long ago. But seeing the interesting combination of personalities as they all gathered around the table made her wonder what it would be like to work with a team like this.

If she stayed, would they make a place for her?

Cassie slammed that mental door immediately. She was not staying. In fact, she should have been leaving in the next few days, but the police had advised her not to leave the state until they figured out who was after her. Going back to Florida would complicate their case and make it difficult for her to stay safe, even more than it would be here. Not to mention the fact that she wouldn't dream of leaving until she found out what had happened to her aunt.

Just because she wasn't able to leave Raven Pass behind her yet, didn't mean it wasn't inevitable though. She needed to remember she was an outsider here, that she had work and a life waiting for her thousands of miles away. While she was going to be around these good people, so that Jake could keep her safe, maybe she shouldn't offer to help too much or get too close, learn anything that would make her wish for their camaraderie. Something she just couldn't have. She had Will, that was enough. She needed to be thankful for what she had and let go of the what-ifs. There was no sense in dwelling there.

"Cassie, come join us." Piper motioned her over to the pizza, still smiling. "We're going to talk about the search for your aunt and how our game plan for tomorrow is going to change from what it was."

Cassie looked over at the table where Adriana had already unfolded a map and was pointing at something.

"Can you show me where you've already searched?" She'd known this area once, had grown up close to her aunt. Maybe she'd be able to help pinpoint where she could have gone.

She owed it to her aunt to try.

"Sure, come on over."

So Cassie took a deep breath, braced herself the best she could, offered a small smile and joined the group.

And hoped it wasn't going to lead to connections, to friendships that would make leaving them break her heart.

Cassie hadn't slept this badly since she'd left Jake, but every night noise, every sound in the dim Alaska night, seemed to come through the windows and to her ears. Beside her, Will slept soundly. At least that was something. She turned over again, closed her eyes and tried to relax.

No success.

Maybe it wasn't the sounds outside that were keeping her awake at all, but the questions she had. For Jake. For herself. They hadn't been able to talk at all after the rescue team left. It had been too late at night, so they'd both agreed to talk again tomorrow. So that unpleasant conversation was put off for now, but the uncertainty lingered.

Why was Jake working with a rescue team instead of in medicine? He'd explained some, but not nearly all of his reasoning yesterday, she felt. Could she ask him for more details or was that prying? She was unsure of the etiquette when addressing one's former fiancé.

But those weren't the questions that kept her awake, though they were the ones that tugged at her heart, made her wish she could go back in time, and…what? Change something?

The questions keeping her awake were more urgent. Why would someone have abducted her aunt? If that was what had happened, which looked fairly likely given the break-in at her house. Cassie didn't believe in coincidences.

She finally gave up the idea of sleep just past three in the morning and headed down the stairs, back to the main part of the house. She'd seen Jake put leftover pizza into the fridge. Maybe trying to eat a little more would help her sleep.

Down the steps she crept, not wanting to wake Jake.

She heard noise as soon as she made it to the living room and there he was, standing from a chair where he'd apparently been sitting by the fire.

"I'm sorry. I tried to be quiet." She offered the words to ease the awkward feeling she had every time they were alone. Though clearly if he was down here, she hadn't woken him up and he'd been awake already.

"Can't sleep?" he asked.

She shook her head. "I thought I'd get a snack."

"There's leftover pizza in the fridge," he offered.

Cassie nodded. "That was my plan." She walked to the other room, looking back over her shoulder at him. He'd sat back down again. Was it too soon to clear the air and try to talk about why she'd left?

Not that she planned to explain why. She didn't understand herself well enough to attempt that. But she could at least apologize…

She took a deep breath, tried to work up her nerve. Maybe she'd talk now, before she got her snack. "Hey, Jake?"

"Shh." He cut her off, but from the look on his face, it wasn't because he didn't want to hear what she had to say. It was because he'd heard something and he was on alert—his shoulders were tensed. He had been sitting with his back against the back of the chair but now he was leaning forward.

"What?" Cassie whispered, but Jake was already up, moving to one of the front windows. Instinctively she stepped back against the wall, into a darkened corner.

He walked from the first window to the second.

This time she heard the noise too, but it sounded like it was coming from the back of the house, not the front where Jake was.

"Jake," she whispered as loud as she dared, motioning with her head behind her.

"Get upstairs. Hide."

His tone left no room for argument as he moved toward the back door and Cassie hurried to the stairs, keeping her back against the wall. He hadn't needed to tell her to go up there. Her son, *their* son, was in that room and nothing would stop Cassie from doing her best to protect him.

As she rushed up the stairs, she tried to pinpoint where she'd heard the noise but all was quiet.

She opened the door of the large closet in the bedroom, pulled Will from the bed and settled him in the corner of it. He slept harder than anyone she knew, something for which she was extremely thankful right now. Then she pulled the door shut behind her.

*Please don't let him find me.* Another prayer. She didn't have time to analyze why praying seemed so natural here. She felt less alone somehow, which was interesting since she wasn't even sure what she believed about God.

Cassie tried to be as quiet as possible, but it seemed

like every time she shifted it was the loudest sound she'd ever heard. She tried not to move so much, made an effort to even slow her breathing down enough that it wouldn't make so much noise either.

She heard a door open, the creaking loud like one of the main heavy doors downstairs to the outside. Relief flooded her and she almost called out to let Jake know where she was. Hadn't he gone outside? So it would make sense if he had that he'd come back in once he'd checked things out and determined everything was okay.

At the last second though, she stopped herself. It could just as easily be whoever was after her. She knew that. So instead she didn't move, didn't make a sound.

Whoever had come inside didn't speak either. Did that mean the chances were more likely that it wasn't Jake? She swallowed hard and hoped her logic was faulty, but somehow she didn't think it was.

There were footsteps, then a creaking noise, followed by another creaking noise. The stairs? Was he coming up to her room? Her heartbeat, already going faster than she was comfortable with, pounding in her throat in a way that made swallowing difficult, sped up even more. Cassie swallowed hard. Waited.

There was silence for a period of time, and she tried to guess how many minutes had passed, in case it mattered later. Two? Three? He hadn't been upstairs long by the time she heard creaking again that seemed to indicate he was going back down the stairs. But he'd been up there longer than was necessary just to look inside her room and see that she wasn't in it. Had he been taking the time to search for her? Or was he setting up some kind of trap in the room where she was supposed to be safe?

Her current line of thinking made Cassie shudder. She wasn't much of a risk taker these days. The amount of risk now being asked of her… It was a lot to take in. More than she wanted to handle.

The stairs creaked again. Wait, was he coming back up? The footsteps grew louder and came closer. Cassie felt her heartbeat skip.

Another door opened.

"Hey!" That was Jake yelling now.

The footsteps moved faster, back down the stairs? Cassie heard the pace quicken like whoever had come inside first was running. Then the front door opened. She heard more running and imagined Jake chasing him, which was her best guess as to what was going on right now. Fear for his life enveloped her. What if he was killed keeping her safe? She wouldn't be able to live with that knowledge.

Easing forward out of her crouched position, she reached for the door and pushed it open again, then stood, looking for something on the shelf to use as a weapon. All she saw were cans of vegetables in dooms-day-prepper sizes. It wasn't unusual for Alaskans to keep emergency food and water stored in closets, in case of earthquakes or other natural disasters that could cut Alaska off from the road system or the port. She grabbed a Costco-sized can of green beans from the shelf. It wasn't much as far as weaponry was concerned, but it was better than the nothing she currently had.

The bedroom was empty, still dark. Did she dare leave Will? She decided the answer to that was no, but crept closer toward the door, where she could lean out of it and see down the stairs and into the living room. From her vantage point, she saw that the door was open.

For the first time, Cassie remembered her phone was in her pocket and called 911 to report that they'd had an intruder. She wasn't able to give more details, but they said they'd come right over.

She started to move back into the bedroom, then movement caught her eye. She raised the green beans.

"What are you doing?" Jake stood in the doorway. He was out of breath, but it didn't quell the emotions in his voice. He cared about keeping her safe. Sure, she'd known he was a good guy and always, *always* did the right thing. But something in his tone just now made her wonder if…

No, he couldn't still care about her beyond how he'd feel about anyone in danger. She shouldn't even let her mind go there.

"Didn't I tell you to hide?" he continued.

She cleared her throat. "I heard noises." It was a lame excuse when she said it aloud. "Did you see him?"

Jake shook his head. "I went outside to check and didn't see anything, but when I came inside I thought I heard something. I yelled and then heard him run down the stairs. He must have come in when I stepped outside, like he was watching me for a chance to come in." He shook his head again. "Beyond stupid of me. I should have stayed inside. Anyway, I stood for half a second longer than I should have, trying to decide if I should come up and check on the two of you or chase him. By the time I decided catching him was top priority, I couldn't catch up." Jake's features were colored with emotion. "He had a car waiting just down the road and he had too much of a head start."

"What kind of car?" Cassie asked, not that she knew what anyone around town was driving these days, so the answer really wouldn't tell her anything.

"A black SUV—a Toyota, I think. It was too dark to be sure."

Just as she'd thought, the information was meaningless to her since she didn't know anyone's cars anymore.

The last thing she wanted to be was a damsel in distress who needed help, but tonight she was at a loss and she didn't like the feeling. "I called the police," she offered as her one contribution.

"The police may want to talk to you again." Jake shook his head. "I'm not sure. Maybe they'll just be able to see if he left any evidence."

She felt self-conscious enough around Jake in her pajamas, though they were a long-sleeved shirt and pants that one of the women on Jake's team had left for her. Her suitcase of belongings she'd brought to Alaska was still in her car, abandoned when she was being tailed. Cassie had to remember to get the car tomorrow. Will would need a change of clothes also, although for tonight he'd been delighted at the idea of sleeping in his blue jeans.

"I think I'll change." She didn't have a bathrobe or anything like that, so switching back into jeans seemed like her best option.

"I'll wait in the hall." Jake folded his arms and leaned back against the wall across from her bedroom door before she could argue. Having him close made her feel stronger, although she wasn't sure she wanted to admit it. When he was here, she felt as though she were on solid ground, could make more confident decisions. Even though she'd been reminded of her mortality multiple times today, being near Jake made her feel she could stop and think while she decided how to work this problem.

She liked this feeling too much. Always had. It wasn't safe to depend on a person that way, was it? To know you were better because of them, to be used to having that person in your day...

Because she'd learned the day her mom disappeared that people weren't always dependable, they left.

It was entirely possible, if she tried to emotionally dissect the past, that it had been part of the problem with Jake—the fact that there weren't problems. He was her better half, the one man she wanted to be by her side forever. She'd always been able to count on him, and that scared her. Shouldn't she have learned from her mother's abandonment not to count on anyone?

Had she invented the problems she'd worried about to give her an excuse to leave? The fact that they'd both wanted to be doctors, that she'd wanted to make her own way in the world. Was it really just as simple as her having a fear of being left, of getting hurt again?

Cassie sighed deeply, letting her shoulders fall. Analyzing it wouldn't do a bit of good. Nothing she could do would allow her to go back and change the past. Puzzling out their history together just confused her when she needed a clear head now more than ever.

So she pulled her clothes back on, resolved that she was going to do the best she could to help solve this case and get back out of Jake's life. As much as she'd messed it up the first time around, she owed him that much.

Now to figure out how she could help when she hadn't the slightest clue how to search for missing persons or how to hunt down attackers.

\* \* \*

The rest of the night passed without incident. Jake knew, because he sat outside Cassie and Will's door as the dusky summer shadows darkened and then lightened again almost in the blink of an eye. He sat there, wondering if she was sleeping, trying to sort out how they were going to handle this situation.

Her attackers meant business, Jake didn't doubt that at all. He stood and stretched, moving toward the stairs to make some coffee, now that it was fully light and a time of day where people were up and attackers would be less likely to strike. Whoever was after her was fairly coordinated, had a plan. Their execution had failed, for which Jake was thankful, but the hard truth was that he'd been unprepared last night. He wouldn't let that happen again.

Movement behind him as he reached for the coffee carafe to fill it with water startled him and he whipped his head around, arms coming up in a defensive stance.

"Easy there, killer." Cassie's face almost cracked a smile. She looked tired, dark circles growing under her eyes. That answered that question. He was almost certain she hadn't slept at all.

"Not funny, given last night."

Her face sobered. "You're right. I wanted to talk to you about that."

"Last night?" He held his breath, waiting to hear if she wanted to talk about the people after her or their son. He needed to discuss Will, but he didn't know if he was ready to face the hurt that conversation would bring. In an odd way, it was easier to talk about the people who were out to get her, or her missing aunt.

Jake busied his hands making the coffee, finding it

hard to see her standing there, all vulnerable and beautiful and so close to him he had to catch his breath.

"I want to help."

He breathed out. He'd been prepped for it. Cassie wasn't a woman to sit on the sidelines.

"It's going to be dangerous, you know," he started, noting the way her eyebrows went up in immediate reaction to his words. He raised his hands in mock surrender. "Hey, I'm making sure you understand."

"Is there anything about my life right now that doesn't strike you as dangerous?"

Something had changed in her since last night. Her fire, one of the things he'd loved about her way back when, had returned with an extra spark. Yesterday she'd seemed defeated. Tired. Today she was ready to fight, and it seemed to bode well.

He was confident in his team, but having her along would help them too. She knew her aunt, knew the areas she was likely to frequent, could tell them about how she would have thought and made decisions if she was on her own or hiking somewhere against her will. With the new information they'd learned about the disappearance likely being intentional and relating to foul play, they'd change how they searched, shift their parameters. Raven Pass Search and Rescue was good at what they did. They'd find Cassie's aunt. Jake wasn't naive enough to be sure she'd be alive when they got there though, something he wasn't sure if Cassie had considered.

"What?" Her facial expression wavered, and he wished he knew her as well as he used to. If he did, he might be able to tell what she was thinking. She was being so brave, handling what yesterday had thrown at her with spunk and grace.

Without thinking, he brushed back a piece of hair from her face. Her eyes widened and she blinked in that way only a woman can, not seeming to know how attractive and innocent she looked.

"Jake…" Her voice trailed off as the impact of years of missing her and of the danger in her life suddenly threatened to overwhelm him, and he stepped closer to her. She lifted her chin, only millimeters, but enough that it almost read like an invitation.

He bent closer, his eyes on her lips.

Stopped.

Their eyes met, and if hers had been unreadable before, he felt like now was the opposite. Her eyes were like clear pools, full of open honesty. He suspected the same could be said of his.

The truth he saw in her eyes, knew was reflected in his own, was this: neither of them was over each other.

But that didn't make rekindling something a good idea. It was still a terrible one. He'd learned his lesson the first time she'd broken his heart, thank you.

He pulled away, turned to the coffee maker and pushed a button to start the brew cycle, then turned around to face her. "Your aunt may not be alive when we find her."

"I know that. Why tell me something fairly obvious?"

"I wanted to make sure you'd considered that before you offered to help." Jake shoved a hand through his hair, shaking his head. And break whatever craziness had come over them that had almost had them kissing in his kitchen a day after he saw her again for the first time in seven years.

"Listen, Jake, I think things through now, okay? I have to."

"Then yes, we'd like your help." He tried to sound as professional as he could, though admittedly he'd probably lost any measure of professional distance earlier when he'd had to fight the urge to kiss her.

But it hadn't just been him, had it? He'd seen it in her eyes too, in the tilt of her chin.

Still didn't make it a good idea. He should have learned from having her hurt him the first time.

He tried again. "Truly, Cassie. It would help a lot to have you there."

The defensiveness in her posture seemed to ease some. Her shoulders untensed. "Thank you."

He nodded.

"I'm going to go get ready. I'm guessing we'll leave soon, right? I don't want to sit around drinking coffee while my aunt is out there, in who knows what kind of shape."

"I've got travel mugs for the coffee. We can go as soon as you're ready."

She hurried up the stairs and Jake went to his own room to shower and change, praying as he did that God would be with their search today. Not only for them to find Cassie's aunt, but for God to keep them safe.

Physically.

And their hearts.


For a minute this morning, Cassie had thought he was going to kiss her.

Then just as quickly as the moment had begun, it

was over and Jake was even more reserved than he'd been the day before. Cassie had avoided being alone with him for the rest of the morning, relieved beyond words when Will woke up, and even more relieved when it was time to go meet Jake's team for the day's work.

They'd pulled into her aunt's driveway and Cassie fought regret at the years she'd spent away from home. What if she didn't see her aunt again? She could never go back and give them more time together, and the thought overwhelmed her.

"We'll do the best we can, okay?" Jake squeezed her hand, let go as quickly as he'd grabbed it.

But it was something, a show of kindness in a day that Cassie could already feel was going to be difficult, and she appreciated that.

She hadn't explained much to Will, who was going with them. Jake had talked to a friend at the police department who agreed that it was safest for him to be with his mom, but that location didn't matter right now. They seemed to be in some degree of danger, no matter where they were, as the intrusion in the house last night had proven. Will knew Cassie's aunt was missing, but she'd been vague about today's events, mostly framing it as a hike they were going on.

He was interested, knowing she'd lived here before. Why hadn't she realized how curious he was about her past?

It further reinforced the need to tell him more of his own history. Like who his father was. She'd spoken of Jake to Will. She hadn't wanted her son to think he didn't have a dad, or wonder too much. So she'd told him stories—the good ones—and about what a good man his father was. Because it was true. Her leaving had never had anything to do with Jake's character. At least not his flaws.

No, Jake had always been perfect. Maybe sometimes too perfect for someone like her to feel like she measured up.

"You're sure you know where you're going up here? It's been a long time," Jake said.

"I'll manage fine." She moved away from him, turned her attention to making sure Will was ready, that his shoes were tied tight enough and that she herself was able to maintain some level of composure. Jake's questions echoed her own. Was she sure that she would be able to help? Cassie didn't even have an answer for herself. But she knew these trails, she knew her aunt, and she had to try.

Most of Jake's team arrived in an old red Jeep. Piper, who was driving, parked it and she, Ellie and Caleb piled out. They were missing one. *Adriana*, Cassie thought.

"Where's Adriana?" Jake asked, confirming that Cassie had indeed remembered the absent member's name correctly.

"She rode with the police. They are meeting us here because they want to come too."

"They're letting her dog ride in the police car?"

Piper shook her head, and then Cassie noticed a leash and a dog jumped out. Some kind of Lab mix, maybe. "Babe rode with us."

"Babe?" Cassie raised her eyebrows, unable to reconcile the serious woman she'd met with a dog named Babe.

"As in Babe Ruth. Adriana's a huge baseball fan, especially the Yankees," Ellie explained.

A police cruiser pulled up before Cassie had the chance to respond, which was probably good because she knew very little about baseball and even less about the Yankees. Will had asked to play T-ball last year for the first time and Cassie had almost signed him up but had to back out at the last minute because she couldn't work it around her job and daycare schedule for him. Yet another thing he was missing out on because he didn't have a dad. Or, well, he did but not in his life.

Another failing that was hers alone to own.

She looked back at the police car. The driver's side door opened, and Officer Wicks, who Cassie had met the day before, stepped out. Adriana climbed out of the passenger side and immediately went to her dog and started petting him like they'd been separated for days instead of maybe half an hour at most, Cassie guessed.

"Everyone ready?" Jake asked the group as a whole, then directed his attention to Officer Wicks. "Officer Wicks, you ready?"

The man appeared to have given up on Jake using his first name when they were working, because he didn't make nearly as much of a face as he had the night before.

"I'm ready when the rest of you are," Officer Wicks answered. "Thanks for letting me join you. I don't intend to interrupt your usual search procedures. I just want to be on hand in case we find…any evidence of a crime scene."

His eyes darted toward Cassie and she heard the unspoken message, gripped Will's hand a little tighter though she hadn't meant to. Jake didn't expect to find her aunt alive.

But Cassie had to believe. Had to try anyway.

Officer Wicks continued. "I also want to be on hand to observe some of the…unorthodox methods your team uses to search, to assure the department and anyone involved in a trial later that you were supervised."

Cassie thought she saw Adriana bristle from where she stood beside her dog. Was that what he meant, he wanted to supervise the use of the dog? She sure seemed to have taken something personally. Or maybe she was one of those people whose facial expressions didn't always display what they were actually feeling.

Officer Wicks looked in Adriana's direction, and to Cassie it almost looked like he wanted to say something to her and then shook his head slightly. Interesting. The vibe between them intrigued Cassie's secret romantic side and she wondered if anything was going on between them, or if it was just tension she was misreading.

"Anyway, I'm ready." Officer Wicks looked back at Jake.

"Okay. Cassie is going to take us on some of the trails her aunt used to use. Follow her. This area overlaps our previous search area to a degree, from what she told me, but then branches off into an area where we didn't go. She sketched out a map for me and I emailed each of you a copy in case we get separated for any reason, or we need to split into groups. Be aware, some of it's pretty overgrown."

"That's good news for me," Adriana mumbled as they all started walking and she came into the line just behind Cassie. Cassie guessed she was in the front because she was leading, and then Adriana was next because of the dog. Cassie was enough of an animal person to think it was cool that the dog could help in some way.

Will looked over at the dog and, reading his mind the way moms do, Cassie reminded him not to pet it and told him that the dog was working.

Cassie looked over at Adriana after walking in silence for a minute, too intrigued by her work with the dog to resist asking the question. "What did you mean earlier about it being good news for you?"

Adriana motioned around them. "In an area like this, the scent disperses quickly and mingles with other scents. The integrity is degraded a lot sooner. In an area like Jake is describing, with thick brush, the scent could get trapped and will linger much longer, making it easier for Babe to identify the scent he's looking for."

"So he's a search-and-rescue dog?"

"Yes."

Though she was trying to keep her hope from rising too high for fear of the crash that would come with disappointment, Cassie felt her expectations lifting anyway. The idea that the dog was trained to do something humans couldn't fully understand intrigued her.

"Mind if I join y'all up here in front?" Jake's voice was barely winded despite the fact that Cassie was keeping a pace that had her catching her breath frequently. Will was up for the challenge—he was the very definition of an active boy—and Cassie knew she shouldn't have been surprised to see Jake not breaking a sweat, face completely relaxed and not betraying any effort whatsoever.

She was also surprised anew by how good-looking he was. He'd been handsome before. But this new fully grown man version of Jake was even more attractive, so much so she was startled whenever she glanced at him.

"Sure, if it's fine with Cassie." Adriana looked at her

and Cassie found herself wanting to tell the woman the whole story. Right now no one but her and Jake knew the truth about Will and it was weighing on Cassie. She needed a friend. Maybe Adriana wouldn't mind being one? She was certainly perceptive enough, in a way Cassie couldn't quantify. Much like the way the dog had skills no one could quite pinpoint, Adriana seemed like the kind of woman who saw things others couldn't. Cassie was certainly under the impression that Adriana knew there was more to Cassie and Jake's relationship than old friends.

"It's fine." Such a multi-purpose word, *fine*. Able to mean everything from *yes, this is great, I don't mind at all* to *actually it's not fine with me at all but sure*.

Her current use of *fine* was leaning more to the second.

"Great." Jake smiled at her, still looking wary, like he was scared to get close to her, even while they were hiking. But the weird vibe from this morning, after the "almost kiss," was gone.

She braced herself for conversation with him, but he looked down instead, started talking to Will.

"So how's it going with you today, little man?"

"I'm not a little man. I'm just a kid. I'm six." Will picked up a stick from the side of the trail. "See this? It's my gun in case we see any bad guys."

She resisted a comment about bringing a stick to a gunfight, but still felt herself crack a slight smile. With any luck, there wouldn't be any bad guys today. Really, she didn't even think they needed luck. It was broad daylight and they were a large group. She didn't feel any of the foreboding that she had last night, and while she knew she needed to keep her guard up, she felt confident that today was, at least, a chance to breathe.

"Have you been on hikes like this before?" Jake was asking Will. Talking to his son and not telling him who he really was. Cassie needed to have a conversation with Will, explain the truth to him as soon as possible.

"No, we don't hike in Florida. Mom just goes to work and I go to school, and then we go home."

Jake's eyes swung to Cassie's. His eyebrows were raised and she heard all of his questions. Yes, she'd once been a more active, adventurous person. Yes, time had changed her. A lot.

"Well, I'm glad you're getting to hike here. I loved hiking when I was a kid."

"I like it so far. Especially because Mom said when you hike, you get snacks. She packed marshmallows for me."

"That's great, bud!"

"My name is Will."

"Not so much into nicknames, are you?"

"Not when they're not my name. But I do like marshmallows. Did you pack any?"

Jake laughed, his face looking more relaxed than Cassie had seen it in years. All of this, the entire interaction between him and their son was too much for her heart to handle. She smiled a little, ignoring the stabbing in her chest, and then focused her attention on the trail, letting Will lag behind her slightly. "You'll stay with him?" She double-checked with Jake.

He met her eyes and nodded.

She pushed her pace harder, letting the burning in her legs and lungs drown out the pain in her heart.

And letting all of it push from her mind the idea that she was being stalked by someone who wanted to bring her pain.

# FOUR

Jake had always considered himself a multitasker. So he was able to talk to his son—still wrapping his mind around that one—and keep half an eye on Cassie up ahead, all the while not letting himself forget that there could be trouble on this hike, more than Levi Wicks would be prepared to handle on his own even though he was an excellent officer.

He was fairly confident they should be okay or he wouldn't have let Cassie bring Will. Exposing Will to danger wouldn't be okay for any reason. But Jake couldn't control this environment as well as he could many others and that fact was making him nervous.

The woods were quiet today, still. Some days the wind blew hard and made it almost impossible to hear the person next to you, but today was the opposite and the hush was getting to him, making him antsy deep down.

"So did you sleep okay last night?" he asked Will, wondering if he knew anything about the events of the night before.

"Yeah, I slept fine. I usually do." He shrugged, used his stick to whack some fireweed growing beside the trail. "Can we stop talking now? I'm getting tired."

The kid said what he was thinking, that was for sure. Something he'd gotten from Jake or Cassie? He'd have said Cassie because she'd never been the type of person to hide how she felt. But he wasn't sure anymore. Who could be engaged to someone, seem like everything was going fine, and then just disappear with no explanation? Come back seven years later with a kid?

Hurt made him want to say he'd never really known her at all, a bitter thought. But he knew none of that was true and wouldn't be helpful anyway. He'd known her well. She'd just reacted out of fear. Or maybe she'd changed her mind about him. Either way, Jake didn't believe her to be capable of deceit.

They still needed to hash this out, and he wanted the full story. Not just about Will but on why she'd left. Her aunt's disappearance and her own jeopardy were getting in the way of that conversation. Maybe that wasn't a bad thing. Maybe God was giving him time to accept the news of his paternity before he delved into the reasons Cassie had hidden it from him, let alone left him.

He hiked along without talking anymore, but he kept watching Will. The kid pressed on with admirable determination. It didn't sound like this was the kind of thing he was used to, but he was doing a good job. It was hard to picture a son of his being raised away from these mountains that surrounded Raven Pass, but Will fit right in here.

Was Cassie planning to just leave when the search was over? And what, have Will fly up in the summers to visit him? He didn't want to be a summer-vacation dad. He wanted to be a real one, starting today.

*God, help me because I'm not even sure I know how.* His dad was amazing, so it wasn't that Jake lacked for inspiration. He just wasn't sure how to put it into play in his own life. A son was obviously top priority over things like work. But he still had a job and needed to do it well. How would that all fit together?

*One day at a time.*

He took a deep breath, looked around them. Cassie was still ahead with Adriana, and Babe was sniffing, working the area like he'd seen the dog do so many times before. He'd been skeptical at one point at the idea of trusting an animal as a full-on teammate, but Babe had proven it was worth it. More than, really. He looked behind him. Piper and Caleb were deep in conversation but their eyes scanned back and forth over the terrain, looking for any aberrations in the landscape that could indicate a struggle, or someone taking the wrong path. Ellie and Levi brought up the rear.

*Help us find her, God.*

"What are your thoughts on this?" Levi's voice asked him only a few minutes later. He must have hiked up ahead of Piper and Caleb.

"On Mabel's disappearance?"

Levi nodded.

"It seemed reasonable to believe it was an accident until Cassie showed up and things started happening. At this point…" Jake trailed off. No need to voice what he was thinking, but Levi seemed to understand. Their chances of finding the woman alive were slim.

Jake had seen Cassie's eyes, knew the hope there that she'd tried to temper. He hoped she could bear up under the storm he feared was coming.

"I agree." Levi nodded and Jake turned to his friend, confused about why Levi had been so ready to accept

Cassie's help to show them Mabel's preferred hiking routes.

"So why these trails? This is where she hiked, but you don't think she disappeared while hiking."

"I didn't say that." Levi said the words slowly. "I don't think she disappeared of her own volition. Or even by accident. But that doesn't mean it wasn't around here. According to Cassie, her aunt hiked every day and told her niece about these trails often. Someone watching her would know her routine, and be aware of the best places to attack."

"What you're saying makes sense, just not for Raven Pass." Jake shook his head. "The man showing up last night was strange enough for this town, but you're saying it may not even have been a crime of opportunity. That someone might actually have targeted an older woman and done some kind of harm to her?"

Levi didn't answer right away. Jake respected the fact that as law enforcement, his friend had lines he couldn't cross, things he couldn't share with him. But he knew from that look that Levi had reason to believe his assumptions were correct. He hadn't found the body, or he would have told Jake and he wouldn't have them all out there.

What did he know then that they didn't?

"We found forensic evidence at the house."

"You know who it was?"

"No." Levi shook his head. "Unless someone has committed a crime, or has some other kind of exception that would make their fingerprints stay in the system, their prints may not be available to match immediately."

"But there are prints."

Levi nodded.

"She had friends though. Surely that explains it."

"Mabel had a .44, like any good Alaskan."

Quite the non sequitur, but okay. Jake nodded.

"There are prints on the safe that match the prints on the door and around the house in other places."

Jake didn't want to consider his next question, or the ones that followed. "And the weapon?"

"Missing."

The farther she hiked, the more the past came back to chase Cassie. Every step through the alders as the trail twisted deeper into the woods and the brushy foliage that gave way to tall spruce trees and thick vegetation seemed to bring her closer to who she had been. Seven years ago.

Her aunt's disappearance hurt even more now that she was back on these familiar trails, battling with what had been and what was true now. The rift between herself and Jake wasn't something Cassie could fix. She knew that. A person made choices in life, but she didn't always get to go back and change them. Still, she wished she could tell her aunt about the situation, get her thoughts on how to handle it.

Why did everyone she love leave her?

Something inside corrected the thought as soon as it appeared. Jake hadn't left her. She took another step, looked at the way the trail was disappearing and tried to remember if they went left or right here.

"I'm hungry, Mom."

Will had caught up to her again. Cassie slowed her pace as she bent to talk to him. "Sorry, bud. I have snacks, but it's not quite time to stop, okay? About another half mile." If she remembered correctly, they'd come to a turnaround point up there. They could stop for snacks and then Jake or Officer Wicks, or whoever was in charge, could decide if they wanted her to keep going.

The truth was that Cassie didn't think it was likely her aunt would have hiked in even this far. She had years ago, but she'd gotten older, and surely that would have slowed her down some. Besides that, she just didn't feel they needed to go any farther. How much did intuition play into situations like this? Cassie wasn't sure.

"You okay?"

Now Jake's voice. She really needed to up her situational awareness for people coming up behind her apparently.

"I'm fine," she answered without thinking, sighed and tried again. "I'm tired. Tired of not knowing if she's okay, not sure if I should let the search go for today… She isn't here, I don't think."

Jake nodded, not commenting. He'd always been good at listening.

"I just…" She trailed off.

"I know."

And she believed in the moment that he did. He knew her fear of what they would eventually find.

They stopped for a snack at a place where the trail widened into a meadow, which had fireweed just starting to bloom around the edges. The sky was bright blue above them and for a few minutes Cassie felt her shoulders relax. Like she could breathe here. But their rest didn't last long.

"We need to leave." Officer Wicks's voice was steel, his expression all-business.

Jake nodded immediately, started shoving Will's pile

of snacks and trash into his own backpack. "All right, let's go."

Will nodded, childlike trust on his face.

Cassie felt none of that trust. She had questions. "Now."

Officer Wicks's directive left no time for her to get answers.

They were back on the trail, hiking at a faster pace this time. Officer Wicks was ahead of the group now, and it wasn't lost on Cassie that his eyes never stopped scanning the path ahead. His hand was at his side, presumably on his weapon.

What had changed? What was going on? Surely someone should tell her, the actual potential victim, right?

She wanted to ask Jake, who was at her side, matching his pace to hers perfectly, which she suspected was intentional. But she didn't want Will to hear the answer.

Did she need to know?

Cassie exhaled, pushed her pace faster and tried to focus her mind anywhere it would land. The gorgeous desolation of deep woods like this. The pace of Babe, Adriana's dog, up ahead of her. According to Adriana, whom she'd talked to while they were taking their snack break, the dog hadn't alerted to Cassie's aunt's scent at all. Which didn't mean she *hadn't* come this way, Adriana had said, trying to leave her a scrap of hope.

Hoping was starting to hurt Cassie more than it helped. No one told you that there was a blackness underneath hope that was nothing more than positive thinking. Was that why Jake put his hope in something more, in trusting God instead of just thinking and wishing for the best?

The foliage started to change again, grew less thick,

the trees less tall. They were close to where they were parked. Half a mile? Give or take?

The first gunshot hit the dust at Cassie's feet, the noise exploding in a sudden sharp snap of sound.

"Will, get down!" she yelled when she knew what it was, tackling her son and rolling into the cover of the alders.

"Was that a gun, Mommy?"

She'd never thought she'd have to answer that question. Her heart pounded, thudding a terrified rhythm in her ears and then there was a weight on top of her. She tensed, almost fought it off and then realized it was Jake. He'd dove on top of her to shelter her the way she had her son.

Without a second thought. Ready to sacrifice his own life.

Cassie wanted time alone to think, figure out what this meant, if anything, but processing time was a luxury people didn't have when there was a gunman in the woods and they were pinned down under bushes with no means of escape.

Another gunshot. Then another. Who were they shooting at? Cassie would have assumed it was at her, but none of the shots were hitting very close, so maybe she wasn't the target after all. Who then? Jake? The people around her?

"What do we do?" Cassie whispered to Jake. The branches were too thick to crawl through, it seemed to her. But wasn't a moving target better than one lying still? Then again, moving could expose Will and she wouldn't let him be hurt.

She never should have let him come today. Why had she assumed the daylight would ensure their safety? Maybe because coming after them didn't make sense.

Unless they had come close to finding something.

Another flicker of hope, even as the shots stopped and the stillness returned to the woods.

Will started to cry. Cassie's already broken heart broke again.

"You're okay, buddy."

Jake's voice was solid, powerful but calming, soothing in a way that washed over her like a swift glacial river.

"Everyone all right?" Officer Wicks's voice.

*No*, Cassie wanted to say. She wasn't all right. None of them were.

*God, why?*

She'd wondered earlier if Jake trusted God because it was a more solid base for his hopes than positive thinking. But was it really? Couldn't the God of the universe have stopped the shots in the first place, rather than just protecting them through it? For that matter, why had He let her aunt disappear if He was really in charge and could change things like that?

Jake's faith hadn't been something that divided them years ago, even though they'd disagreed on issues. Like whether or not "waiting" for marriage was fully necessary.

But now Cassie felt further from him, even though his body was just above hers, pressed against her back like a shield.

How could he believe in a God who cared but let bad things happen?

"We're okay over here," Jake answered for all three of them.

Physically, Cassie supposed, it was true.

"Why didn't you shoot back at them?" she asked the officer when she saw that his weapon was drawn.

"I never had a clear shot. I saw muzzle flash that way." He gestured to a rise in the land that Cassie could see would have made a good place for a shooter to hide. "But you should never shoot at an unknown target."

Cop shows didn't always get it right, Cassie realized. She opened her mouth to apologize for questioning his judgment, but he was already on his phone, calling the incident in and asking for officers to canvas that hillside and see if any evidence was left behind.

Jake climbed off her and Cassie let Will move away from her. He wiped another stray tear from his face, but besides that, he'd stopped crying quickly. Kids were resilient, people said. She was extremely thankful that appeared to be true.

But kids weren't invincible. And while Cassie had never dreamed she was really allowing Will to be in danger today, she was certainly not going to put him at risk again. If that meant she had to lock them both up inside some kind of safe house, she wouldn't fight it. Whatever it took to keep him safe.

Running appealed to her, straight back to Florida. But she knew their safety there would only be an illusion.

"I'm hit." Ellie's voice wasn't very close, and Cassie had to look around to find her. She was ten, fifteen feet away. She must have been behind them on the trail.

"How bad?" Jake had started moving that way as soon as she'd spoken up. Now he bent over, looked at the site.

"Not badly. Just a graze on the outside of my left arm."

Not far enough away from her heart to make any

of them breathe deeply. If the shot had been six, eight inches to the right…

Cassie pulled Will close to her, running her hand through his hair. To reassure him or herself, she wasn't sure.

"You okay, bud?"

"I'll feel better when we are back inside." His little voice was honest, a quiver in it. Cassie squeezed him tighter, then looked to Jake, who was looking over at her.

"Let me help Ellie. I'm a nurse," Cassie said.

"No. You need to stay down. I'll take care of it."

Jake held her gaze for a minute, but a look she once would have been able to read was perplexing to her now, so much time had come between them. Finally he glanced away, swung his backpack down off of his shoulders and rummaged through it. For a first aid kit, she was guessing.

Cassie scanned the area around them, fought against full-body shakes, only somewhat successfully. It wasn't safe to just stop here. It couldn't be.

"We need to move," Officer Wicks spoke up. "Jake, do what you can quickly and we'll take better care of it when we get to town. Sorry, Ellie." He shrugged but she nodded, understanding their situation.

They started hiking again, faster this time, and Cassie kept her eyes roving, looking for a threat she knew was out there somewhere.

Someone had shot at them today, and could still be watching even now. She had a son to keep safe, to keep raising. She couldn't afford to be an easy target for the shooter.

And yet any moment she could be.

Cassie walked faster.

# FIVE

No way was Jake letting his son walk into something like that again. The determination beat against his chest, in rhythm with his heartbeat, as he hiked down the trail, conscious of the weight of responsibility pressing on him. He was the leader of the team, should be the protector of his son, and they'd walked straight into some kind of trap.

Not a trap, because no one had told them to go there. They hadn't received any anonymous tips. They'd investigated the area because Cassie had suggested it. Surely it didn't mean she was in league with whoever had her aunt?

Jake glanced back at her, dismissed the idea immediately. It was a coincidence he was uncomfortable with, but it was explained away in many more logical ways than Cassie having changed so drastically, or having put her son in danger. More likely, one of the cars was being tracked or one of the phones was tapped. Or, even more possible because it was easier to pull off, someone was watching them.

"I'm going to go ahead and check out the cars and

make sure nothing has been sabotaged." Levi motioned down the trail. "Can you handle things from here?"

"Yes."

"Jake, I don't think we're going to find her aunt, at least not alive. I need Cassie to stay alive."

So did Jake. Just not for the same reasons. He nodded though. "I have a .44 in case of bears."

"And other threats?" Levi seemed to be taking his measure, weighing whether or not Jake was willing to protect Cassie no matter what. Jake squared his shoulders, did his best to communicate his answer.

Levi nodded. "Thanks."

It was a job Jake would have done anyway—he didn't need to be asked or thanked, but he nodded back and watched his friend hurry down the trail.

Jake looked back at the group with him. Piper and Caleb were walking in front and in back of Cassie and Will, respectively. His team was already helping him. Adriana was right behind Jake, Ellie behind her. He noticed she was keeping a good pace, so her wound wasn't slowing her down.

"Are you okay, Boss?" Adriana asked him. He smiled at her teasing nickname. He was the leader of the group, but he wasn't anyone's boss, not really. A team leader wasn't the same thing.

"I'm not the one someone's trying to kill," Jake muttered, the words making the situation even more real. He turned right when the trail came to a fork, glanced back to make sure everyone followed him. When he did so, he noticed the look on Adriana's face, her eyebrows raised, expression questioning.

"I know." Her words were quiet.

Did all of his team suspect that he still had feelings

for Cassie? Or just Adriana? The woman reminded him of her dog sometimes, able to understand things, sense what most people couldn't.

It was eerie. Extremely helpful during searching. And just as annoying when it came to his personal life.

Then again, having someone else know…

He nodded. "Thanks for asking. I'm as okay as I can be." He considered his words carefully, not wanting to share too much with a team member.

She smiled. "She's a pretty cool woman. Tough. She's the one people talk about, isn't she?"

"What?" Jake didn't have to feign surprise. He had no idea what she was talking about.

He turned ahead, scanned the terrain before them. No threats that he could see, though the unseen ones were even scarier, always looming there unable to be neutralized.

"When they're talking about why you don't date…" Adriana trailed off. "Okay, you really don't know what I'm talking about. I'm sorry, Jake. It's really not appropriate of me to pass on gossip anyway. I shouldn't have said anything."

"Don't worry about it."

His shoulders relaxed, relieved to have that conversation over. But the effects still lingered. People talked about him? Jake supposed he shouldn't be surprised. Raven Pass was a small town, full of Alaskan moms who would be happy with their single daughters marrying a paramedic who always planned to stay in town. He'd taken to turning down dates, so it followed reason that people must speculate about why. And it wouldn't be hard. He'd dated a little, about a year or so after Cassie had left. But he'd never made it past one date with anyone, and finally the last woman he'd been out with he'd had to apologize to and tell her he couldn't date because he was still in love with his former fiancée.

So yeah, they probably talked.

The parking lot finally came into view up ahead and Jake exhaled. They'd made it this far. He could see Levi and another officer bent over cars, looking underneath and at engines.

"What's the verdict?" Jake asked as they approached.

Levi shook his head. "No tracking devices, so that's not how he found us."

Of course, that would have been too easy. Find the tracking device, get rid of it, problem solved. However else the shooter was doing his surveillance was going to be much more difficult to mitigate.

"Do you need us around here?" Jake asked as the others caught up to him. He stole a glance at Cassie. She was still holding Will tightly to her side, but she looked more composed than earlier, even if her shoulders were still so tight they practically came up to her ears.

"No."

"Good. I'd rather get her inside."

"What about the rest of your team?" Levi asked, eyes on Adriana and her dog. "Are they finished searching for the day?"

Jake didn't speak up at first. He gave them all a second to think, then turned to his team. "I'm going with Cassie today and am going to figure out something better for security than hoping the bad guys miss."

Cassie opened her mouth to argue. Yes, he knew she wanted her aunt found. But he was starting to think Levi was right. This was no longer a rescue mission—it was a recovery. Living people, potential victims, took priority. And for Jake, Cassie and Will took priority over any aspect of this case. He shook his head and she closed her mouth.

"We're going back out, on one of the trails near here but not where we just were. We've got the email you sent, Jake, so we've got search parameters and quadrants and will work through some of the other options for where she could be." Caleb was the one who spoke up, but beside him Piper and Adriana nodded.

"You're not going anywhere, right?" Jake turned to Ellie. "You need to get checked out by a doctor, someone with more on hand than antiseptic wipes and Band-Aids." He had more than that in his first aid kit, but still, she needed an actual doctor for wound care.

Ellie nodded. "No arguments here. I'm going to do that, take some Tylenol and get some rest."

"Good. We'll keep communicating with the active searchers," Levi said, looking at the group who was heading back out, "and with you too, Jake, so you know where we are."

And could be kept current on events and potential escalating danger levels. He heard the unsaid words.

"All right."

Jake unlocked his car, let Cassie and Will climb in, which they did wordlessly, and shut the door behind them. Then he turned back to Levi. "I appreciate what you're doing." For the first time, Jake wished he'd gone into law enforcement instead of medicine and rescue. Not because he actually felt his skills would be best used there—no, he was where God wanted him, he knew. But he wished he could be more current with the investigation and be the one on the front lines. He'd have to settle with his friend keeping him updated. And he'd keep his focus on making sure Cassie and Will were safe.

In fact he was already working on ideas for doing just that.

Cassie helped herself to Jake's kitchen and fixed lunch for all three of them. No point in being hungry *and* cooped up in a house that was the last place she would choose to be.

Well, the crosshairs of a potential killer was the last place, but that aside, facing Jake was still one of the hardest things she could think of doing.

Will ate his lunch with only minimal complaints about the bread on his sandwich being wheat instead of white, and then started to yawn. It had been an exhausting day so when Cassie suggested he go lie down to watch a movie, he didn't argue.

A check on him fifteen minutes later revealed what she'd been expecting. He was asleep with his stuffed animal, taken from their bags, which were now in their room. Jake had arranged for a friend to fetch them from the rental car and to take care of getting the vehicle back to a local agency.

Cassie smiled from the doorway of their room, then frowned. The window shade was open, and someone looking from outside could probably see her son stretched out on the bed. Defenseless. She walked into the room, shut the blinds, then looked over at Will. He'd had a scary day. She could only hope rest would help.

Cassie looked away from him and turned to go back downstairs. Jake was right in front of her.

She startled.

"Shh, I'm sorry, I thought you knew I was here. I

didn't mean to scare you." His voice was low, barely above a whisper. Why did it still send shivers straight to Cassie's toes when she hadn't chosen him all those years ago? Surely her abandonment of him and their dreams should have made her reactions to him lessen over the years.

Instead the opposite was true. She was more drawn to him than ever.

"It's okay." She crossed her arms over her chest. He dropped his hands from her shoulders, where they had been, and looked down at the floor.

"He's sleeping?"

She nodded.

"Then we can't put this off anymore, Cassie. We really need to talk."

He'd had time to absorb the news, but she still couldn't read the emotions on his face. His eyes though…those betrayed one bit of his feelings.

He hurt. Worse than if she'd slapped him. *Of course* he hurt. He'd missed out on six years with his son because of her. And still he sheltered them both in his house, and had demonstrated today that he wouldn't hesitate to keep them safe, even if it meant using his body as a shield.

Had she realized when she left exactly what she was walking away from? The fullness of the kind of strong man Jake was? Part of her liked to think that she hadn't known. But no, she had. She'd loved him for every bit of it and she'd still walked away.

And that was part of what told her she was irretrievably broken.

She exhaled, deep. Slow. "Okay, let's talk."

"My office is right there." He motioned to the next

room, the door of which was shut. "If you'd rather be up here next to him than downstairs and farther away."

Cassie felt fairly safe in the house, but she wasn't sure she could trust her judgment anymore about risk. She never would have expected someone to break in the night before and she'd been completely stunned by the attack today. "Yes, let's stay up here."

Jake nodded. "Okay." Then he hesitated. "You go ahead and I'll make us coffee and then come back, okay?"

Cassie wasn't ready for this. But it wasn't fair to him to put it off any longer. She nodded.

The office was pure Jake, a room with a large wooden desk and bookshelves covering every wall. She'd almost forgotten how much he loved to read, for the build of his body made it seem he spent every waking moment outside chasing adventures. He was more well-read than most people, but not pretentious about it. He just genuinely liked gaining knowledge, figuring things out.

She hoped he didn't view this conversation like some kind of fact-finding mission, drilling down into every idea presented, questioning everything. It was the one thing she'd remembered complaining about when they'd dated. He had the meticulousness of someone who'd once wanted to be a doctor, the curious mind of a scientist. And her feelings couldn't always be analyzed or quantified. She'd wanted someone to just...*get* her.

"Here you go." Jake walked in a few minutes later holding two cups of coffee in mugs from Seldovia.

"You finally went, huh?" she asked him. They'd planned to tour the little town near Homer, Alaska, on their honeymoon. The one that had never happened.

Jake shook his head. "No. My parents went and brought these back as souvenirs and then didn't want to move them when they left the house."

Surely he had more mugs than just these two. And he'd chosen them because…

A nod to their past? The kind meant to cut? Meant to ease the blow of finding out how she'd betrayed him with her secret?

Cassie had to stop analyzing and just wait and see how this went. He had a right to be upset, and she needed to let him start the conversation at his own pace.

It was another time she wished she could pray. But she still couldn't reconcile Jake's faith with the evil she'd had such a firsthand view of lately. How could both exist? Evil go on unchecked?

"So what happened?" he asked as he settled onto one end of the brown leather sofa against the back wall. He kept his voice low and Cassie appreciated it. Will was a hard sleeper, but she didn't want him hearing this conversation, in case he woke up.

"I don't know."

"You have to know."

She did, didn't she? Cassie sighed. "I…"

"Okay, while you think about it, let's start backward. Did you know you were pregnant with him when you left?"

Cassie looked up at him. His jaw was tight, his lips in a straight firm line like he was bracing himself for the damage her words might do.

"No. I didn't know. I never would have left without telling you if I'd known."

He exhaled and sat back against the couch. At least she could give him that much reassurance. What she'd done, not telling him, was inexcusable, but it hadn't been calculated. It just hadn't seemed like news someone should deliver over the phone, and she hadn't been brave enough to face the situation in person by coming back to Alaska. And she'd been embarrassed. Ashamed.

"Okay," Jake said, his voice still steady.

"Everything was going well." Cassie stated what had been obvious to both of them, once upon a time.

Anything in his face that had relaxed tightened again, but there was nothing Cassie could do to change the truth, no matter how much it might hurt.

"It couldn't have been going that well." The first hint of bitterness crept into his tone, one she'd never heard before. Sure, they'd argued. Jake wasn't actually perfect despite the fact that he seemed to be so often, even to her. But this voice was different than any she was familiar with. Harder. Harsher.

"It was." She took a deep breath and reminded herself not to get defensive. He had every right to be upset by the situation. "It was going well and I loved you, and I was happy."

"Then what happened?"

Cassie hesitated. The life she'd envisioned for herself hadn't turned out anything like she'd dreamed or planned. So how did she admit she had left him for something that had never materialized? She guessed by just putting one word in front of the other, like the verbal explanations that she needed to offer were footsteps that had to travel a long way. One step at a time.

"I realized you were going to stay. And I wanted to leave."

"For med school? Cassie, we were both going to leave for medical school. We had a plan."

They'd both been accepted to a good school in Washington, and Jake was right, they'd had the next decade of their lives relatively planned. Undergrad, medical school, residency at schools hopefully close together, but even if they had to be apart, it would be okay because they were strong. Their love would handle the separation.

If only they'd known how the next few years would turn out. How wrong their idealistic hopes in their relationship had been.

"You were always planning to come back, Jake." Cassie kept her voice soft. "You love this town and it loves you back. I…was always just going to be the girl whose mom left her. The one lucky enough to have Jake Stone look her way. I didn't fit here like you did, and I didn't want to try."

"So rather than give me a choice, you just cut and run?"

Cassie hated to admit it, but yes, she'd run. Sometimes running seemed like the best escape route. A truly brave person wouldn't think so. But Cassie had never claimed any extraordinary level of bravery.

"Jake…" she started, but he was shaking his head.

"I tried, Cassie. I tried to come in here and make things comfortable. I tried to do the best I could to handle this." He gestured with his hand between the two of them and toward the room where Will slept. "But that's it? You didn't want to live here? There has to be more."

There wasn't more. Wasn't that enough? The fact that she'd blatantly chosen her dreams over the man she'd promised once to love forever?

And then in a great twist of irony, instead of being a doctor in a big city saving people in an emergency room, she lived in a medium-sized city in Florida—a state she hated, but it had been far from Alaska and her past—working as a pediatric nurse and barely making enough money to pay for the apartment she was raising their son in. Alone.

At the time, she'd felt she was saving Jake as much as herself from future pain. She'd felt her mother's abandonment acutely. She'd known that it was due, at least in part, to her mother wanting more than Raven Pass could offer. What if Cassie was like that too? What if she grew to resent Jake and even her baby for her not being able to leave town and follow her dream? She hadn't wanted to hurt Jake like that, not when she knew what it felt like to be abandoned. So she'd chased her ambitions. Left him behind, even if in her mind she felt like it was what was best for him too.

But dreams sometimes didn't turn out. If her aunt were here, Cassie would complain to her about the fairy tale she'd told her every night when she was a kid, after she and her dad had moved in with her, a story of long-lost love and a princess rescued by a daring hero. She'd wanted to believe that was possible in real life. It wasn't.

"That's all there is." Cassie shrugged. "I was…" Should she tell him the truth? Did it matter anymore? She didn't want another chance with him because she didn't deserve it and he deserved better. But something in her wanted to come completely clean. "I was wrong, Jake. And I'm sorry." Then she set her half-empty mug of lukewarm coffee down on the table by the sofa, and walked to her room without another word.

# SIX

Jake had thought Cassie would eventually have to come out of the room she and Will were staying in. But she stayed there for the entire afternoon and long enough past a normal dinnertime that he finally had to admit she wasn't going to face him. At least not today. He suspected, after all the tension of the day, she'd fallen asleep.

The explanations she'd given him felt hollow, left him feeling worse than he had before. Somehow he'd always imagined there was some big reason, something that justified shattering their future without his input.

He moved to the back windows, looking outside and making sure nothing out there gave him cause for alarm. Next window, same thing. He couldn't shake the fear that someone was going to come after her again. It was *when*, not *if*. And he wanted her safe even if she'd broken his heart. Back then and now. He'd gone into today expecting to feel better somehow, to understand. Instead the truth was empty. She hadn't talked to him back then about her dreams, or her concerns, had left instead, and neither of them could get the last seven years back. Even if they wanted to. And after something like this…

Still, he knew not all the blame lay on her. Not really. She'd called him not long after she left and he hadn't taken her call. Had she been trying to tell him then?

She hadn't even brought that attempt up in her defense, he'd noticed. She was perfectly happy to take all the blame. But the truth was, she had reached out. In a small way, but still, she'd tried.

And he'd been too hurt to answer, then too upset to call back.

So they'd both helped destroy what they'd had.

Jake knew he'd still probably love her forever, would maybe never be able to settle down with anyone because every woman he'd tried to show interest in was a poor substitute for what he really wanted—*who* he wanted. But he was finally willing to admit they weren't good for each other and had maybe never been meant to be together.

If only they'd figured that out back then and come to a mutual decision. If only he'd stuck to the truths he'd known were right and honored her the way he should have.

But Will was a blessing, wasn't he? He couldn't bring himself to wish the kid out of existence. His son. No, Will was something out of this whole experience to be thankful for. He'd rather have his son and be missing seven years of his life than not have him at all.

*God, I don't know how You're going to work this out. Can You fix this kind of pain? No, I'm sorry, Lord, I know You can. But will You?*

Jake heard nothing in reply.

He made himself a sandwich. Ate it, and then called Caleb. He'd said he could give him some backup if necessary, and Jake needed at least a few hours of sleep.

\* \* \*

Just past one in the morning, Jake got up, fully awake. He reached for his phone, thinking it may have roused him. No missed calls or messages. He'd expected one of the police officers to want to talk more. He'd have to call in a few hours, when people were starting morning shifts. Before he'd fallen asleep, he'd been thinking about Will and wondering if there wasn't some way to separate him from Cassie and keep him safe. She wouldn't like it, he knew, but it was starting to seem like the best option.

He was Will's dad. He had some rights too, which was another thing Cassie was going to have to talk to him about. He wanted to be in his son's life.

Even if he had to leave Alaska?

He tried the question on for size. He loved his work with the rescue team and wasn't sure how he'd make a living and provide for his son otherwise. So quitting full-on wasn't an option for him…but part of the year? He could make sacrifices in order to really get to know Will, have his son know him.

Sleep wasn't going to come back, not with thoughts like these going through his mind right now. Jake threw back the covers, then pulled on jeans and a shirt. Besides, this way Caleb, who was downstairs on the couch, could get some sleep. Jake appreciated his friend giving him some much-needed backup, but he was okay now.

He opened the door to his room, then walked down the hall, pausing outside Cassie and Will's room.

Opening the door was probably some kind of violation of privacy. But now that he'd had some rest and could think clearly, his protectiveness—and the fears that went with it—kicked in. Was there a chance they'd been attacked last night and that's why she hadn't come down? He didn't think so; he'd heard nothing.

But now that the thought had popped into his mind, the worry vibrated inside him, wouldn't let go.

He eased the door open.

Will was asleep on the bed, sprawled across it, his small hand across the pillow next to him.

Cassie. Jake's heart thudded and he blinked in case his eyes weren't seeing something in the darkness.

"You should really let someone know if you're going to check on them in the middle of the night. You could scare them otherwise."

Cassie's voice. She was curled up in the chair by the window, a blanket over her huddled form.

"I'm sorry. I just needed to know you were okay." Jake didn't regret his decision to come in. Surely she understood that their protection was a higher priority than dancing around whatever propriety demanded at the moment.

"I'm fine. Sorry I worried you." She shifted in the chair. "Will was taking up the whole bed and I didn't want to wake him, so I've been sleeping here."

"Sleeping?" She sounded awake to him.

Cassie shrugged. "Enough. Off and on. You're not the only one worried." Her eyes went to the window, maybe subconsciously. Jake hated that the threat weighed on her at all hours, but he was glad she wasn't letting her guard down. It was safer that way.

"Okay, well, I'm sorry. Glad you're all right." Jake moved for the door.

"Jake?"

He swallowed hard. Stopped walking. Something

in her voice sounded like their past, guard down, years erased. It tugged at him. "Yeah?"

"I'm sorry."

Not just for tonight, but for more than that. He could tell by the weight of her whisper.

"I know." He hesitated. "I forgive you." And he did, for keeping Will away from him, even for hurting him in the past. But if there was one thing the last day had made clear to him, it was that they'd had their chance and anything between them was over. For the sake of their son though, he had to live his faith and let go of any bitterness over the lost years with Will. His faith taught him love was the most important path in life. He loved Will.

All these years he'd thought he wanted a second chance with Cassie. While he'd always love her, maybe what he'd really needed was forgiveness. For both of them.

"And I'm sorry too," he said, for whatever had gone wrong that was also his fault, for the choices he'd made that had led to Cassie thinking she had to leave.

"Thanks, Jake."

He walked out the door and down the stairs, ready to keep watch the rest of the night. He certainly wasn't going to be sleeping anymore.

When Jake reached the living room, Caleb looked up at him, questions on his face.

"Everything's fine," Jake said, though it was debatable if it was true. He and Cassie were both broken inside, he knew that, from past hurts. Maybe tonight was a step toward healing but neither of them was fine yet, not in Jake's opinion. But Caleb would be curious about how things were going safety-wise.

"Good. Are you planning to stay up now?"

"Yeah, I'm done sleeping. Do you want to head up to the other guest room to crash or go home?"

"Upstairs is fine. I've been walking a lot to stay awake and keep an eye on things outside. So far nothing seems out of the ordinary."

Jake was thankful for it, he just wasn't taking chances after the night before. "Thanks for the help."

He took the spot on the couch his friend vacated, thoughts still running wild. He reached for the table by the sofa and eased open the drawer and pulled out a notebook. He might not be able to get much done with the case now in the middle of the night, but he could make some notes to remember for tomorrow.

Priority number one was finding somewhere safe for Will to go, at least during the day. Cassie wasn't going to let him out of her sight at night, that had been clear after checking on her. Jake might be trying to keep both of them safe, but as far as Cassie was concerned, she was the one watching over the kid. He could respect that. But during the day Cassie might still want to help, now that there was a tenuous peace between them again. Surely there was an option that would work for everyone.

He broached the subject with Cassie that morning while pouring her coffee. He'd used the French press this morning, which was her favorite, or at least it used to be.

"We need to talk about Will."

"What about him?" Her tone was guarded, and he didn't blame her. Yesterday's conversation... It could have gone better.

Jake shook his head and poured himself some cereal. "Nothing big, sorry if it sounded that way."

Cassie opened the cabinet with the bowls and grabbed two of them, then reached for the cereal when he was done. It was the kind of early morning routine couples did all the time, and it affected Jake more than he would have thought it would. It was surreal, still, to have her in his house like this. Like a little flicker of an idea for how it might have been if not for all that had gone wrong.

"Okay, what then?" she asked.

"He's got to stay with someone else during the day."

"No."

"Cassie, you were there yesterday. It was dangerous and I don't want it to happen again. He doesn't need to be exposed to a threat like that."

"I agree, but I'm the best one to protect him."

"Are you?" He let a few beats pass and watched her face. Her expressions flickered from one end of the emotional spectrum to the other until she finally seemed to settle on cautious.

"Tell me what you had in mind."

"I called the police chief this morning and explained the situation to him. His son-in-law is a police officer also and is on leave this week to spend time at home with his family. They offered to let Will stay with them where someone can make sure he's not in the line of fire." Not that he was expecting any more firing. He was certainly hoping there wouldn't be, but as yesterday had proved, it was better to assume the worst.

Cassie nodded, but still didn't say anything. She looked back toward the stairs, like she was thinking of Will, and left the empty bowl and the cereal on the counter. He was still asleep, Jake guessed. Her own bowl she carried to the table and sat down, then started to eat.

So was she still thinking, or…? The Cassie he'd known was confident, bold, which meant she usually responded immediately and had her mind made up quickly.

Then again, she'd made her mind up quickly and told him no, hadn't she? So maybe it was best that she took a little more time to think it through. Jake had confidence in her as a mom, but this was an area where he knew he could help, or at least connect her with people who could.

"It's for the best, Cassie," he said quietly, as he walked toward her, not meaning for her name to come off of his lips quite so gently. She couldn't tell, could she, how much he still cared by his tone? He hoped not, because any ridiculous feelings he had didn't need to be acted upon. He knew that.

Then she was facing him, her bright green eyes searching his. "You really think so?"

The idea that she cared what he thought made his heart beat faster even as the alarm bells in his brain went off. He couldn't care that she cared, couldn't let himself get close again.

*It's already going to hurt enough when she leaves, with your son*, he reminded himself. But he couldn't quite pull his eyes away from hers. He nodded, slowly. "Yes."

Her lips parted and he fought to pull his eyes away from them. She sighed. "Okay."

"Okay? You'll let him stay with them?" he clarified.

Cassie nodded. "Yes. I still want to help and you're

right, his staying with me is putting him in too much danger. Even if I stayed here during the day, he's probably still safer with an officer's family than with me and I want what's best for him, not just what I want."

"Great." He looked away from her, and whatever moment they'd had had passed. "We'll take him there this morning and then you and I will head out with the team."

She nodded, then focused her attention back on her cereal.

Jake took a deep breath and asked God to help them find her aunt, preferably today.

# SEVEN

Will had been more than cooperative at the idea of playing with new friends during the day instead of being with his mom, Cassie thought. Of course, he was six now, not nearly so interested in her whereabouts and spending time with her as he had been at five. Every year seemed to bring more longing for independence from him, and made it clearer to her that boys needed their dads, whenever it was possible.

She needed to tell Will. Jake hadn't pressured her about it, though he had to have it on his mind, she thought as they pulled away from the police officer's house in Jake's car. She appreciated the way he'd handled this.

Perfectly.

No surprise there.

They met up with the team in a parking lot farther from her aunt's house than the trailhead where they'd met yesterday. But Cassie knew from the time she'd spent living and hiking in Raven Pass that it was basically the third point of a triangle, with the other two being her aunt's house and the trailhead from the day before. She hadn't seen any maps, but she assumed the search team must have some since they'd talked about breaking into areas to search.

"So are you guys still thinking my idea could be right, that she hiked from her house on one of her normal trails and then something happened?"

Jake didn't answer right away. Cassie turned to look at him, noticing that the expression on his face was nothing short of grim.

"You don't think it was an accident though, her disappearance," she surmised, not needing verbal confirmation anymore. His facial expression had given her enough.

"They're working it as a murder investigation. That's what Levi Wicks went over again when he called."

"He called you and talked about it?"

"Yes, he's my friend and he knew I wanted to know."

"Well she is my aunt, so you should have told me. I would think you'd have a basic sense of decency and know that without needing to be told." Cassie felt her voice rising, felt her mind telling her to stop talking before she dug herself any further into a hole with Jake, who had really shown her a lot of grace since she'd been back in town.

"I would have thought you'd have the decency to actually say goodbye before leaving town and not coming back for over half a decade, but here we are." His voice had lowered, but it wasn't intimidating. Jake had never yelled at her and apparently wouldn't start even now. But it was flat. Devoid of any warmth.

Cassie was sorry for what she'd done, but she'd already said so. It hurt for him to throw it in her face like this, and she wondered if this would evolve into some kind of never-ending penance. Cassie made mistakes, and she apologized or learned from them, and then she moved on. She knew this particular mistake was bigger than most, and she knew Jake had a right to be angry, that moving on from it might take a little longer. But she hoped he wouldn't keep using it as punishment.

Wasn't that the whole problem with Jake in the first place though, his inability to move on? His well-sunk roots into Raven Pass soil made it impossible to go on to the next adventure, like Cassie had always longed to do.

He didn't like change. He'd probably never get past this, the hurt she'd caused him, either. For the last few days she'd wondered how he could so easily forgive her and act like the past hadn't happened. In a way it had seemed too good to be true, but it was Jake and he'd always seemed that way to her.

Now at least she knew. He hadn't forgiven her.

She met his eyes, nodded once. At least she knew where they stood. "Let's go."

He climbed out of the vehicle without another word and they started hiking, through the big meadow where the trailhead started, and toward the tall spruce trees that seemed to swallow up the trail without a hint of where it was going. But Cassie knew the way, even if she and Jake got separated.

She'd be fine. With or without him.

Just like she always had been.

Jake didn't mean to be setting a pace worthy of some kind of sports-conditioning program, but he'd always worked off frustrations with exercise, and *frustration* didn't begin to describe what he was feeling right now. With himself, with Cassie.

He squeezed his eyes shut for an instant and tried to

pray but he was still too upset, all his boiling emotions too close to the surface.

One foot in front of the other. Another step and another, his hiking boots pounding the ground. Cassie was upset about her aunt. She was in danger, which wasn't something she was accustomed to. There were all kinds of excuses and explanations for her behavior and the hurtful words she'd said, but had he accepted any of that? No, he'd just exploded in a low-voiced sentence of words designed to hurt.

They'd hurt her. And he was sorry.

She wasn't ready to hear that yet though, so he just punished himself with a pace that made him more out of breath than he'd been in years. She kept up fine, and he wondered what she had been doing to keep in such good shape.

Not that it surprised him. She'd always been able to match him and she'd never been the kind of woman who made Jake feel like he had to wait for her. No, Cassie could handle herself fine in any environment and it was part of why he'd fallen in love with her in the first place.

She kept pace with him for another ten minutes, as they wound through the spruce on a side trail so narrow he wasn't sure he'd have found it without her direction. It was then he started to notice that she was getting out of breath and he slowed. Rain had begun to fall; some was even finding its way down through the tree canopy.

"I'm sorry," he said, knowing she'd know what for. She'd always been able to read his mind, or at least it had seemed that way, and with how little had changed between the two of them, he suspected that hadn't changed either. The raindrops on the tree limbs were the only sound for a few seconds until she finally spoke up.

Cassie nodded. "Me too."

Jake stopped walking and gently turned Cassie to face him, his hands on her upper arms. "You've already apologized for what you did." He looked her in the eyes. "Another apology isn't needed and I'm sorry I made you feel as though it was."

He'd only wanted to face her so she could see his expression and know how sincere he was about her not needing to apologize anymore. He hadn't meant to fling an accusation at her, and he intended to keep a check on the emotions that had fed that outburst. She didn't deserve that.

The two of them facing each other like this had made the world almost still, except the gentle sound of the rain, the way it was falling on the curls that usually edged around Cassie's face when she was wearing a ponytail. It was dangerous, feeling like he and Cassie were the only two people on earth, and the only two people in this stretch of Alaskan woods.

Chemistry had never been an issue between them. They'd always had more than Jake had known how to handle.

Jake caught his breath, didn't move. He knew all the reasons he should be careful not to give her the impression they could pick up where they left off because they couldn't.

Cassie moved closer, her eyes on his lips, her chin tilted up.

Her lips met his and it was like all the yesterdays were gone and they were back, six years ago, lips touching just like this. Gentle, tentative and then bolder.

She'd been his once and this kiss said that she still was, somehow, despite the mistakes, the years, the regrets.

Jake kissed her with every ounce of himself that had missed her over the years, and she responded.

Nothing had ended between them then at all. They'd been put on pause.

Jake slowed his kiss, had to make himself pull away, because this wasn't the time or place. They separated and he had to catch his breath.

"If you apologize for that I may never speak to you again." Cassie's voice was breathless too and Jake squeezed his eyes shut, loving the sound of it, the memory of her lips on his.

"Later. We have to talk about that later," he said quietly.

Cassie didn't answer.

"Seriously, Cassie."

She finally nodded. "Okay. We'll talk later."

Jake swallowed hard, unable to formulate any more words at the moment. His train of thought had certainly narrowed, to Cassie and loving her, kissing her, spending the rest of his life with her...

His mind tried to caution him from letting his heart carry his thoughts away because he'd tried this once and had never been the same after. But at the moment he had no desire to listen to the caution. Instead he grabbed her hand, squeezed it gently while he met her eyes and then nodded, like a promise.

And hoped that this one would turn out better than the promises they'd made last time.

Cassie couldn't breathe, couldn't think. Jake had kissed her. No, she realized, as she ducked around a bush of salmonberries, she'd kissed Jake. He hadn't moved away, and he'd been a willing...participant...in the entire kiss, but she'd started it.

Oh, how she'd started it. And with it she'd restarted all kinds of worries and fears in her mind. It had been easier, in a way, to pretend the spark between the two of them had died, that she'd killed it all those years ago, but clearly that was a lie.

Cassie just didn't know what to do about it, here and now today. So talking about it wasn't something that was high on her list of priorities, but she knew Jake was right. They had to talk.

If she'd talked to him before she left, like he'd mentioned earlier, how different would things have turned out? Would they have really had a happily-ever-after, living in Jake's parents' house together, married like they'd planned, with Will and a little sibling maybe? Her heart squeezed and she had to blink back the tears edging over the corners of her eyes. You couldn't go back. Wasn't that what she'd been telling herself for years now?

Except it almost looked like she had the chance now. Would she take it? Could she?

Cassie felt adrift and wondered if this was one of those times that Jake would pray and if she could learn to.

*Um, God, we could use help figuring out what to do*, she tried as a tentative test.

She didn't hear anything back, but she did feel her shoulders relax a little. *Huh.*

They hiked on without talking, taking game trail after game trail, winding so deep into the woods that Cassie was getting nervous and hoping she could find their way back out. This part of the woods had been one of her favorite spots as a child, for the way the wilderness seemed to swallow a person whole. For that same reason now, Cassie felt her muscles tensing, her heartbeat growing faster. Fear had crept out of the corners of her mind, where it had been temporarily banished while she'd been kissing Jake, and had taken a more front and center spot now. It washed over her and she wasn't able to stop or even slow it. Goose bumps shivered down her arms and she could almost smell fear.

No, not fear. Something else.

"Jake." She stopped walking, her nose registering immediately what took her mind a few moments to realize.

The smell was decay. And how many people walked this way or used this trail?

She'd feared her aunt was dead and had wondered if the hurt could actually get worse if it was really true. It could. It did. Despair hung on her like a too heavy blanket, scratchy and hard.

And then Cassie moved to the side of the trail to throw up. Jake kept walking.

"Stay there," he told her, pulling his .44 from his chest holster and handing it to her once she'd stood up and regained a tiny bit of equilibrium. "Use this if you need to."

He had taught her to shoot with either this one or one very similar when they were in high school. Cassie nodded and sat down, a few feet away from where she'd been sick, in the shelter of some berry bushes.

Her aunt had loved salmonberries. That was probably why this had been one of her favorite trails. When Cassie was a kid, they used to walk this trail and pick them together, and then her aunt would make jam.

Her aunt was gone.

Why had Cassie left?

It was too late to fix any of it, her regrets about the time spent away, all the years she'd said she'd visit one day and hadn't. Cassie had let her aunt down, let herself down.

Tears threatened to overtake her, but fear kept them at bay for now. Because one other question wouldn't leave her alone no matter how much she tried to think about other aspects of what was going on.

If Jake and the police were right and her aunt hadn't died of natural causes, then someone had wanted her dead.

Why?

And if they'd done that as intended, why would they come after Cassie? She had nothing they could want, barely any money in her savings, and what she would inherit from her aunt amounted to the tiny cottage on half an acre. Nothing worth killing over.

It didn't make sense.

Cassie lowered her head and cried.

# EIGHT

Jake had seen his share of people who had died. It was part of being a paramedic and on a search-and-rescue team. And in a small town, he had even seen people die whom he'd known in life. But seeing Cassie's aunt crumpled among a patch of fireweed shattered him. Cassie's sobs in the distance wrenched his gut. He felt the pain and weight of her hurt almost like it was his own.

Because it was. He did hurt when she hurt. Always had. Because he loved her.

Jake bit back a groan. Another realization he wasn't ready to face, and it had to take a back seat for now since dealing with the fallout of this discovery took priority. He pulled his phone from his pocket. No service. He took the backpack off, eased the SAT phone out of the top pocket and dialed Levi's number. Jake's team was out searching, and they would be his second call, but he figured law enforcement should know first. And the sooner the Raven Pass Police Department got here, the sooner Jake could leave and take Cassie with him. He was worried about her, and more than just emotionally. It wasn't unheard of for someone to go into le-

gitimate medical shock after an event like this and he
wanted to avoid that with Cassie if he could.

"I found her." He kept his voice low. "Near Bold
Mountain, on the side closest to town."

Levi asked a few more questions about location, her
condition.

"Dead, and not recently." The smell was unbearable.
Jake couldn't bear to look at her and hadn't even needed
to take her pulse to confirm that she was dead. He then
gave Levi directions to the trailhead and their location.

"I'll be there as fast as I can. You don't have to stay
right there next to the body. Living people take priority and Cassie's still in danger so get her somewhere
sheltered nearby."

"I'll do that," Jake promised.

He next call was to Caleb, to whom he told the same
information, but faster since he was walking back to
Cassie and eager to focus on her.

"You okay, man?" Caleb asked.

Jake couldn't remember really *needing* his team-
mates for anything personal before. He knew he could
count on them during a search and didn't hesitate to
put his life in their hands. But he hadn't really talked to
them much about his personal life or counted on them
to care about it.

The fact that all of them seemed…sensitive to his
current situation was unusual. But he appreciated it.

"I think so. Thanks for asking."

He ended the call and made his way back to Cassie.
Or tried to. He didn't see her anywhere, and the tall
fireweed and other vegetation obscured her from view.

If she was still there at all.

Could it have been a trap, Cassie's aunt's body being

right there where they could see it? Had whoever killed her meant for Cassie to find the body and then planned to overpower her in her grief? His heart pounded faster as he scanned the area and then started using his hands to press weeds to the side so he could see better. Where had she been?

"Cassie?"

He waited. Nothing. The panic that had been growing exploded in his chest and Jake realized again how much things weren't over between them. Not even close. "Cassie!" Louder this time.

"Here. I'm down here." She stood up, unfolding herself from her place among the brush, about fifteen feet farther than where he was standing. Her face was red, tears under her eyes smudged with some kind of makeup. Mascara, maybe. Cassie sniffed.

"It's her, right? And she's really gone?"

Jake nodded, slowly. He couldn't bring himself to say the words out loud, but the nod seemed to be enough for Cassie to have to fight back a fresh round of sobs.

"Sweetheart…" His words betrayed him, but he ignored it and held out his arms. This wasn't the time to think of all the reasons they couldn't be together.

There were some of those, weren't there?

Still, not the time. Cassie moved toward him and he wrapped his arms around her as she pressed herself against him and cried into his shoulder, like she was giving her tears to him to carry. Jake just stood there, held her for another few minutes before he remembered what Levi had told him to do.

And he hoped he wasn't too late.

"We can't stay right here, Cassie. Levi is worried about your safety. The fact that your aunt is dead doesn't put you in less danger. If anything, the danger is worse now because whoever killed her won't hesitate to kill again. It's a sort of point of no return."

Cassie nodded, brushing away the wetness from her eyes. "Okay, where?"

Jake looked around the meadow. They could sit down like she'd been doing and probably not be seen, but he wasn't as comfortable with that option. It wasn't defensible. They'd be better off among the trees.

"This way." He unwrapped his arms from her, but didn't break contact as he slid his hand down her arm and then grasped her hand in his.

He felt her flinch a little. Met her eyes. "Is this okay or should I let go?" He swallowed hard, the charge between them almost a tangible thing.

Cassie nodded. "Don't let go." Her words were almost softer than a whisper. But firm.

He didn't let go.

They hurried together through the tall plants, toward the edge of the forest but not in the direction they'd come from. Jake wanted to be off the trail, even though it wasn't a very obvious trail, just to make their chances better.

"Here is good." He motioned to the base of an old spruce, whose branches tangled in such a way that they'd be sheltered from the back, more or less, but have their view to the front open to the meadow and only slightly obscured by the tall vegetation.

Cassie nodded and sank down beside him, laying her head on his shoulder.

"Jake… Thanks."

He nodded.

She looked up, tears in her eyes. "Do you know how…she died?"

"No. Looks like a blow to the head, but we don't know if she fell or if someone hit her. The coroner will let us know eventually."

She rested there, quietly, warm against him, not speaking, just staying in the moment.

She lifted a hand to his chest as she leaned closer to him.

Jake held his breath, tried not to move. It had been so long since she'd touched him like that, since he'd felt so close to another soul.

And she was grieving. Not thinking clearly.

He moved her hand away. Cleared his throat. "No matter what, I'm glad I could be here. We…we should never have stopped being friends at least. I'm glad I can be one for you now."

And he felt her pull away, not physically. Her head was still on his shoulder. But he felt the tension gather in her body, the stiffness in her shoulders.

He could have sat there forever, forgetting the present and living in the past, maybe making one of his old mistakes all over again if she'd asked him to. But he wasn't that man anymore, and didn't want to be. God had forgiven him for the past, but he wanted to do better in the future, not just for him, but for Cassie.

Or…whoever he ended up with.

Because maybe there was just too much between them to be able to move on. Maybe they'd had their chance.

Maybe all he could hope for now was the chance to keep her safe and one day get to know his son.

Maybe second chances didn't happen after all.

\* \* \*

Cassie had stayed curled up against Jake, willing herself to get the strength to pull away from him, but she couldn't. Even if he'd made it clear where they stood, emphasized the fact that they were *friends*, which apparently nullified that earlier kiss, she still felt stronger when she was with him and she wasn't sure she could withstand the onslaught of her circumstances right now without him beside her.

So she did the easy thing and stayed still, even though it broke her heart a little more because it reminded her of the love with Jake she could never have. But what was another crack in a heart that was already broken beyond repair?

The police eventually arrived. Cassie and Jake watched them from afar until they could see Officer Wicks—Levi, she was beginning to call him in her mind, like Jake did—looking around, like he was trying to find them. Then they emerged from their cover and walked to where he was.

Cassie didn't pay attention to what the men said, even though she did want to know what had happened to her aunt. Instead, here in the moment, all she could do was breathe and listen to the rhythm of her heart whooshing in her ears. *She's gone. She's gone. She's gone.*

By the time Jake steered her back to the trail and said something about how they were free to leave, the rhythm had progressed to a full-on migraine, her head pounding along with her heart. Her stomach felt queasy again, but not the kind being sick could ease.

*God, why?*

They walked the trail down silently. Cassie led them back the way they'd come, surprised at how easily the directions came to her again. It was like she'd traveled this trail hundreds of times in her memory, not just the a-couple-times-a-year treks with her aunt to pick berries, Strange. Or a side effect of grief sharpening her mind and memory? Cassie didn't know.

"Do you want to go home?" Jake asked in the trail-head parking lot. There were police cruisers there; one of them was parked next to Jake's car. The officer there nodded to them and even in her mental fog, Cassie appreciated that men had been stationed there to make sure no one was lying in wait at the car or had rigged it to hurt them somehow.

"No," Cassie surprised herself by saying. "I want to go to my aunt's house."

Jake nodded, adding no words. She knew the police had finished their investigation there already.

Cassie heard Jake on the phone, checking on Will. That made sense; it was much later than they'd planned to be done. Almost dinnertime.

She couldn't imagine being hungry.

The drive there didn't take long, and Cassie kept her attention to things outside the windows rather than have to face Jake and talk to him. It wasn't the most crushing blow of the night—his reminder that what they had was friendship at best—but it was another blow when she didn't feel like she could take any more.

When they pulled into the driveway, the door to the house was still open.

"Don't the police usually fix doors? Or put crime-scene tape up?" Cassie mumbled, her mind focusing enough to get the questions out.

"Stay here." Jake reached for the door handle, then turned back to her and she understood. He didn't want to leave her. She was tired of this, tired of wondering what was a trap and when she should go with him and when she should stay, and she was exhausted and grieving. And. She. Could. Not. Do. This. Anymore.

Of course she didn't have a choice, so she took a deep breath and got out too. "I can go with you. I can do this."

Did he believe the words any more than she did? She stepped from the truck, exhaustion making her sore down to her bones. Again, she wished she could trust God. But she couldn't.

Right? Maybe it was a subject that deserved more consideration and thought from her. But all she knew was that Jake was holding himself together well. A friend of hers she'd known years ago when they competed in high school running events in the state—Summer Dawson—had gone through a scary time a few years ago but had seemingly held it together fine. And Cassie knew she was a Christian, like Jake was. Could it be that easy? Trust that someone else was in control and then you didn't have to carry the weight of everything on your own?

Cassie walked toward the front door, gravel crunching under her feet as all the times she'd done this before, walked to her aunt's home, paraded in her mind like a newsreel of memories. She'd seen her aunt for the last time. Talked to her for the last time.

So many lasts. So little hope.

"This shouldn't be like this," Jake muttered as he looked closer at the door. He shook his head. "Back to the car. I wanted to see for sure before we called anyone, but this is new."

Cassie walked back to the vehicle, her mind waking up a little more and kicking into gear to remind her to be aware of her surroundings. Will needed her. She couldn't let her guard down, not even now.

Jake put the car in gear once they were both inside and he'd ended his phone call to the police. Cassie wasn't even buckled yet; she'd thought they were waiting for the police to arrive. "What are you doing?"

"Not sitting here with you in the car like a stationary target, that's for sure." He shook his head once, seriousness etched on his features. Today had taken a lot out of him too, Cassie could see, now that she was paying attention. So maybe the trusting-God concept wasn't a cure-all. How did it work then?

She wanted to ask Jake, but not today, not after how close they'd been, only to find herself ripped away from him again, this time not from her own choice to run, but from his intentional distancing by calling them *friends* so pointedly.

Instead she said nothing, just looked out the window as they rode around town. Jake pulled out his phone again. It didn't seem to be synced with any Bluetooth, so Cassie frowned and waited to hear whom he was talking to.

"Hey, it's Jake. Everything still okay there? There's been another break-in at Mabel Hawkins's house. It's likely whoever is behind all of this is still in town, so I just wanted to make sure… Yeah, I know you know what you're doing. Overprotective. Yeah, maybe. I've never had a kid before. Pretty sure when there's a crazy criminal in your kid's town that's linked to his family, paranoia is expected. All right, thanks, man. I appreciate it."

Ah, the officer who was letting Will stay at his house.

"He's okay?" Cassie confirmed.

Jake nodded.

"Yes, and I told him...you know, about Will being my son. Just to make sure he understands how important his safety is to me."

At least she was thankful for the fact that the search yesterday hadn't led to her aunt's body. In retrospect, that was another reason she shouldn't have brought him with her the day before. Even though she'd hoped her aunt wasn't dead, she knew it had been a possibility, and Will being present for that would have scarred him.

*Thank you.* She found herself whispering to a God whom she'd mentally debated the existence and trustworthiness of a hundred times over. But she still felt compelled somehow to talk to Him. Odd.

"Why is this happening?" she asked against her better judgment as they made another turn on a side street and Jake glanced at the dashboard clock. The police must have told him how many minutes it would take to get to her aunt's house, and he was killing time until then.

Bad phrase. *Wasting* time.

"This with your aunt?" Jake seemed surprised at the question. "We don't know, Cassie. They're still compiling ideas so far, and motive and opportunity and all that kind of stuff."

Here was her chance to just keep quiet, not follow through with the conversation she knew she wasn't ready to have. Not with him, when it involved opening herself up and making herself vulnerable by admitting she might be wrong about something as important and personal as faith. "Not about that." She heard herself keep talking before she'd consciously decided to. "*Why* the grand scheme? Don't you believe God has a plan? How could this fit?"

He didn't answer. For a minute she wasn't sure if she'd offended him.

"I don't know." His words were barely audible. They were pulling back into her aunt's driveway and a squad car was out front, reminding her again that this wasn't fair.

*She* certainly didn't know how it could possibly make sense, but she'd thought Jake would have an answer. Wasn't that what faith did? Gave a person answers?

"What do you mean? You don't *know*?"

"Trusting God doesn't mean He explains Himself to me, Cassie. There's a verse in the Bible about how His thoughts aren't ours and His ways aren't ours. Somewhere in Isaiah, I think. So no, I don't know why this would happen." He put the car in Park. "I wish it hadn't. But I'm not God and He has a plan."

*Hmm.* It wasn't the too-easy explanation she'd been anticipating, been ready to shoot down. She knew better than to believe that life came with easy answers. Maybe she'd been hoping he would offer her some so she could continue to discount his faith like she'd done before.

How much had their difference of opinion in that regard played into her decision to leave? She'd never wondered before, but didn't have time to follow up on the thought now, as a police officer she hadn't met yet was waving them over to the house.

"Who is that?" she asked as she followed Jake there. He looked familiar.

"Judah Wicks. He's Levi's brother and also a police officer."

That explained why she'd thought she'd met him. He

did look something like his brother, but broader and taller and a bit more serious. Levi smiled more. This guy had no laugh lines.

"Jake, thanks for calling this in," he said as they approached. "And you're Cassie?"

"Yes. Cassie Hawkins, nice to meet you." Manners kicked in automatically and Cassie felt an unexpected stab of pain. Her dad hadn't taught her manners. That had been her aunt's doing. As a kid she hadn't realized how much responsibility her aunt had voluntarily taken on when she offered to have her brother and niece move in. It had changed Cassie's life for the better, but what an adjustment her single aunt must have had to make.

*And did I ever even say thank you?*

"So what's going on?"

"I've done a quick look around the house. There's a mess, but it's safe. Structurally sound, nothing I can see as far as danger. I'd like Cassie to walk through it with me to see if she can help me identify if anything is missing. Last time it was broken into and someone made a mess we chalked it up to a fit of rage of some kind. Now that someone has returned and done the same thing, we need to try to figure out why they were here," Judah Wicks explained.

Cassie nodded. "I'll do it." Any way she could help. The drive to be involved had grown stronger with the knowledge that her aunt was dead. Maybe it was some kind of desire for revenge, which of course she wasn't going to get, but being involved would make it feel more like she played a part in bringing whoever had done this to justice, and Cassie wanted that. Badly.

"If she goes, I'm going."

Judah raised his eyebrows but nodded at Jake without hesitation. "Of course."

As though she needed Jake there for protection when she was walking around the house with a man who had a gun on his hip and a build that would dwarf a great number of NFL players. It was sweet of him to want to be there though. Although she couldn't understand why he'd go to so much trouble for someone he'd pointedly called a *friend* just a few hours before.

Judah stopped them both inside the front door and handed them each a pair of nitrile gloves. "Put these on. We're still waiting for a forensics team to come out from another town, so we don't want you compromising fingerprints. Ideally you'll touch as little as possible, but just in case."

They both pulled the gloves on.

The living room was a mess, Cassie discovered as they stepped inside, and she looked to the left. The kitchen and dining room, on her right and opened to the main living space, were messy but not quite as bad. Drawers had been opened and left haphazardly with no pattern. She'd heard once that professional thieves knew to start with the bottom drawers so they wouldn't have to close drawers behind themselves, but this wasn't professional if that was the case. Some drawers were pushed in almost all the way, some were fully open and some were in between.

Someone had been looking for something.

But what?

# NINE

Jake followed Cassie, careful not to get in her way or distract her. She seemed more focused now than she had been earlier, though he wasn't sure if that was a good thing. Earlier she'd been in full self-protection mode. Even though it hurt him to see her that way, he wasn't sure it wasn't best for her.

Now she was prepared to help however she could. He was proud of her. Scared for her. Frustrated beyond all reason that he couldn't get his head straight when it came to her, no matter how much he tried.

"What were they looking for?" Cassie asked Judah.

Judah raised his eyebrows. "Why do you assume they were looking for something? Do you know what it could be?"

Jake liked Judah fine most of the time, though he was closer to his brother. But he didn't like the way the man was practically implying that Cassie had something to hide, or knew more about this than she was saying. While she frowned, Jake jumped in.

"Of course she doesn't know. She's asking you be-cause she looked around and saw the signs. Her aunt was already gone by the time someone did this. Obviously they were looking for something."

Judah shot him a warning look. "I'm asking Cassie."

She threw Jake a glance that indicated she appreciated his support. She'd been hard to read today, leaning up against him one minute and freezing him out the next. He couldn't figure her out.

And he didn't need to. They weren't a couple, weren't even close anymore.

So clearly following her around the house like she needed him was a logical thing to do.

"Anything missing that you've noticed yet?" Judah asked Cassie, giving Jake a sort of warning look that wasn't necessary. He wasn't planning to say anything else.

Cassie shook her head and moved from the main living area into a hallway. She hesitated in front of the study and then walked in. "This is a mess."

It was an understatement. The desk drawers had been haphazardly opened and half closed like in the other rooms, and there were books all over the floor, some open, pages fluttering, some shut, all of them piled up at least a foot high on the floor.

The shelves were empty.

Had someone flown into a rage and destroyed the order on the bookshelves for no reason? Jake didn't know how to analyze something like that and wasn't convinced Judah was equipped to either. It seemed like something a forensic psychologist would need to work on.

"Why would someone mess with her books?" Cassie frowned and moved toward them, bending down by the pile. She slipped one back onto the shelf and then looked up at Judah. "Am I allowed to fix these? I mean, they're not like evidence, are they?"

"You can fix them. We'll fingerprint them in case, but I doubt the placement of the books matters."

Cassie kept setting them on the shelves, book after book, until the floor was clear. Jake didn't remember going into this room before when he'd been invited to her aunt's house, so he felt like it must have been a special room for her. He understood Cassie's desire to straighten it up.

She was lining up the front covers of the last couple of books with the rest of their row and stopped. Frowned. "I don't remember this row not being full. She has…had…tons of books and never left blank spaces on the shelves."

"Where are the rest of the books?" Judah asked.

Cassie moved to the closet and opened it. There was a box on the top shelf that she pulled down and then unpacked on the desk, in neat stacks. The overflow books seemed to be mostly literature books, classics and a couple of anthologies. She took out three books and fit them into the empty space on the shelf.

"That's better," she said quietly, then frowned at the shelf. "Still…what if…" She met Jake's eyes like she was looking for something, though he didn't know what. He nodded his chin down slightly in encouragement. She looked at Judah. "What if they took some of the books?" She winced. "I know that must sound ridiculous."

"Stranger things have happened. You're here because I trust your eyes, Cassie. I've heard you knew your aunt better than anyone and that means something. If something strikes you as off, even if you can't articulate why, it's worth looking into."

"I'm sure she wouldn't have left her shelves like that,

with some books off. She was pretty particular about this room, actually. I wasn't allowed to borrow her books without permission, like it was her own kind of library." Cassie wore a slight smile. "She used to keep a list where I could sign books out, after she'd given me her permission to read them. I didn't read every book she had, but I read this list enough times to remember most of the titles." She opened the top desk drawer. Jake moved closer to see. The contents were disorganized, but she pulled out a few typed pages of paper.

"Here they are." She set them on the desk, then started scanning the pages. Stopped. Glanced at the shelves. Looked back down.

"I know what's missing."

Jake and Judah both waited. Jake could feel the room grow even more still as they braced themselves for whatever she was about to say.

"But it doesn't make any sense. She actually has some valuable books in this collection."

"Cassie, which books?" Jake spoke up, hoping to keep her focused.

"She had a few self-published books about Raven Pass. Those are what's missing."

Books about the town?

"Let's look through the rest of the house," Judah suggested, clearly dismissing the idea that the missing books were relevant to the investigation.

None of the rooms past the library down the hall had been touched, which in Jake's mind gave credence to Cassie's idea that the books had been taken intentionally. Judah seemed baffled. He was a nice enough guy and Jake didn't get the impression he disbelieved Cassie or anything. Just that her observations didn't jibe with his assumptions about the case.

"When the officers tasked with the recovery come back to town, we will fingerprint the house and see if forensic evidence indicates anything," Judah said as they all walked toward the front door. "And we will call you if we need anything else."

"Okay." Cassie nodded but seemed hesitant.

Jake reached for her hand and tugged her along with him onto the front porch. "Thanks, Officer Wicks. Keep us posted if you will."

"As much as I can." Judah nodded. Jake suspected a call to Levi would probably get him further with information, but he appreciated that the other man at least seemed to understand why they cared so much.

Cassie followed him to the car and they both climbed in. When he shut the door and reached for his keys, he turned sideways enough to see that Cassie's eyes were flashing fire at him.

"Whoa, what's the matter?"

"I wasn't done talking to him and you pulled me out of there like I was yours to control." She rubbed at her hand, at the spot that he'd held. Like doing so would wipe away all evidences of physical contact that had been between them.

He took a deep breath. "I know you weren't done. I can tell."

She opened her mouth but he shook his head and kept talking. "Cassie, stop. Trust me, okay? I know you had more questions, but Judah wasn't the man to ask. He wasn't impressed with the books being missing, and I don't think he was going to listen to any more of your speculations. I, however, am happy to listen, and we're going to go pick up our son, feed him some food, and then after he goes to sleep, you and I are going to discuss it and come up with our own plan of action, okay?"

"Our own plan..." Her eyebrows were raised, the look on her face slightly wary.

"I think we should look into it. The books, I mean. You know which ones they were?"

"I memorized the three titles on the list. The ones that are missing."

"Well either your aunt hid something in one of those books, which is possible, though you'd think they'd have taken it and left the book itself—or there was something in one of the books they were interested in."

"Something worth killing over? I wondered all of that too, that's why I wanted to talk to Officer Wicks. But it doesn't make sense. Why not get the books from the library? Surely they have them."

"Did she make notes in her books?"

Cassie nodded, eyes wide.

"So there may have been notes."

He saw the question asked again in her eyes, from earlier. *Something worth killing over?*

Very possibly. They were close. Jake could feel it. Her aunt's death hadn't been random or a crime of opportunity, not if the house had been gone through like this and things taken.

And Jake was confident that he and Cassie would be able to figure things out.

Cassie couldn't remember ever being flooded with relief quite as much as right now, as her son ran to her open arms while Jake waited in the car for them.

"Did you have a good day?" she asked, bending to kiss his cheek and inhale the scent of his hair.

"It was so fun! They have a bunch of wooden swords and we fought bad guys all day."

Relief was quickly replaced by alarm and Cassie felt her eyes widen as she looked up at Officer Thomas. "Bad guys?"

"Imagined only." He shrugged. "Boys, you know?"

Especially a boy whose dad was a police officer, and a boy who had been shot at by some faceless villain the day before. Yes, it made sense to Cassie, even though she'd rather her little boy had been filled with thoughts of…she didn't know, caterpillars, or worms or something. Maybe boys were supposed to know about bad guys and things like that at six. Cassie didn't know, but yesterday still bothered her more than she could say. She should be thankful, she supposed, that he was processing his feelings well, acting the part of the hero in pretend play. The psychology classes she took in college would have said it was a good sign.

Still, her heart hurt.

*Why?* she asked again, about the whole situation. Again, no answers.

"Thank you for letting him stay here."

"No problem," Officer Thomas said. "He's welcome here tomorrow too."

Cassie nodded slowly. She wanted him with her, but…he'd been safe today, while she'd been at risk on more than one occasion. Either she stepped out of the investigation, even the informal one she and Jake seemed to be conducting on the side, or she trusted someone else to provide some of Will's care.

"We'll have him here about the same time. Thank

you." She hoped her words conveyed all the gratefulness she felt.

Officer Thomas nodded.

Will hurried off to the car. Cassie followed him.

He talked all the way home—or rather, back to Jake's house. Jake Stone's house was not home and never would be.

"So can I?" Will asked her, clearly for the second time.

"Can you what?" Cassie tried to focus.

"Can I have a wooden sword?"

She opened her mouth to say no, a knee-jerk response she wasn't proud of but wasn't going to deny either. "Maybe so, bud. Ask me again when we're home, okay?"

Now she felt Jake's eyes on her, despite the fact that he was supposed to be driving and, you know, paying attention to the road. Cassie stared out the passenger-side window, his unasked questions boring through her like his gaze. What did he expect? That because she'd told him the truth about Will she'd just…pick up her whole life and stay here?

She did have a job. Not the perfect one, but a job. Same with their apartment. Will's school was good though, one of the best in their part of Florida, hence the reason she'd chosen the apartment in the first place.

Raven Pass offered what? Bad memories piled on top of other bad memories?

Not all bad, Cassie knew. But she didn't want to think about those right now.

Instead she went on some kind of autopilot mode and fixed Will dinner at Jake's house again. Over dinner, she asked if he remembered how she'd told him he had a dad somewhere. Jake had gone out of the room; where, Cassie didn't know.

"I remember. You said he loved me a lot but he didn't know me."

A slight embellishment on Cassie's part. She'd known Jake *would* love him, if he knew about him, and it was important to her that Will knew he had two parents who cared about him.

"Right. He didn't know you and it was my fault. I didn't want to share you."

Will frowned. "You're supposed to share."

"I know, sweetie, and I'm sorry. I'm…ready…" she was not ready, not even close, but she knew it was past time, so she kept going "…to share you with him now, okay?"

"So I can meet him?" Will's eyes widened.

"You have, baby… It's Jake."

Cassie braced herself, waited for the fallout she certainly deserved.

"Really? This is awesome! I'll bet he knows how to make wooden swords!" And Will jumped up from the table and went in search of the dad he'd just discovered.

Cassie was left alone, her stomach churning with questions about whether she'd handled this right, or could have done a better job of damage control for her past choice to leave Jake out of Will's life.

*You told him?* Jake mouthed in her direction when he came in a few minutes later, Will attached to his side like a koala.

Cassie nodded.

A shadow flickered across Jake's face but he nodded too.

"Can we play a game? All three of us?" Will was

practically beaming, and Cassie wondered when she should finish explaining things to him. Like the part where even though he had a dad, Cassie was only planning on Will seeing him a few times a year.

How on earth was she supposed to do this?

Instead she said nothing for now, just kept running over options and scenarios in her mind. She and Jake played a few card games with Will until it felt like they'd all settled in enough that he should be able to get some sleep. After the last hand Cassie leaned back and took a deep breath, ready to wage the war for bedtime that seemed to be happening more often the older Will got. He sometimes seemed to think that because he "wasn't sleepy" he might not have to listen to the rules about what time he was supposed to be in bed with the lights out. The past few nights had been exceptions. He'd been so exhausted that he'd conked out as soon as his head hit the pillow.

"Time for bed, Will," Jake said before Cassie got around to it and she almost stopped him. Why, because she was Will's mom? Jake was his dad.

This was much more complicated than she'd ever really thought through, even in her most anxious moments.

Instead of fighting when she had little fight left, she sat still, kissed her son on his forehead when he came over to her with arms outstretched.

"Dad is going to tuck me in." Will smiled up at him, skipped off and left Cassie behind.

With her heartbreak, regrets and an overwhelming feeling of being alone.

"You should have waited for me to be there." When he was done tucking Will in bed and came back downstairs, Jake wasted no time telling Cassie what had been on his mind. He'd been working in his study earlier, detailing some of the search notes for the last few days, when he'd been attacked by a six-year-old boy who'd excitedly declared that Jake was his dad.

He was elated Will knew and happy he didn't have to keep it a secret anymore. He hated secrets.

But she still should have waited for him. He tried to be understanding and not overreact about the entire situation, but the frustration was all building over this one issue. He could feel it, identify it logically, and still it was hard to deal with.

"Couldn't you have let me be part of that one thing, Cassie? I've missed everything. And you had the chance to share this with me because I was right here in the same house and you still couldn't do it?"

The hurt flickering in her eyes wasn't lost on him.

But what was he supposed to do?

*God, how are we ever supposed to work this out?*

"I'm sorry." Her voice was soft, but something in her tone made him meet her eyes. She wasn't self-abasing or being manipulative with her apology to elicit sympathy. She was really just that sorry.

Jake nodded. "Thanks." Focusing on something else for now might be a better idea, he realized, and moved to sit in his favorite chair. Probably he should have sat down before having that last conversation at all. Two people sitting always made for more equal ground in discussions, whereas one standing made it feel unbalanced from the get-go.

"So about those books," he started.

Were those tears she was blinking back? He thought

they might be, but didn't know if they were for her aunt or the way they'd both handled things with Will.

Maybe both.

"What about them?"

"Do you think the library has them?" Jake couldn't say he'd ever searched the library for books about the town. He'd been born in Anchorage and then brought back to his parents' home in Raven Pass at just a couple of days old, so town history was something he'd assumed he knew.

If someone was stealing books for information and potentially killing over it, he suspected he didn't know everything there was to know about the town.

"I would think so." Cassie shrugged. "Which means stealing my aunt's was worthless unless she *had* written things down in them."

"Did your aunt know any town secrets?"

Jake was mostly joking, but Cassie looked lost in thought.

"Cassie?" He called her name, but she still didn't respond. He waited.

"I would have said no." She shook her head. "But... I don't know... She was so strange about that office, Jake. Why *did* she make me write down books I checked out like a real library? Was she really that obsessive? Or did she not want me to read certain books?"

"You never read the ones about Raven Pass?"

"No."

"Do you know anyone who did, or anyone she might have shared them with?"

"No. She kept them to herself, as far as I know."

Jake was out of questions for now. "We need to go to the library and check out those books."

"Tomorrow after we drop Will off?" she asked, so casually that it felt as if they'd always been like this, a real couple, discussing their kid.

Of course they were a real couple doing just that. Only he'd missed six years of these types of discussions.

"Sounds good."

She caught his eyes, whether on purpose or not, he wasn't sure. It was like there was something she wanted to say but she was hesitating.

"Cassie…" He trailed off, memories of six years ago, of the kiss today, of the way he'd tried to tell her they were just friends all swirled together.

Along with guilt. Because surely she'd left for a reason. He'd tried to tell himself for years that if he'd done anything wrong, he would have fixed it if she'd asked, but was it true? Or had he driven her away somehow?

They'd had plans. Dreams. They'd finished high school and had been accepted to a college in Washington, but they'd both decided to do one year of general education courses in Anchorage first. They'd been halfway through that year when they got engaged. They'd just finished it when she left.

"What else?" Jake asked.

"What else, what? About the books?" Her expression said she knew what he meant, but that she was still afraid to go down this road again. It hurt to relive—he got that. But maybe if he understood, they'd finally have some kind of closure and could figure out how to work well together parenting Will, from however far apart they lived.

"About when you left. Please tell me why. The whole truth."

She opened her mouth to talk when Jake heard the

first noise that sounded out of place. Then he heard a creak, a scratch against the siding of the house. Something he wouldn't have noticed before this week, but that now sent alarm bells off in his head.

"Get upstairs."

Cassie was already on her way. A feeling of déjà vu swept over him.

Last time Jake had sent her up there, the man had come inside hunting them, or at least Cassie, when Jake was outside trying to find him. And Jake was putting them all in play the same way. The guy after her was smart, Jake realized, as he moved to a window to see if he could see anything outside. He saw nothing out of place, just dim, hazy midnight sun. The culprit probably expected his noises to draw Jake outside, away from Cassie's side, as they had before.

This time he might get to Cassie. And Jake wasn't going to let that happen. He grabbed his cell phone off the side table by the chair and took the stairs two at a time. Barely winded because adrenaline was coursing through his veins, he made it upstairs just as Cassie was starting to shut the door.

"I'm coming with you." He kept his voice low but saw Will stir on the bed anyway, a shadow in the dim room. His blackout curtains darkened it well. He walked into the room, picked Will up.

"Get his pillows," he told Cassie and opened the closet door with his foot.

"What are you doing?" she whispered after she'd slid the pillow into the closet where Jake was heading with Will and he'd settled their son down on the floor in the back corner. He was glad he kept this closet fairly empty.

"Keeping us safe," he answered as he dialed the police department and described the situation. Five minutes, they told him, and they'd be there.

Jake hoped the guy hung around for five minutes. Then maybe this could all be over, and they could get on with their lives. His breath caught in his throat when he realized that once the danger passed, Cassie would leave again. But at least she'd be safe. Maybe even happy. And that was what Jake wanted.

"Shouldn't you go out there?"

"And let them get to you? No. I'm staying here."

Jake felt his heart pounding in his chest. From fear? Or proximity to the only woman he'd ever loved? Cassie leaned closer and he felt the pace of it quicken even more. That answered that question.

"I'm scared, Jake."

Her voice was low, quavering. He didn't think she'd admitted that this entire time, though she'd already been in enough situations where it would have been appropriate to admit that it was the truth. Without thinking, he reached for her and tugged her close, right up against him in the darkness.

"It's okay. The police will be here any minute."

"That's not what I mean."

Jake frowned, loosed his arms a little, but when she snuggled closer—something he wouldn't have thought possible—he tightened them again. *God, please help me understand why she feels so good in my arms if she's not supposed to be here. Am I supposed to be getting over her? Or asking for another chance?*

He swallowed hard. "What are you scared of?"

"This."

Jake listened hard for sounds outside the closet that would mean they were in trouble. He heard nothing. Though he felt plenty, like he was in trouble in here.

He wanted to ask her what she meant by *this* but he knew full well what she meant. And she had to know it too.

"We aren't just friends, Jake," she said, her voice bolder than he could ever remember hearing it. Not brazen though. Just confident. Irresistibly so.

And she was right. They weren't just friends.

That didn't mean being anything more made sense.

But he couldn't tell her she was wrong.

All he could do was keep listening for trouble. Keep breathing.

And keep trying not to kiss her again even though it was all he wanted to do right now. Jake closed his eyes and swallowed hard, temptation filling him.

If there was any hope of them being together again one day, he wanted things to be different this time. He wanted to honor Cassie and show her how special she was. That meant kisses were going to be a little more limited. Given out carefully.

And not in dark closets.

"I don't think I ever stopped loving you, Jake."

The words he'd always wondered about hit him with the velocity of an unexpected freight train.

His phone rang. It was Levi's cell.

"You're here?" he asked by way of greeting.

"Yes. We saw a truck driving away in front of your house, but no one else here. No sign of anything."

"I'll come downstairs and talk to you." Jake stood and Cassie looked at him questioningly.

"That's Levi Wicks. They don't see anyone out there but I want to check it all out for myself before I go to bed."

"I'll come with you." She stood too and there they were, achingly close again.

"You need to stay inside in case Will needs you, okay?" Or in case of a sniper who'd positioned himself somewhere outside and was lying in wait. Either reason was solid.

"Okay, I'll stay in the living room downstairs," she said as she followed him out of the closet. He watched her look back at Will and hesitate.

"Leave him there for now. It's safer."

Cassie nodded.

Jake talked to the officers downstairs, but it was as Levi had said. There was no sign of attempted entry, and there were no suspects on the premises. They hadn't recognized the truck, and it had been too dark to get a license number.

He felt cheated. Like they'd come so close to stopping the man or men behind this and then only been taunted. And left to recover from the adrenaline crash that came with wondering if this was it—the end of being hunted one way or the other.

When the police drove away, he came back inside and told Cassie what he'd learned, which was fairly close to nothing, but she seemed to appreciate knowing anyway.

After about a minute of silence, letting the news soak in, Cassie stood. "I guess I'll go try to get some sleep." She seemed hesitant and he suspected she might want to pick up the conversation where they'd left off, but he couldn't handle any more tonight. He needed a break. So he just nodded and watched her walk back up the stairs.

"Cassie?" He couldn't stop himself. She paused on the fourth step from the bottom.

"About earlier?"

She waited.

"I'm sure I never stopped loving you."

# TEN

Despite the weight of so many events the day before, or maybe because of them, Cassie slept better than she had in ages. If there had been any more suspicious noises throughout the rest of the night, she hadn't heard them. She stretched, blinking her eyes to try to get some moisture back into them. Then she glanced at the clock.

Past nine o'clock. The library was open by now and they needed to see those books. Cassie fumbled her way out of the covers she'd heaped on top of herself and carried a pile of clean clothes to the bathroom where she took the fastest shower she could and then braided her hair. She never did her hair this way in Florida, but it seemed natural here just to braid it wet and have it out of the way, hanging over her shoulder and down in front on one side just like it had when she was in high school and too busy adventuring to worry too much about her looks.

Of course, Jake had always thought she was beautiful. She'd never doubted that. He'd been good to her, good for her.

And he still loved her. What was she supposed to do with that information? It didn't change the fact that she'd left and didn't deserve him. And it certainly didn't erase all the obstacles.

What Cassie couldn't decide was if it made it harder or easier.

"Wake up, sweetie." She shook Will gently until he finally blinked his own eyes open.

"It's morning already? I barely slept."

Cassie laughed, thinking of the way they'd carried him into the closet, and then how she'd moved him out after she'd come back upstairs for the last time, sure that danger had passed, at least for the moment, and not wanting Will to wake up in the closet and ask questions. By moving him, she'd effectively kept him from knowing that anything strange had happened last night, and after the trauma he'd endured with the gunshots the day before, she was happy with that.

"It's morning and you get to go back to the house with the swords." She kept her voice light, and sure enough, that was all it took to launch Will from bed and send him into a flurry of tooth brushing and clothes changing.

By the time they got downstairs, Jake was dressed too, sitting in a chair, drinking his coffee.

"You guys all ready?" He smiled and Cassie thought she read in his look a hint of teasing at how late she'd slept. Well, let him tease her. She felt amazing and after the last few days she didn't even feel bad. She'd needed that extra rest.

"Ready." Cassie nodded to confirm.

"Breakfast?"

She patted the small backpack she'd slung over her shoulder. "I packed granola bars."

"Those are not breakfast." He made a face and

walked to the kitchen, pulled two plates out of the oven and handed one to each of them. "I made waffles and kept them warm for when you woke up."

"You *made* these?" Cassie confirmed as she set her backpack down to take the plate.

He shrugged. "I've had to eat all these years, you know. How did you think I did that without learning how to cook?" He laughed, and Cassie and Will sat down at the counter on a couple of stools. Cassie guessed the library would still be there in five minutes, but it had been a long time since anyone had made breakfast for her. She certainly wasn't going to let that go to waste.

When breakfast was finished, they piled into the car and drove to Officer Thomas's house to drop Will off. When Cassie moved to get out of the car to update the officer on the other possible attempted attack last night, Jake held out a hand to stop her. "I've got it, okay?"

His face was so hopeful, like he wanted to have this chance to be involved in Will's life, be the one to drop him off, that Cassie couldn't say no. She nodded. "Okay."

She hugged and kissed Will, and he made a face about the kiss on his cheek like he always did. Then he and Jake were off and she sat waiting for a few minutes until Jake returned.

"Everything okay?"

"He's got it under control." Jake let out a breath. "It's a huge relief to have him out of danger during the day."

It was, Cassie had to admit, if only to herself.

They drove to the library and were there within minutes, one of the perks of a small town. Cassie didn't bring up anything about their conversation the night before. Despite what he'd said, she still felt some kind of hesitation in Jake. There was something keeping them from a second chance, but she didn't know what it was and wasn't sure he did either. Besides, they had too much to think about right now, trying to figure out why her aunt had been killed.

And by whom.

They parked in front of the library, a building with a gorgeous mural of Fourteen-Mile River painted on the side of it. That was one thing Cassie had missed in Florida. The municipal building artwork in Alaska was special.

Had she admitted to herself how much she loved it here and how much she missed it? Cassie didn't think so.

"Don't tell anyone why we're looking," Jake said to her, his voice low as he held the glass door for her at the library's entrance. She nodded, but wouldn't have thought of it if Jake hadn't told her. She'd always felt safe in libraries, maybe because her aunt had taken her so much when she was a kid and encouraged her to read.

Still, danger reached every corner of Raven Pass she'd been in so far. Cassie needed to remember not to let her guard down, and to assume that the threat could find her anywhere.

"Hello." The librarian, Mrs. Carpenter, had to be at least as old as the building itself. At least that's how she seemed to Cassie, because she couldn't remember a time without the woman working there. In reality, she was probably only a few years older than Cassie's aunt was…had been… But her hair had gone white early, so when Cassie was younger, she'd always assumed she was ancient.

"Hi, Mrs. Carpenter." Cassie smiled.

Jake frowned at her. Apparently he'd not only meant to keep quiet about what they were looking for, but he would have preferred for them to slip in unnoticed entirely.

*Oops.*

"Anything I can help you with today, dear?" she asked, then her eyes behind her glasses clouded over. "I'm sorry to hear about your aunt."

"Thanks." Cassie darted a glance at Jake. He still wasn't looking much friendlier. "And no, we don't need help," Cassie said and watched Jake's face relax as she said so.

"All right, just let me know." Mrs. Carpenter went back to her work on the computer.

Cassie walked with Jake to the back of the library, where the books about the town were. She pulled the slip of paper from her pocket that she'd written the books' names on last evening to assure herself that she wouldn't forget them.

They searched the shelves. The library had all three books.

Finally something was going their way.

Jake pulled the books from the shelf and nodded to one of the study tables nearby. It sat under a window, with a view of Fireweed Mountain. Cassie followed him over there and they sat, the books stacked between them on the table. Something in Cassie's stomach felt heavy. These books, while not the exact copies that had been stolen, somehow felt like one of the links she had left to her aunt.

And maybe the reason for her death? Cassie didn't

know how, but it made sense. Why else would someone have taken them?

But what kind of notes could have been worth killing someone for? And why would the killer have gone after her too?

"I wish you hadn't said hi to the librarian," Jake whispered.

"Mrs. Carpenter? Why?" Cassie frowned. "I didn't tell her why we were here."

"Yeah, but librarians talk, you know? When was the last time you were in here?"

Cassie couldn't answer. She didn't even remember.

"I don't want her to notice our presence and tell someone about it. We have no idea who it is we're trying to protect you from, and we can't afford her talking to the wrong person."

It made sense to Cassie.

"Sorry, I'll be sneakier."

Jake raised his eyebrows. "It would be hard not to be sneakier than that."

Cassie made a face, then looked at the stack of books again. Reached for one of them.

She opened the first book. It didn't tell her too much she hadn't heard. Raven Pass had been founded over one hundred years ago by miners, but they hadn't lasted long in the Alaskan climate and their settlement had come to ruin. Settlers tried again in the 1930s, when another gold rush farther north inspired people to try in many different places. One of them found gold then, or so the legend went. But no one knew for sure because the gold had disappeared around the time of a grisly double murder.

Cassie had forgotten, somehow, the legend of the

Raven Pass gold. Odd, because she could remember people talking about it, especially the elementary school–aged kids, around Halloween. The whole town had been fascinated by it. Eventually talk had died down some, but it was still one of those things everyone in Raven Pass knew about, just by virtue of being from there.

Jake was looking through another one of the books, but he stopped reading and looked at her. "Your aunt didn't know about the gold, did she?"

"The legend?" Cassie whispered back, conscious to keep her voice at a library-appropriate level, and of the fact that someone could be listening. "Of course she did. All of us do."

He shook his head. "That's not what I mean. Did she know more about it?"

She'd barely talked to Cassie about it. That didn't really speak to someone who had extra information about the subject.

Unless it did. Unless she'd been keeping something from Cassie. Was it easier not to talk about the subject at all than to try to be selective about what information she shared?

Which fit with the aunt she'd known. Cassie didn't know what to say, didn't know what to think.

Chills went down her backbone the more she thought about it, and the idea of sitting in front of the window was awkward.

"Can we leave?" she asked Jake, swallowing hard. "I feel…weird."

*Like someone was watching her.*

He nodded. "Let's make copies of the pages about the treasure and the rumors."

"Out of the whole book, you're that sure it's what it has to do with?"

"What else about Raven Pass could lead to someone being willing to commit murder? The gold and the legend make sense."

Cassie knew he was right, but it didn't make sense at all. Not really. Not with everything she remembered about her aunt. She shivered again and moved away from the window.

Somehow it felt like someone was out there. And whether Cassie was being paranoid or not, she couldn't shake the feeling, couldn't stop her skin from crawling.

Would she ever feel safe again?

Making copies didn't take long and Jake was able to do it without asking for help. He was relieved by that. He didn't want the older woman talking about why they'd been there researching.

As it was, no one would ever know. He finished making copies of the last book, only the sections about the Raven Pass gold and the legend that surrounded it, and then returned the books to the shelf. Cassie followed along behind him, not saying much, but clearly not wanting to be alone.

"Are you okay?" he finally asked her as he pulled the finished copies out of the machine.

She shook her head. "No." Her voice was even quieter than the library called for. "I feel weird. Like when I'm near a window, someone's watching me."

"Which window?" he asked, not willing to take chances.

She nodded her head toward where they'd been sitting earlier. Jake walked over to it, careful to keep Cassie out of the line of vision from anyone outside.

But he didn't see anything out of place. Just the town itself, and the mountains on one side. This was the back of the building. The car was out front.

"I don't feel it anymore," she mumbled, then shrugged. "Maybe I am just being overly anxious."

Jake wasn't inclined to think so. Cassie wasn't the kind of woman who was naturally suspicious and concerned. If she'd felt like someone was watching her, there was a decent chance someone had been. Then why not now?

He wanted to get her back home. They could look at this information there, and while he had no illusions that his house was bulletproof either figuratively or literally, it was his home turf and therefore easier to defend and to keep Cassie safe in.

"Ready to leave?" He tried to keep his voice casual, but it did nothing to ease the tension he could see in her jaw.

"Yes, please."

They walked to the front of the library together.

"Have a good day," the librarian called. So much for sneaking out unnoticed. The woman saw everything.

Jake didn't want Cassie outside for long unprotected, even though he was pretty sure that now *he* was the one being paranoid, so he unlocked his vehicle from the entryway of the building.

"Don't waste time getting in the car, okay?"

Cassie nodded. "Okay."

For a crazy second, Jake thought maybe he felt it too, the sensation of being watched, but it was the tension overwhelming him. He wasn't the one in danger, Cassie was.

He didn't hear the concussive blast of the rifle shot until it had already kicked up part of the sidewalk a couple feet from his feet.

"Car, Cassie, now!" he yelled and looked around to try to figure out where the shots had come from. Which left him a still target, but they weren't after him.

"Jake!"

"I'm trying to find the muzzle flash."

He saw it, somewhere on the hillside just above town to the south, just before he felt a searing pain in his arm. The force made him flinch sideways and he felt himself falling.

Then he hit the sidewalk hard and his head hurt, hurt, hurt.

Until it was all black.

He was behind her, taking too long to get to shelter, when Cassie heard the second shot and then saw him fall. Cassie didn't hesitate, but ran in his direction, knowing if he wasn't unconscious, he'd yell at her for heading toward danger instead of away from it. The fact that he didn't protest, and his eyes didn't open, told her how bad it was.

*Please don't let him be dead.*

She hurried to his side. She could see the bullet wound, which looked like more of a graze. At least there was that slight bit of reassurance. He wasn't going to die from that wound, not unless she couldn't get him out of the line of fire. She tugged at him but he was too heavy. She looked behind her, toward where the shot had come from.

Nothing. No hint of movement. Wasn't she the one in danger? She could be in their sights right now, kneeling on the hard concrete sidewalk that was digging through the knee of her pants. Cassie could imagine the scene. She was vulnerable, no question.

So why wasn't anyone shooting?

"Jake, you have to wake up." She shook him.

Still nothing.

"Jake. Now!" She raised the volume of her voice as she felt frustration building in her. Not toward Jake, he couldn't help it, but at the entire situation. Doubt clouding her mind, she reached for his wrist and felt for a pulse on the off chance she was wrong, and something had been fatal. The fall, maybe. Her own heart pounded as she waited for her fingers to feel the reassuring thump of his heart rate.

There it was. He was alive and breathing, she now saw when she looked at his chest. All of that was good news. He was just very, very unconscious.

Movement out of the corner of her eye caught Cassie's attention. There, coming from the side of the library, one hundred feet away, maybe, someone was heading slowly in her direction.

She opened her mouth to ask for help, human instinct overriding her caution. Until her brain finally registered that the man coming toward her was dressed entirely in black and had some kind of firearm strapped to his waist.

Not help. Someone she needed to run from.

Cassie glanced back at the car, right there, so close but doing her no good. She wondered if the librarian had heard the shot, but even if she had, here in Alaska she might just figure it was a hunter too close to town.

Cassie could leave Jake, which is what she knew he would want, but she wouldn't. Not now. She'd done it once and paid for it every day since. This time, she wasn't going to make the same mistakes.

"I. Am. Not. Leaving. You!" She punctuated each word, gritted out through her clenched teeth, with a tug on Jake's shirtsleeve. On the last Jake's lashes fluttered. Then his eyes went wide.

"Hurry!" she yelled at him and he stood, slowly, but enough that she was able to pull him toward the passenger side of the car. She climbed in the driver's seat, took the keys he offered and floored it out of the space just as the man who'd been coming closer started running at her. Cassie exhaled deeply, then startled as she realized there had been another man she hadn't seen. He was dressed the same way, all black, nothing identifying about his features, running for the front of the car.

"Don't stop," Jake ordered.

Cassie kept driving but felt herself tensing as the figure moved to the center of the road. "I can't hit him."

"He'll move. Go, Cassie!"

She hit the gas. The man dove out of the way at the sound of the engine revving and relief flooded her. She drove without saying a thing for at least the next sixty seconds and then finally managed to put a thought into word form. "Are you okay?" Not wanting to take her eyes off the road, but needing to see for herself that he was really awake, alive and sitting next to her, Cassie glanced in Jake's direction quickly.

Her own heart jumped, skittered in her chest. Adrenaline, surely. Not a reaction to Jake.

Everything in her wanted to go straight to Will and pick him up, but even though a glance in the rearview mirror showed no one following them, Cassie wasn't taking any chances.

The first couple of attacks in broad daylight had been easy to explain away, at least for Cassie. First, she'd been alone during hours that most people weren't on the streets. Next, they'd been in the woods. No witnesses there except for the other people in the group.

But attacking outside the library? Shooting onto the actual sidewalks of Raven Pass? Cassie couldn't remember this kind of attempted violence in town ever. Not at any time during her childhood. She supposed at some point years before that a double murder would have had to have taken place in order for the whole Raven Pass treasure legend to be true, but even that was rumored to have happened in the mountains outside of town.

She wasn't safe here. Cassie pressed her foot down a little harder on the gas.

She shouldn't have come here. She pressed harder.

"Cassie, you've got to slow down."

His voice was calm. Steady but firm, and she let her foot off the gas immediately. "I'm sorry. I just can't…" She trailed off. Her voice was wavering, and her hands were tight on the steering wheel. Being in this kind of danger wasn't something she was used to.

"Drive us back to my house, okay?"

She had been driving with no destination in mind, but she was close to the edge of town. Cassie suspected she was subconsciously heading for Anchorage, though of course leaving town wouldn't solve any problems and she'd never leave without Will anyway.

For that matter…would she leave again ever? What was waiting for her in Florida?

Emotions still running high, she stole another glance at Jake.

"We should get you to a doctor," she said. His face looked pale, and she could tell he was hurting.

"I'm fine. Between the two of us, we can clean the wound and patch me up."

"Jake…"

"You're a nurse, right? I'm an EMT. Head home." His voice was strained, and she didn't want to upset him, so she did as he asked.

Maybe it was okay to admit that she cared about him still. Almost losing him today had made that hard to deny.

He caught her looking this time, and looked back at her. She turned her eyes back to the road immediately.

"So someone knew we were at the library…" Jake trailed off. "Did they know what we looked at? Or just that we were there? No one saw the books we looked at, not even the librarian."

"Are you thinking she let someone know that we were there? Like on purpose?" Cassie couldn't picture the old librarian being involved with any of the people who wanted her dead.

"No, but I heard the door open and close a few times while we were in there and saw some other people in the library."

"Of course, it's the library and it's morning. I would imagine that's one of their busier times." Cassie pulled into Jake's driveway, finally, and let out a deep breath when she had put the car in Park.

"My point is that she saw us come in and easily could have made a comment to someone that we were there, and they could have guessed what we were looking at."

"Like a coincidence thing? You think someone came in at the same time and passed the information along to whoever is after me." She frowned as she said the words. Were they even after her? It was starting to seem like they were after Jake.

"It could be that. I was thinking more like someone could have been following us and watched us from a distance in the library."

Cassie shivered, remembering how she felt someone had been watching them.

"Are we going inside to continue this conversation in the house? Personally I'm partial to the house as it has water and I'm extremely thirsty, and there are some bandages in there. I'd prefer not to bleed all over my car."

Cassie felt exposed on the walk from the car into the house—Jake's garage was too full of tools and other equipment to park inside it—and right now Cassie wished she could tease him about it instead of dealing with this serious situation.

Once they were inside, she wanted to clean his wound and bandage him, but he insisted on stopping in the kitchen for water first. "Someone watching from inside the library, like you said, someone who maybe followed us there and came in afterward, could explain how I felt like I was being watched."

Jake seemed to be considering the idea, as he leaned against the counter and took another long sip from his glass. "You thought it was coming from outside though. It could just as easily have been whoever shot at us."

"True." Cassie had to concede the point. "But I'm also not used to pinpointing where someone might be watching me from. I just know when I have a general creepy feeling come over me, you know?"

That seemed to make sense to Jake.

"Either way, there's a small chance today was purely a target of opportunity, but it seems like a strange place for an attack if it was."

"It's much more likely we were attacked because we're getting closer," Cassie said, lowering her voice some even though they were the only two people in the house.

"I agree." Jake nodded. "Which means…"

"We need to turn the investigation over to the police and stay out of it?"

Jake shrugged. "I was going to say that it means we need to be extremely careful. Someone is tracking you."

# ELEVEN

Cassie seemed to be thinking over his words, but told him to go into the bathroom so she could look at the bullet graze where his first aid kit was. He'd listened to her and made his way into the large guest bathroom downstairs, and she'd followed him in, but then he'd thought better of letting her touch him when his thoughts about her were already so confused, and had resisted her efforts to see it, clean it or put any kind of antiseptic lotion on it.

"Just let me see it." Cassie reached for his arm again, her tone growing more frustrated.

Jake tugged his arm away as she stretched out her hand, barely moving it away in time. He almost wished he was wearing long sleeves, but then again with the way she was taking this so seriously, she'd probably make him peel his shirt off. Not something he wanted to do in a small room alone with Cassie. Just thinking about it made him swallow hard and wish he had something else to focus on right now.

"It's fine, Cassie."

"I still think you need to go to the hospital. How are you supposed to keep me safe if you have an untreated concussion, or if this wound goes septic, hmm?" She stepped closer.

Jake stepped backward. She was cute when she was mad. He'd never tell her so, since it was far from politically correct and would only make her angrier, but it was true. He tried not to smile.

Apparently not hard enough. Her frown deepened.

"Do not laugh at me, Jake Stone." She stepped closer again.

He tried to move back, but there was nothing behind him but the bathtub. She'd blocked him into the room. Despite her warning, he laughed, and tried to deflect from the fact that he was so overwhelmed by her closeness right now that he didn't care about a stupid gunshot wound or a little head trauma. "You know, I'm a paramedic. I do know some of the same stuff you do. Concussion protocol, wound care..."

"And you're also proof of the fact that doctors or people in the medical field make the worst patients. You can't treat yourself and you know it. Now hush." She grabbed his arm, far enough away from the graze that it didn't hurt. Her hands on his arm brought all his focus there, and all he could think about were her fingers on his skin.

So he hushed. Didn't say a word.

She examined the wound first, then proceeded to clean it, apply triple antibiotic and then dress it. All things he could have done himself. And without the overload of emotions.

If she hadn't left, they could have been married by now. He'd thought it more than once before, but it kept surfacing, probably because he couldn't for the life of him figure out why they weren't. On his end, were there any real reasons not to start something again? Other than the fear of being hurt.

Fear was no way to live. He'd almost died today.

Maybe that was why when she came near, he caught his breath, was fully aware of how close their faces were with her leaning down like that, and how easy it would be to press his lips to hers and pick up where they'd left off with that kiss yesterday...

But it wasn't wise to do so. Not in this room alone, emotions high from the day. He'd determined to do better this time. So he decided to talk instead.

"About today..." he started.

Cassie shook her head. "I don't want to talk about it yet."

Her voice quavered at the end and Jake stopped speaking. She looked over at him, relief relaxing her features. "Thank you."

He nodded. Then couldn't resist. "I'm okay, Cassie. God protected me."

She snorted.

And he felt himself pull away.

"What did that mean?" he asked, wanting to stay calm. She'd said several things about God during their relationship and engagement that he'd been a little concerned about, but she hadn't grown up in church like he had. Jake had been raised in church and had trusted Jesus to save him when he was seven years old. Cassie...

At the time Jake hadn't known much about Cassie's story, faith-wise. He wasn't one to preach, but rather to lead by example. In hindsight, he wished he'd pushed a little more, asked more questions. He'd been in the dark then about her deepest beliefs, if she had any at all.

And the same was true now, he realized.

Dread settled in his stomach as all the pieces fit together. Her lack of knowledge, comments like this, the way she'd pulled away from any attempts at spiritual conversations when they'd dated before. "What, Cassie?" he asked again, needing to know now. He had years' worth of questions he feared might be getting answered right now.

Did Cassie even know Jesus? Jake wasn't judging. He didn't think doubts defined a person's faith. But the fact was…he wasn't sure she'd ever given him any reason to believe she trusted Jesus personally. She'd only been very tolerant of his faith, he now realized.

"I just don't know why you say stuff like that."

"About God protecting me?" That seemed obvious to him. He was alive. She was alive. Surely she could see how that provided some evidence of God at work, especially when one considered how many other times they'd been attacked in the last few days.

"If He's God, why doesn't He just stop it all, Jake? Why?" She'd stopped doctoring his arm and was pacing the bathroom, looking back at him now and then. Her shoulders were tense, in a defensive posture, like this was something she wasn't fully comfortable talking about.

Now that he let himself think about it, Jake remembered her asking before about how God could let bad things happen, but he'd written it off as a common struggle some Christians have.

Now he was wondering…

"Cassie, it comes down to this. Do you trust Jesus?"

She stopped. Looked straight at him. "No, Jake, I really don't."

And he didn't know what to say to that. Instead he prayed, right there, his arm bandaged, head pounding, sitting on the closed lid of a toilet while the woman he'd wanted to marry stood in front of him telling him that they never should have planned to get married in the first place.

Why had he never realized Cassie didn't believe?

*God, why did I fall so deeply in love with her if I was never supposed to have her?* He'd no sooner articulated the prayer than he rejected part of its premise. He had full confidence they were supposed to be together. Or… were supposed to have been at one point?

All confidence faded.

*I love her, God. But she doesn't love You.*

And they had a son together. But she wasn't a believer.

What did he do with that?

"Cassie." Jake took a breath, focused on her, on the fact that there was a real person in front of him, one he loved very much, who didn't understand how much the God who created the world loved *her* personally. "I don't want to fight with you, but I promise, God can handle your anger, okay? He's real and He gets what we are feeling better than we do. You can ask Him all this stuff."

"Even if I'm not sure I believe in Him?" Her face was defiant, but he saw in her eyes a flicker of hope he chose to cling to.

"Talk to Him, Cassie. And think about this week, okay?"

"My aunt was killed. Not died in her sleep or anything like that, killed. Homicide. You know the coroner is going to confirm that. That's what happened this week."

"And even though we've been shot at multiple times, we are okay. Will is okay. Even the fact that you left before could have saved your life—what if you and Will had been with your aunt the day she was taken? Look at the other side here and maybe you'll see God at work, Cassie."

"I may not." She said it like a warning. But she didn't argue, and Jake thought that was positive.

"Just try, okay?"

She nodded and then moved back to him. "How is your head? Any double vision?"

He let her keep nursing him for now, even while his heart pounded along with the churning in his stomach. He still loved her. But he couldn't let himself think past being her friend for now, not when she didn't believe like he did. Even if the Bible didn't say not to marry an unbeliever, he'd known too many people who had divorced over faith issues. When he did get married, he wanted it to be forever.

But he also wanted it to be with Cassie.

*God, help me. And help her believe.*

Cassie turned over in the bed again and pushed the button on her cell phone to see the time. 2:28 a.m. At this rate, she might not sleep at all tonight, if she didn't fall asleep soon.

Jake's words from earlier, about God's protection, kept rolling through her mind. It was crazy how much shifting her perspective, to tentatively wondering if his explanation could be right, made her see things differently.

Could it be true that God had protected them?

Yes, she admitted finally as she turned over another time, back to the side where she'd started just now.

But still, why let the bad things happen in the first place? That was a question she couldn't seem to answer. Would reading the Bible help, or would it just push her further away?

It was important to Jake that she believed. They'd been in some kind of dance all day long, since that kiss. Toward each other, then away. Together. Away. Jake was pulling away again and she knew it was because of the faith issue. Cassie also knew from all the times she'd spent listening to Jake's pastor preach in church during high school that she couldn't make decisions about her own relationship with God—like if she wanted to have one—based on someone else. It was a personal thing. That much she understood.

But she didn't understand God. And she wanted to.

But maybe she wasn't supposed to.

Her head was starting to hurt, whether in sympathy to Jake's injury or from all the thinking, or more likely exhaustion, she wasn't sure. Cassie rubbed her forehead and rolled to her stomach, burying her face in the pillow.

*Okay, God, if You're real, I'll give You a chance to show me, okay? Just make it clear. Like maybe help us with this case. And help me get to sleep.*

Cassie sank deeper into the pillow and felt herself drifting off.

She woke up to crying, but slowly, like her body had been so deep into sleep it had to shake off several layers of mental blankets to even make it to this dazed, half-awake state.

There was a shadow at the foot of the bed holding Will, who was crying. She tensed but instantly relaxed when she realized it was Jake. Holding their son.

Cassie blinked her eyes to wake up, to get used to the darkness, and to try to reconcile what she was seeing.

She wanted to be with this man forever. Why did she keep trying to deny that? The way he held Will so carefully amazed her. Still, it wasn't helping Will who looked to be having one of his rare, but occasional, night terrors.

"He won't stop crying." Jake's voice was heartbroken and puzzled. "Does he want you?"

"Sometimes he can't wake up. It's like his mind gets stuck." Cassie reached for him and sat him up. "Will, buddy? Can you hear me?"

It took a few seconds but he eventually nodded.

"Okay, it's time to go to sleep now."

He started to cry again. Cassie wanted to cry too. She was exhausted, and when she was awake, she was thinking about her aunt and the fact that she'd never get to see her again. Memories of her aunt brought back remembrances of nights like these. It had been her aunt who'd woken up with her, who'd tucked her in at night. Her dad had done what he could but he'd been grieving her mom's abandonment and he'd been so busy with work. Much of her comfort as a kid had come from her aunt.

"Want me to tell you a story?" she asked as she thought about Aunt Mabel. She'd told her the same bedtime story nearly every night. It had been years since she'd heard it, and she'd never thought before to tell it to Will, but being up here in Alaska made her nostalgic. And it was a tiny piece of her aunt she could hold onto. "Listen, my sweetheart, to this tale. For from it, you will learn how to do the right thing, and from the truth, never to turn."

The familiar opening slipped off her lips like she'd told it a thousand times instead of just listened to it. Memory was a funny thing. Cassie snuggled her son closer and continued.

"Once upon a time there was a princess who was as kind as she was beautiful. Her hair was golden, and the men of the kingdom were enchanted with her. One night, while she was sleeping in her castle at the base of a mountain, a man stole her away to his mountain cave. The man who had planned to marry the princess was brokenhearted and determined to find her. He pushed through crowds of trees and devil's club to trace the steps her captors had taken. He climbed mountains."

Will smiled a little. "I climbed a mountain."

"You did," Cassie agreed. "Part of one, anyway. Back to the story, okay? Ah yes, the prince. So he climbed mountains. He ignored the promise of other thrones if he'd abandon his quest and followed straight ahead instead. He was not stopped by rivers, and he even pursued, like true north, his princess, into the heart of darkness where she was kept. He navigated the maze to the dungeon. Left, right, left, left, and there she was alone and cold. He gathered her in his arms and kissed her, but he didn't just stay there. He took her back to the town, where the people had loved her, and they were married there."

"I saw a throne once," Will mumbled as Cassie settled him back down onto his pillow, since he'd looked to her like he was sleeping. And maybe he was, he certainly wasn't making much sense.

"Okay, sweetheart." It was better to agree with him when he was like this.

"When we were hiking. There was a throne on the rock. We turned there and walked a *loooooooong* way…" His voice trailed off and Cassie smiled at him. Then her smile fell.

She looked at Jake.

They had turned, abandoned a trail at a rock that, according to Will, had looked like a throne. They hadn't continued straight ahead.

Shivers crawled down her arms, then back up again. "You don't think…"

He nodded slowly. "Your aunt knew where the Raven Pass treasure was."

Cassie whispered back. "And she told me how to find it."

# TWELVE

Jake led them to the room where they'd talked the other night and Cassie had been so sure there wasn't any kind of second chance for them. She wasn't sure how she felt now. Sometimes she was positive Jake still cared, and at other times she knew she'd destroyed what they had beyond repair years ago.

Right now she didn't know what she thought. The look on his face… Her stomach jumped if she paid too much attention. But he sat in a chair after she'd taken the couch, which seemed to imply he didn't want to be that close to her.

*Stop analyzing.*

Cassie started talking so she'd stop thinking and overthinking. "Thanks for calming him down before I woke up, or trying anyway." She offered him a smile as she sat. "It was so weird seeing someone else hold him and take care of him… I missed that, raising him alone. And I'm sor—"

He cut her off before she could apologize again. "You've already told me you're sorry. It doesn't change the past, okay? Just let it go. I'm trying to."

Was it that easy for him? Because it wasn't for Cassie.

Her shoulders sagged as she attempted once again to take the grace he was offering her. It didn't seem real, the way he was willing to forgive her for it and move on. But then again, that's what his church taught, and what Jake said that the Bible taught too. Jake took his faith seriously, so maybe Cassie should understand his behavior.

It was strange to Cassie that Jake should have been so surprised by her own lack of faith. She'd never meant to give him the impression while they were dating and then engaged that she agreed with him. But she was respectful and had assumed that meant something to him. Still, he'd acted strange since she'd told him that no, she didn't trust God like he did. Or at all, for that matter.

She hadn't read enough of the Bible to know if there was a reason that the faith aspect could be a deal breaker for him, but it was bothering him to some degree.

"So tomorrow…" Cassie decided it was better to stick with a neutral subject, and this was the only one they had. The rest of the possible topics of conversation were littered with unseen landmines.

"We need to get back to the trailhead and see if we can find the treasure."

"For real, Jake, isn't it time we involve the police? Especially because I'm starting to wonder if you were the target of the gunshots all along. Maybe they'd planned…" She stumbled. "…to kill you and then take me like they did my aunt. To try to make me help them find the treasure. They must assume I know where it is."

He shook his head. "We still have no proof. We only have a guess. And you saw how Judah looked at us last night. I may send a text to Levi, just as a courtesy to a friend, but the department as a whole is not impressed with our working theory. Besides, the fewer people who know, the safer you might be. Remember the library—someone must have seen you there, tipped someone off."

Cassie knew he was right. She'd seen the look on Officer Judah Wicks's face when she mentioned her idea. He didn't seem to be a man given to guesses or hunches; she could tell from the brief dealings she'd had with him. Best-case scenario would be they turned over their idea to the police, and the authorities ran with it, catching their culprit. Worst-case? Their information stirred up more trouble, more risk. Possibly for nothing, if their theory wasn't correct.

It was better not to say anything. After all, nothing they were doing was illegal or even unethical. Unwise? Possibly. But Cassie had grown desperate to try to find whoever killed her aunt whatever way she was able. Her only hesitation was Will's safety, but the situation they had worked out right now with him staying with that other family was going well.

Of course, the father, who was a police officer and the reason Cassie felt comfortable with the deal, had to go back to work in two days. They had tomorrow, the next day, and then that option would be taken from them and Will would be back with Cassie. She'd be out of the investigation then, formal or informal or otherwise. She'd lock herself up in this house with her son until someone else solved the case if she had to, but she wouldn't expose him to any danger if she could help it.

"So…"

Cassie hadn't realized until just then that Jake was sitting there, watching her as she thought. She had a feeling every idea she'd considered, every emotion, must have been displayed clearly on her face, because he looked hesitant, like he knew she was having second thoughts. And third thoughts.

"I think you're right," she heard herself say before she was sure she was ready. "We need to go hunt some treasure tomorrow."

"Okay, so let's look at the map and mark the places we think relate to the fairy tale, shall we?"

He pulled up an internet satellite map system on the laptop he'd brought to the chair with him. Cassie could barely see it from where she was on the couch, because of the angle of the screen.

Jake glanced her way and noticed her problem. "Sorry," he said, then picked up the laptop and moved next to her. Not so close that their thighs were touching, but on the same couch anyway.

Cassie felt her breath catch ever so slightly and wished she could roll her eyes at herself without Jake noticing. What was she, sixteen with a crush?

No, this was the same man she'd had a crush on when she was that age though, which was maybe why her feelings were so strong. Jake had been her first and only love. Men had asked her out in Florida, but she'd used Will as an excuse, going on one or two first dates before giving up on the proposition entirely. She was focusing on being a single mom, she told people.

*She still loved Jake.* That was the truth. She'd been close last night, when she said she wasn't sure. But now she was. Fully, completely sure. She felt her shoulders relax as the tension left her body.

If they could just get past this, find the treasure, get some assurance of safety…

Then was there a chance? Jake's words had led her to believe there was, last night. But he'd not indicated anything of the sort today. Cassie believed some people who were truly in love with someone else never did get their happily-ever-after. Even if both of them loved each other. Relationships failed for a lot of reasons, or never got fully off the ground. They had enough reasons between them to ruin several relationships.

The biggest was the way she'd kept Will from him. But he insisted she didn't need to apologize anymore, so that meant it was in the past, right?

That maybe they had some kind of future?

"Do you see this line right here?" Jake motioned to the computer screen and Cassie turned her attention back to it. Yes, there in the trees, a thin line of tan seemed to go into the woods and then disappear.

"Yes."

"Part of that is where we were the other day. But judging by the directions in your story…" He frowned. "Can you say it again for me?"

"I'll do better than that. I'll write it down if you'll bring me some paper." She smiled up at him and he handed her the computer while he went to get a notebook. She studied the aerial view of the location as he did so. Strange to think that the location of the treasure could have been photographed by satellite. Of course they couldn't see the treasure or any indication of where it was, not from the altitude of the picture, but the general topography, trees, rivers were all there—it was strange to think it was there too, hidden.

So close. Still so far.

"Here you go." He handed her the notebook and sat back down, taking the computer from her.

This time he sat closer to her, and whether he'd done it on purpose or not, it was distracting her to no end.

Cassie reminded herself she was an adult and could certainly pay attention no matter whose thigh was pressed against hers.

She swallowed hard.

She could pay attention, right?

"Okay…" She took the pen Jake held out and started writing the story down as best she remembered it. Some of her aunt's word choices had varied. It wasn't like a poem that had particular lines, just a story. The only part repeated perfectly was the bit at the beginning about remembering what you heard.

"She really was trying to get me to remember," Cassie observed as she wrote those lines. "But why?"

Jake shook his head.

"I don't remember her talking about the treasure or the legend ever, which means she talked about it a lot less than the average Raven Pass citizen. Why spend every night then telling me how to find it?"

"She clearly didn't take it. She would have been too young or not even born then." Jake sounded like he was thinking aloud, but Cassie nodded because she agreed with him.

"Right. We may never know," Cassie offered, though she hoped that wasn't the case. But still, it was better to be prepared for the possibility than to be heartbroken if it turned out to be true. Bracing against unrealistic expectations was something she'd caught herself doing many times since her happily-ever-after with Jake hadn't happened. Yes, that had been her fault, but it didn't seem to matter.

"I think we will." He sounded much more confident than she felt. He continued working at the computer, pressing buttons, zooming in and surveying the land and then zooming out again. He finally printed the general area and together they highlighted the basic trail it sounded like they should take. Where directions were vague, they highlighted large chunks of Alaskan wilderness.

It could take days to thoroughly search the area, longer than that if they accounted for the time needed to look in extremely small spaces. But Cassie didn't think that would be necessary. *The heart of darkness* in the story could only be something like a cave, of which there weren't many in this part of Alaska, or possibly an old hollow stump hole, which sometimes seemed like vast holes in the ground, or a mining shaft. The entire area around Raven Pass, especially on the north side against those mountains, was known for having been active during at least one of the gold rushes. Cassie believed there were mining shafts that hadn't been explored since the time of the murders and the gold's disappearance, but she didn't know how difficult it would be to find them. Terrain could have changed, trees could have grown up. Even with the "throne" Will had noticed as a starting point, they could still have a considerable amount of trouble finding it from there.

Could her aunt have tried to show people where the treasure was and then been unable to find it? And why, after all these years, did someone know her aunt might have a clue to the treasure's location? Cassie just didn't know. She should probably stop speculating because it was starting to give her a headache.

Or that could be because it was the middle of the night and she wasn't sleeping.

"I need to go back to sleep," she finally said when fatigue had overwhelmed all of her senses.

"Sleep well."

Jake reached out to squeeze her arm and Cassie stopped. She'd been starting to stand, but his touch made her lose all motivation to leave.

"Thank you," she said in a whisper, meeting his eyes. "You didn't have to do any of this. You didn't have to try to keep me safe, or try to figure out why someone killed my aunt, but you are." She shrugged, suddenly feeling self-conscious and too vulnerable. Late nights made her feel this way. "Anyway, thanks."

"Cassie…"

She couldn't read his tone, couldn't tell from his voice what he wanted. And it was impossible to say who moved first, but one minute they were sitting side by side on the couch and she was talking, and the next she leaned into him, or he'd leaned into her, and they were kissing again, all the familiarity and magic of the past mingling with something that made her stomach flutter—hope of having a future.

Tired or not, Cassie didn't want the kiss to end. She kept her eyes closed, kept saying with her lips what she was still too afraid to say with her words. Jake said everything back to her.

And then he pulled away. Shook his head.

And she knew by the look in his eye that she had been wrong to think the words he'd said last night meant what she wanted them to. He was sure he still loved her, he said.

But that didn't mean they had a future.

She swallowed hard, brushed at invisible lint on her jeans. "I'm sorry, I don't know…"

"It wasn't just you." His voice was thick with feeling. "We can't do this, Cassie."

And somehow she thought maybe if she fought for

them this time, maybe if she didn't give up so easily, things would be different. "I won't leave again, Jake. I'll be here, like I promised last time. We can start over, but better, you know?"

She waited, but all he did was shake his head.

"I can't, Cassie."

She stared in his eyes till she saw it. The faith issue. It was a bigger deal to him than she'd anticipated, and it was something he hadn't known to be true the last time around.

Could they not get married because of that? It was *that* important to Jake? She wanted to be angry, but it was part of who he was. His commitment to doing what he felt was right was part of why she loved him; Cassie knew that. To change him would be changing him in such a fundamental way that he wouldn't even be the same person she was in love with.

He was being true to his beliefs. She admired him for it.

But it still broke her heart.

She stood. Nodded. "I understand." Another hard swallow. "Don't worry about it, okay? We can still figure this out together. I still want Will to know you. We'll be friends. Like you said, right?" She nodded again and turned to the door.

Then she brushed a tear from her eye.

She'd almost had the fairy-tale ending with Jake, and she'd been the villain in that story who stole it from herself by leaving. She should have known a second chance was too good to be true. She should never have gotten her hopes up.

Because the thing about hopes?

They hurt the worst when they come crashing down.

\* \* \*

Jake sat in the dark for another half hour after Cassie left, trying to figure out what he could have done differently. Well, not kissed her for one, but she'd been sitting there, looking gorgeous, and he had told her the truth, he did still love her. He was every bit as in love with her as he had been years ago. But none of those feelings changed what was right, and she didn't believe the same way he did.

It shouldn't have been a deal breaker, not in his opinion, not when they had a son together. But truth was truth and it didn't change no matter what your preferences or situations or circumstances. Hadn't he been saying that for years? Here was his chance to live it.

When he'd thought out their situation from every angle, and spent some time praying too, Jake finally went back to bed. He slept lightly though. Too many things on his mind to do otherwise.

By the time he got downstairs for breakfast just after six o'clock, Cassie was already awake and scrambling eggs.

"Did you sleep okay?" he asked as he started toward the coffee maker to brew a pot only to find she'd already made enough for both of them. Jake blinked, the contrast to last night, the bad way it had ended, hurting him somewhere in his chest.

She shut off the burner she'd been using and separated the eggs onto two plates. She handed him one and then pulled bread out of a toaster, placing it on each plate before walking to the table. He followed.

"Not really." She finally answered the question as she reached for a jar of strawberry jam she must have put on the table earlier. She met his eyes and he blinked against the unflinching nature of her gaze. He didn't know what he'd expected after last night, maybe for her to be embarrassed, or upset with him, he wasn't sure. But he hadn't expected this. She seemed bolder. More confident.

One thousand times more beautiful and irresistible.

"I'm sorry about that," he said and then put jam on his own toast. Cleared his throat. "About the search today…"

"Do you want to start as soon as Will wakes up?"

He nodded.

"I can get him up if necessary. He has to be woken up for school usually."

"That…" He was about to say it wasn't necessary when he realized that if they didn't leave soon, he would just be sitting here, staring at Cassie after shattering any chance things between them could ever go back to how they used to be. He couldn't handle this level of awkward. Breakfast was hard enough. "That would be great, actually."

"Okay." She finished her breakfast without saying anything else to him and then started up the stairs.

She and Will came back down minutes later. Will had some quick breakfast, and Jake loaded them in the car only saying what needed to be said. He didn't feel much like talking this morning.

As he pulled out of the driveway, a shiver went down his spine. Things between him and Cassie were so strained that he felt even more pressure not to let anything happen to her today. If she was hurt it would crush him no matter what, but he did not want last night to be the final real conversation they'd had.

Surely he was overreacting. But none of the reassurances he tried to offer himself would stick. Because he wasn't being paranoid. Someone *was* after Cassie, they might want her dead, and he had no leads yet on who it could be. Neither did the police. He'd texted Levi enough times that his friend had finally sent him a message that said, Nothing new to tell.

None of it sat right with Jake. It had been too quiet, too easy and calm since the last attack—the gunshots outside of the library.

It made him feel like the danger was a rubber band being stretched and stretched and sometime soon…

It would snap.

# THIRTEEN

Nothing improved after they dropped Will off.

"You remember we only have a couple more days before he stays with us again, right?" Cassie asked Jake, her voice completely void of any extra warmth. She wasn't rude. Just matter-of-fact and not especially… friendly.

Ironic, since that's what they'd established they were. *Friends*. Funny how much of a step back that could seem like.

"So we just need to figure out who was responsible for your aunt's death before then."

"Sure, we'll solve a decades-old legend superfast and eliminate our need for childcare." Jake didn't look at her, but he could hear the roll of her eyes.

Then she sighed. "Listen, Jake…"

He felt his shoulders tense, unsure of how this conversation was going to go. But he waited anyway.

"I'm sorry about that. It's not your fault that I…got the wrong idea, and…you know…" She shrugged. "Anyway, we're adults. We were in love once. We share a son. I can be nicer than I have been this morning and I'm sorry."

He wasn't sure what to say. And just as he opened his mouth to do so, movement in the rearview mirror caught his eye. They'd just passed a narrow driveway and someone was turning out of it, toward them.

"You're buckled, right?" Jake double-checked with Cassie.

"Yes, why?"

His worst fears were realized when whoever was tailing him advanced. He couldn't see the driver well, but he could tell he was wearing a hat, low over his eyes. It was a white sedan, something like a Honda Accord, and its intentions were clear to Jake.

The road was narrow and wound up the mountain toward the trailhead. The mountainside itself was on the right and there was a guardrail on the left. Then it just dropped off. There was little room to maneuver if someone was driving aggressively. The car behind them qualified for that description now.

"What on earth?" Cassie's voice was breathless but not full of fear yet. She hadn't realized that whoever was tailing them was part of the group that was after her, or was the one person behind her. He wasn't sure quite how many people were involved, only that Cassie had said she'd seen more than one individual during the attack at the library.

There was only one person in the car behind them. Was his partner up ahead somewhere, or in town? If Jake knew, it could change how he drove. Should he keep going in, knowing they'd be alone in the trailhead parking lot and still needing to face the person behind them and possibly more people if others were involved and waiting somewhere, or turn into a driveway on the side of the road and try to change direction?

He wasn't completely sure either one would help.

Then the white car smashed into his bumper. They were thrown forward and back and Cassie's screams pierced his ears.

He wasn't going to be able to get away if the white car tried again. It accelerated, moved to the right edge of the road. If the car ran into him now, they'd be pushed directly against the guardrail on the left and the side of the mountain.

Jake hit the gas.

The car behind them slowed down.

"Are they gone?" Cassie twisted around in her seat, breathing hard, her eyes wide with pure fear.

"They are. Don't worry, okay?"

But she wasn't a child and she wasn't the kind of woman who would blindly accept reassurances. She knew they were still in danger and she wasn't going to act like that wasn't the case. Not even when he tried to offer comfort.

"Where did they go?" Now fear was creeping in the edges of her tone, and Jake felt it too, the sensation that something was coming, that a weight was pressing in on them.

They weren't safe. No matter how much of a relief it was that the car had gone.

The next pullout, Jake was taking it and driving back down the mountain. He could take Cassie and Will and just keep them safe in his house for as long as this lasted.

He said as much to Cassie as he kept driving up the road, which was too narrow to turn around in yet. He kept his eyes on the rearview mirror.

"You know you can't do that forever."

"It wouldn't be forever," he argued. "Surely the police will find them eventually."

Cassie shook her head. "You said yourself that they weren't looking at anything even related to why we think she was taken. Not the treasure or the legend or any of it. It could be literally years before they look there. Or they might close the case first." Her voice raised a bit in pitch, turned tight. He knew how much she'd loved her aunt and hated that she was having to deal with the lack of closure that resulted from not knowing who had killed her or being sure why it had happened.

"Still, I need to turn around." The pullout should be in the next half mile or so, at least he thought, but he eyed the next driveway on the right anyway, tempted to use it to turn around. He didn't want to be sitting still for that long, just in case the white car came at them from farther down the mountain at a high rate of speed.

"No."

He looked over at her, and blinked. That's how firm her voice had been.

"Jake, please. We are so close."

"I've got to call the car in anyway and let the police know." Was he really considering carrying out today's plan? When it was clear someone knew what they were doing?

No. He couldn't.

"Cassie..." He trailed off. He glanced her way and then back to the road again. Her expression made it clear she wasn't pleased, but he was much less concerned with her happiness than he was with her safety.

He'd just looked up at the rearview mirror to confirm no one was behind them when a car came flying at them down the mountain. This one was black, a crossover.

And it edged over the line toward him.

"Jake, watch out!" Cassie yelled.

Jake jerked the wheel hard to the right and worked to keep the car from crossing the edge of the road while avoiding the head-on hit from the other car. It happened so fast he didn't know how he was able to react at all. Maybe God's mercy.

The car still rammed them, despite his efforts. It spun Jake's vehicle almost forward, and swung it to the right. He fought with the wheel but couldn't control it, couldn't stop it from spinning.

They hit the side of the road hard, then the black SUV knocked them again.

Jake's head smacked the steering wheel before the airbag deployed and threw him backward, and for the second time in two days he felt himself lose consciousness.

*Please, God, no.*

But nothing changed. Jake blacked out, aware of Cassie's yelling beside him, and completely powerless to help her.

When she woke up, Cassie felt like...gravel. Hard. Uncomfortable. All of her hurt. Cassie's eyes were dry, sandpapery. Her throat was scratchy. She swallowed. Licked her lips and swallowed again, desperate for some moisture.

She blinked, and saw that she was in the dark somewhere. And it was bumpy. She blinked some more, feeling much heavier than when she normally woke from sleep. Was it a side effect from the accident she'd been in? Or had someone drugged her? As her eyes focused, she was able to see that she was in the trunk of a car. Her hands were bound behind her by something that felt tough and plastic. Not rope, maybe something like zip ties. Her eyes weren't covered, because she could see variations in the dark and as they adjusted to the dim light, she was able to make out shapes in the trunk itself. It was fairly good-sized, she had room to stretch out. It was clean—there was nothing in there with her that she could use for a tool to escape.

Will. Was he safe? Cassie didn't know for sure but she hoped so. She was alone in the trunk and for now that encouraged her. She remembered being hit while she and Jake were driving to the trailhead to search using her directions and to see if they could find a location for the treasure. In retrospect, they never should have headed to do that alone.

How many mistakes would they make in their attempts to investigate? Come to think of it, probably no more now. Because their investigation was officially over. She'd been caught by whoever had been after her. Chills chased up her spine. Was this it, the last few minutes or hours or even seconds of her life? Cassie had no way of knowing and the thought tortured her.

*God, help me.*

What did she want help with? Her current situation? The mess she'd made of her relationship with Jake? Or life in general? Or her unbelief?

*Can You help me believe, God?* Much to her surprise that was what bothered her most. She'd thought about what Jake had said last night, when she couldn't sleep. She felt oddly pursued by a God she hadn't been sure existed. Like maybe He did want her to know Him and maybe He had been working on their behalf. But surrendering and trusting was so against her nature. When you trusted people, they let you down. Look at how her mom had let her and her dad down. How Cassie had then taken her own hurts and let Jake down, and by extension Will, who didn't know his own dad because of her fears.

*God, I have really messed up. I don't know how I could be scared to trust You because clearly I'm not doing a great job without You. I believe You're real. I believe what I've heard in church over the years, that You sent Jesus to die in my place and if I trust that, I can live with You in Heaven and know You here, right now.* Cassie was surprised at how many snippets came back to her from church services she'd sat in and conversations with Jake. She was surprised too at how she didn't feel like she was talking to air, or to the trunk walls, but really like she was talking to… God?

*Help me believe more, God. Help me, okay? And if You can help me out of this too…that would be really good. I want to raise my son. I want to tell Jake I still love him. And more than that, I want to show him.*

The car hit a pothole and Cassie was thrown against the top of the trunk. Impulse had her jerking her arms to shield her head, but she couldn't get them in position with how they were bound. Instead she hit her head.

Wincing from the pain, she closed her eyes again. But not to go to sleep or to give up.

She needed to figure out a plan for when whoever had her opened up that trunk.

Because she had too much to live for to go down without a fight.

The car edged to a stop after another little while of driving. Cassie was hopeless enough measuring distances when she hadn't been unconscious for part of the time and left tied up in a trunk, so she didn't know how far they'd gone. Her head hurt and the accident itself was fuzzy in her head. She did remember heading up the road to the trailhead. The white car. Being tailed. She frowned.

The car that had been behind them had backed off, she remembered that. But she hadn't been completely relieved since she'd still felt like something was coming.

Sometimes she hated being right.

She heard footsteps crunching outside the car. Her heart rate sped up. She couldn't imagine seeing who'd been behind all this and her stomach churned at the idea of the terror they'd put her through, and the fact that they'd killed her aunt.

Unconsciousness couldn't be summoned though. So she had no choice but to face this.

The trunk opened and daylight spilled in. The light hurt her eyes.

*Please, God, I'm not ready.*

"Get out."

The voice was gruff, a male voice she didn't recognize. Somehow she'd assumed whoever killed her aunt was from Raven Pass, but this voice wasn't familiar to her. As soon as she had the thought, she remembered that a good portion of the rescue team had moved to Raven Pass after she'd left town. There were likely more newcomers also. Cassie not knowing who the man was didn't mean her aunt hadn't known him.

"My hands are tied so it's hard to move. Untie them."

The gruff laughter was void of any actual humor. "No."

Cassie kicked her feet forward to roll herself over

as best she could, but finally the man reached in and grabbed her by the arms and lifted her out.

His strength scared her. She didn't want to die, but it would have been easier in the car crash. It terrified her to think of dying at the hands of someone with that much raw strength.

Her eyes still burning and dry, Cassie blinked against the daylight. They were in a parking lot, but not the one for the trailhead she and Jake had been heading to. "Where are we?"

"Near the gold. You're going to take us to it."

"We were heading to where we thought it was. You need to take me there. Of course, all that assumes I would actually help you find it." Neither honesty nor sarcasm were likely to hurt her at this point. At least she didn't think so. They'd already abducted her. It could only get worse if they had her son.

Fear stabbed her chest. She had to cooperate. If she didn't, they'd look for more ways to threaten her, and endangering Will wasn't an option. "Okay, I will show you. But truly, I don't know how to get there from here."

"You were going to a trailhead not far from here." His voice was low. Rough.

Cassie frowned. "I don't know where we are."

"Half a mile north of where you were going. Farther north on private property. Don't worry, your boyfriend won't look for you here. Neither will the police."

Any flicker of hope she might have entertained wavered, but didn't go out. She knew God now. And while she didn't know a lot about Him, she hoped maybe He would rescue her.

Right?

"Get me back on that trail and I'll see what I can do," Cassie said, hoping her voice stayed steady.

The big man nodded once.

Cassie started walking, her hands still behind her back, her heart beating hard and her mind trying to figure out how she was going to get out of this.

# FOURTEEN

Jake's head hurt, throbbed with pain. He blinked himself back into consciousness, thinking in a detached way as he did so that getting what was likely a concussion two days in a row wasn't helpful to his brain.

When he was finally awake enough to panic, he looked to the passenger seat. No Cassie.

The police pulled up behind him just then, and Judah Wicks got out of his car.

Someone had called them? Jake certainly hadn't.

Judah Wicks walked over to him, talked to him about the accident while his head throbbed in pain. Was Jake hurt? Yes. Where was Cassie? Jake didn't know. He answered the questions like it wasn't him talking, like he was somewhere outside himself absentmindedly wondering if this was what utter panic felt like.

She wasn't with him, and the people who had taken her had already committed one murder.

*God, please keep her safe.*

Jake made himself focus until Judah drove away, after assuring him they'd look for Cassie. Judah had wanted to get Jake medical attention, but he'd deferred, told the man he'd take care of it himself.

After a deep breath, he put the key back in his dented but still functional car and got ready to drive.

They had a head start on him, but Jake wasn't going to quit until he found Cassie.

First though, he needed help. His mind was fuzzy, but that much was clear.

Jake opened his group text and texted his search-and-rescue group. Cassie's been taken. Meet at the trailhead from three days ago. Then he texted Officer Thomas, the man who had Will, and updated him in case the danger had heightened for his son in some way. He was relieved to receive a text back from him almost immediately. Will was fine, having fun, and Jake didn't need to worry about it.

Something he was finding out as a father—it was nearly impossible not to worry about your kid.

His phone rang. Not Cassie, saying she'd wandered off after their accident and was fine. Not even an unknown number that could be the start to finding out where she was and getting her back.

It was Adriana. Jake slid the phone icon to answer. "Did you get my text?"

"Yes. I'm on my way to you with Babe and he's ready to find her. Do you have something of hers he could smell to establish her scent?"

"I can find something." His car smelled like her. Half his house smelled like her. Cassie's presence was everywhere in his life and had been for days. And now she was gone. He had to make himself focus, and only did so by reminding himself that Cassie was counting on him right now.

"We're going to find her, Jake."

Adriana's voice was confident. Firm.

He nodded even though she couldn't see him, not sure if he believed her or not.

"Did you hear me? We are going to find her. I'll see you at the trailhead, Jake. And bring your A game. This team needs everyone and that means you can't be distracted right now with imagining what might have happened to Cassie in some made-up, worst-case scenario, okay? If you love Cassie, and I know you do, bring the Jake I know who is ready to handle this. Not this shell of a guy and not the cautious guy from the last few days. Bring my boss, okay?"

She hung up before he could tell her that basically everything she'd said was technically insubordination on some level. Or before he could say thank-you.

He exhaled.

*God, even my realizing she didn't believe in You was halfway a relief. God, it gave me a chance to step back emotionally, since I want the woman I marry to know You like I do. But I do love her, God. I'm still waiting for her to trust You because I want to obey You in who I commit my life to, but Lord, if she ever does, she's the woman I want to marry. I don't want to be afraid of loving her again, or afraid of trusting, or of anything else. Please keep her safe, help her to trust You, and bring her back to me.*

*Please.*

Jake took another breath, then lifted his head and put the car in gear, then gunned it to the trailhead, gravel kicking out behind his tires as he started.

By the time he got there, the rest of his team was already assembled and waiting. Several members of the Raven Pass Police Department were there too. Levi

Wicks and his brother Judah, Christy Ames, and another man Jake didn't recognize.

"Where do we search? Do you have quadrants in mind?" Ellie asked.

He shook his head. "It's going to be really unusual." He looked at Adriana. "I still want you to search with your dog like you usually would. If my plan goes against the dog's nose, go with his nose, okay?"

She nodded.

"The rest of you, Cassie knows where the treasure is, approximately."

"Uh, Boss, what treasure?" Piper raised her eyebrows. "Wait…" She frowned.

"The treasure in the legend people talk about?" Caleb finished for her.

Jake nodded. "Sorry, I forgot I didn't start at the beginning." Adriana had told him they needed him as their boss, and he needed to get it the rest of the way together. "Cassie figured out what her aunt knew that was worth killing over. She knew how to get to where the rumored Raven Pass treasure was buried, or hidden, we aren't quite sure which. There was an old fairy tale she told her that had directions in it."

He opened his phone to photos, where he'd taken a screenshot of the story as Cassie had written it down for him last night, then texted it to the group. "We're assuming this is the starting place. That's the assumption Cassie will be acting on."

"You think they took her to show them where the treasure is?"

Jake nodded. "Yes, because I believe that's why her aunt Mabel was abducted also."

Adriana frowned. "Then why kill her?"

"Maybe she wouldn't show them." Ellie shrugged. "I wouldn't."

"Your life is more important than that, just for the record," Jake said to her and everyone else, hoping Cassie understood that too. Why *hadn't* Mabel told them though? Jake hadn't figured that out. She would have known that she was more important also.

*Please don't let Cassie make the same mistake.*

"So does everyone understand our objective? Find Cassie." He hesitated, realizing for the first time the danger he'd be putting his team in. Cassie was clouding his vision. *God, help me see clearly.* "But..." He trailed off. "I understand if some of you want to bow out of this search. Your position on the search-and-rescue team won't be affected as today is outside the realm of our normal operations."

"We're coming, Boss. Now stop talking and let's go find your girl." Adriana started off first, Judah Wicks at her heels. Jake appreciated seeing the law enforcement officers spread themselves out among the search-and-rescue team so no searchers were without an officer and his or her weapon to protect them.

They followed the directions past the throne, but the trail all but disappeared. The directions from there were vague until wherever *the heart of darkness* was, Jake noticed when he looked at the story again. True north meant to go north. They'd have to cross at least one river, maybe two, or the same river more than once. He wasn't sure quite how literally to take the words.

"We should split up," Levi finally said after the group had started down several trails only to turn back when they became impossible to navigate.

"Fanning out will make it possible to cover more

ground anyway, and potentially approach a dangerous situation from multiple sides," his brother Judah spoke up.

Jake considered it and nodded. "Okay. No groups without an officer?"

Levi nodded.

Levi stayed with Jake. Judah went with Adriana. Christy went with Piper and Caleb. The other officer, whose first name he'd learned was Luke, was paired up with Ellie.

The woods seemed quiet after they split. Initially Jake could hear some of the noise from other groups, but then nothing. His heart thudded even harder in his chest. Someone was going to find her. He believed that. They'd assembled too good a team not to, especially when they had an idea of where her captors would most likely be headed. The question wasn't that. It was whether or not she'd be alive when they got there.

"Where did they park, Jake? If they took this trail?" Levi spoke up and Jake stopped in his tracks. The thought caught him that off guard. The black SUV that had hit him hadn't been in the lot and neither had the white car. Had another car been working with them? There had been several other cars.

"Do you think there's a third car involved?"

Levi shook his head. "I don't know what to think. It's possible but it's a lot more logical they parked somewhere else."

"Where else is there?" Jake asked as he was already pulling up the satellite view he'd looked at with Cassie the night before. He could barely think back to that, it hurt too much to think of the note on which they'd ended. Still, he studied the landscape. Levi leaned in too and both of them stared.

They saw it at the same time; Jake could tell by the way Levi tensed.

"There. What is that?" Jake asked.

"I'm not sure." Levi was staring at the same narrow road through the trees that showed on the satellite. It wasn't large enough to be any kind of official trailhead parking. But it was north of where they were, well within a mile. It was possible they intended to have Cassie take them to try to find the gold but didn't want to risk using this trailhead. They had to have known that as soon as Jake regained consciousness he'd come after her.

Which raised the question—why hadn't they killed Jake? Had they assumed the accident had done it? Had they not had time...

"Who called in the wreck earlier, do you know?" Jake asked his friend.

Levi shook his head. "Judah said it was a guy who saw it happen. He called it in and one of the other officers talked to him in person and took his statement."

That made sense. Jake hadn't understood why the guys who had caused the wreck hadn't finished the job with him when they were taking Cassie away, but if someone was there at the scene and saw it happen, murder was a bit harder to get away with.

"The witness saw them take Cassie away. How was she?"

Levi shook his head. "Unconscious, not responsive. We don't know anything else yet, so let's not speculate, okay?"

Jake forced himself to think about other things,

things that weren't Cassie's limp body, maybe alive maybe not, being carried away from him. He'd promised to keep her safe and he'd failed at that. How was he supposed to forgive himself if he didn't get her back?

Summoning all the courage he still possessed, Jake nodded and glanced back at the satellite map. "It's a long shot, but let's head in the direction of the spot we noticed on the satellite."

"You think they parked there and came this way?"

"I'm almost sure of it."

"Let's go."

It was ironic, really, how one of the activities Cassie had loved to do with her aunt had factored into this week back in Raven Pass to such a great degree. Here she was, hiking again. Without her aunt, but here in town because of her aunt. Wondering if what had happened to her aunt was about to happen to her.

It felt eerily like walking in someone else's shoes as she walked down the trail. She was grateful she'd dressed in light long sleeves and long pants. It was unusually warm for Alaska, in the high seventies she'd guess, but the trail was overgrown, barely able to be called a trail from the place where the man who'd abducted her had parked. The branches of the trees scraped against her and the fabric kept them from scratching her skin.

As she walked, she felt oddly calm, whether from shock or from God kind of cushioning the emotional blows she should be feeling, Cassie wasn't sure. She knew though, that she felt strangely confident. The treasure was in these mountains and she knew how to get to it. Roughly. And she would find it and let them have it if it meant they would let her go.

No, she amended as she pushed through the branches of several spruce trees that had grown together, it wouldn't mean they'd let her go. She wasn't naive enough to think it would. But it might be possible for her to get away from them when they were distracted by the gold.

Cassie wished she knew more about what it was supposed to look like. Were they talking gold nuggets, basically? She assumed so from the talk she'd heard occasionally around town and what she read in the book yesterday. The story seemed to imply that the gold had been hidden straight from the mountain, not processed in any way. So it might not be a stunning sight even if it was worth a substantial amount of money. She'd have to be ready to create her own sort of diversion if the gold itself wasn't enough to distract them into complacency.

"Speed up."

The harsh voice of her captor behind her startled her forward and she tripped on one of the rocks. A hand wrapped around her arm almost instantly, jerking her back to a standing position. It was a stark contrast to how she felt when Jake helped her, when his hand was on her arm.

She'd thrown away more than she'd known years ago. But she wasn't giving up on getting him back yet. If the faith issue had been the only one between them, that was solved now. If it had only been an excuse and he really hadn't forgiven her, or he just didn't love her anymore… Well those were possibilities but she would cross those bridges if and when she came to them.

Thinking about him now wasn't helping though. Her

focus needed to be on the treasure and getting there as quickly as she could, as it appeared her captor was getting impatient. She had been walking at a slower pace than usual, thinking that the extra time to think might help her tactically somehow. He'd noticed and now she felt like he was watching her more carefully, so that had been a risk that hadn't paid off.

"Let's go."

The muscles in her legs were burning—there was nothing false about her pace now, she truly couldn't hike much faster. She forced herself to though, needing not to enrage him to the point that he hurt her or lost his temper. The man looked like he could crush her without much effort.

*Help me, God. I want to get back to Will. And Jake, if he'll have me.*

She prayed, that sentiment and more like it, as she pushed herself down the trail. When they reached a river, she looked back at the big man. He just stared at her. "Is it across the river?" he asked.

Cassie nodded.

"Then cross it."

There was no rope, nothing to aid her across the river. Except farther downstream there was a branch that overhung the water a little, and that might possibly be used to hang onto during the crossing. Cassie walked down that way on the gravel bank and discarded that plan. The branch was barely hanging onto the tree and could fall off any moment, and the water was deeper at that part of the river, swirling into eddies.

She walked back to where she'd been at first, thinking the shallower part might be easier.

"Do you have a preference where we cross?" she

asked the man. He shook his head, then gestured with his meaty hand. "Just cross it."

His voice was rough. Hard.

And getting swept away in the current was preferable to being at his mercy. Cassie felt her eyes widen at the thought and she looked down immediately, then looked back at the river, trying to appear natural when so many thoughts were swirling in her head so fast, the current of them almost as powerful and dangerous as the river itself.

She was facing an impossible choice, she realized. But she did have a choice. Option number one meant trusting that her captor would have some degree of honor, or decency, and not kill her the moment she showed him where the gold was. All of that assumed she could stay alive long enough to do that. It felt like his temper was on a hair trigger and at any moment he might explode and that would be the end for her.

Had her aunt died that way? Violently and suddenly? Cassie wanted to know, and didn't.

She swallowed hard and blinked back tears.

Option two meant surrender to God, and hope, and everything that Cassie wasn't good at. Add to that the practical aspect of surviving in the frigid water. A decade ago she'd been trained for wilderness situations by her daily activities in Alaska. She'd grown soft working in Florida, in a climate-controlled office and far from the dangers and adventures of the backcountry. Just crossing the river would be much more difficult for her now. She knew well that the temperature was enough to give someone hypothermia if they spent much more than a few minutes in it. And as a nurse, she understood hypothermia better than most. It was a fairly peaceful way to die, if one had to make choices about things like that, but it was unforgiving. Once you started down its road, it seldom let someone turn back without medical intervention, and by virtue of what she was considering and the danger she was in, medical intervention would not be an option, maybe for hours.

Still. It was her only hope. And if hope wasn't worth holding onto…what else was there?

Cassie walked back to the tree trunk. "I'm going to use the tree."

The big man nodded, folded his arms across his chest. It seemed he was willing to use her as a guinea pig and then decide his own route based on the one she took. The spinelessness of a man who would be willing to sacrifice a woman for his own safety or gain made her sick. She wanted to tell him that, that he made her want to throw up, but in case her plan didn't work and they ended up back together, she'd better not antagonize him.

The first step into the water was the coldest, and Cassie stepped back out immediately, her gasp reflex making her inhale sharply. She took a deep slow breath and tried again, letting the water rush over her hiking boots and soak through. Then she reached for the tree branch, her hands tightening around the wood of the branch itself, the leaves tickling her forearm. She took another step deeper into the river with her left foot, then her right. The water was above her ankles now. Cold, it was so cold. Her hiking pants soaked in the water and it crawled up her leg. The tree branch held. She continued across, the water now past her knees. On her thighs. She had to squeeze her eyes shut for a second and grasp for all her courage again because the cold made her want to cry. But she had to get across, or let herself be swept away.

Or…could she cross the river without him and manage to hide out somewhere? Cassie hadn't considered that option, but now she saw there was a chance. Probably not much of one if she let herself be swept away in the river, but it was an option and possibly safer than…

The branch snapped, the swirl of glacial blue water tugged harder against her, and Cassie felt herself being pulled down, into the churning water, and downstream.

Cold. That was the thought first and foremost on her mind. The water was ice cold like a thousand sharp icicles puncturing her skin all at once, all over. She heard herself screaming and then forced her mouth to close as she passed the man who was running into the water after her. She was his living map, she knew, and he wasn't likely to go without trying to get her back.

The thought was terrifying.

The current swept her farther downstream, around a curve, and when she was out of his sight, Cassie started to fight the water with her arms, desperate to gain buoyancy and get herself to the shore, where she could hide. She cupped her hands together and pulled the water with even strokes, slowing her breathing so she didn't panic. She was five feet away from the shore. Four feet.

She paddled harder. The current tugged her back out.

She wouldn't have much time in this water, she knew. That's why the entire plan had been a gamble.

*Please let it have been a smart one.*

The shore was closer now and she swam again, against the tug of the water. One more chance. She had what she guessed was one more chance before the cold and exhaustion would team up against her, bullies that they were, and prevent her from reaching the shore safely.

Everything depended on this next try.

Cassie swam hard, and she swam not just for her, or for Will, or even Jake, but for hope and for the new life she had now that she'd trusted God.

*See? I'm trusting You now, God, so please come through for me.*

Her hands reached out and she grabbed another branch. It was thin, but it was flexible, and it held long enough for her to stand up in the thigh-deep water and pull herself the rest of the way to the edge with hesitant steps.

The first step on shore, Cassie almost cried. She'd made it, but she wasn't safe yet, couldn't rest yet. Instead of collapsing there, Cassie walked inland some, into a thick cluster of fireweed, and curled up in a ball. She had to stay warm. But she couldn't build a fire, not without being detected. Instead she prayed the sun was enough to keep her warm, and tried to stay awake.

But she couldn't. She fell asleep with a prayer on her mind, hoping she wasn't foolish to, for once in her life, trust and hope and wait.

# FIFTEEN

Using the story Cassie had written out, as well as the satellite map, had gotten Jake and Levi halfway to where the treasure supposedly was from the trailhead, at least according to his entirely unscientific estimation. They were standing now at a riverbank, staring at the glacial river. It wasn't the largest Jake had ever seen, but it was silty and fast and that made it dangerous.

"You're sure you want to cross this?" Levi asked from a few feet away where he'd been looking out, trying to find a good path across the water. Some river crossings on hiking trails in Alaska would have ropes stretched across them, to help hikers get over them safely. Even with the ropes, it wasn't rare for someone to be pulled down by the current, held under by the heaviness of the silt, and then drowned. It was even more likely here without anything to aid in the crossing. Most Alaskan rivers were angry churning blue, filled with rocks that dared someone to not take them seriously, and offered death as a consequence of carelessness.

This one fit that profile. And Jake had too much to live for to die right now. But the story had said to cross the rivers they encountered. He pulled the wrinkled paper from his pocket, the one Cassie had written last night in her own handwriting.

"He was not stopped by rivers," Jake read aloud, then shrugged. "It sure sounds like we are supposed to cross it. It doesn't say to turn around or find another path."

"And you're sure this story really means something and is going to lead us to gold?"

Levi was trying to believe him and be supportive, Jake could tell, but he still wasn't sold on the idea, as Jake had known he wouldn't be. It was beyond their usual encounters with criminals, most of whom knew what they wanted. They were dealing with something unknown here, a legend. While Jake believed he and Cassie were right about their theories, he understood Levi's hesitation.

"I'm sure, but besides that, Cassie is sure. She'll follow what the story says."

"So we have to cross."

Jake nodded. He walked up and down the bank, trying to figure out where Cassie would have gone and if she'd have made it. Because the gold wasn't the point, and the men who had been after her weren't even the point for Jake. He would rather find Cassie safe, and if she hadn't made it across all the way...

"Do you think she would have made it—if she crossed this?" he forced himself to ask his friend, not sure he wanted to hear the answer.

Levi looked out again, then spoke up over the roar of the river. "I don't know. It's an intense current and she's been gone for a long time. You think she could do something like this?"

"She could if it wasn't too deep." Cassie was strong,

Jake knew, but once water was over someone's knees, their strength started to make less and less of a difference. It was simple science as far as how deep someone could go before being overpowered. If the water was too deep, she wouldn't have stood a chance. Which meant if she had crossed, she should have done it right about where they were standing, in the middle of this clearing, straight across.

Still…he didn't see footprints. Would he see some between the rocks, on actual soil?

Maybe. He walked the river again, this time more toward his right. A tree branch overhung the water by about a foot or two, the end of it snapped like it had broken clean off the rest of itself.

Surely…

Cassie would have known better than to cross here, right? he asked himself as he looked down at the deeper water. Using the tree branch as a way across would have been tempting, especially with her having had experience crossing rivers with rope before. She would have defaulted to the way she knew how to cross safely and that was with something to hold onto. But the river here was deeper and the current angrier than in the other locations. If the tree had broken…the water would have been up to her waist, Jake was guessing. Far too deep for her to stand and hold her ground against the flow if she'd lost her handholds.

How long ago had the tree broken? Jake wished he'd studied something that would answer that question for him, instead of being a paramedic and having only worst-case scenarios for Cassie scroll through his mind. Mindless facts he'd once memorized, about drownings and water in the lungs, and the evidence of drownings in autopsies—those were the things he was thinking about now, and pondering them in conjunction with Cassie wasn't something he wanted to do. They weren't helpful, and he needed to do something to help. For years he felt like he'd let her down by not coming after her. He'd let his own fears, his own desire to be wanted and not rejected keep him from trying to get her back, and he'd learned. Maybe too late, but he had learned.

She was worth fighting for. And if her lack of belief in God was all there was between them… Jake would keep loving her and pray every day that she came to know the truth. He would try harder to be an example of a good Christian, to show her what it meant to be a person of faith. He would try to gently lead her, not pressure her. But he would not, could not give up on her again.

"She crossed here," he mumbled, knowing the truth clear down to his soul. He bent down to study the dirt. There, the slightest impressions of the soles of someone's shoes.

He heard noise behind him and turned his head. Levi.

"Did you find something?" Levi asked.

Jake nodded. "She crossed here."

His friend's eyebrows rose. "Because of the tree? You think it went farther out and then…"

Jake shook his head. "No way to know for sure. But I think she went here for some reason."

"If she was trying to escape someone, would she take her chances being swept down the river?" Levi asked.

Jake didn't know. Cassie wasn't a huge risk taker, and she'd struck him as even more careful now, since having Will. But if it was the only chance she'd had to escape, he knew she was brave enough to have taken it.

"Maybe," he answered.

"So do we cross? Or do we go downstream, hoping to find her?"

Jake struggled for an answer. "If she did go down the river, we still don't know which bank she'd have ended up on. She wants to know who killed her aunt. Would she have made an effort to cross?"

Levi didn't answer and Jake hadn't really expected him to. No one knew her as well as he did, and if he was asking questions, then so was everyone else.

All he could do was search all the options. "Let's start with this side, go downstream a bit and see what we can find," he said to Levi.

The other man nodded. "Okay. I'll update the other officers with our general position in case we run into trouble."

"Or…" Jake trailed off. "We could split up?"

Levi shook his head. "No. I've seen how that movie ends."

Jake laughed, appreciating the bit of humor. It was a good coping mechanism, lightening the mood. "Thanks. Okay, we'll go together. Downstream."

The brush was thick, and bushes grew along the riverbank that Jake didn't know enough about to identify, but there were several different kinds, of varying heights. The advantage was that if she'd come out of the river at any point, they should be able to see evidence in the trampled brush. So far, there was none of that right next to the river, or ahead of them either, which meant that no one had pursued her, at least on this side of the river.

Not a complete reassurance that they didn't have to be on guard, but it did make Jake breathe a bit easier. Someone was still out here, he knew, but maybe not in the immediate vicinity.

He said as much to Levi and Levi shook his head. "If someone was tracking her and walked through the river, right along the edge, we'd see no evidence."

Which meant the man who'd taken Cassie could be anywhere. Jake's small bit of hope disappeared again.

Finally, it occurred to him to pray. Ironic that he'd pushed Cassie away because of her lack of trust in God. But when it came down to it, did he trust God either? Not as much as he wanted to, that was for sure. He was an imperfect man who could only keep trying to do better every day.

*Forgive me, God, for not asking earlier, and please help me. I don't want to give up hope. Please.*

They continued on, each step in the spongy ground too slow. Neither of them wanted to end up in the river by accident, so it was slow going. Every minute that passed was a minute Cassie might be in danger, and Jake hated knowing that.

"Did you hear that?" Levi asked.

Jake hadn't. He stopped.

Something rustled in the bushes. Up ahead, off the riverbank about twenty feet. Would she have taken shelter so far away from the river?

Or was it whoever had abducted her in the first place, lying in wait?

Or burying a body?

Jake worried his heart would stop at the last thought. Not another one he was going to let himself have again. No, he was trusting, remember? Trying to hope.

So he called out her name. "Cassie?"

The rustling stopped. He held his breath.

"Jake?"

Her voice was watery, weak, and every thought he'd had earlier about hypothermia and the dangers of the river came back to him. Jake fought again against the threatening feeling of hopelessness, knowing that with God there was always a chance. Never a reason to doubt. Always hope.

"Cassie!" he called again louder, hoping she'd answer so he could pinpoint exactly where she was. Beside him, Levi was looking around too, scanning the area for Cassie and for threats, Jake guessed.

"Here."

He saw the fireweed waving ahead of him, moving just enough to give it away as her location and he walked there. Levi came with him, but hung back slightly, which Jake appreciated. He wanted to see her first, know how she was, and he was desperate to know if she was all right.

She was, and she wasn't.

She was curled in a ball on the ground, the fireweed surrounding her like a tall curtain that came up from the ground. She'd been protected from being found by whoever had been after her, probably because she'd been so far off the river, and not on any obvious trail. Her choice of location had likely saved her life, and Jake thanked God for the intelligence he'd given Cassie so she could make that choice.

But while physically unharmed, she was soaked through—her clothes clung to her and her hair was wet too. She must have been pulled all the way under in her fight with the water.

This though, this he could handle. He wished he had equipment, but he could assess her at least, knew the signs of hypothermia, and no longer felt entirely helpless. A small mercy.

"How are you feeling?" He kept his voice even, reminding himself that if there'd ever been a time for professional detachment, this was it.

"I'm okay…" She sighed. "Sleepy. Just sleepy."

She wasn't shivering. That alarmed Jake. It was a warm day and the sun was out, which would help her, but there was a little bit of a breeze. Maybe she'd been protected from it enough by the fireweed, but he still had concerns. She needed to dry out.

"We need to get you warm, okay?"

"I can't…clothes are wet…"

Jake heard the slight slurring in her words that time and knew he'd been right to be concerned. They were there in time, but they had to act.

Building a fire could give away their location to anyone who was after her. He knew Levi had a weapon and more than enough training to use it. While Jake wasn't law enforcement, he'd grown up in the Alaskan woods and knew how to use a gun as well and had his own for bear protection. They were covered where that was concerned, but it wasn't enough to make him cocky about their chances. Bad guys could have guns too. It wasn't an automatic win for the good guys.

"How many men took you?" he asked her as he bent beside her to feel her pulse. It was fairly strong, better than expected. Jake breathed a prayer of thanks while he waited for her answer, continued to assess the situation. He removed his sweatshirt and tugged it over her head, instructing her to take off her wet shirt underneath. He turned around to give her privacy.

"Only one. I only saw one. He was so big." Her voice trailed off again. "I had to get away."

So he'd been right. She'd braved the river. Jake pulled her toward him, did his best to hug her though the angle was awkward and she was half asleep. "You're going to be okay, all right? You've got this, Cassie."

"Not sure I do, but God does."

He stilled. Swallowed hard.

"What did you say?"

"God… I'm trusting, okay, Jake? But I need to sleep."

"No. No sleeping." Jake looked at Levi, who'd been standing by, waiting. He stood up, kept his words soft in case Cassie was still awake enough to listen. "We need a fire, like half an hour ago," he muttered.

Levi nodded. "I agree. She sounds hypothermic, right?"

Jake nodded.

"It's a risk," Levi said. "But everything is at this point. It seems worth it."

"How should we do this?" Jake knew the fire would make them more visible to anyone looking for Cassie. It was daylight, so no worries as far as the light giving them away, but the smell of smoke traveled on the wind and someone skilled in tracking would be able to pinpoint its general location.

"We'll just keep watching out, maybe take turns wandering around the site here, seeing if there's anything unusual." Levi shrugged. "That's all we can do while we wait for help."

Jake nodded. "Okay. I'm going to get some sticks

for a fire." He glanced down at Levi. "You won't leave her?"

"I promise." Levi met his eyes and Jake knew his friend would watch her not just like anyone who needed police help, but like someone who was special to Jake.

When Cassie had left him in Raven Pass all those years ago, he'd tried to turn inward, back off from his friends. Instead God had kept pushing him to make new friends and he'd ended up with some of the best. Including Levi. Jake had to smile. "Thank you."

Levi nodded.

Jake wandered away and gathered the wood, alarm gathering in him when he didn't see Levi when he came back.

"Levi?"

Nothing.

"Cassie."

Nothing.

He couldn't remember where she'd been, not exactly. The scene reminded him so much of…yesterday? The day before? When they'd found her aunt Mabel's body and she'd hidden in some fireweed much like this. So much life had been crammed into the time between then and now, and yet this felt oddly like déjà vu.

Was she there, just unseen as she had been at first? Or had something far worse happened?

Levi being gone didn't bode well.

Jake kept looking around. He glanced at the fireweed, deciding he would try again there in a minute. He'd walk to the river now and make sure Levi hadn't gone down there, maybe even with Cassie.

He found Levi on the edge of the river, unconscious.

Jake gritted his teeth and bent beside his friend. His heart rate was good. Jake didn't see any bullet wounds, or any sign of head trauma. So either he'd been hit on the head or possibly drugged. He couldn't tell which without more assessments and tests, which he couldn't do out here.

Jake reached down and dragged him farther from the edge of the river. He'd gotten tangled in the branches of a small tree. Otherwise, he might have fallen in entirely. So he'd been…attacked and shoved toward the water? What had made the attacker leave?

Cassie? Could she have been awake enough to help? Jake wasn't sure. She'd been in bad shape.

He glanced at Levi again. Tugged him a little farther from the water.

"I'll be back. Sorry, buddy." He pulled Levi's phone out of his pocket and texted the police department to let them know their approximate location and that Levi needed help. Someone messaged back that they'd be coming.

One problem taken care of. Maybe two if they sent medical help along for Levi. They might come with supplies that could help Cassie too. Jake's knowledge wasn't much good without actual tools to put it into practice.

He hurried back to the fireweed.

"Cassie?"

Nothing.

He bent down on his knees, crawled through the bushes, sure she must be there. She'd fallen asleep, he told himself. He was just overlooking her hiding spot, which was good because it meant whoever had attacked Levi would have been unable to find her too.

He searched and searched. Found nothing.

And finally had to ask himself…why had Levi been so close to the river?

Jake had the sick feeling he'd let Cassie down again. This time though, he was going after her.

He ran toward the river, hoping he'd come up with a plan as he went.

She was so very tired. And cold. She was cold.

Should she be cold, Cassie wondered, if she was hypothermic? She'd always understood hypothermia to be a warm death. Maybe then she wasn't dying.

At least not from hypothermia. She had many other options, sadly.

She looked across from her in the raft. The big man from earlier had been joined by another man, which was why they'd been able to overpower Levi before he'd even been able to get his weapon out. She'd felt sick as she watched the big one grab him in something like a headlock and then drop him, shoving him toward the water as the other man pushed the raft with himself and Cassie in it out into the river. The big man had jumped in at the last minute and it was just the three of them. The two men had oars and were fighting the current to the other side, where they thought the gold was.

Her aunt. Maybe Levi. Maybe her next. And where was Jake? How many lives would be lost because of some gold? Did people's greed have no bounds?

It was something she wanted to learn about, if she lived. Why did God create people if they were going to be so messed up? She'd heard Jake mention the phrase *free will* but it wasn't something she understood. Maybe she never would.

*Please help me get out of here.* She tried to pray,

but she was so tired. Tears crept into the corners of her eyes and everything in her was still even though the men were yelling at each other, the river seemed to be yelling at all of them, and even the weather was joining in as this morning's sunshine had been replaced by gathering clouds.

It had been too hot. Now a storm threatened. She could add lightning to the list of threats she was facing.

"Row harder!" the big man yelled at the other.

"I brought you the raft. I've done enough to help you, don't you think?"

"I said row harder!" His rage was growing, Cassie could feel it and it terrified her. She wanted to hide back in her cluster of fireweed, even though that would only be false security. After all, it hadn't kept her from being discovered earlier. The men had come soon after Jake had left, as if they'd been watching her the whole time.

"Row yourself!" the other yelled.

Cassie watched in horror as the big man hit the other with a paddle, so hard she saw the man's eyes roll back in his head as his arms flew backward, his body off balance, and then he fell over the backside of the raft into the river.

She looked at his lifeless body, tossing in the water, hitting the rocks, then back at the big man.

"Get his paddle and row."

Cassie did.

Fighting with terror and determination, she rowed as hard as she could. The river tossed them where it wanted, but eventually they were caught on a rock close enough to the other side that with some maneuvering, the big man was able to lean over and propel them to shore using his paddle as a pole.

"Get out," he ordered when they'd banged up onto the rocky edge.

Cassie did.

She swallowed hard. Eventually she was going to have to defy him if she wanted to live. His temper was a liability, one she could use against him, if she was smart.

And careful. She'd have to be very careful.

Cassie climbed out, feeling her heart beat in her chest, hard and strong and tired.

She was so very tired.

"Find. The. Treasure."

Cassie nodded, eyeing the clouds above them. She heard a rumble in the distance. If it rained, their footprints would be destroyed, and any chance of someone like Jake tracking them would be diminished. She couldn't afford to draw attention to herself enough to mark their trail in any other kind of way though. She'd seen what the big man's temper could do and she wasn't about to trigger it unless she could use it to her advantage.

*Please let the rain hold off.*

The bedtime story in her head, Cassie remembered they'd likely have to cross at least one more river. The story had said *rivers*. Was there another river? How big would this one be?

She found out before too long. It may have been a branch of the same river, or this may have been the confluence of two, Cassie wasn't sure. But there was another river, stretching in front of them.

"This time—" the man grabbed her arm again and she tried to hide her shudder "—we are going together."

Swallowing hard, Cassie nodded and they stepped into the water.

Her mind shouted alarms as they kept stepping deeper and the water crept up and up her legs. Muscle memory remembered falling, the feel of the swirling current pulling at her, throwing her into its swift downstream flow. Her chest tightened and breathing got harder. There was no real danger in crossing the river right now. So far the water was only at her knees. Easily crossed. Not a danger like the last crossing. They were in the middle of the river now, so the chances of it getting deeper were slim.

*Help me, God. We can do this. Right?* she asked, not expecting an answer, but she felt reassurance settle over her anyway, soul deep, in a way that bolstered her confidence even more.

Then they were out of the river, on rocky ground again.

"What next?" the man asked.

"We go north."

"And after that?"

"We have to go north first." Cassie tensed as she said the words, afraid the man would be angry she wouldn't answer him, but she'd understood all at once that if she gave him all the directions, he'd have no need of her. In order to keep herself useful, she had to leave him needing her.

For now, he seemed satisfied with that answer. Maybe it was the fact that she'd kept her tone soft and hadn't been forceful, or maybe God had helped her. Either way, Cassie was relieved. The landscape grew more and more treeless as they climbed higher up the mountain than they'd been earlier, winding through alpine tundra. It looked like an area that could have once held a successful gold mine. Cassie walked north, thankful for the survival and navigation classes she'd taken during her high school years.

The next phrase she thought was a directional clue. It had been *into the heart of darkness*, which she assumed meant some kind of cave. An opening into the mountain of some kind. Maybe even a mining tunnel?

She saw it up ahead, in the distance, but instead of relief at getting them to the right place, Cassie felt fear grip her, hard and unrelenting.

She was about to become superfluous. He'd need her for the directions through the tunnels that she suspected were inside the mountain and that the story referred to when it said *left, right, left, left*. But after that… Time was running out to make her escape or figure out another plan. Overpowering her captor was out of the question, but there had to be something she could do.

"See the mining tunnel?" Cassie gestured to it.

The man nodded. "It's in there?" He was breathing heavily, anticipation making him lean toward her in a way that was even more intimidating than before.

Cassie nodded, about to open her mouth to explain the mazes, so he'd know he still needed her. But she wasn't fast enough. She saw one big fist of his coming against her head and she was unconscious.

Jake kept the story out as he hiked, like it was a literal map that he could see points on, as he moved ahead. He'd crossed the second river now and was making his way north. Soon, if he'd gone the right way, he should see whatever was described as *the heart of darkness*.

Was Cassie inside yet, and even more importantly, had her abductor harmed her in any way? They'd want to see the gold before they killed her, at least Jake thought so. But Cassie had seemed terrified, not just hypothermic, when he'd found her. And for her to have braved the river's current rather than try to overpower her captor, the man must be terrifying. Because Jake knew Cassie, and the woman wasn't scared of much. That was part of why he loved her.

He walked the trail he felt sure she must have walked just a short while before and wondered if officers had made it to Levi yet. He hoped so. He knew his friend would feel awful when he woke up, but again, that was another reason for Jake to be reminded to take these men who had Cassie seriously. His friend was no easy man to overpower.

So far the rain had held off, for which Jake was thankful, but now he felt drops starting to fall, first on his arms, then on his head as they hit hard enough to feel through the baseball cap he wore.

There. He could barely see a dark spot on the mountainside up ahead, but it was enough to see it was likely the *darkness* described by the story. He hurried in that direction and came to a cave. Not a cave, a mining entrance. It was cool and dark, many degrees colder than the warmer air outside. Cassie's hypothermia came back to the forefront of his mind. She was battling more than one enemy and he could help her with neither right now. Jake hated being helpless.

The tunnel was so dark he couldn't see, and he didn't want to use a light and give away his presence. Jake stepped out again, back into the light where he could read the story on the paper.

"Left, right, left, left."

He could remember that. He stepped back into the

darkness and crept forward. He put both hands out and decided it felt like a standard kind of mining tunnel, at least from the little he knew about them. It was about two feet wide, maybe less. Just enough for him to walk through, but passing someone would require flattening your body against one wall while they flattened theirs on the other. People were smaller in the 1930s so they'd likely made tunnels to fit how people were built back then. That also explained why he had to stoop a little; his over six-foot frame would have scraped the ceiling if he'd stood at his full height.

He kept going forward, not noticing any place where he had the option to make any turns. The story indicated that there should be some. He'd just begun to wonder if he'd missed them at some juncture when he came to the first option. Straight or left.

Left.

He made the turn, followed a tunnel that felt identical as far as specs to the one he'd just left.

Another juncture, maybe five minutes later. Right.

At the next intersection, there were multiple ways to turn. Straight. Left. Right.

He turned left, remembering the story. And then he could hear voices. They were low, in the distance, but they echoed enough on the walls of the tunnel that he could make out some of the words.

One of the individuals was angry. A man. His voice was low and full, maybe the man who'd nabbed Cassie. Anther voice was higher pitched. Female.

And older. Familiar.

Jake frowned, struggled to place it. He'd heard it somewhere…

He crept closer, mindful of how sound echoed, and

tried not to make any noise. He needed surprise on his side if he was going to help Cassie at all.

Even then, their odds weren't good. But he wasn't giving up.

*Help us, God.*

Jake held his breath, and kept walking.

# SIXTEEN

Cassie heard them talking well before she opened her eyes. In fact, she kept her eyes shut longer than she should have, listening. Waiting to see what the situation was.

"We should have stayed at the entrance. You took her in before I got here, without my say so, and who knows where we are in this stupid cave. I told you we needed her for the directions!"

The voice was female. Familiar. Cassie kept listening. Then peeked her eyes open the slightest bit.

The man shrugged. "She stayed out longer than I expected."

"Because you're an ape who hits harder than you think. Don't think I didn't notice that Lowell is gone. I'm assuming you killed him too?" She made a noise of disgust. "Your habit of killing people whose help we still need is infuriating."

"You asked for my help."

His tone was growing deeper, more menacing. Cassie remembered the scene earlier, in the raft, and felt herself tensing, though she tried not to let her facial expression change. She was supposed to be unconscious.

And she had been when they got into the cave. But she'd woken up after her captor had taken the first left turn. He'd guessed correctly. The next turn he'd gone right. Simple human instinct, to vary your guesses. And he'd guessed right. But the next turn he'd gone right again. That's when he'd stopped and the woman had found him. From a tracker? She doubted cell phones got signals inside the mountain. Had she been waiting? No, if she'd known how to get there, they wouldn't have needed Cassie, or her aunt.

She must have been nearby. Or the big man must have stayed with Cassie outside the cave for as long as it took the woman to get there and the woman had followed them without Cassie hearing her voice till now? Cassie had faded in and out, maybe, during the first couple of turns.

So she had a guess as to where they were in relation to the treasure, but she wasn't sure. That put her at a disadvantage.

Her only current advantage was that they thought she was unconscious. She needed to keep that going as long as possible.

"I asked for your help and so far you've only hurt." The woman's voice was cold. Unfeeling.

Cassie felt the man's rage, heard it in the cry he let out, and then a gunshot exploded, its noise reverberating off the walls in an echo of piercing sound.

A huge thud. Cassie's eyes flew open, found the man in the light from several lamps that were lit nearby. He lay bleeding on the ground, eyes unseeing.

Dead.

A woman stood over him, maybe ten feet from

Cassie. They were in a wider spot of the cave, not narrow like most of the passages.

It was the librarian, Mrs. Carpenter.

"Hello, Cassie."

"You…" She trailed off, hating how stereotypical she sounded, but her thoughts clamored over each other. She couldn't think. This woman was old. Not that old, but too old to…

To what? Shoot people? Clearly not.

All her preconceived notions about the person she'd been running from were shattered; one of them was lying dead on the floor, bleeding out nearby, the tinny smell of his blood overwhelming her. *He* had been who she'd pictured when she lay in bed afraid at night. And while she knew she and Jake had seen a man at times, so it might have been the big man, or the man called Lowell, or both as at the library, this woman, from what Cassie had heard in the last few minutes, had been behind it all.

"Why…"

The woman shook her head. "No one should have had to die, Cassie, don't you see that?" Her voice was prim. Proper as well as aged. She was one of Raven Pass's citizens who'd been there the longest. Her family, Cassie's family and a couple of others, they'd been there at the beginning.

"Why, then? You killed my aunt." She hated the words as she said them, rage threatening her as she realized that physically, she could overtake this woman.

"Don't do it, dear. You'll only end up dead, and I still won't have my treasure, and we will all be unhappy, don't you see?"

"You…"

Mrs. Carpenter shook her head, the lamplight glittering off her widened eyes. "I didn't do that. He did." She gestured. Then shrugged. "I didn't mean for her to die. I just wanted her scared enough that she would tell me. That *brute*—" her tone turned disgusted "—ruined that avenue and I was forced to look for other ways to find the treasure."

"You took the books from her house," Cassie accused, knowing without confirmation that she was right.

The woman nodded. "She always did take such good notes in her books. But while the margins were filled with confirmations of what I suspected, there were no directions. So I had to get your help."

"I'm not helping you." Cassie folded her arms across her chest. Waited while the older woman stared at her.

Even now, she struggled to believe this was the person who'd been after her, who was responsible for her aunt's death.

Why? She had so many questions. She may as well ask them now.

"How did you know about the notes?"

The woman's smile was nothing short of smug. "Your aunt told me, dear! I'm a friendly sort, as the town librarian, and she would come in regularly to do genealogy research. That's what tipped me off to your family's bad history."

Bad history?

She was curious about that too, but wasn't going to let the woman get away with dodging her question. "Okay, but what about the margin notes? You talked to her about them?"

"I told her one day how some library patrons marked up the books, and she said she only wrote in her own personal books. I knew by then she was doing a lot of digging on what had happened back in the day to the treasure. So I pressed her on that, and she revealed how she was taking notes about it in her own copies."

Cassie fully expected the gun to train on her then, but the woman's arms didn't move. She laughed a little, and it wasn't an evil sound like Cassie would have imagined. It was normal, light. Which made it even eerier.

"What did the books say in the margins?" Her curiosity was too great. And maybe the woman would answer, if she thought it would motivate Cassie. It wouldn't. But it was worth a try.

Her eyebrows raised. "You don't know? Surely she told you."

Cassie involuntarily shivered at the implication her aunt had kept things from her. But Cassie knew it was true. Hadn't they guessed her aunt knew where the treasure was? Of course there would have been other secrets tied to that, but if they didn't relate to Cassie, she hadn't needed to know. She couldn't be upset with her aunt for keeping that secret.

"Your family, Cassie. It's your family in the legend. They were the murderers."

She blinked, feeling the words like a slap across the face.

Mrs. Carpenter smiled, clearly pleased with her reaction. "See? So let's not be so hasty to judge here. People do nasty things for gold, Cassie. I'm no different than your relatives, the people you came from."

Cassie searched the statement for truth, struggled against it, fought to deny that her family had had anything to do with it, but she wasn't sure it wasn't true. They'd been there when the town was founded. Her aunt had reacted strangely to the treasure, kept it a secret and died refusing to give it up.

Had she been trying to make up for the wrongs that had been done by their relatives years before?

"So take me to it, dear. Like I said, I never wanted anyone to die." She shook her head.

Cassie stood, slowly.

Finding the treasure would at least give her closure, before she likely died. That was the worst-case scenario. Best-case was that someone found her here, that help arrived and she got to go free and Mrs. Carpenter spent the rest of her life in jail. The idea of the aristocratic lady behind bars was almost worth the terror.

But not worth the loss of her aunt. Not worth the heartbreak of knowing her family line had possibly done something so awful.

"This way," Cassie said and did her best to lead them back to where they could follow the directions of the story again, back to the entrance of the tunnel. She walked down the dark path, the light from the lantern Mrs. Carpenter carried giving her enough illumination to have shadows and shapes she could make out. Cassie wanted to cry. All these years she'd thought her mom was the worst of her family, and had been terrified she'd repeat her mistakes and leave the people she loved.

Then Cassie had done just that, in her effort to not repeat her mom's mistakes. She'd ironically done the same. What about these relatives? Was she destined to make their mistakes too? Not murder. Cassie was no killer. But betraying people for gold? Letting greed get the best of her?

*God, who knows? Help me. Am I more than my history? Their history?*

There in the tunnel, Cassie knew undoubtedly that she was not alone. God was with her. God was answering her, in her heart. Not in words but in steady reassurance.

No, she was not those relatives.

She was not her mom.

*You are mine.*

It was a Bible verse, part of one she remembered from a sermon she'd heard when she'd been dating Jake. From the Book of Isaiah, maybe?

She was God's. Not defined by any of that. But defined by Him. Cassie held her shoulders straighter. Kept walking, and begged God to help her, one more time.

The gunshot was the last straw. Jake could wait no longer. He crept toward the voices and was rewarded with the sight of Cassie. Her eyes were wide and she was talking to a woman. When the woman turned, Jake recognized her as the little old librarian.

People never stopped surprising him. Mostly in bad ways.

He watched them, listened and moved back into the shadows as they moved in his direction. They were close to the treasure, but not quite there and Cassie would be at a disadvantage, trying to find where they'd gotten off course.

He expected it to take a while for her to find it, but she made the turns well, like she'd been waiting for this all her life, and with the bedtime story, maybe she had been.

*Good girl, Cassie.*

The two women were ten feet in front of him, almost close enough to touch, but he was so careful not to make any noise that they hadn't heard him. There was a possibility the older woman couldn't hear well in her older age, which would work to his advantage.

"There," Cassie said and Jake crept as close as he dared.

He saw them both, leaning toward the tunnel wall. Not at the end, not in any obvious place, just a little notch out of the wall of the tunnel about as high up as a man would carve if he was reaching up but not to his full height.

Cassie reached up there, came down with first a slip of paper. He watched her facial expression flicker as she read it, and shoved it in her pocket.

Someone tapped Jake on the shoulder. He jumped. Levi. Judah. Adriana. Piper. Piper made the classic shh-signal with her hand.

Jake's face must have asked his questions because Piper pointed at Levi. He must have come to and led them there. Jake nodded, then waited, and all of them watched the scene in front of them.

"That's it? That's not the treasure, is it?" The woman raised a gun at Cassie. "Give it to me."

Jake made himself wait. If he hit her from this angle, the gun might discharge, killing Cassie.

"It's up there. That's a note to me."

The gun lowered.

"Get it down." The woman's voice was firmer now. Steely. "Actually... If it's there, then that means I don't need you anymore."

She raised the gun again. This time more purposefully. Levi tapped Jake, motioned for him to move left. Jake did.

"Freeze!" Levi yelled.

The woman whirled around, caught off guard.

"Raven Pass Police, put down your weapon!"

The librarian turned again to Cassie, gun at the ready.

Levi, Judah, someone, Jake didn't know, pulled the trigger.

The woman fell, hit somewhere center mass in the stomach. That threat was disabled. Cassie stood pressed against the opposite wall, having been less than two feet from the bullet and no doubt terrified.

Judah hurried toward the librarian, ready to perform first aid. Jake glanced at her as he rushed over to Cassie. Mrs. Carpenter might be going into shock, but Jake had a feeling she'd make it. Good. He'd rather see her live out her days in prison than die here. And he didn't want his friends to deal with the guilt of having had to end a life, though their shot had been justified.

But right now, Jake cared mostly about Cassie.

"Cassie." He reached for her and she came into his arms, wrapping hers around him and burying her face in his neck. Sobs racked her and he felt her tears soaking his shirt.

"She was behind it all along, Jake. How could someone do that? How could they be so greedy?" More sobs. "And the murders that started the legend? Apparently some relatives of mine did it. I don't understand. How could people do that?"

Jake didn't have answers for her questions, so he just held her until she ran out of tears.

"We're going to get her out. A helicopter is meeting us outside," Levi told Jake, motioning toward the injured woman.

Jake nodded.

"I want to get out of here," Cassie told him.

"Want to get the treasure first?"

She hesitated. "Can I…?" She sighed heavily. "Yes. I can do it."

He tilted his head, unsure of what she was thinking. She reached into her pocket and handed him the note he'd seen her pull down from the shelf that he assumed held the gold.

My Cassie,

If you find this, I'm likely gone. My apologies for handling this badly. I tried to tell you many times during your life, but the time never seemed right. You were always worried about becoming your mother, but you aren't her mistakes, dear. And you aren't our family's mistakes either.

The legend is true. There was a double murder, over some gold. But neither person who died was responsible. They were innocent, the ones who had found the gold. Your great-grandfather killed them, stole their gold.

He died not long after, in World War II, and never got to use the gold he'd stolen. He told his wife, who was racked with guilt. The story was passed down and rests now on me. One day, the hope was, someone in the family would be brave enough to return the gold to the town of Raven Pass. Neither man who died had a family so that gold is the town's. I almost brought it back. That's why I'm here in this cave today. But I can't do it, so instead I'm writing this note. If you find it, then possibly the paranoia I've had about someone asking me questions about the gold isn't paranoia at all. My life may be in danger, but, Cassie, even still I cannot find it within me to just turn the gold in to the police. I can't take people thinking ill of my dead family.

Be stronger than me, dear. If you find this, you can find the gold. It's where this letter was. Do the right thing, Cassie. Give it back. But let the comments roll off you. You aren't your relatives or their mistakes. You aren't even your past, dear.

I love you. Forgive me, dear.
Mabel

Jake brushed a tear from his own cheek, his heart so connected to Cassie's he felt he could feel her pain as his own. "I'm sorry, sweetheart."

"She died doing what was right though." Cassie sniffed. "In the end, she was braver than she thought."

Jake nodded. "She was, sweetheart. She was."

They walked together two feet forward, and Cassie reached up, pulled a small box off the shelf and opened it. Jake shined a flashlight down in.

Gold nuggets. Enough of them to be worth hundreds of thousands now. Maybe more. His eyes widened.

"I'm going to give it to the town, Jake. I'm going to do what she asked." Cassie nodded.

"And then?" Maybe it was the wrong time, but he had to know. Was this going to push her away, make her leave Alaska? Was there any hope at all?

"And then...if God wants me to, I thought I might

stay here. Raven Pass would be a wonderful place to raise our son…" She trailed off. "And I'd like to raise him with you."

"I would like that too, Cassie. Only one thing…" He reached for her again, pulled her into his arms. He knew sometimes men went down on one knee, and he'd done that before, but right now he just wanted to be as close to her as possible. "I want to marry you, Cassie Hawkins. I want to wake up next to you every day and know before God that our love is honoring Him. I want to raise Will with you and who knows how many other kids."

"I would like nothing better."

She lifted her face to his and he met her lips in a kiss. Long. Slow. Just enough of the past to remember that it had led them there.

But mostly, promise for the future.

# EPILOGUE

The sun was shining and Cassie was dressed in white, ready to marry the man she should have married years ago. Then again, maybe it was good she hadn't. God had done so many things in her heart and taught her so much that she never would have learned otherwise. It was time, Cassie thought, to stop thinking about what she wished she could change about her past and start being thankful for the future.

At her side, Will tugged on the skirt of her dress. "Do I really have to wear a tie?" He made a face. His bowtie was lopsided, but he looked adorable in his suit. When she and Jake had gone home a month ago and told him that they were going to get married, he'd done a loud war whoop and run around the house like a crazy person. He'd come out of his shell so much in Raven Pass, partly from being around other boys his age outside of the school environment, and partly from the confidence that came from having his dad in his life, Cassie thought.

"You have to wear a tie." Cassie pulled him close and kissed his hair.

"Mom." He rubbed at the spot where she'd kissed

him, creating an even messier appearance than he'd had a minute ago. "No more kissing."

"I'm going to kiss your dad in just a few minutes, during the wedding," she reminded him, having done her best to explain how weddings worked the night before, since he'd had questions and had never been to one.

He wrinkled his face. "Kissing is gross."

She smiled. "Hey, buddy?"

He looked up at her.

"Thanks for being excited about our move. You're going to love it up here and I know your dad is so happy we will all be a family."

He nodded. "Uhh, me too, Mom. Can I go play now?"

That was what she got for expecting seriousness out of a six-year-old. Cassie laughed. "Not now, the ceremony is starting."

She heard the music that was their cue. Will was walking her down the aisle, toward his dad and their future. It had seemed appropriate, especially since he was the only family she had left.

They walked down the aisle and Cassie's eyes met Jake's. The way he looked at her, all love and warmth and faithfulness, was more than she could have dreamed or hoped for, but she'd learned in the past month of being a Christian that sometimes God works that way.

*Thank you. Thank you so much*, she prayed as she walked, one foot in front of the other.

"Dearly beloved, we are gathered here today to celebrate..." the pastor started, a nice man she'd met during hers and Jake's premarital counseling sessions the last few weeks, but all Cassie saw was Jake.

And in his face she saw forgiveness. She saw a future instead of a past. And she saw hope.

They repeated their vows and he held her hands and then finally, *finally*, it was official.

"You may kiss the bride."

Their lips met and inside Cassie's heart she knew she'd never felt as loved as she did right now. They kissed and kissed until there was laughter from the guests and then Cassie felt pulling on her dress again.

"That's about enough kissing," Will said dryly. "Come on, someone told me we get cake now!"

Cassie and Jake laughed, and he took her arm in his, then they walked together, as a family, out of the church and into their new life.

Together.

\* \* \* \* \*

SPECIAL EXCERPT FROM

🌿

**LOVE INSPIRED** SUSPENSE
INSPIRATIONAL ROMANCE

*A K-9 trooper runs into danger while trying to
help her missing twin.*

*Read on for a sneak preview of*
Tracking Stolen Secrets *in the Alaska K-9 Unit
series from Love Inspired Suspense.*

Alaska K-9 state trooper Helena Maddox headed up
the grassy embankment within Denali National Park,
looking for any sign indicating her estranged twin, Zoe,
had been in the area recently. Upon reaching the crest,
she knelt beside her K-9, Luna, a Norwegian elkhound.
She ran her fingers through the animal's fluffy silver-
gray fur before opening the evidence bag and offering it
to her partner.

"This is Zoe. Seek Zoe. Seek!"

Luna buried her dark face in the bag, taking in the
scent of a scarf Zoe had left behind well over a year ago,
then lifted her nose to the air, sniffing as the gentle July
breeze washed over them.

"Seek Zoe," she repeated as she released the K-9 from
her leash, giving her room to roam.

Gazing upward, Helena caught a glimpse of the tallest
peak in America. Denali never failed to steal her breath.
Today she couldn't see as much of the mountain as she
would have liked, thanks to the low clouds hinting at
an upcoming storm. But this wasn't a leisurely visit.

She'd driven straight from Anchorage after receiving the uncharacteristic call from her fraternal twin sister.

*Helena? I'm in big trouble*— The connection had abruptly ended, and each time Helena had tried to call the number back, the phone went straight to voice mail. Zoe's full mailbox was not accepting messages.

Why would Zoe be out here? Was she working at one of the hotels? That made more sense than the thought of her communing with nature.

She glanced around again, searching for Luna. The dog's zigzag pattern indicated she was still searching for Zoe's scent, her hunt drawing her several yards away.

Helena was headed toward Luna when the sharp crack of a rifle rang out. At that exact moment, she was hit hard from behind and sent face-first to the ground in a bone-jarring thud.

*Don't miss*
Tracking Stolen Secrets *by Laura Scott,*
*available August 2021 wherever Love Inspired Suspense*
*books and ebooks are sold.*

LoveInspired.com

# LOVE INSPIRED
INSPIRATIONAL ROMANCE

## UPLIFTING STORIES OF FAITH, FORGIVENESS AND HOPE.

---

Join our social communities to connect with other readers who share your love!

Sign up for the Love Inspired newsletter at **LoveInspired.com** to be the first to find out about upcoming titles, special promotions and exclusive content.

---

## CONNECT WITH US AT:

Facebook.com/LoveInspiredBooks

Twitter.com/LoveInspiredBks

Facebook.com/groups/HarlequinConnection

**HARLEQUIN**

*Heartfelt or thrilling, passionate or uplifting—Harlequin is more than just happily-ever-after.*

With twelve different series to choose from and new books available every month, you are sure to find stories that will move you, uplift you, inspire and delight you.

# Get 4 FREE REWARDS!

### We'll send you 2 FREE Books plus 2 FREE Mystery Gifts.

**Love Inspired Suspense** books showcase how courage and optimism unite in stories of faith and love in the face of danger.

**FREE** Value Over **$20**